BLIGHTED HEART

BLIGHTED HEART

PRIMORDIALS OF SHADOWTHORN

Blighted Heart.

Copyright © 2021 by Jessaca Willis

ISBN: 978-1-953072-02-3

ASIN: B08KKDJG52

Front cover art by Evelyne Paniez, www.secretdartiste.be
Editing by Sandra Ogle from Reedsy.
Proofreading by Kate Anderson.

❀ Created with Vellum

Arcathain Capital
Castle of
ARCATHAIN
Drayfil Shore
Gravenburg
SHADOWTHORN & EVVE

N
NW
NE
W
E
SW
SE
S
The Wardens Camp
Beyrn
Labyrinth
OWTHORN
Ushines
The Dark Sea
The Heart
The Eyve
FORGOTTEN
FOREST
OF EYVE

To my brother,

You helped develop this world with me,
So you should at least get some of the credit, right?

CONTENTS

THE WARDENS

WARDENS OF QAEUS, SHADOWTHORN

I am dying.

Someone has reached their hands into my stomach, their fiery fingers clutching onto my ribcage and wrenching on my bones until I am split in half. At least, that is what it feels like. Pain, hot and blinding, sears through my abdomen and arouses me from my already fitful slumber. I writhe where I lie, unaware of my surroundings, of the time of day, and only dimly aware of why the space between my chest and hips seems to be nothing more than a gaping wound filled with molten lava.

Darkness pools in my thoughts. Sharp teeth glisten there. Bloodred eyes taunt me, blinking through the shadows where I cannot avoid their ever-watchful gazes. Fangs tear into flesh —*my* flesh, and I'm jolted by the sudden reminder of the demon that bit me. The demon that *killed* me the moment its wretched maw latched onto my side.

But if I am dead, why is my heart still thrashing inside me? Why can I hear it thumping against my head like someone is pounding against my skull? Why do I feel the stickiness of warm blood coating my entire stomach and seeping down my thighs?

My weary eyelids flutter open, but my surroundings are no more than a blurred wall of white and gray as my vision adjusts to the sharp light. I turn to my other senses instead. Despite the brightness, I can tell that I am inside. The scent of damp leaves is muted behind something stringent and musty, like a cellar that's been cleaned with ammonia. But the creaking of old trees is too audible for me to be tucked beyond the thick stone walls of a place like that, a place like a dungeon, like the one back at the Castle of Nigh. Relief floods through me at the realization that I am at least still safe from there, and the last few hours continue to awaken in my mind. My sister and I being imprisoned by Alphonse and the Magistrate. The executions that awaited us once we reached the Capital. Our escape into the Shadowthorn.

The fresh open air isn't the only thing that's changed from the last time I held consciousness. Even in my fitful slumber, I'd been so keenly aware of the cold blowing around me, that at times I'd been certain I was falling from a cliff instead of nestled against a reserve of warmth. Pressed against one side of my shivering body, it had been my refuge from the wind, a chiseled rock wrapped in warm velvet that had smelled of cedar and moonlight.

That warmth is gone now, leaving my body to freeze on the slab of ice I lie upon. But the cold doesn't last long. Within moments of awareness returning to me, the hot iron in my belly churns. Pain engulfs me in heat that surges from my head to my toes. I arch against the ice beneath me, fingers clenching around the slab and trying to anchor myself in place, to allow the cold to soothe the roaring flames of agony. But fire this hot cannot be tamed by ice.

Hands grasp my shoulders. The calloused fingers are rough, snagging on my black leathers, but with my vision still a hazy grayscale, I have no way of knowing who they belong to. My teeth grind, as if I can bear through it, as if I just need to last long enough to be seen and mended by a healer. But I forget that I am dying already. Soon, the demon's bite will be the end of me, its toxin will slither into my heart and I will rot from the inside out until my blood runs black and curdled.

The hands press me gently back against the cool softness beneath me, something that I only realize now feels vaguely like a cot. Whoever the person is, they offer no soft words of false comfort, no lying reassurances that I'll be all right. They simply release me once the pain has subsided and my muscles cease clenching. It's better this way. I can bury myself in the silence and try not to think about what led me here. I'd rather not spend my final moments in this world thinking about how I'd failed as a daughter, failed at being a Crusader, at being a lover, and how I couldn't even enjoy the freedom I'd escaped to for more than five minutes before I failed that too.

Eventually, my body as well as my mind become too numbed to worry about anything. The dark depths of unconsciousness beckon me like a warm bed, but just before I can tuck myself in, a commotion stirs from the opposite end of the room.

"Over there," a man commands, the roguish tone both familiar and strangely soothing. "If you're certain the boy doesn't need your immediate attention—"

"He's fine." The woman's voice is chilling, silvery. Like a dagger cutting through the air. "He is not the one bleeding."

"Yes, yes, yes. Of course," the man mutters. "See to it, then."

With the pain temporarily dulled, my vision finally starts to clear, and I begin making sense of my surroundings. I was right about being inside, but it's not stones that encase us, nor is it thick wooden panels. Canvas hangs over thick beams and poles, creating a small pavilion that glows dimly beneath the sun's dulled shine. It's either dusk, or we are still inside the

Shadowthorn, judging from not only the pale glow of the room, but also the silence of the surrounding area outside.

My fuzzy, drowsy gaze catches on a candelabra in the center of the room with a dozen lit tallow candles. Squinting away from the painful glares, I instead turn to the shadows I find more soothing near the end of my cot.

A young man, a cloak of darkness seeming to ripple around him, leans against the edge of my bed, his back barely grazing my leg. I blink, forcing myself to focus until he comes into view more clearly. My heart lodges in my throat when he does

I recognize him instantly. His gnarled, demonic arm would be unmistakable anywhere, but it's his eyes that have left me the most scarred. They are night and shadows in solid form. The eyes of a killer. Of my parents' murderer.

The moment I think it, part of me realizes that's not the whole truth, part of me remembers that it wasn't him I'd found lapping up my mother's and father's blood. But it had been him who'd charged me after the other demon died. It had been him who Dimitri had chased away. And it had been him who'd followed me to the Castle of Nigh and seemingly led an attack on the catacombs, quite possibly all in the effort to kill me and finish what he and his demon-friend had started.

It strikes me then, that he looks different than he did in the catacombs. That day, he'd been coated in black from horn to toes, and even the human bits of him could've passed for demon during the attack. I suppose he'd been slathered in something, but what? And actually, I'm not sure I care to know.

Now he bears more semblance to the way he looked the day he terrorized my home. His horns are longer, the darkness that used to only take up his arm has since bled across half of his chest.

Seeing him here, now, a whole new kind of pain ravages me. He might not have sunk his teeth into my parents' flesh, but I didn't see him stop the other demon either.

Hatred burns so fiercely inside me that I challenge the sun for heat. My voice is low, my clenched jaw clipping the words to razors, as I finally managed to speak. "What is he doing here?"

The demon-man scoffs—he actually *scoffs*. As if *I* am the offensive one here. As if *I* have anything to apologize for, to repent for. My parents are dead because of creatures like him. I had been mere seconds away from meeting the same fate, by his hands, until Dimitri arrived. And my Uncle is just letting him be here.

"What is he doing here!" The words claw their way from my throat like ravaged beasts set loose for the hunt. I jerk my leg to kick the demon-man off me, but the motion sends another flare of pain burning through my abdomen.

I shriek out through gritted teeth before anyone can answer me, my head twisting to the side.

"Halira!"

My sister's voice is so addled with concern that I almost don't recognize it.

Kalli rushes from across the room and brushes my forehead with the soft of her hand, though her sharp tone shows nothing of the same gentleness. "Help her!"

I pry my eyes open through the pain to spot the person she's barking at. Imryll—the woman I've just learned to be my mother's sister—stands across the room hovering over Silver who lies atop a table. The leathers that should be covering her thighs are split open, her pale skin shining through a sheet of blood, but I can't tell what kind of wound she bears: sword or demon.

The sight of her and the others brings back some of my recent memories. The last few hours are buried behind a haze, but I wade through it like a staggering, wounded animal. My arrest, my imprisonment alongside my sister, our narrow escape, and the battle that ensued once we were inside the Shadowthorn.

Dimitri leaving. Me murdering the Magistrate's son…my cousin, Alphonse.

Just as I recall the way I commanded the lightning from the sky, the bulk of Güthric's shoulders nudge beneath the canvas door flap, something gangly strewn over his arms. He swings the form down to another cot, and Alphonse's angular face peeks out from his tussled, dark hair.

Knowing he is dead was one thing, but seeing him now, the proof of my vile power, churns what's left of my stomach to curdled milk.

"We should've left him," Imryll bites out, her hands gliding over Silver's thighs as if she was smoothing a poultice over the wounds.

The wave of pain settles again, and I blink through the tears as I relax my rigid spine. As I blink through weary exhaustion, my gaze settling on my aunt and her work, I notice the shadow of her hand is too far away from Silver's leg to be touching it. If she's not applying a poultice…

The air between them seems to ripple with energy. Silver's fingers dig into Imryll's shoulder as my aunt lets her druid magic flow. From this angle, I can't see what she's doing, but I recall through my haze of consciousness someone telling another to tend to someone who'd been bleeding, and suppose they'd been speaking about Silver.

"Leave him?" says the familiar voice from earlier, and it's then that I notice my uncle Adrien is in the room as well, rummaging through a cupboard for bandages. "I'm not leaving my nephew unattended in the Shadowthorn to be ripped apart by demons." Humor softens his angular features when he turns around, gauze in hand. "Even if he always was a little shit."

"He will come for him," my aunt warns, and I'm too

exhausted to be able to guess who she's talking about at first. "You know he will. He will want his son back."

Imryll doesn't need to name the man in question after that. For all the animosity he held toward his bastard son, my uncle Esmond—the Magistrate of Arcathain—has never abandoned Alphonse, even when he could've. A man with that much power and status could've sent a bastard to the most remote part of Arcathain to live a quiet, secluded existence and never faced the shame of him again. And yet, he gave him a station in the Shadow Crusade. Granted, it was a position far from the Capital, but it was still preferable than living the life of a troglodyte.

"Let him come," Adrien says, and from this angle, with the ghost of pain still fraying my hold on reality, I almost mistake him for my father. They even share the same honey brown eyes and roguish grin, the one saved especially for conversations regarding their tyrannical middle brother, Esmond. "It could be the blessing I've been waiting for all these years. Maybe he'll pardon me for saving his son."

Saving. My thoughts snag on that single, hopeful word. I test my voice. "He's…not dead?"

Adrien's laugh is bright and short. "Not yet, though I'm sure an arrogant young man like him will have more difficulty surviving hearing that he was bested by a young woman, an *evil* magic-user, at that."

"That's enough," Kalli snaps at him, her thick ropes of hair whipping like vipers about her shoulders as she twists.

Adrien holds up his hands. "It's all in good jest, my dear. I'm quite proud of my *evil* magic-using nieces."

If it wasn't for the black raven who swoops in to settle on my sister's shoulder, I fear the growl in Kalli's throat would've turned her animalistic. With another toss of her hair, she returns her attention to me, but it's not long before her eyes flick to the end of the bed.

"You've served your purpose, beast," she says crossly. "You can leave now."

Kalli does not yet know that the man she's speaking to, the man breathing the same air as us, the one still leaned against my bed with his arms crossed, is one of the demons responsible for our parents' deaths. Her hatred for him wasn't bred the day they died, but rather over decades and centuries as Arcathainians fled from the Shadowthorn and the demons residing there.

Ryven snorts before I can tell her, a bored scrunch to his nose. "And you could say thank you. But, apparently, just because we *can* do those things doesn't mean we're going to." He resettles against the bed, making sure she and I both know that he has no intention of leaving.

I can't contain the volcanic wrath churning inside me any longer. Having him this near me is like bathing in my parents' blood, like frolicking through their bones and lying with their rotting corpses. It's repulsive. It's blasphemous. It's inherently, irrevocably wrong, and I need it to stop. Every molecule of my body screams for distance, for release from the months of pent-up rage and grief. I need to scream.

"Thank you?" I say, voice quaking behind my vicious snarl. On shaking arms, I push myself up to stare him directly in those bottomless eyes. "She will never thank you for what you did to us, to our family. Murderer. Wicked *thing*. You will suffer for what you did to them."

The sneer he'd reserved for Kalli widens with an emotion I cannot read. My own vision is too clouded and bloodied with the red I want to see running from his orifices.

"What are you talking about?" my sister asks, taking a cautious step closer toward me, toward him, so that she might be between us.

"He killed our parents!" I hurl the accusation at him like a brick plucked from the already tenuous fortress of my body. I watch it smack into him just as my walls come crumbling down, another cleaving sensation of pain ripping through my abdomen.

"He what?" Kalli grits out beside me, but my uncle is shoving her aside.

"Ignore her. She's delirious," I think I hear him say between my guttural shrieks for someone to make it stop, to make the pain go away, to kill me now rather than make me suffer through this until the end.

As someone—presumably my sister—presses my bucking shoulders to the cot, Adrien lifts my shirt. His fingers are ice to my singed skin, a burning sort of cold that almost seems more unbearable than the fire igniting inside me. "Imryll, we're going to need you over here."

Leather soles shuffle over earth. More hands splay across my abdomen. Voices warble and I catch phrases like:

"I'll do what I can…" and

"Why does my sister think…" and

"There's more to the story…" and

"He had nothing to do with their deaths…"

But my screams cut off whatever's left of the conversation, the pain making it impossible to hold onto even the parts that I manage to glean, until an hour or more has passed, or at least long enough that the room seems dimmer than it had been.

"There." My aunts voice, quiet and ethereal, sounds like mist clinging low to the ground. "I've done what I can to stop the bleeding, but the pain will still come."

"I know," says my uncle.

Instead of focusing on how much more pain there could possibly be, I swallow the dryness on my tongue and try to change the subject. "Where are we?" My voice is barely more than a rasp. "What is this place?"

Adrien appears beside Kalli, serving as a shield between my sister and the half-demon before either of them can strike. But he ignores their blazing gazes, and instead says to me, "We are still inside the Shadowthorn. This place doesn't have a name, but the people here, we call ourselves the Wardens of Qaeus."

"*The Wardens of Qaeus?*" Kalli's lip peels back. "That title makes it sound as if you're protecting him."

"For a time, that was our undertaking. I suppose some might say it is still. I prefer to think of us as shepherds. For as long as I have been alive, and likely longer, the Wardens have done what they can to keep the Primordial as far away from mankind as possible. There is more to that story than the time we have now, but to answer your question, in that sense we are protecting him. From himself."

The crease in Kalli's forehead deepens. "A lot of good that has done anyone. The only way to protect Arcathain is to kill the Primordial, not *shepherd* it as if it were a harmless lamb."

This time, it's Ryven who responds. He squares his shoulders, dropping his arms from his rigid and bare chest as he presses against my uncle to look directly at Kalli. "Qaeus is a Primordial, an ancient and powerful being who, you might not know, is held in high regard by the druids. You might want to mind the way you talk about her around here."

"Her?" I manage to wheeze.

"High regard?" Cool rage flashes behind Kalli's eyes before anyone can answer me. She twists to face Ryven. "That monstrosity has taken thousands of Arcathainian lives!"

"Leave the outrage at the door, children." Adrien's arms shoot up, bracing Kalli and Ryven on either side of him. "You know how I despise politics."

With an acquiescing sigh, Ryven turns away, his arms crossing again seemingly in an effort to contain any other disagreements roiling inside him.

My sister, however, does not back down. She remains solid in her stance, her gray eyes as piercing as double-edged swords.

Adrien pivots to her, his voice low and pleading. "We've just left one battlefield, Kalli. Instead of leaping into another, might we tend to the wounded and leave the fighting for another day, hmm?"

If Kalli had planned to retort, my uncle's plea seems to leech the bluster right from under her. Her expression wilts as swiftly as a morning glory greeting nightfall. I know what she's thinking. She just risked everything—her station, her reputation, her livelihood—just to ensure my safety and prevent our executions. But now, bitten and fever-chilled, I'm as good as dead. Where does that leave my ambitious sister? Is she destined to live the rest of her days here as a fugitive, with the *Wardens of Qaeus*, a group she already seems to loathe as much as anyone could loathe anything?

"Who else is here?" I ask, wondering what kinds of fugitives Kalli will find herself among. Arcathainians or druids? Mages?

Adrien seems to understand the deeper meaning of my question. "Most of us here are those who have fled Arcathain for one reason or another, though there are still some druids among us. But not many. Most of the druids still reside in the Forgotten Forest of Eyve. Before the Blight, the Wardens studied Qaeus, kept her busied and distracted in the remotest regions of Arcathain so as to prevent her from killing ruthlessly."

I can't even begin to imagine the scene he's describing. All accounts of the Primordials are of gigantic, vicious creatures.

"But when we lost the Primordial," my uncle continues. "Once the Shadowthorn swept over the lands, most of the druids who had ventured into Arcathain fled back to the safety of the Eyve."

I wonder what he means by the *safety* of the Eyve. Has the Blight not reached their borders yet? Or do they have defenses against the curse upon the lands?

Prepared to ask him more about it, I gesture with my hand,

but the movement flares a stinging burn across my knuckles. I hiss at the pain, my hand flexing so as not to put any more strain on whatever gash has broken my skin there.

Adrien grabs my wrist, my bloodied hand coming into view as he brings it closer toward him for examination. It's only then that I remember where the injury came from. Alphonse disarmed me with a swift flick of his thin sword, and I only survived what came next because of a strange surge of magic that had erupted from within me.

"You're hurt," Adrien mutters. "Imryll? There's a lot of blood over here."

My aunt is at my side in a matter of moments, but as appreciative as I am for her swift tending, the cynical part of me can't help but think that she's wasting her time and energy. Bleeding or not, there's only one way this ends for me, and it can't be very far off by now.

"It's fine," I say, jerking my hand from both of their grips. "Finish healing Silver. And Alphonse, if you think he'll survive." At their confused expressions, I add, "We all know that I'm a lost cause now."

Adrien's mouth cracks open as if he's going to correct me, but then his lips curve into a sympathetic smile. He and Imryll exchange a look, one that I don't understand.

"What?" I ask, the emotion of the room shifting.

Kalli squeezes my shoulder, the two of us locking eyes. Her raven tilts its head at me, like even it knows what she's about to say. "I thought you overheard earlier."

"Overheard what?"

Her eyebrows lift, her expression unreadable. "Adrien says there's a cure. You're not going to die."

A BLIGHTED HEART

WARDENS OF QAEUS, SHADOWTHORN

"**W**hat are you talking about?" I manage to grit out, my gaze a hot iron searing into my sister's cool eyes. "Kalli, there is no cure. Once someone is struck by a demon, it's only a matter of time before—"

"Not exactly," Adrien offers.

Imryll snatches my bleeding hand again. I'm trying desperately not to look at it. The sight of blood has always made my stomach watery, but especially since out of the corner of my eye, I swear I can see bone. *My* bone.

Imryll rests my palm in hers, her other hand hovering over the backside of mine to create a perfect, warm little pocket for me. Even from this short distance, I still can't see or hear any signs of magic that I might've expected. There is no sparkle or illumination, no hum or crackling of the air. Not like when I called the lightning. There are only two indicators that she's healing me with druid power. The first is the tingling sensation that pricks my knuckles; it starts at the edges of the gash and works its way to the center like she's brushing the wound with a small, invisible flame just over the top of my skin. The second, and by far the most convincing, is that before my eyes, my skin begins to knit itself back together. This time, I can't bring myself to look away as the bone disappears beneath the flesh, and the darkest depths of the wound close. The pale, shimmering skin is still splotched with blood, but otherwise renewed.

My aunt releases my hand, and I flip it before my eyes. The gash is gone. And though the blood still remains, I see only the faintest pink line to indicate that any injury had been there before.

I've never seen anything like it before in my life. To think of how effortlessly she just performed the use of her magic, how useful such a skill could be, it leaves me stupefied with wonder and conflicted by the boundless possibilities.

I can't bring myself to look down upon my stomach, but the wound there feels different too, as if her magic reached further than just my hand to nurture every wound in my body. That wound is different. Though I think the puncture wounds have repaired, the toxin still seeps beneath my flesh like black, writhing worms. I feel the evil clawing beneath my skin, but I don't dare look at it.

Faintly, I hear Kalli ask our aunt, "Is it you, then? Can your...druid magic heal her?"

It's not until her second question that I'm able to pull my attention away from my healed hand and back to the people standing over me. But everything is starting to make sense now. If Imryll can cure wounds that have ripped down to the bone, surely, she can remove the demon toxin from my blood. And maybe that's exactly the sort of *safety* my uncle talked about in the Forgotten Forest of Eyve. If that is where the druids live, and they can cure the blighted, then it's no wonder they returned to their homeland.

The curious look exchanged between my aunt and uncle, punctuated by Ryven's loud and condescending snort as he leans back against one of the posts holding the pavilion together, suggests that Kalli and I have jumped to the wrong conclusion.

"Not everything in life comes so easy," Ryven says.

Kalli whirls on him, indignation chilling her rigid expression. "Do not mock me for drawing conclusions. I have lost my brother to the Blight. My parents. I am not about to lose my sister, as well."

Ryven shoves himself off the post. "You think you're the only one to have lost loved ones? We've all lost people. But some of us have the luxury of living outside of the Shadowthorn, outside of the prison walls that Arcathainians put in place to keep others trapped, while the rest of the Broken Realms moves freely across the lands."

"I don't care about your people!" Kalli roars. "I'm talking about saving my sister!"

"Children, please," Adrien says, pivoting to face them both.

He holds his arms out again to placate them, but it does very little. He needn't worry so much, though. My sister is not a fighter in arms, but one of words. I don't know the half-demon well enough to be able to analyze him but judging by how comfortable he has appeared here—leaned in various places throughout the room—I'd venture to guess that this is as much of his home as it is my uncle's. An outpost, at least. Adrien has already requested they leave the fighting out of it, and I don't get the sense that Ryven is in the habit of disobeying him.

My uncle turns to Ryven first, his shoulders slumping with exhaustion. "There are finally people here who can understand you and your plight, and your first instinct is to antagonize them?" Just as I'm starting to wonder what he means by that exactly, he returns his attention to Kalli, composure restored. "Please forgive his manners. Not only has the blight sickness made him moody, but he's not used to social interactions."

My eyes widen. What could my uncle possibly mean by that?

Kalli's eyes narrow on the two of them, and she draws her own conclusion. "He's blighted as well?"

"Indeed." My uncle nods. "Ryven, here, is in much the same predicament as your sister—" Then, seemingly remembering my presence, or perhaps my consciousness, he directs his gaze at me and adds, "As *you*, Halira. Ryven was attacked by demons and left for dead, but his druid blood combats the demon toxin, giving him time to find a cure, time to expunge the toxin from his veins, just as the druid blood in you does, as well."

"That doesn't explain his manners," Kalli murmurs, so quiet that I think I'm the only one to hear her.

But my aunt is still close by and answers her with an arched, slender brow. "Once the toxin spreads throughout the bloodstream, speech becomes impaired. Cursed. Imbued with dark magic that only a druid can understand."

"But," I say, sitting up a little. "You can still understand me?"

Adrien looks sorrowful. "Only for a short while longer, I'm afraid. Your speech is already becoming…muffled, raspy. Soon, I will hear only the shrieks and yowls of shadowcreatures when you speak."

At first, I think he's joking. He must be. We've been carrying on a conversation for minutes now—Ryven, a part of that—and my uncle has been conversing with all of us…

But the more I replay the words, I realize Adrien hasn't replied directly to anything Ryven's said. He's spoken at him a few times now, but never as a direct response. And Ryven hasn't responded.

Horrified and frightened, I turn to my friends across the room for confirmation. They're close enough that they've likely heard everything said so far, and can tell me if I'm already difficult to understand.

Silver purses her lips together and gives a single swift nod.

Güthric's smile is apologetic when he shrugs. I look up to my sister last, momentarily forgetting that we share the same druid blood because I'm too afraid that soon I will lose her too. When I reach for her hand, she squeezes it, and I hear her reassurances without her even needing to speak them. We will get through this together. She will not let me die.

Kalli's calculating gaze turns to Ryven. Her eyes roam from his curved horns, to the leathery wings of shadow that hang behind his back, and finally down to his blackened, repulsive arm. "Is that where it happened?"

The half-demon nods, and one thing becomes clearer to me than anything else.

"Is that…is that going to happen to me?"

The question makes Ryven shrivel into himself. He hunches forward, the marred arm tucked against his chest like he has any hope of hiding his disfigurement. If he wasn't one of the creatures responsible for my parents' murders, I might feel sorry for him. But my rage is too deep, and my self-pity already expanding, all-consuming. It drags me down into its darkness like a pit of quicksand. The more I writhe in my fear, the deeper I sink into despair.

I don't want to die.

Having even a little more time to obtain and administer a cure is far more preferable to death, but I don't want to become one of the very things I despise, the creatures I've been trained to kill.

My friends followed me into the Shadowthorn, but what would they think of me then? What do they think of me now: a druid girl who thought she was Arcathainian but is now turning into a demon?

If Dimitri had stayed with us, I wonder what he would have thought. Just as quick as that doubt comes to life, I shred it to pieces. Sure, when he'd first discovered I was different, he didn't respond the way I would've liked him to. He was frightened, his ethics warring with his heart and with every bit of truth he thought he knew. I can't blame him for that, for being who he is.

But I want to. When he thought I was dying, he should've been by my side. That's what a true friend—a friend you've known since childhood—would've done. It's what lovers do. It's what I would've done for him.

If he had only known that wasn't the end, I wonder if he would've stayed.

I turn my rageful eyes to my uncle, suddenly realizing what all of this means. "There is a cure, and you just let Dimitri believe I was going to die."

Adrien holds his hands up in defense, a gesture he apparently uses often. "It's not as simple as you think."

"It is! It takes a breath to say: *There is a cure.*" I ignore the screaming fire in my belly, using it to enflame my outrage instead. "You could've told him! He would've come with us—"

"He was leaving you, Halira." The raven on my sister's shoulder makes her appear all the more severe. Her tone is colder than ever, sharper. Her words are hot daggers to my already mangled heart. "He said so himself. Besides, you know how he is. Duty above all. He was never meant to be here. Never meant for *this* life."

I know she's not trying to hurt me. In her mind, she's simply stating the facts. The only problem is, they are a truth I have not yet decided to face, nor do I know if I ever will. As long as no one talked about it, I could continue ignoring the burning in my chest, I could pretend it had nothing to do with Dimitri's betrayal, his rejection of me, and everything to do with the demon toxin slithering its way to my heart.

But my sister's words serve as another reminder of the loss we've shared today. It's not just a boy I'm leaving behind, not just one person, but everything. Regardless of whether I survive this...this Blight, my life—all of our lives will be changed forever. Despite years of separation and sparse encounters, it appears Kalli and I have followed the footsteps of our uncle. We can never return to Arcathain, not unless we want to be hung as the mages they mistake us for.

I should be grateful that we have somewhere to run, a place to call home among family, but it's too soon for appreciation. It's still too shocking for me to comprehend. I've done nothing wrong but exist.

"So, there is a cure," Kalli restates before flicking a hand at Ryven. "But I'm gathering from *his* still-blighted state that you do not possess it." It's another realization that I hadn't come to yet, and one that continues to splinter the remnants of hope in my chest. "Why did we even come here then? You took us deeper into the Shadowthorn, closer toward danger, not a solution. This place is surrounded by demons. Soon, they'll find us and—"

"They won't. I assure you," Imryll says, her voice ringing like crystal. "This camp is protected by ancient druid magic. The Wardens were established by the druids to protect the Primordials, but their shadowcreatures are unruly. They needed a safe haven in case the demons ever turned on them. This camp is protected; no demons may enter."

"What about me?" I ask softly before pointing across the room to Ryven. "What about him? We're demons now."

Adrien's reassuring grasp cups my shoulder. "Only partially. Your humanity is far greater than any darkness trying to burrow inside you. You will be safe here."

"Only if we have the cure," Kalli adds. "So why are we here? What are you not telling us?"

I glance to my uncle when he clears his throat. "I brought you here because you are my nieces and you needed help. Bringing you to my home was the only way I could help you."

"It's not the only way. You said there is a cure, and even if you don't have it in your possession, you seem to think we can obtain it. So stop dancing around the topic and tell us how you plan on helping her or we'll figure it out ourselves. We've gone our entire lives without either of you." Kalli cuts both our aunt and uncle down with a glare. "So prove yourselves useful now. How can you help me save Halira?"

Adrien eyes the rest of the room before saying softly, "I can offer you the heart of a Primordial."

Kalli looks at our uncle as if he thinks she is the dumbest person to ever live. "You're saying you have in your possession one of the fallen Primordials' hearts?"

Before Adrien can answer, the canvas doors are pulled apart, drawing the attention of the room. A figure—a man—ducks beneath the pavilion, someone who I'm determined to pay little attention to until he straightens. I recognize his long face, the thick sideburns that make his ears stand out and almost give him a primate-like impression.

Saimenimus, a man who most thought dead after the attack in Ashenvale. Most, but me. But even my jaw struggles to stay closed. After everything that happened, after being accused as a mage, escaping the prison cells at Nigh, fleeing into the Shadowthorn, being bitten by a demon, and striking Alphonse down with a lightning bolt, I honestly hadn't even had the chance to remember that Adrien had taken Sai with him that day in Ashenvale.

The former Crusader's cocky grin tilts up the side of his face. "I was told the Wardens returned with some familiar faces."

Out of the corner of my eye, I watch Silver blink away her disbelief while Güthric smiles that great, toothy grin of his. He bounds across the room in two strides before enveloping Sai in his arms.

"Okay, big guy," Sai wheezes, patting Güthric's broad back. "I know you missed me, but surely, you wouldn't want to squeeze the life out of me after only just learning I'm still alive."

At that, Güthric releases him, riling his thick, brown head of hair as he steps back. Sai shoves him farther as if he's annoyed by the attention, but it's obvious he's enjoying it. He's missed us as much as we've missed him.

"What happened?" Silver asks, interrupting them before the tomfoolery can become more rambunctious.

There's an arrogant tilt to Sai's head. "You didn't really think those demons could take me, did you?"

Güthric's grin becomes demonic itself.

But Sai notices me on the cot across the room before he can explain the past few days. He strides to my bedside, filling the space between my sister and uncle. At first, I mistake his hobbling gait as he makes his way toward us for the same booze-addled stagger that I've come to associate with him, but it's not until he's hovering over me that I realize I smell no booze wafting from him like usual. I try looking down at his leg, but from this angle, it's no use.

Fortunately, he sees me trying.

"Ah," he says. "I see you're starting to piece it together."

He gestures down to his leg as if any of us can see what he's talking about, but he's covered head-to-foot in leather armor—a shabby shade of gray that, I realize, is thinner than our usual Crusader garb.

"Courtesy of the shadowbeast that *you* took down." He winks, ignoring my bulging eyes and the flare of concern that pricks my skin. Does this mean he's turning too? Does this mean he's a druid like me? "I haven't had the chance to properly thank you for that yet. If I had died back then—or if I still die," he adds, a playful glare cast at Adrien. "At least I'll go knowing I was avenged."

"You're not going to die," Adrien assures him.

Relief swells then, blanketing the gnawing concern that had started to eat through me. "Happy to avenge a friend," I say softly. His crooked smile skews more, but I have to ask, "Does that mean you're a druid too?"

"Me?" Confusion crosses him. "Oh, no. Sorry. You misunderstand. I wasn't bitten or scratched. Just flung to my death when I tried attacking that…that *thing*." The memory folds over him like a shadow and his lip pulls back.

"He suffered a broken leg and a cracked skull," Adrien adds, a hand planting gently on Sai's shoulder. "Both of which have been healed, so you have nothing more to fear."

"So the man says," Sai murmurs out of the corner of his mouth before returning his attention to Adrien. "And yet, I'm still not allowed a single tankard of ale."

"As I've said before, we do not keep spirits or ale here. Nothing that would impede the mind." Something wicked flashes in his eyes then. "But I promise you, there are other ways to enjoy oneself."

The smile on Sai's face curls in a devious challenge. Then, he shakes his head at me. "Can you believe my luck? Me? Stumbling into the only *sober* secret society of fugitives ever to exist."

"Do you know many secret societies of fugitives?" Adrien asks wryly.

"Too many to count," Sai replies, another wink aimed at me. "And I assure you, it is an unspoken code to allow every form of debauchery and depravity within *all* ranks of fugitive groups. After all, what's the point in breaking the laws if you can't break them all?"

My uncle feigns a thoughtful reflection on the matter. "Perhaps I'll consider it."

I grin at the two of them despite myself, despite everything I've just lost, learned, and am still grappling with, despite the noxious toxin bubbling inside me. But there's something heartwarming about seeing the way these two near strangers can banter like they've known each other for ages, something about the glint in Adrien's eye that brightens every time Sai riddles off another smart retort, that makes everything else seem distant and unimportant.

"Am I the only one who can remain focused here?" Kalli scoffs, shoving Sai back so that she has a clear view of our uncle. "Do you or do you not have the heart of a Primordial?"

Adrien shakes his head. "No. Not exactly. But—" Kalli's eyes flash red, but it's her raven's sudden outburst and flapping that causes Adrien to hold up his hands. "That being said, I do know the whereabouts of one."

Uncomfortable as it is to move, as blinding as the pain can be when I put any strain on my abdomen, I attempt to sit up. "Do you mean you know the location of Qaeus?"

The question brings Silver upright as well, her legs swinging over the edge of the table as everyone in the room eagerly awaits a response.

"Yes," Adrien says at last, the word resounding in the air with power and meaning, like a spell or incantation that's just set into motion our futures. At the very least me, but perhaps others as well.

I look to my friends, to the people I've spent the last few months with training to kill the Primordial, never once realizing just how soon that day could come. No one in the Shadow Crusade knows the location of Qaeus. It is one of the reasons they send units into the Shadowthorn regularly, because until they find the Primordial, we can't put a stop to the Blight it's unleashed.

And here Adrien is, with the knowledge that could save the country—perhaps even all the Broken Realm.

"Incredible," Silver breathes the word as quiet as snow drifting over a meadow. "We can finally kill it then. Arcathain will know peace, at last."

Güthric's grin is all gapped teeth and brutish menace.

"*Her*," Adrien corrects, muttering so quietly that I almost don't hear him. By the time I register that he's assigned the Primordial a gender, my aunt is already speaking.

"Sorry to be the bearer of ill tidings," Imryll says. "But none of you will have the opportunity to slay Qaeus because she is already dead—may the gods rest her spirit."

"Dead?" I choke on the word and all that it means. Qaeus can't be dead because if it is—if *she* is—then that means Arcathain is doomed. If it's not the Primordial allowing the Shadowthorn to fester and expand across the continent, unleashing demons upon the innocents, then who is? And better yet, how can they be stopped?

"We don't know that Qaeus is dead," Adrien counters.

Imryll looks at him as if to say he's only lying to himself.

The rest of the room exchanges confused glances, all except Ryven and Kalli. The half-demon has spent all this time staring at the ground, looking miserable ever since Adrien last spoke to him. But irritation flickers across his expression now, his jaw tightening, and I get the distinct impression that he's heard this conversation one too many times before and can no longer abide it.

Meanwhile, my sister, who is only just hearing about all of this for the first time, squints her eyes. "You said *heart*. Not that you knew the location of the Primordial itself, but only its heart."

"*Her* heart," Adrien corrects.

I balk, unable to even focus on the increasingly glaring reality that the Primordial I've been taught to fear and hate my entire life is apparently feminine by some means. "Just the heart?" I ask.

"Yes," Adrien answers. "However, the heart still beats. At least, as far as we can tell it does. The Shadowthorn surrounding it is too thick to be able to get very close, not without great risk. But even from a distance, the rhythmic thrumming of the beating heart livens the darkness, the vibrations palpable in the air like placing a hand atop a beating drum." Pointedly, he looks at Imryll. "Qaeus is very much alive."

Imryll doesn't deign to give him a response, assured by her own conviction of what she knows to be true. Instead, she turns away, striding across the room to begin her examination of Alphonse's supine form.

"I don't understand," I say. "How is that possible? A heart can't function outside of a body... And if Qaeus doesn't have one, then Imryll's right. The Primordial is dead, and if she's dead—"

"I apologize, dearest niece," Adrien says, cutting me off with his sympathetic tone. "But someone will need to translate for you. It appears the demon toxin has completed its course. I am no longer able to understand you, and neither will anyone else without druid blood." With a stroke of his short beard, he adds thoughtfully, "It won't be long now before the sickness settles in." My eyes must bulge as large as the moon and sun because he adds quickly, "Try not to worry too much. You have been injured. A foreign substance—a deadly one, at that—invades your bloodstream. Your body will fight it off, but in so doing, your senses will be...compromised. Nothing too serious. A fever that will likely last a week or so. Mild disorientation. Possible hallucinations."

"Hallucinations?" I've never had to think about it before, but the idea that I won't even be able to trust my own sight terrifies me to the point that I start to tremble. I look from him to my sister.

Adrien waves off my concerns as if I'm fretting over something as trivial as the weather. "I still cannot understand you.

However, know this, I have no doubt that you've endured far worse than fever-induced hallucinations by now in your life."

My mouth hangs wide as I look up to my sister again. She notices my gaze but mistakes my silent plea for her to comfort me as a request to translate the question I'd asked earlier instead. Or perhaps she doesn't mistake it at all. Kalli has never been one to be easily deterred once her sights are set.

"Halira asked how it's possible for Qaeus to be without her heart when we have been sending hundreds of Crusaders into the Shadowthorn to kill her for centuries." Those weren't my words at all. They are heavily influenced and reworded with Kalli's own interests in mind. I guess that answers that.

"This is just a theory," Adrien begins, still combing his fingers through the wiry patch of umber hair hanging from his chin. "But we believe the Primordial has—in a sense—deteriorated. Just as mage magic has." He says it as if it's a well-known fact, but as far as I'm aware, such a belief has never been more than conjecture. When Qaeus broke through the wall bordering the Forgotten Forest of Eyve, some speculated the failings of magic, but just as many wondered if it hadn't been an intentional choice by the mages. They did, after all, flee shortly after it fell, so it's not hard to fathom that they could've disrupted the spell on the wall on purpose to release the Primordial to rid the realm of humans so that the mages could claim all of Arcathain instead of the fraction they wound up with.

And I'm honestly not sure what to believe anymore. I didn't even know druid magic existed up until today.

"What evidence do you have of this?" my sister presses.

Adrien frowns, his head bobbing from side to side. "Evidence? I'm not sure we can call it that. I definitely doubt you would. But there are strong correlations. For example: the existence of humankind." He pauses, as if that alone will convince us. Seeing our dubious expressions though, he quickly adds,

"Think about it. If the Primordials have been here since the dawn of time, ravaging the world and unleashing such darkness upon us, how would anyone have survived for this long?"

"Magic," Kalli answers glibly.

"Perhaps," Adrien says. "Or perhaps the Primordials have changed over time. And before you ask in what ways, I'll spare you the breath. I do not pretend to know the specifics. The Wardens records don't date back far in history, so our knowledge of Qaeus is limited, let alone the rest of the Primordials."

My sister grows increasingly intrigued, the creases in her forehead shifting from ones born out of frustration to curiosity instead. "How far back do they date?"

Adrien doesn't answer at first. His lips pull taut, as if he's afraid to even utter a response. But he finally does. "Other than a few general entries that indicate very strongly that the Wardens existed before the wall fell, most of our records begin that same day."

The room all but gasps in unison. If I could feel shock, I'm sure it would pulse through me right about now, but the entire day has been one surprising revelation after another and my body no longer has the reserves to express much of anything, especially not while I'm lying here on the cusp of another wave of pain.

"How is that possible?" Kalli says, a lethal chill clipping her words. "If the Wardens have been around as long as you suggest, why didn't they—"

"I'm afraid we do not know," Adrien says gently. "And it doesn't matter right now even if we did. That is just one of the many reasons we have to believe that the Primordial is fading."

Something raw and cataclysmic implodes behind my sister's eyes. Lengthening through her spine, Kalli squares off with our uncle, the large raven on her shoulder hardly even budging, as if the creature is a part of her. I blink at the two of them for a long moment, wondering how I never noticed it before. The bird entered her life, what? Eight years ago? Nine? When did they become so in-tune? How was she able to hide their closeness all this time, especially while she worked in the Capital?

"The Blight grows stronger." Every word is sharpened to a point, my sister's tongue a wet stone to the wrath she wields. "The speed at which the Shadowthorn consumes the land has hastened, the creatures growing bolder as they venture out into the neighboring villages and slaughter families by the dozens. Every day we lose more people."

It's left unspoken that our parents are among the dead whom she speaks of, but the somber weight that settles over the room is proof enough that everyone knows what she is insinuating.

Our uncle's head dips. "The Shadowthorn does expand. I cannot contend that. But it is a symptom of the Primordial's corrosion, not an indicator of her growing strength."

I watch the firm line in Kalli's brow twitch. When she doesn't protest further, my uncle continues.

"Centuries ago, when the mages spelled the wall to contain Qaeus in the Eyve, they inadvertently disrupted the channels of magic that flow through the earth. Or at least, that is what many among the druids believe. In all that time while they were trapped with the Primordial, never once did she strike them. Never once was she hostile. To hear some describe it, she was as gentle as a lamb. It was as if she'd forgotten odious nature. And after a while, they grew to forget it too.

"But the longer the severance lasted, the weaker the mage's magic became until one day the spell simply dissolved. The druids describe the Primordial that day as if she had been lit aflame from the inside. In an instant, Qaeus was full of rage once more, and flung herself through the stone wall like a caged animal desperate for escape. The mages—the cowards that they were, and likely still are—couldn't face Qaeus' wrath again. So they fled, thereby severing the flow of magic in the lands yet another time.

"It is believed that the mages now suffer for it, that their magic continues to wane the longer the continent remains broken. Soon the day will come when they'll have no magic left."

The story reminds me of something Maxwell would've enjoyed hearing, the kind of thing he and I would've lost ourselves in if we had stumbled across it in the library. The sudden memory of him drives another stake through my heart as I wonder how my friends are doing at Nigh. Is Maxwell contentedly tending to the forgotten tombs in the library? Has Dimitri been accepted back into the ranks, or is he facing punishment of his own? And I know I shouldn't think about her, but my thoughts drift to Fox as well, to the life she chose over our friendship, and I wonder if she's happy or if she regrets anything at all?

Of course, by now they might not even be at the cathedral still. The Magistrate had every intention of rejoining the Shadow Crusade with the rest of his legion. Part of me wonders if those plans are still in motion, if he's already left the cathedral with the Shadow Crusade, or if the journey has been postponed in an attempt to retrieve the presumed dead body of his son.

But then I remember the disdain he held for the Shadow Crusade, the futile mission he believed us to be upon, and the conviction for which he believed in his own plans to infiltrate the mages of Illashore. The only reason the Crusaders ever returned to retrieve the fallen was to gather the shadowsteel weapons and create more necro-ink to arm the next batch of Crusaders. If the Magistrate has no intention of continuing our cause to slay Qaeus, it's doubtful he'd waste time retrieving a dead body, even that of his son's.

Besides, if he knows the mages' magic is fading, he'll want to attack before they have a chance to remedy the issue.

Sai's nervous chuckle is born when he sees impatience and frustration winding Kalli's lips taut. "And I know *I've* heard this story before, so I'm well aware of where you're going with it, but maybe it's time to tie all those loose ends together for everyone and tell them how this relates to the topic at hand?"

Adrien smiles fondly. "We believe the same thing to be happening to Qaeus. I've been to the site. I've seen the dark mass that beats with the rhythmic pulse of life, and I know the Primordial's body has deteriorated, just as the magic has. It's that very decay that has caused the Blight on Arcathain. It's that decay that the demons crawl from. And it is that decay that must be stopped. Not the Primordial herself."

I drown in the information I've received today, like a babe being tossed around through wave after wave, lost out at sea.

Kalli unfolds her arms before crossing them almost instantly. "What does any of this have to do with Halira? You said there was a cure, but you don't possess it. You said that the heart of Qaeus would help, but that no one can go near it. You have left unspoken how, exactly, the heart could heal her, as well as how we break through the barrier to get close enough to it."

"I like her," Sai whispers, holding his hand up to his mouth as if it's a secret meant only for me. But from where he stands beside Kalli, and with how loudly he speaks, I doubt she doesn't hear him.

Adrien sighs, his shoulders drooping low. "Well, there is a reason for my omissions, dear niece. From here, the lines between what I am sure of and what I think could possibly be true, are far starker. I am hesitant to give you too much hope without the proof that I know you'll desire. But, if you trust me and my estimations, I believe I know the answer to curing the blighted. Or at least, I know where the answer lies." He pauses, waiting for Kalli to interrupt him or protest, giving her the choice of hearing only fact or allowing him to share with her his analysis. When she doesn't say a word, doesn't so much as unfold her arms or move a muscle, he inhales sharply. "The Blight stems from the Primordial's heart, as I've mentioned—from where it touches the earth. That's where the darkness seeps. It is that same toxin that creates the demons and fiends of the Shadowthorn, the same toxin that's inside Halira and Ryven now."

I'm not even sure how to feel about that, but my sister shows no uncertainty when she says, "Okay," and indicates for him to continue.

"Think of what hearts do in our own bodies. They are the muscles that pump our blood throughout our veins, our organs, our entire system. Some valves channel the blood out into the body, and others are receivers, where the blood flows back into the heart." Looking around the room, he checks to make sure everyone is still following him. "I believe, if the blight blood—or toxin, or whatever you want to call it—can flow *from* the Primordial's heart, then wouldn't it stand to reason that it can flow back into it?"

Fascination and hope bubble inside me like rapids. If what my uncle is saying is true, then despite Qaeus' death or deterioration, there is still a chance that Arcathain can be saved. Still a chance that *I* could be saved.

Unfortunately, I make the mistake of noticing Ryven in the corner of the room as he rolls his eyes and shifts ever so slightly away from the rest of us, thereby promptly squashing any hope I'd allowed myself to feel. He's heard this story before, perhaps dozens of times, and for some reason, he finds something disagreeable about it. I wonder just how long he's been blighted, how long he's tried holding on to hope that he will be cured, only to keep waking up as he is.

"Great," Kalli says, the excitement in her voice clearly a

farse. "And how exactly do we *put the Blight back* into Qaeus' heart?"

Adrien's head dips to the side. "Well…"

Kalli cuts him off. "Let me guess. You don't know. I'm beginning to think you know very little."

"It's a good wager," Imryll remarks.

"True," my uncle replies, angling a playful glare at my aunt before returning his gaze to meet my sister's. "But I'm not without a means of discovering."

"What do you mean?"

Adrien clears his throat. He glances over his shoulder back to Ryven, whose breathing intensifies beneath his gaze. "There might be someone who knows how to channel the Blight back into Qaeus' heart. Perhaps now it's time we venture to—"

Startling the room, Ryven shoves off from the table he's been leaning on. "I'm not going back there." His voice is low, almost animalistic.

Adrien crooks an eyebrow at Imryll. "Translation?" There's something about his expression that says he already knows, but Imryll replies anyway.

"He said he's not returning to the Eyve."

"*He* might not have to," Adrien says, turning toward Imryll with a worrying look. "We have options now that Imryll is here. If she is willing to help."

My aunt straightens from where she's hunched over Alphonse's body. As far as I can tell, his breathing has steadied, and I don't know whether to feel disappointed or relieved.

Imryll's head dips. "By death's whisper, I am sworn to protect my nieces. I cannot say whether the Elders will have knowledge of a cure, but if my niece's life is on the line, then I will gladly seek them to find out." She speaks to us now, Kalli rigid at my side. "Besides, as I mentioned in that fetid dungeon, there is nothing I want more than for *all* of us to return home."

I don't have to see Kalli's face to be able to imagine the

disgust that curdles her expression. "The Eyve is not my home." Then, rolling her neck, she softens the edge of her voice. "But, if going there gives us a chance at saving Halira, then I am ready."

"I will go as well," Silver says, and the sound of her vocalizing her support warms my dying heart. After everything she's learned about me, she would still stand by my side. It is all I've ever wanted from a friend, and it is an area where Dimitri and Fox have fallen woefully short.

Güthric grunts beside her, clasping a fist to his chest.

Emboldened by them all, I push myself up to sitting, biting through the pain that slices through my abdomen. "When do we leave?"

The room whips to face me, but it's Imryll who speaks, and though she stares at me, her words are meant for others as well. "I'm afraid not all of us will be."

"I—I don't understand," I stutter. "You just said you wanted us to return to the Forgotten Forest of Eyve with you. Why wouldn't I—I'm coming with you. It's my life in the balance."

"If you were to join us, you'd only slow us down. As Adrien mentioned, you will be quite ill for the next week as the toxin takes root in your system. You will become delirious, dehydrated, and exhausted, certainly not fit for travel. It is best that Kalli and I go now while your body works through the worst of it. By the time the toxin has settled, we will have returned, hopefully bearing news on how to proceed in finding a cure."

"I feel fine," I protest through gritted teeth, and it's only partially a lie. True agony was when the demon's fangs plunged into my skin, raw and searing heat filling me up with a burst of fire. Now that Imryll has healed what she can, most of the pain has gone away. There's still a deep, nagging ache that becomes a sharp shooting twist whenever I move, but the pain is quick to settle back to something almost ignorable. Swinging my legs over the side of the bed, the world tilts, my head spinning, but I try focusing on my aunt. "The pain has already subsided."

To my surprise, it's not Imryll to protest, but Kalli. She drags the back of her hand across my forehead. "Look at you. You're sweating already. The fever has already begun."

Imryll nods. "It is the first symptom of the blight sickness and it will continue to worsen until the fever breaks."

My sister watches me, her gray eyes pleading, if not also commanding. Looking up at her now, she reminds me more of our mother than she ever has, and only because I know how stubborn she can be—and because I'm sensing that Imryll is much the same—do I relent. With one arm supporting my shoulders, Kalli guides me back to the cot. Already my perception is off because it feels like I'm sinking past the mattress, or like the sides of it are rising up around me, swaddling me in a cage that I won't be able to claw my way out of.

I try steadying my breath so as not to cause any alarm or give either of them any more reason to deny me, but I have no intentions of staying here. Uncle or not, I refuse to stay with someone who has been offering sanctuary to the very half-demon who helped kill my parents—Adrien's own brother. I don't care what excuses Adrien has allowed himself to believe, I won't stay here with that *thing*, especially not while my sister and aunt set out to help me. I'm not as helpless as they might believe. I am a trained Crusader now. I've battled demons, small and large, and lived to fight another day. Besides, how could I let my sister—a woman who has never trained a day in her life to combat demons—traverse the perilous Shadowthorn without me? Crusaders with years of training fall to the evil beyond the dark border every day. She is ill-equipped, and I can't let her risk her life on a whim that mine might be saved, not unless I'm willing to also put myself in that same risk.

But none of them need to know that. They need to believe the opposite. If Kalli so much as suspects I intend to do anything other than rest, she'll do whatever is in her power to ensure that I remain stuck here. This cot could become more than a cage of my imagination. I could be shackled to the bedposts or dosed with enough valerian root and chamomile to knock me out for the duration of the fever.

So instead of protesting further, I close my eyes and pretend to acquiesce.

"You said not all of us will be joining you," Silver says at last. "I couldn't help be sense that you meant us."

Imryll nods.

"We won't slow you down. We are Crusaders, trained to traverse the Shadowthorn and fight any of the demons that you may encounter."

My aunt clasps her hands together. "As honorable as such an offer is, once we arrive at the wall, you would be left in the Shadowthorn while we continued into the Eyve, and that is a place where no one can survive, not even the valiant Crusaders." Sensing the question in the air, she elaborates. "Only those with druid blood may cross the into the Eyve. After Qaeus left, we used our own magic to ensure that no one could send her back, and that no human could come running to us for safety, after having abandoned our people so entirely to a fate that they thought would be the end of us."

The room falls silent, her words powerful. All this time I've been raised to hate the mages for the way they abandoned us to the Blight, but I'd never once considered how Arcathainians had done the same to the druids—to *my* people.

"We don't have to enter the Forgotten Forest of Eyve," Silver counters, leaning into the shoulder Güthric offers to hobble off the table. "We can wait outside while you speak to your Elders."

"Not an option," Imryll says sharply.

Adrien steps forward then. "If you thought the Shadowthorn was dangerous near the border towns, let me assure you the real horrors dwell deep, *deep* within the dark expanse."

"You wouldn't survive awaiting us once we're at the border," Imryll adds plainly. With a swivel of her head, she returns her attention to my sister. "Get some rest, Kalli. We leave first thing on the morrow."

Then that's when I'll leave too. If they won't willingly allow me to accompany them, then I'll do so from afar, a safe enough distance back until we've put enough distance between us and the Wardens that they'll have no choice but to bring me with them. I won't slow them down. If Ryven can function despite the blight sickness, if he could fight the demons in Ashenvale and barely break a sweat, if he can whisk damsels into the air without so much as breaking a sweat, then I can manage to walk through the woods.

I will not hinder their pace. If anything, I will propel them to move quicker. There is no one who wants to find this cure more than I do.

From the depths of my slumber, I become aware that someone is standing beside me, watching me as I sleep. My heart quickens, galloping inside my chest, a horse trying to race through the thickest mud, only becoming more frantic as it struggles to gain any real traction. Grogginess and pain keep me from launching myself to my feet and bolting from the room. Where would I go even if I did? The musty air is a quick reminder that I am nowhere near home, trapped instead somewhere deeper in the Shadowthorn than I've ever been aside from my trip to Ashenvale. I may know and trust my uncle, but I also know the kind of company he keeps. Fugitives. Murderers. The blighted on the brink of becoming demons. If I fled this medical tent right now, there's no telling if I would have anywhere safe to run.

It leaves me with few options: fight or remain motionless and hope whoever is here means me no harm. I'm in no condition to attack. Despite the relief Imryll's healing powers offered me, the demon toxin enjoys reminding me of its presence with a wringing of my guts every so often.

I opt to keep my eyes pressed shut. Ever so slowly, my hand

creeps closer to the dagger that's always secured to my thigh, and I silently give thanks to Tor, my brother, for always being here to protect me, even when he's not.

It takes every ounce of restraint in me not to flinch when the stranger brushes their fingers through my sweat-dampened hair, tracing the white locks to where they pool on the cot beside my head. With the stranger's increasing proximity, or perhaps my awareness of them, a new scent reveals itself, a comforting kind of aroma that has no scent at all. It's like walking into one's home after being away for a time, one I hadn't even realized had been a scent associated to my family's cottage, but the moment the smell wafts beneath my nose, I recognize it in an instant.

My eyes flutter open then, but when I tilt my head to confirm my suspicions, my sister is already leaving the room, white ropes of hair tapping quietly against her cloak.

With the sudden understanding that this was the closest thing to a goodbye Kalli plans to give, I bolt upright. Pain flares and I bite down on my tongue to keep from screaming, but I can't afford to succumb. If Kalli came to say farewell, that means she and my aunt will be leaving soon. And if I don't hurry—

My upper half sways forward while my lower half becomes watery. I fall from the cot a good few feet, crashing to my knees on the dirt floor with a painful thud. My momentum carries me even farther, my shoulder colliding with the compacted earth, my cheek slamming into the ground. It's like someone is a turbulent ocean swaying madly beneath me. I can't decide if closing my eyes or keeping them open is worse because everything is moving, and my stomach cannot handle it for much longer.

But as much as I want to curl into a ball and sink back into the comfort of oblivion, the panic that has coiled around me at the thought of being left behind won't let me. If they leave without me, I will be stuck here with the half-demon who was going to kill me the day our parents died, and I'll have to wait for my sister and aunt to return. It could take weeks. Weeks is too long.

Convincing myself that the protesting of my body is only this loud because I've been sedentary for so long, I clench my jaw and crawl back to my knees. Once I've regained stability even remotely, I push onto my heels. My abdomen is warm, but the searing pain has already diminished and it's far easier to ignore now, especially as my heavy head acclimates to being upright again.

For the first time since arriving, I actually notice Alphonse resting on a cot across the room, *actually* look at him. He hasn't budged since our arrival. Buried somewhere deep and cobwebby inside me, I suppose I feel some guilt for what I've done to him, for how satisfying it had been to finally get my revenge, but more than anything, I am awed by the impact my power had on him, at the sheer might of the magic I called upon when I needed it most. It's wrong to revel at someone else's expense, especially considering Alphonse has been unconscious for several hours at least, but I can't help the pride that swirls in my chest as I gaze at his immobilized form. If only I had been able to do that years ago.

Slowly, I draw my attention away from my cousin and back to the room around us to search for my belongings. I'm still dressed in my Crusader leathers, the same ones that are now shredded at the waist by an imprint of fangs that seem far too large for me to have survived. But my shadowsteel battle-axe is missing. If I'm going to stagger after Kalli and Imryll, I'll need a viable weapon to protect myself until they're far enough away from this place that I can reveal myself to them without fear that they'll make me return.

Fortunately, I don't have to look far. I find my shadowsteel axe hanging close by on a rack holding cloaks and a scabbard.

"Come on, Halira," I mutter to myself, seeking to uncover the strength and willpower I need to muster to move with any sort of precision. "You survived the demon scourge in Gravenburg. You survived the attack in the catacombs. You killed a behemoth monster in Ashenvale. Standing on your own two feet should be nothing."

On wobbling, quaking knees, I begin to rise. A rush of cool air blows through me, making my very joints ache and moan. I want nothing more than to hobble back to bed and climb beneath the covers until I am so warm that I could be on fire. But nothing but a slow death awaits me in that bed, and the ever-crippling fear that it's impending without me doing anything about it.

I stagger over to the wall and snatch my axe from the stand, nearly knocking everything else over in the process. The blade is heavier than I remember, the silver seeming to hold less of a shine. As I examine the curve of the blade, my eyes drift to the horned skull of the Primordial Khunas centered on the hilt. At about the same moment my delirious mind convinces me that the skull actually winks, I stagger for the exit. Despite what Adrien and Imryll think, I can ignore the fever-induced hallucinations. They will not hinder me.

Outside of the pavilion, I brace myself for the blinding light of day, only to remember that we are deep inside the Shadowthorn. Outside of what I learned about the Shadowthorn during our trip to Ashenvale, everything else I learned during my time at Nigh. There are seemingly two times of day inside Qaeus' reach: dusk and darkness. Fires crackle in the nearby pits, but they've diminished enough to confirm that the night has just ended, a new day beginning to emerge.

Either not many people in the confines of this place have arisen yet, or the camp is sparsely populated. Perhaps even both, because as I scan my surroundings, I see no one but

Kalli, her back to me, a black raven perched on her shoulder as she strides through the camp, already a long distance ahead of me.

She disappears around a corner and my breath catches. I've already lost more ground than I intended, so I don't delay any longer despite the quivering earth beneath my unsteady strides and the tents that dance around me like frolicking, taunting imps.

I swipe my axe at them whenever they get too close, the blade tearing through a canvas or two, but I don't stay long to find out if I've disturbed anyone. I reach the corner Kalli took, and stumble around it just as quickly.

I follow her through the encampment, its reach wider than I expected for a ragtag bunch of fugitives, and use the various beams and corrals I run into to catch my breath as needed. But I never stay long. I can't. Kalli moves with the same unwavering purpose she carried with her to the Capital, as if her task of locating the cure is remotely as important and timely as the decisions she's made at the Senate on behalf of all Arcathainians.

When I round another corner and find Imryll and Kalli standing just on the other side of the next building, I skitter back the way I came and press myself against the wooden hut. They were holding their bags, their conversation kept quiet so as not to arouse anyone nearby unnecessarily.

"Can you take the form of an animal yet?" I hear Imryll ask and it takes me a moment to register what she's saying. The events of the last few days and the constant onslaught of new discoveries are murky inside my muddled mind. But at the mention of transformation, I recall Imryll's first appearance, how I'd summoned her with the mere mention of her name, and she'd appeared in a gust of feathers and wings, a great raven come to our rescue by the command of magic that had been unknown to me then.

"Not reliably," Kalli answers. "Besides, I'm not sure how helpful becoming an owl would be in this situation."

I have to actually swallow the outrage that threatens to pour from me. I have to be hearing her wrong. Surely, I've just underestimated the power of the hallucinations, for that is the only logical explanation for thinking I'm hearing my sister—a woman who just the other day denied that anything strange or magical had ever happened to her—admit that she can become an owl.

Beneath the hurt of realizing she hadn't trusted me with such information, lies another churning, bitter sensation that I'd rather ignore. Unlike Kalli, I have not mastered—nor even glimpsed—learning how to become an animal.

"No matter," Imryll replies. "Then we will travel by horse."

I look back around the corner as my sister asks, "What horse?"

With a gust of something akin to wind, but something far more charged and exhilarating, a change begins, one that causes my sister, a woman of expert stoicism, to gasp. Imryll hunches forward to all fours, her thin arms extending, her midsection lengthening. Her skin changes from sleek smooth-ness to something velvety. Before our eyes, our aunt becomes a horse, her fur matching the cream of her skin tone and her mane as white as the moon.

A shrill whinny shrieks from her lungs and echoes in the quiet encampment.

The moment the transformation is complete, Kalli resumes her usual flat affect with impressive agility. "You're lucky I know how to ride."

Suddenly, my throat clenches.

No. No. No.

I can't believe it's taken me this long to realize what they intend. They mean to travel by horse—I know Imryll said as much earlier, but the repercussions of such a decision hadn't reached me yet. If they travel on horseback, I won't be able to keep up. Even if I was at my best, which I'm slowly starting to accept that I am not, my two human legs cannot compete with the gallop of four. I'll be left in the dust, lost days behind them as they race through the expansive Shadowthorn to the wall of the Forgotten Forest of Eyve. I'm not even sure of its location.

To follow them now would be foolish.

It would be reckless.

But what alternative do I have? To stay here while they go on some epic quest to save me? To return to living a simple, boring life, like taking up beekeeping—if they even have bees in the Shadowthorn—or maybe fletching like my father? I won't just stay here while Kalli goes to visit with the family I never even knew we had, to the home our mother never told us of, and I certainly am not staying here where a demon lives. I don't care what story Adrien's decided to believe about that day; I'd rather die in the Shadowthorn than be in the same compound as him.

Frantically, I search the nearby structures for any signs of a barn or a trough or even saddles slung over a banister outside of one of these buildings. If Kalli and Imryll will travel by horseback, then so will I. I wouldn't say I'm well-practiced, but I have some experience with it. Throughout the years, the butcher often had a horse on hand to aid with deliveries, transporting large carcasses, and things of that nature. On occasion, Dimitri and I would take their mare out for a ride, chasing hares and ducking beneath low hanging branches, until neither of us could feel our backsides from the ride, nor our face from so much laughter and excitement.

When the aching reminder of his absence brushes up against me, I refocus myself and search for hoof marks in the dirt. But I find none. Not a single indicator that there are any horses living here.

I suppose that's not too farfetched, considering we are still inside the Shadowthorn…

My attention snaps to Kalli as she chucks a satchel over one side of the horse. She kicks off the ground with a grunt, her leg swinging up and over the horse's rear until she's slid into place on the horse's bare back.

"Piss on a mage," I curse under my breath, just as Kalli's heels thump against the horse's belly.

With no time to think about the consequences or even to consider my other options, I tear around the corner and chase after them.

We barrel out of the town, not a single one of us ever looking back, which I suppose I should be grateful for. Kalli and Imryll are so singularly focused that they have no awareness of me staggering after them.

For a while, I convince myself this is working. Even though they're greatly outpacing me, at least I have their tracks to follow, and eventually they'll have to stop for a break. That's when I'll finally arrive and reveal myself.

But it doesn't take long for that thought to crumble to ashes like a torch with nothing left to burn. Within a matter of minutes, the white horse—*my aunt*, I have to keep reminding myself—is putting more and more distance between us until she finally blinks out of view behind the thick bramble of dark slithering trees and underbrush. It's not too long afterward that I become too winded to breathe, a whiny rasp grating in my throat and making my lungs feel like I am breathing smoke rather than fresh forest air.

My disoriented steps continue to slow to a crawl as the forest comes alive around me. The blackened branches reach down for me, their twisted claws hooking in my hair and scratching my skin. Closing my eyes, I bare down on the thought that it's not real. The trees do not move. They do not have claws. But when blink up and see a flash of red, I wonder if it's the trees I should be so fearful of. With the sky lit gray behind them, the branches look like fissures on dusty glass. They move with a volition of their own, the forest contorting around me like a living, breathing thing. I'm no longer convinced it's not. If all of this stems from Qaeus' heart, who's to say it's not alive?

Just then, the leaf-covered ground bucks. My knees give as I fly forward, trying desperately not to whack myself with the blade of my sharp axe as I crash to the cold, dark ground. Dizzily, I raise my head, only to let it fall back down to the earth when it starts to spin again. I am caught in a cyclone of nausea and weakness too powerful to overcome.

With my ear pressed firmly into the dirt, I swear I can almost still hear the rhythmic beating of Imryll's hooves as she and Kalli gallop away; I can almost feel the Shadowthorn breathing against my cheek, my belly.

"What *are* you doing?" a male, aristocratic voice calls from somewhere distant, and yet all around me at the same time.

I scramble to my feet, but my head is so much heavier than the rest of me and I nearly fall over again. I bury my axe into the ground instead and use it to support myself. A bead of sweat drips down my forehead as my eyes strain to focus on the approaching man.

At first, I almost can't see him, his dark hair and armor blending in so fluidly with the shadows around us. But the sharp angles of Alphonse's face as he steps into view are unmistakable. There's a hobble to his gait that hadn't been there before. Wicked pride flickers at the realization that I caused it, my lightning did.

At least I'm not the only one impaired.

"You have no idea where you're going. Do you?" he asks, irritation prominent in his noble tone.

"Alphonse?" I say, struggling to find every strangled word. "What are you doing here?"

Wincing to some unseen discomfort, he rubs his chest. "You tell me. There I was, sleeping soundlessly—mind you, on a dreadfully cold and uncomfortable thing they called a bed—when I was rudely roused by my inept cousin bumbling around the room, mistaking herself as some kind of covert lioness, when in reality she was as loud as a charging bull."

I'll show you a charging bull I'm tempted to say to him as I think back to how easily I'd struck him down the other day. But I'm still struggling to stand, let alone speak. The butt end of my axe digs deeper into my shoulder as my ability to hold myself upright continues to diminish.

"But," he continues. "Seeing as I was unable to discern my surroundings with any sort of familiarity and noticing the effort with which you put into skulking about, I opted to follow you in your escape. It seemed a wise decision. Whatever danger you believed awaited you, presumably the same awaited me."

My raspy voice finally awakens. "We weren't in danger, you fool." I wish I could see his face more distinctly, watch the way he scowls at the insult, see how he holds himself back for fear of evoking my wrath again. But the shadows cast down by the trees distort his features, as does the realization of what I've just said. Do I really believe that to be true? That we were in no danger with the Wardens, despite the company they keep?

It's not a truth I can allow myself to admit. Not now. Not when I'm on a mission and already losing ground. "I'm following my sister," I tell him.

With his teeth still biting down on the venom he'd like to spew at me, he responds. "I noticed you were following them." Then, straightening, his voice takes on a smugger tone. "But to where, I wondered." When his arms spread wide, indicating to the thick trees around us, I notice his scabbard is empty. Or at least, I think it is. The way it jostles against his thigh makes it appear no heavier than a flap of leather. Either his sword wasn't retrieved after our fight, or he didn't take the time to look around the medical ward like I had before he left. "As far as I can tell, you're headed deeper into the Shadowthorn. Not toward safety. And at the rate you're going, well, you'll make a nice demon meal once you find the Primordial, I'm sure."

It's not an outright threat, but my body responds to it like it is. The darkness inside me stirs and thrashes at the very idea that death could befall me. Anger swells so swiftly that I might as well be a tidal wave bent on destruction.

Baring my teeth, I shove myself off my axe, fury fortifying me with the strength I need to stand tall and glare at him straight in the eyes. "You should head back to camp. You don't even have any shadowsteel on you."

Something like shock or fear bulges behind his eyes. He glances down to the vacant scabbard at his waist, and upon corroborating what I've already told him to be true, and perhaps irritated that I'm right for once, he pinches the brim of his slender nose.

As my mind adjusts back to reality, the fever giving me a reprieve from its mind tricks, I can finally see my cousin more clearly. The necro-ink symbols he wore the day earlier remain almost entirely intact, aside from one of the lines that should be below his eye. Those are more faded than the others, seemingly wiped away as the ink has been dragged further down his cheeks than it would've been normally. There's noticeable wear in his chest armor, particularly in the center, a faded gray that I realize is exactly where the lightning speared him.

"I don't understand," he says slowly, emphatically, as if he's irritated with the way every one of those words make him sound weak. Vulnerable. At my mercy. "How are we this deep in the Shadowthorn? The last I recall, we were still near Nigh, but I've been in this place enough times to know that Nigh is at least a day's travel. How did we get here? How is there a camp this far under the Primordial's reach—one that, might I add, I've never before encountered?" Without any real answers to his questions, staying silent is easy. "Why have you brought me here?"

My jaw pops open. "I didn't bring you here."

But it's like he doesn't hear me. "When my father hears that you've abducted me, have no doubt that he will bring the force of the entire Arcathainian Legion to search for me, and when he finds you—"

"I didn't *take* you. Your Crusaders left you for dead." At seeing him flinch at the words, my own anger simmers. "If it weren't for our uncle—"

"Uncle Adrien? That vagrant? What does he have to do with any of this?" The confusion only lasts a moment before clarity flashes in his expression. "He was there. During the attack. I'd almost forgotten."

It hits me then just how much of the previous day's events he's missed, and how little time I can afford to spend catching him up.

I shake my head. "Never mind. It doesn't matter. You're wasting my time."

It takes more effort than it should, but with a firm grip and a mostly solid stance, I'm able to pull my axe from the ground. I pivot away from Alphonse, intent on leaving him where he stands so that I can pick up Kalli's trail again.

"And just where do you think *you're* going?"

I growl, tossing my head back. "I already told you. I'm following my sister. If you don't want to head farther into the Shadowthorn without a weapon, then I suggest you head back to the Wardens and leave me alone."

He barks a laugh, one that quickly becomes a fit of coughing as he clutches his chest once more. It takes him a moment to recover, but when he does, he's just as arrogant as always. "And you just expect me to let you escape? Have you forgotten your place? You are my prisoner. I will not leave without you. The two of us are returning to Nigh and…"

Another bout of nausea coils in the pit of my stomach, one that overpowers any notion of outrage I might've lashed out with. I clutch my own stomach and try not to think about the slithering inside my belly, the warm oiliness rising to the back of my throat.

I blink through tears and stare at Alphonse, still on a rampant tirade. There's no getting through to him. I don't know why I even try. Everything I say, he just argues against it. It's in his nature to be belligerent and quarrelsome with me; it always has been. It's as if every breath I take, every word I speak sets him off—

Every *word*…

Realization smacks into me like I've just walked into a stone wall.

"Wait…you can understand me?"

Alphonse glares as if I've just insulted him greatly. "Of course I can understand you. What kind of preposterous question is that? Your voice carries like a shrill piglet crying out for its mother."

I barely register his insult, too dumbstruck by what this conversation might mean. I mull over everything my aunt and uncle told me about demons and druids, about the blight sickness that's ravaging me from the inside and changing me on some biological level.

"But…you can't. Uncle Adrien said that only druids would be able to understand me now."

Alphonse scoffs. "*Uncle* Adrien is a filthy criminal who keeps the company of thieves and whores." It's like he doesn't know our uncle at all. Or at least, not the full version of him, only the version his father has shared about him, of the man who's an offense to the entire country. "As much as I would love to never hear your voice again," he adds. "Unfortunately, I'm plagued by your perpetual prattle."

"You don't get it," I say. "If you can understand me, why couldn't Silver or Güthric, or even Sai, for that matter?"

I bite my lip, recalling the way they all stared at me like I had already become a deranged demon that would pounce on them the moment they took their eyes off me. My thoughts drift back even further, to the day I ran into Adrien at Ashenvale and his strange, one-sided interactions with Ryven. The more I think on it, the more certain I am that Ryven never bothered speaking to him, nor any of the others. He used hand motions and his facial expressions to convey everything that he'd communicated to them.

But he spoke to me. I was the only one who could understand him.

Realization rips through me anew, making my eyes bulge as I return my gaze to Alphonse. "You're part druid."

A muscle in his jaw muscle twitches. "I beg your pardon?"

"It's the only explanation. Why else would you be able to understand me?"

"Because you're speaking clear as day."

"I'm not though," I assure him, but I'm soon swept away in an onslaught of childhood memories.

The Magistrate had never been kind or warm to anyone, but he seemed to reserve a special place in his heart for the loathing he reserved for Alphonse. I can recall times when he'd enter a room with Alphonse close on his heels, and my Uncle Esmond would slam the door in his face, feigning unawareness of his son's obvious presence. On the rare occasion they'd come to visit, I can recall at least three times when Esmond loaded up his carriage and left without the boy, not even realizing he'd done so until Alphonse had chased him halfway down the road screaming at him for leaving him again, as if it were an occurrence that happened all too regularly. More often than not, Alphonse would be referred to as *bastard* by his father rather than by his first name. And the longer I think about it, the more it all begins to make a depressing sort of sense.

"It's no wonder you never knew your mother," I say, just as breathless from the exertion as I am from the realization. "She was probably a druid. Maybe your father knew, or found out afterward, but—"

"Lies!" Alphonse jaws tear open in a snarl, his shoulders drawing back as he devours the space between us. "I will not believe a single word that spews from your vile, treacherous mouth, *mage*."

I shove his shoulders, and stumble back from the effort just as much he does. "I'm not lying to you, Alphonse. I'm simply telling you what you missed while you were unconscious. I was bitten by a demon. I should be dead by now. If I were merely a human, I would be. But druid blood isn't as susceptible to the toxin. It slows down the infection, but Arcathainians cannot understand me anymore, not as long as I remain infected. The only way you would be able to understand what I'm saying right now is if—"

His finger shoots outward, a solid line as stiff as a sword. "Don't you dare say it."

"Whether I say it or not doesn't make it any less true."

His snow-white pallor burns hot and bright, the scowl on his face etching deeper into his perfect complexion with dark, heavy crevices that mimic the bare, blackened Shadowthorn branches hanging over us.

A new realization occurs to me, one that draws out a cocky grin. "Oh, I get it. All this anger and frustration. If you're part druid, if you have magic in your blood, then you'll have to persecute yourself once you return to Arcathain. Maybe we can walk to the gallows together—"

"Shut. Up."

"Saying our last prayers to the gods—"

"I said stop."

But I don't. I can't. Not after all the years that he lorded over me, made me feel small and weak. Worthless. Pathetic. I was raised better than to kick a wounded animal while it was down, but my parents' gentle teachings escape me now. I'm a gleeful to torment him, and if that should scare me, then maybe there's something more wrong with me than I realize because it doesn't.

"That is, if you ever return." Delight fizzes inside me, a babbling brook that sends thrilling chills down my arms. "Perhaps we'll even get lucky and they'll hang us together, and I'll get to watch with morbid satisfaction as you finally meet the death you should've ages ago."

"That's enough!"

Without warning, Alphonse lunges for me, fingers outstretched like claws that want to slice open my jugular. My bravado of words does nothing for the nausea wracking my body and silences my reflexes, weakening my movements. I'm too slow to dodge his grasp, too delirious to revisit any of the training I received during my time at Nigh, nor the few times Tor tried teaching me.

My only reaction is to flinch when his body collides into mine and we tumble backward.

We slam into the ground as if it were concrete. The impact defies sound, a cataclysmic boom that ricochets throughout my entire body and leaves my bones groaning like the wounded survivors of battle.

But this battle is only just beginning.

Alphonse pins me down with his hips, a cold hand clutching my chin. I'm still dazed by the sudden flip of the land, still disoriented and aching from the fall, that when his fist cracks into my cheek like a solid chunk of ore, I don't even see it coming. Pain bursts below my eye, filling my jaw with a deep ache that makes me wonder if I'll be able to talk again. I blink up through the black branches, to the gray sky beyond, and only see red.

We've been here too many times before. I've taken this beating more than I ever should've. And though I might not be able to beat him, I can at least fight back.

Before he can swing again, my senses awaken. Gritting my teeth, I rear my hips and send his unsuspecting body catapulting over me. He lands in the blackened leaves with a whoosh of air from his lungs, and I scramble to my feet to stand over him, to relish in the power of *him* being the one on the ground this time, not me.

Staring down at him, I do my best to ignore the writhing Shadowthorn as it encroaches on us. There is no distinction between what is real or not, no way for me to discern if the blinking red eyes that have appeared in the canopy are the eyes of hungry fiends or just a figment of my fever-addled and wrathful imagination, no way to tell if the swinging branches are blown by wind or have a mind of their own. The more I try to make sense of it, to decide what's real or not, the more my head pounds with the thunderous beatings of a thousand horses' hooves.

I'm so distracted by the lurching realm that I almost fail to notice Alphonse staggering to his feet. His struggle is as visible as mine. The way he rubs the faded mark in his chest armor reminds me that he, too, is still recovering from the other night. The lightning I shot at him had a long-lasting bite.

Not long enough, my rage says. It's the first time since I've been bitten that I've called it that, treated my anger like it is its own sentient being. Right now, it feels like it. I spent our entire childhood telling myself that I didn't want to fight him, that I never had. He was always the one to instigate any feud between us and I was docilly willing to go on about our lives believing that me not wanting to fight him made me the better person. I convinced myself that I was showing him kindness, that my act of pacifism would maybe inspire him someday to treat others with more care.

How naïve I had been. It was not an act of kindness I was doing him, it was one of empowerment, enabling him to continue being the scared little boy whose only ounce of power came from the lineage that didn't even want him.

He'd meant to kill me. After having me and my sister arrested and forcing us to flee our homeland, he hunted me down like an animal and would've been all too elated to slaughter me right there in the Shadowthorn if I hadn't inter-vened. If I hadn't stood up for myself and everyone else he's ever stomped all over.

Even if it wasn't clear from the fury reflected in his eyes now that he still means to kill me, the time for complacency is over. The era of retribution has come. I will not die so easily. I will not let him win. If only I could summon the lightning I'd possessed the other day, I would end this, here and now, knock him down and leave him for dead the way he'd want to leave me. How satisfying that would be. But I already know I'm too weak. The lightning isn't even a distant purr beneath my skin; it's static silence. My delirious mind can't even focus long enough to try to summon the storm.

Before he can regain his footing, I square my hunched shoulders, steady my staggered breaths, and charge. I'm not as stiff as I'd like to be when my shoulder slams squarely into his stomach. I cause myself more pain than I do him. But the blow lands, only, instead of stumbling backward, the two of us fly through the air. I hadn't noticed the knoll behind him. My fever hadn't allowed me to.

We hit the sloped earth with a resounding thud that makes my bones scream an echo of the pain they endured during our first fall. The impact sends us sprawling, detangling our bodies and sending each of us on our own rolling and tumbling path down the hill. Limbs flailing, my battle-axe is flung from my hand, and I'm only deftly aware that might've been for the better when on the next rotation my weapon arm is bent into my chest at an angle that sure would've split me open if the axe had still been in my hand.

The bottom of the chasm comes fast and hard, the earth covered in oblong rocks that clatter where we land. I can no longer tell the difference between which parts of me are fever-sick and which are battle-weary.

Blearily, I push through the pain and try shoving myself up, only to have my hand slip through the loose earth, sending my jaw to the ivory rocks beneath me. When they snap and crack on impact, it's then that I come to the unfortunate, terrifying conclusion that these aren't rocks at all.

Fear coils around my heart like a frightened snake rearing to attack. I look over the expansive grave of bones that we've stumbled into. I want to believe they're the remnants of live-stock poached from the dozens of fallen Arcathainian villages riddled throughout the Shadowthorn, the discarded pickings of small animals that wandered over across the darkened border. But I know better. Growing up with Dimitri, the ward of a butcher and one of the main hunters residing in the Wallows, I've seen my fair share of animal carcasses. To the trained eye, their bones are distinct. On more than one occa-sion during his hunting treks, Dimitri had been able to identify an animal purely by the carcass left behind. I never looked longer than I needed, but even I don't need Dimitri's proficient gaze now to point out that none of these skulls resemble any woodland creatures, let alone livestock. The large, mostly round skulls are human.

Fear stills my shaking limbs, and I push myself off the ground, aware of Alphonse doing the same not too far away from me.

Something clings to my fingers, wiry and sticky. I don't want to know what kind of human excrement it might be, and

I brush my hands hastily against my pleated leather armor, scanning the area for any signs of the beast that could've accomplished this massacre. Tracks in the dirt, disturbed foliage, snapped branches—anything to indicate that something large has been through here. When I find none, and when the pesky threads tangled in my fingers won't scrub clean, my gaze falls to my hand. The translucent fibers glisten in the early morning haze, thin and sinewy. A spiderweb, tackier than the mortar used to seal a stone wall and stronger than any I've ever had the displeasure of encountering before, weaves two of my knuckles together.

And like everything else in this forsaken land, the string is as black as death.

The ground quivers, a gravelly rumble that rattles the bones before us. Alphonse and I exchange a worried look, one that reminds me just how doomed we are. Neither of us are in any condition to fight. Even as we stand here, I can sense my focus waning, another bought of hallucination veiling my perception with nonsense and misdirection. Alphonse, too, is debilitated by his own demons. He leans slightly to one side, his elbow cradling the rib right where my lightning struck him and a new abrasion fresh on his cheek and leaking down his jaw.

Another tremor rolls through the boneyard like a wave crashing on the shore.

Then another.

And another.

Each one is more powerful than the next, ridding us of any hope that whatever shadowcreature is moving about might've been headed anywhere else but here, let alone that it might be small enough that either of us could stand a chance. The behemoth from Ashenvale surfaces to memory, a beast that had practically stood as tall as the homes nearby, with long, thin slashing arms. Not even it created such a raucous when it moved. Not like this.

Despite all odds, or maybe because of them, our training kicks in, and Alphonse and I move toward one another, our backs almost flush against each other. The thunderous steps keep coming, becoming more distinct, more resolute, more sinister as they approach.

A shadow fills the pit like an ominous cloud passing through the sky overhead. Our gazes climb the shadow, dragging over the hundreds of bones scattered between us and the opposite side of the chasm, until they crest the top of the hill and snag on the eight-legged creature looming there, its fangs dribbling with hunger.

ARANEAE UMBRA

SPIDER'S DEN, SHADOWTHORN

The shadowspider swivels its repulsive head, the two-dozen black, beady eyes never once blinking as it stares down below. Watching. Waiting. My knowledge of spiders is limited. Though they have eyes, I'm not sure they can actually see, or if their sight is based on heat, on movement, or if they're one of those creatures that relies on the reverberations of sound or on scenting their prey. And since I have no way of knowing whether the beast has spied us yet, I don't dare move. My bones become iron rods in my skin. And as long as that creature stays up there and far, *far* away, we just may survive this yet.

To complicate the matter of my limited understanding of spiders, this isn't just any spider. The shadowcreature looming at the top of the hill is gargantuan in size. For all I know, it could be the Primordial Qaeus, whose vague descriptions refer to her as hideous and as large as anything ranging from a tree to a mountain. The shadowspider wouldn't even need to scale a building to climb it; it could simply stretch one of its slender, oily legs over and lift its heavy body atop the thatched rooftop.

Like all the creatures of the Shadowthorn, its skeletal form is coated in darkness, the spider seemingly having crawled up from a black lagoon of death and decay that still drips from its flesh.

Its two fangs press against each other, and I start to fear that it might have caught our scent after all.

"Where is your axe?" Alphonse mutters through gritted teeth beside me, his lips not so much as twitching as we both gawk at our impending demise.

The axe will be of no use to us now. I'd been holding it when Alphonse and I fell into this death pit and it had been flung from my grasp. But since Alphonse followed after me without a single shadowsteel weapon on him, it will be our only chance at survival. I search the hill behind us for any glint of silver I might find there, but my careless twist catches the spider's watchful attention at last. The screech that fills the chasm is grating and shrill, like the tip of a sword being dragged up my spine. I spin back around, finding the spider reared on six of its eight legs before it crashes back to the ground with a mighty tremor that rattles the trees. It launches itself into a barreling descent and my heart quickens.

The spider moves too fast to fathom. Its spindly legs pierce through the foliage like arrows loosed through air, but they're drawn back and knocked again faster than any archer's aim. There will be no outrunning the beast, but Alphonse and I scramble backward anyway.

The shadowcreature lands at the base of the knoll with another quaking boom, one that clatters not only the bones around us, but also the ones inside my body, the ones that I had turned to steel but have since been boiled to quivering puddles of broth.

I stumble as I turn around, falling face-first against the hill, my mouth filling with what I tell myself is just oblong rocks or extremely stiff grass. Lifting my head, I try to catch my bearings, to push myself back up off the ground so that I might stand a chance at scaling the hill before the shadowspider reaches us.

But something flat and hard cracks into my nose when I look up.

"Sorry," Alphonse says, any hint of remorse absent from his voice. I plummet back into the pit. "But one of us needed to be sacrificed."

My back slams into a cold sea of bones, my head colliding with something solid. Everything hurts, even my lungs as they strain to draw air. Some of the bones shatter beneath me on impact, but the more formidable ones, the newer skulls and ribcages that the spider has picked clean more recently, those ones leave bruises. They awaken the aches inside me that Imryll healed from the demon bite. They make my stomach boil, turn my blood to liquid fire.

I groan from the burning fever that ripples over my entire body.

Distantly, I'm aware of the rumble shaking furiously beneath me. I know it means that the spider is advancing with predatorial speed, that I should roll over, jump to my feet, and prepare to fight. But all I can do is lie here. Out of all the horrible things Alphonse has ever done to me, this, by far, stings the most. He has all but killed me himself. He might as well of stuck a dagger into my heart and I don't know why I'm still so surprised after all these years.

Blinking back the tears, I watch with jaded horror as my cousin drags his hobbled body up the knoll without ever once looking back, never once showing any signs that he feels remorse, even if he did what he believed he needed to do.

I'm about to yell something profane at him, when the shadowspider's head appears over me.

I become as rigid as stone, as still as the dead bones beneath me.

As the shadowcreature dips its face closer, its insect-like fangs twitching as it nears, I hold my breath and try steeling the thrumming of my heart, try forcing myself to a false death that might be convincing enough that the creature will leave me alone. The shadowspider's head is so large that its fangs drag over my aching cheek and stomach at the same time. They trail down the rest of my body, the beast moving farther and farther so that it can smell the length of me, until I can see nothing but the ribbed underside of its breast hovering above me.

It's not until then that I remember Tor's dagger strapped tightly in the hilt at my waist.

While the creature is still distracted, its fangs skittering over my leathers and the places where my skin is bare, I reach for the hilt of the weapon that's always strapped at my side. Once the leather binding is within my grasp, once I can feel my brother's presence beside me like a ghost guiding my hand, I become as swift as a coursing river.

I jerk the dagger free and plunge it into the shadowspider's underbelly, stopping only once the hilt makes me.

The giant beast shrieks. I cover my ears to shield against the shattering sound as the spider writhes and draws backward. I flip onto all fours to watch as the creature skitters away, retreating back toward the hill it plummeted down, and I have just enough time to relish in my victory before dread seizes me again. Instead of climbing back up the hill, the shadowspider halts its mammoth body at the base. Leaking inky blood all over the necropolis, the beast screeches again, a cry that sounds more like vengeance than one of pain. Its beady eyes fix with lethal focus on one point in the arena before it: me.

Adrenaline pumps through me with renewed vigor. I shove

myself away, scooting back on my hands and rear, desperate and wild. I ignore the bones splintering beneath me, the ones puncturing my palms, my thighs, as I drag myself blindly through the graveyard.

The spider rears on its hind legs and something shines from its underbelly. A poisonous lump fills my throat when I realize I'm staring at my dagger. When I covered my ears, I must've left it buried inside its mark, foolishly forgetting to keep it close in case I needed it again. It's still gouged inside the shadowspider stomach, staunching some of the bleeding, but the way the creature charges makes me think it's nothing more than a sliver in its side.

Something heavy lands beside me, making the bones jostle and casting me in shadow. I peer up just as two arms wrap under my legs and around my back, dark wings unraveling around us with diaphanous shine.

Ryven hoists me into the air, backlit only by the dark gray sunlight that sifts through the blighted trees. His bat-like wings catch air like sails on the ocean, carrying us off the ground and away from my demise.

"What are you doing out here?" Ryven growls. "You shouldn't have attacked it. It smelled the demon blood in you—it would've left you alone."

Watching its meal be stolen from it, the charging shadowspider becomes enraged. It uses its amounting speed to rear again, its gaunt and crooked legs aimed and ready for the both of us.

"Look out!"

But my warning comes too late. With a precision that would've been impressive under any other circumstances, the shadowspider spears one of Ryven's wings on an updraft. The half-demon roars, a gut-churning cry that sounds as if the dead have risen, and the two of us are sent plummeting back down to the ground. We crash into the bumpy sea of human remains and I can almost see their terrified faces, hear the final screams that burst from their lungs in the moments before they met their deaths.

I refuse to be one of them. Despite the throbbing of my skull, despite the way the world seems to tilt left and then right and then left again as if I am on a pendulum, I muster the will to roll onto my stomach. My arms protest, they insist they have no more energy to spare, but I grind my teeth and shove them beneath me anyway.

By the time I'm up on all fours again, a fresh coat of sweat dripping down my back and my breathing ragged, I find that I'm halfway across the field of bones from where the shadowspider now stands over Ryven. It takes me a moment to gather why the half-demon man isn't moving, but then I see the horrendously sharp and angular leg that's pinning his wing to the ground.

Ryven's square jaw is twisted in agony, his arm reaching across his chiseled chest and to the space beside him where is wing is penetrated by the large leg. As the shadowspider crouches closer, its fangs dancing over his face as it had mine, I realize this is my chance to run. With the creature distracted, I might be able to drag myself out of this pit and back to somewhere that resembles safety.

At the thought, my stomach twists like a hundred coiling snakes. That is exactly what Alphonse did. He left me to die so that he could live. Had I not recognized the injustice of that when it had been me left in the spider's den? Can I bring myself to admit the injustice of it now that the roles are reversed between me and the half-demon man who killed my parents?

Before I can decide whether to help him or myself, the fight flashes back into Ryven's dark eyes. He kicks the dagger still buried in the spider's abdomen and half of the beast's body collapses. As it shrieks and writhes, shriveling and expanding, dragging its crumpled body away, Ryven's wing finds the release he needs. He pulls himself off the ground and squares away with the shadowspider, but his injured wing hangs limply from his back, his shoulder hunched from the pain and weight of it.

He bends to retrieve something from the bones. I'm too far away to tell what it is at first, my vision muffling again from fever, but when he twirls the item at his side, the shadowsteel gleaming in the rogue tendrils of light, I recognize Tor's blade in his grasp and indignation consumes me. No one touches my brother's dagger but me, especially not the man responsible for our parents' deaths. Who does he think he is, swooping in like some dark Crusader? I won't allow him to save me again. He already intervened once in Ashenvale, possibly in the catacombs as well. He does not get to be the reason I am an orphan and the reason why I'm still alive.

My hands bunch into fists at my sides as the shadowspider rises and faces Ryven once more.

I should run. It would serve him right for everything he's done. If the bones around us are any indication, death by shadowspider is about as gruesome of a demise as I could've ever hoped for him. If I fled now, I might have enough energy in me to stagger away to safety. But to where? The Wardens is the only place that could offer such security, and it is not where my heart tells me to go. My journey to the Forgotten Forest of Eyve cannot just end as swiftly as it has begun. For whatever reason—call it arrogance or stubbornness or perhaps something more profound like fate—I am driven by a need to continue forward. Such a sensation, such determination and motivation are unfamiliar to me. They are the characteristics more commonly associated with my sister. Where I spent years in the Wallows bemoaning my life but never once doing anything to change it, Kalli set out with a plan. Through sheer determination and aptitude, she secured herself a seat at the Arcathain Senate.

Perhaps it's because such a profound sense of direction is so strange to me that I know I can't go back. The Wardens would keep me there *for my own good*, they'd say, despite every instinct in my blood telling me that my path lies in the Forgotten Forest of Eyve.

The shadowspider before me screeches, drawing my attention back across the graveyard. How many of these fallen tried to outrun it? How many had it hunted down only to drag back to its collection? As long as this creature lives, I will never be assured that it won't follow me, that it won't find me in the middle of the night somewhere and stab me with its sharp leg like it did Ryven's wing.

Besides, I can't leave now. Not without Tor's dagger.

With a sudden rush of realization, I remember that the dagger isn't the only weapon at our disposal. I scan the hillside for a glint of silver. My eyes roam over the skid marks left behind by Alphonse's and my tumbling bodies. They ignore the deeper gouges and grooves where my cousin dug the toes of his boots into the mud as he abandoned me and fled. And just when I'm about to give up my search, right when I convince myself it must've been another hallucination and that I wasn't even carrying the axe, something shimmers behind a tall patch of blackened grass.

I clamber up the slope, faintly aware of the eyes following my back. Whether Ryven thinks I'm abandoning him or not, I do not care; with the pounding skittering of the giant shadowspider's footsteps, I have little time for thinking about anything other than focusing on my path. The window of opportunity to intervene is dwindling. For every stride and leap it takes for me to reach my weapon, Ryven is forced to defend himself—and with nothing more than a dagger, at that.

I know those odds. I faced them already. And if it weren't for the half-demon—

Stubborn pride and heartache clamp down on the thought before it can finish. Staggering, I finally reach my shadowsteel axe. As I clutch the pole, power thrums into my grasp and up my arm with the jolt of a thousand sparks. Baby bursts of lightning and fire. They dance through me until I am nothing more than static charge before fading into the background of my being. There may still be much for me to learn about wielding such a weapon, but whenever this axe is in my hands, I feel invincible.

Looking back down to the pit, I pay attention to the strategy and pattern of Ryven's motions. Every time the shadowspider draws near enough to sink its fangs into him, he slides under the beast's belly and springs up behind it. For a creature of that size, it's fast, but not fast nor limber enough to follow. It shuffles around to face him again, charging, its fangs bared and glistening, only to be thwarted again when Ryven ducks beneath it once more.

I catch the half-demon's eye, a silent look telling me to be ready. He's stalling. He knows as well as I that he doesn't stand a chance against this horrendous creature. I can't help but wonder why though. The day my parents were murdered, he'd torn the other demon to shreds with his bare hands. The shadowspider may be larger than that demon had been, but I would think he'd still be able to do some damage with a dagger. Or perhaps he's more injured than I thought.

After sliding down the slope, I crouch low, the boney ground cool and knobby against the knee I'm propped on. I creep toward a boulder along this end of the clearing, trying not to disturb the bones discarded at my feet. Fortunately, on the outskirts of the pit, the human remains are sparser and easier to navigate around, even if the blighted blood coursing through me makes my head sway and fills my feet with lead.

Once I reach my position behind the rough boulder, I catch Ryven's eye across the clearing. He's been glancing my direction on every rotation, every dodge and maneuver that keeps him alive. When my gaze snags on his, dark and bottomless as a chasm of death, my head bobs to indicate that the time has come.

Something swift and dark shifts in his gaze before I duck away unseen.

I try steeling myself against the nausea bubbling in my gut. My axe sways overhead in my frail grip. The sharp blade of my weapon towers above the height of the boulder, and surely, if anyone were to look—if the shadowspider were to scan the arena for any signs of foul play—the creature would see my axe sticking up high, and the stealth I was attempting to achieve would be forfeit. But judging from the clambering steps and jostling bones, the beast is still too immersed, too intent on killing the man that has made a fool of it time and time again, to notice anything but him.

This time when I hear Ryven sliding through the brittle bones to dash beneath the shadowspider, he bellows, a deep and guttural sound that carries over the ravine and tells me to be ready.

The two of them charge. Tucked behind the boulder, I cannot see them, but I feel the power in their strides as the ground quakes beneath my feet and the boulder hums at my back.

Ryven smacks into the large rock, his fist pounding twice as if it's some signal we've agreed to. "Now!" he shouts.

Twisting around, I spring from the ground, my feet scaling the boulder in two swift strides. I'm not sure where such agility came from, nor the sudden burst of energy that's flooding through me now, but I don't question it. Now is not the time for doubt. Doubt is the enemy of necessary risk-taking.

Once I'm midair, the shadowspider's bulbous head before

me and my axe swung over my shoulder, ready for a devastating blow, all notions of doubt disappear. I may have few experiences with the lesser-known demons of the Shadowthorn, but I've already bested one of them—in much the same way, I might add.

The shadowspider cocks its head, recognition flashing behind the dozens of beady black eyes at the very moment I bury the sharp blade into its skull. The creature rears, and I hold tight. I ride the beast down as it hitches, the last vestiges of life shrieking from its lungs and wreaking havoc on my eardrums. When the shadowspider finally collapses, it is nothing more than a shriveled heap of darkness resting among a tapestry of its fallen victims.

At some point in the commotion, my dangling body that clung to the hilt of my axe was swung to the top of the creature's head. It's a good thing too because now that the fight is over, the blight sickness thrashes through me with renewed vigor. Suddenly, it's as if I hardly have the capacity to breathe, let alone leap from boulders and swing my hefty shadowsteel around.

This illness doesn't make sense. It comes in waves and flashes, ones without rhyme or reason. Some are powerful and knock me to my knees, while others are distant cries that make my muscles ache with nearly forgotten memories of past injuries.

Biting through the exhaustion, I drag myself to my feet and try shoving on the handle of my axe so that it might loosen from the deep gash in the shadowspider's skull.

It's no use though. I can barely stand upright, let alone crank away at the weapon that had been so heavy when I first received it that I'd nearly toppled over and carelessly sliced through the onlooking Crusaders. I have no more energy to muster. Collapsing to my knees, I rest my head against the pole of my weapon, close my eyes, and let the hazy air fill me.

My eyes snap right back open though when I feel the creature moving underneath me. It's a subtle, rocking motion, one that mimics breathing. But that can't be right. I look to my axe again, making sure it's shadowsteel I buried into the beast's skull and not just some regular weapon.

But then I hear a soft grunt, one that sounds far too human to be anything that dwells in this wretched place, and the faint thud of footsteps walk up behind me. Well, *human* might not be the best description.

Ryven extends his hand to me, the one opposite his torn wing. I smack it away and stay firmly planted where I am.

"Whoever said I needed your help up?"

A humorless laugh leaks from his crooked grin. "You seemed tired. I thought I would help."

"Of course I'm tired!" I bark, pressing my palms into my knee and forcing myself to stand. "I just fought one of the largest shadowcreatures I've ever seen, while simultaneously fending off the blight sickness that's left my mind and body tormented by fever, all occurring immediately after I fled my homeland, was betrayed by my best friend, lost my boyfriend, and became an outlaw. I think I've earned a moment to rest."

Relishing in my point, I lean against the hilt of the axe, but as if to prove that he is the pettier one among us, Ryven shoves my hand away and I almost flail face-first off the shadowspider's head.

"Hey!" I say, catching my balance. I turn around to find both his hands are gripped tight around the rod. "Don't touch that. It's mine—"

With one great heave, he pulls the axe from the shadowspider's head. He feels the weight of it in his hands and I'm frozen as I watch, unsure of what he'll do with it. After all, he's lunged for me at least once already, hunted me down across Arcathain. What's to stop him from finishing the job he meant to end months ago?

To my slack-jawed surprise, he hands the weapon to me, pole-side and arches a brow. "I forgot how much rage rules the recently-blighted."

Ignoring his irritatingly unhelpful and slightly condescending words, I snatch the weapon away before he can think better of offering it to *me*. Doesn't he know that the balance is not settled between us? He stole the two most important people in the world to me. He and his demon companion gutted my parents in my home, and he would've done the same to me. I don't know why he's with the Wardens, why my uncle has seemingly turned a blind eye to his vicious tactics, but I won't be swayed.

"This changes nothing," I assure him, the axe held out between us just daring him to strike me.

"I didn't assume it did." There's a melancholic tone in his voice, one that almost makes it seem as if he actually hopes things *will* change between us someday. It makes me grind my teeth together all the harder.

The axe is heavy in my shaking hands. It pulls on my shoulders, making me hunch from the impossible weight of it. He watches me, awareness in his gaze, the both of us knowing exactly the decision I'm contemplating.

And although I could attack him now, slice his throat from ear to ear—behead him, for that matter—my attention catches on the black scales creeping up his bared arm, to the poison leeching his human life away, day by day. And despite my wrath, despite wanting to slay him a hundred times over, my treacherous heart actually weeps for him. For the plight that has befallen us both.

"How long..." I start to say, but I can't finish the question. I'm not even sure what I'm asking. How long has he been blighted? How long has it taken for his arm to become what it is, for wings to sprout from his demonic back and horns to sprout from his lush head of hair? How long before he loses whatever humanity he's still clinging onto?

"A couple months," he answers, the hard knob in his throat bobbing.

My mind makes quick sense of his meaning. It was only a couple of months ago when my parents were slaughtered, and I'd first encountered him.

"What did you mean earlier, about rage ruling the recently-blighted?

He shrugs, but winces at the strain it causes his tattered wing. "Just what I said. At the onset of being blighted, it's like wrath rules over your ability for rational thoughts."

If it wasn't so painfully obvious that he is lost to whatever memories he has from his own early days as one of the blighted, I might have a mind to be offended at the insinuation that I can't be rational. It does shed some light on the past day or so though. I'll be the first to admit that I've always been a bit impulsive, especially when tempers are rising, but I had been surprised by my quickness to lash out at Alphonse after he followed me away from the Wardens and into the Shadowthorn. I'd chalked it up to years of silencing my indignation and allowing him to perpetuate his hateful atrocities, but perhaps the demon toxin is equally to blame.

Ryven's words echo in my mind again and this time something new occurs to me. A few months ago, he was suffering from blight sickness. It would suggest that a few months ago, he was operating from maddening wrath and irrational thoughts.

Anger flares beneath my skin, molten and volatile, as I realize what he is trying to suggest. He can't blame his abominable actions on the blight sickness; I won't let him dodge the fault that I know to be his.

But before I can lash out at him, another flicker of silver

catches my eye in his hand. My brother's dagger, streaked in thick, inky blood rests in his clenched fist.

"That belongs to me, as well," I growl, anger pulsing through me so hot that I can feel my skin steaming against the cool air.

Ryven scoffs, seeming almost offended. "It's hereditary, then?"

My brow knits together as I resecure my axe along my back. "What is?"

"Your family's inability to say thank you."

I only have a split second to react when he tosses the dagger to me. Not that I was ever in any real danger, considering the dagger would've hit me flat against the chest, hilt and blade at the same time, if I hadn't caught it first. But who throws a dagger at someone who just saved their life?

"You have an interesting way of expressing gratitude yourself," I snap, and I make quick work of resecuring Tor's dagger back into its sheath at my hip.

When Ryven snorts, I glance up from where I'm hunched, watching him through lowered lashes as he stares at me in disbelief. "We both owe each other then."

Something dark and wicked claws up my throat. It's only because of what he said—about recently-blighted being governed by rage—that I manage to clamp it down and refrain from lunging at him with my claws out.

"I owe you nothing," I mutter.

Never will I thank him. Not for this. Not for Ashenvale. Not for anything. Expressing gratitude for saving my life would be the same as thanking him for killing my parents. After all, if they were still alive, I wouldn't even be in the Shadowthorn; I'd still be back in my cottage, dipping cords into wax and hanging candles with my mother; I'd be slipping away from work to find Dimitri, trying to convince him to ditch skinning his next deer and join me in sneaking in to watch the horse races or gambling in the streets on a game of dice.

Pivoting away from the half-demon, I slide down the shadowspider's sleek side.

Ryven follows, stepping off the creature rather than sliding down it and landing in a clash of bones beside me. I make a point not to look at him, but I can still see his steadiness from the corner of my eye, the thick thighs that are supporting the toned weight of him far better than mine are capable of supporting me. It makes me dizzy. And weak. And oh, so very irritated.

"You fought well," Ryven says into the silence.

I glance at him sidelong, expecting to find a teasing look about him because I hadn't fought well, and I knew it. I'd barely been able to fend off Alphonse, let alone the shadowspider. The only reason I'm even still standing is because Ryven arrived when he did. Not that he'll ever hear me admit that.

His expression twists with amusement, a lazy smile spreading to reveal the points of his teeth. "Did I say *well?*" he amends, as if he can hear my thoughts. "I meant to say you fought bravely."

A bubble of laughter climbs up my throat, and I almost forget myself, forget all the horrible things this half-demon is responsible for. Almost.

Disguised as me clearing my throat, I swallow the burst of amusement as swiftly as it came and focus instead on steadying myself where I stand. By now, I'm sure Kalli and Imryll are long gone, but their tracks shouldn't be too difficult to follow if I can drag myself out of this pit.

"How bad is it?"

I meet his pitiful gaze with vehement ire. "You should be worrying less about me, and more about that tattered wing of yours."

He snarls at my mention of it. "That demon should've ripped it clean off."

The image is so graphic, so violent, that I have to bite back another bought of nausea. I may not have wings, but the idea of having a limb ripped clean from my body sounds like the most excruciating kind of pain I could ever imagine. I'd rather have my throat slit, or die in a fire, or be bitten a dozen times more by demons.

"These things"—he shifts his uninjured shoulder for emphasis, the thin black wing whipping open with the movement—"they've been more trouble than they're worth." Then, growling low to himself, he adds, "Do you think—" He cuts himself off, his twitchy posture making it obvious that the question he's about to ask makes him uncomfortable. "Do you think you could heal it?"

My eyebrows rise all the way up to my hairline. "You're a druid. Why can't you do it?"

"Because I'm blighted. The infection has burrowed too deeply. It's cut off my connection to the natural world. I can't take the form of an animal. I can't change the weather. I can't heal."

If he were anyone else, my stony disposition might crumble upon hearing the hopeless frustration in his voice. I know what it's like to lose the things you hold dear, but it's for that exact reason—for the role he played in my own misery—that I feel nothing for him now. He deserves all the suffering he earns. In fact, it will be all too fitting for him to succumb to the demon toxin inside him. It will be far worse than any death I could've ever conjured for him.

"Even if I could heal you, I wouldn't," I say, lacing every word with sinister contempt.

He shakes his head, muttering something to himself that I decide I don't care to hear him repeat. "I suppose we better find that cousin of yours then before we head back."

"Cousin?" I say, whirling on him again. "You saw Alphonse?"

Ryven nods, a dark shadow cast across his features. "I found him running through the forest, screaming for help. He showed me how to find this place."

"H-he actually returned?"

"Well"—a wry, devious grin—"not without protest."

With a slight jerk of his head, Ryven beckons me to follow him up the slope. He makes it look easy, even with the wing dragging behind him like the train of a dress. When he slows or stumbles, I can tell he's faking it. I try not wondering about why. Instead, I think about Alphonse leaving me behind, what I'll do when I see him, how far away he might've made it, and where we'll find him now. It's not until we're halfway up the hillside that I realize Alphonse could be all the way back at the Warden's camp by now, and that Ryven could mean to bring me back there. I won't allow it though; I don't care how much he insists, I'll—

The moment we crest the top, I have to purse my lips together to prevent the eruption of laughter threatening to burst from my lungs. Alphonse is hovering fifteen feet off the ground, tangled in a massive, silken web that bridges the gap between two black oak trees as old as time itself. Glancing around the area, I'm surprised to find that it's not the only spiderweb up here. The forest is sticky with them, reminding me of the long candlewicks my mother would hang before the candle-dipping commenced. Some days, our house would be littered in them, draped from every hook and beam and making it nearly impossible to walk about without running face first into one of them.

Despite the prevalence of the webs, somehow, I'd managed to be oblivious to them all. We both had, too consumed in our hatred for each other. If we hadn't fallen into that pit, I wonder how long it would've taken before the shadowspider sprang on us.

Alphonse thrashes against the spiderweb constraints, still operating from the fear that his life depends on being able to escape before the shadowspider can kill Ryven and I, and set its sights on him. He's so thoroughly focused that he hasn't yet noticed the creature has already been defeated, let alone the two of us walking up to him.

When he finally sees us, there is only a flash of panic behind his hazel eyes before he notices the grin splitting my face in two. A glower cuts quick and deep into his expression. "Oh, I see what's happening here. Okay, you've had your fun, now let me down!"

With a crooked smirk, Ryven moves to oblige him, but I hold my hand out, my palm inadvertently pressing against his bare chest. He looks down at my fingers, and reflexively I withdraw them, turning my attention to my treacherous, sniveling cousin.

"Why should we?" I spit, my teeth bared. My hands plant on my hips and I'm grateful for the stability I find there. "You left me for dead. Why wouldn't I do the same to you and leave you here to be discovered by whatever other monstrosities dwell beneath these trees?"

A fragile smile answers, one meant to seem friendly and disarming, but I notice the fear ticking at the sides of his mouth. "I—I wasn't abandoning you. I went for help. See?" He tries pointing to the half-demon behind me, but the web's hold on his arms prevents him from doing much other than flexing his fingers in Ryven's general direction before they spring back against the elasticity. "I brought him. You're saved. No harm, no foul."

"That's not the way I remember it," Ryven snarls, glancing at me with a look that's meant to refute the unbelievable claim. As if I needed confirmation. Alphonse's stinging words cannot be forgotten so quickly.

"Piss on a mage, Alphonse. You really expect me to believe that? What kind of fool do you take me for?" I don't let him answer, even though he looks as if he wants to. "You told me I was to be sacrificed, so that *you* could live. You left me to die."

The friendly façade crumbles. "Oh, come off it. What would you have me do? You were bit by a demon, Halira. You're going to die anyway. Why wouldn't I sacrifice you?" Scowling at the ground, his voice becomes barely more than a whisper. "You would've done the same."

My nostrils flare and I glare into the side of his face, and I don't know what bothers me more. The idea that he thinks me as cruel as him—a man who dedicated an entire youthhood to tormenting his youngest cousin—or if I'm more irritated that he might be right. If he had been bitten, if it came down to his life or mine, could I really say that I wouldn't choose my own?

Will I do the same now?

I might've, if it hadn't been for the conflict that his last choice of words causes me; I might've left him here to rot and never turned back.

But even I know that's not true. There's a reason I couldn't leave Ryven at the shadowspider's mercy, just like there is a reason I can't leave Alphonse to die here. Call it weakness. Call it a foolish heart that has too much empathy for the world, but no matter how much life takes away from me, no matter how much it makes me suffer, I can't seem to bring myself to relish in the suffering of others. No matter how much they've wronged me.

In one swift motion, I draw the axe from my back and swing, severing the left side of the web. Then the right. Alphonse drops to the ground. Bewilderment hollows his expression as he stares up at me.

"I guess I wouldn't have," I say, my voice cold.

Slowly, Alphonse rises, never once dropping his gaze from mine, not even as he frets with the remnants of web clinging to his body.

"Come on," Ryven says. "Let's head back to camp. It's not that far—"

"I'm not going back there." When he squares his broad shoulders to mine, seemingly blocking me from taking any path but the one that leads us back, I glower. "I'm not letting my only remaining family fight for my life without me fighting with them."

"You're ill," he reminds me.

"So are you."

Ryven crosses his arms and shoots me a dry look. "I was infected three months ago. The blight sickness lasted a week, just as your aunt told you last night. I am not the one suffering from weakened muscles and fever visions."

"Fever visions?" I try, feigning ignorance. "I don't know what you're talking about—"

But Alphonse chimes in, plucking a particularly sticky strand of webbing from his elbow. "So that's what was wrong with you. You've always been an atrocious fighter, but I wondered why you were so dreadful earlier."

Fingers tightening around my axe, I move to lunge for him, but Ryven grips my weapon before I can swing it. He stops me, jarring my shoulder and sending a ripple of dizziness through me that I fight to ignore. This illness, this weakness, why can't it be more reliable? I keep thinking maybe I've seen the worst of it, only for it to flare again at the most inopportune time.

Ryven's dark eyes bore into me and from this distance I realize they're not as bottomless as I once mistook them to be. His are a burnt shade of russet, a smoldering firepit and tree bark heavily shaded. I shrink back from the compassion I find reflected there, from the softness imbued in his voice. "It'll only get worse. Wandering the Shadowthorn while impaired in any way is a fool's errand."

I shove him away, surprising myself when I make a point of not pressing into the arm of the injured wing. "Then go back to the Wardens. I'm going to the Forgotten Forest of Eyve."

As I stagger forward, headed back to the place where Alphonse and I first began our scuffle, back to where I last saw my sister and aunt galloping in the distance, I fully expect the two of them to disappear into the darkness behind me. After all, on different occasions, they've both wanted me dead. Ryven, back in the cottage, and Alphonse just moments before. Letting me go about my reckless mission alone would ensure they get what they wanted.

So when I stumble on what I'm fairly certain to be another hallucinated dance of the earth, I'm surprised when Ryven's hands are there to grab me before I fall. Without a word, without a snide remark or an *I-told-you-so*, he helps me to my feet and continues walking the same direction I had been.

Dumbfounded, I just stand there, watching him lead the way.

"For the record," Alphonse says so close behind me that my heart startles to a lurch. "I would've headed back to camp, but seeing as it's dangerous to wander these woods alone, I'm stuck with the two of you."

My head jerks around to face him, stunned by the eager curiosity that flashes in his eyes suggesting otherwise. Maybe he has personal reasons for journeying forward. Perhaps he's finally given thought to what I said about his mother's likely druid heritage. Whatever his reasoning, I'm far more interested and suspicious of the half-demon marching ahead of us. He and Adrien had made it clear the other night that Ryven had refused to return to the Forgotten Forest of Eyve, and yet now he needed little to no convincing at all.

I watch the backs of his and Alphonse's heads with dubious

unease as the two of them continue along as if nothing is unnatural about this trifecta. They both tried killing me. I tried killing Alphonse no more than a few days ago, and I have dreamed of Ryven's death more times than I can count. The three of us journeying through the Shadowthorn together makes about as much sense as a lamb wandering into a pack of wolves who are being hunted by a bear.

Suddenly, a frightening, guttural growl rumbles from somewhere deep in the Shadowthorn behind me, and I'm reminded that as long as we remain inside the boundaries of the Blight, the three of us share a common enemy.

With his arms folded, one hand reaching up to press against his lips, Alphonse eyes the blackened root in Ryven's hand with haughty skepticism. "I'm not eating *that*."

I lean forward to get a better view of it myself. "What was it? A carrot?"

Ryven sniffs, a sound caught somewhere between derision and amusement. "It's a beet."

I tuck a grimace behind the plastered smile I'm forcing. The movement makes me wince, the bruise on my cheek from where Alphonse punched me still sore. "*Blighted* beets. As if they couldn't get any worse." Catching the way his expression levels at me, I add hastily, "I'm sure they taste delicious."

"Who cares how they taste," Alphonse bellows. "I know the two of you are already doomed, but I will not succumb to the same fate by ingesting infected vegetation. Really, the mere suggestion is simply irresponsible and barbaric."

With a low snarl, Ryven tosses his forage to the ground beside the small fire. "Despite the rumors you've been foolish enough to believe, the food that grows here isn't poisoned."

An incredulous snort blows from Alphonse. "Right. And the Primordials were once gentle giants who believed in peace and harmony."

"They did," Ryven growls, his eyes seeming to blacken. "For centuries they lived in harmony with my people. Your people have spent so long trying to kill them that you've forgotten everything about them."

I raise an eyebrow. "*Our* people," I correct. "You forget, demon-boy, we're one of you. Druids by blood, as much as I'm loathe to admit it."

Now it's Alphonse's turn to bare his teeth. "Didn't you learn your lesson last time about spewing that vile rumor about me, or do I need to remind you again that I am not to be slandered?"

"Here we go again," Ryven mutters. He slumps to the ground with a knife in hand, ready to begin preparing the beets, while Alphonse and I get lost in another heated debate.

It's been like this for the last day and a half. When we aren't walking in silence through the blighted underbrush, the canopy so densely packed and mangled in some places that it's nearly impossible to see past my own arm's reach, we spend the rest of our breaths bickering. I should've expected nothing less from the company of a spoiled rotten son of a Magistrate and a disgruntled half-demon.

"When will you get it through that thick skull of yours?" I groan, my tongue so fatigued from having to say the same thing over and over again. "There's only one explanation for why you can understand us, and don't you dare say—"

"It's the necro-ink!" Alphonse exclaims. He points to the freshly applied batch on his face for emphasis, but I can only roll my eyes. "I told you, it protects me from the lies of shadowcreatures like the two of you!"

Growling my frustration is the only outlet I have at this point. There's no reasoning with him. He says the same thing every time: *it's the necro-ink*. No matter how many times I assure him that I am not a demon—not yet anyway—nor how many times I remind him that none of the others in that medical tent at the Wardens could understand me, Alphonse still blathers on about the multitude of ways that fiends can tamper with a Crusader's perceptions.

"The first unit I ever lead as general into the Shadowthorn was ambushed by fiends. Some of the newer recruits hadn't been adequately prepared. They weren't wearing their necro-ink. The fiends stole my voice and whispered into my Crusaders' ears, convincing them that—"

"Yes, I know," I say, exasperated. "You've recited this story ten times in just as many hours."

I can't endure his presence any longer.

But when I stand and start to storm away, I accidentally trip over Ryven's wilted wing where it lies spread out behind him on the ground. He arches back, an agonizing roar ripping from his lungs and skittering down my spine.

"S-sorry," I utter hastily, human decency getting the better of me. I lift my toe up and scurry away from his injured wing as quickly as possible. "I didn't mean to..."

Ryven falls forward to his hands, the flames of the fire just a lick away, but he doesn't seem to even notice them. His corded back rises and falls with every strain it takes for him to breathe, every ragged breath.

My hands curl into fists at my sides. I've never been one to bask in another animal's pain, no matter how vicious a creature could be. I once begged Dimitri to let a wolf go free, despite it having ravaged one of the village's livestock. I told him that the sheep herder would never have to know if we'd lost the tracks or simply stopped following them, but it wasn't in Dimitri to outright lie, especially not to our own people, nor was he the kind of man to allow empathy into his heart when it came to a kill. Humans came first and foremost. Animals were just game, leather, and wool.

I wonder if he'd see me in much the same light…

Before the sore ache of memories that revolve around Dimitri can close in around me, I fix my attention back on Ryven. Watching him in agony feels a lot like watching that gray wolf as it was struck by Dimitri's arrow. The creature had yelped, only once, but it beheld the instinctual will to survive. It kept running, crashing through the forest, snow misting beneath its frantic, trampling footsteps. Dimitri had knocked a second arrow, and I knew better than to beg even if what we were doing didn't feel right. The predator that we had so feared —that our village had vilified—was fleeing from *us*. And that meant *we* were the dangerous ones, the ones who had come into its territory and hunted it down.

The arrow had cut through the wind, a straight path to the wolf's heart, and I could've sworn I felt it lance through my own the moment it struck.

Piss on a mage.

"I can try to heal you," I grit out, thoroughly frustrated with my bleeding heart and the unhelpful memories of a painful past I'd rather forget. "If you're willing to walk me through it."

Ryven's dark gaze cuts to mine. He watches me, the pain reflected in his big, russet eyes seeming to calm at the mere sight of me. It ignites again when his gaze wanders down to the bruise.

Sighing and seemingly unaware of the anger bubbling up inside the half-demon that will soon be directed at him, Alphonse stands. He smooths his hands over his plated leather armor, readjusting the white phoenix sigil on his chest. "Yes, well, while the two of you are busy playing *mages*, I will be searching yonder for a place to relieve myself."

"I don't need to warn you what happens if you wander too far, do I?" Ryven growls.

Alphonse waves him off. "Yes, yes. Shadowcreatures. Evisceration. It's all quite perilous, but needn't I remind you that I am the general of the Shadow Crusade. I am fully aware of the dangers that lurk in these woods."

Ryven opens his mouth to launch into what I'm sure would've been an accurate testament of just how nightmarishly underprepared Alphonse is, especially the deeper we venture into this largely unchartered territory, but I plop on the ground beside him, effectively cutting off his view of my cousin.

"Let him go," I say, listening to the bushes rustle as Alphonse wanders through the thicket. "Besides, I'm sure we'll hear his screams before anything actually kills him."

"That might not be soon enough," he says, angling an eye at me.

I shrug. "Then I suppose he should've listened." Before I actually start enjoying the conversation, I snap. "Now, are you going to tell me how to do this, or am I going to change my mind?"

A snort accompanies his half smile, but then he swivels on the ground so that his back is turned to me. "Most healing spells work best when there's contact between the caster and the injured."

My brow twitches. "So...I need to touch your wing?"

He nods, a rapid motion, before tensing every muscle in his body.

"Isn't that going to hurt?" I ask, a foolish question, given his reaction, but one I need to ask anyway. This magic, there's still just so much I don't understand about it.

"Yes."

I await further instructions, but when none come, I infer he's waiting for me to make my first move. He plans on guiding me through this step by step, which makes me worry how many steps there may be.

Sucking in a dubious breath, I come onto my heels to get

into a better position, one that will grant me greater mobility to work along the length of the wing should I need to—not that I know what I'll *need* to be able to do; I've never used healing magic before and am only basing my assumptions on the healers I've seen applying poultices and bandages to wounds.

Up this close, I'm able to finally see the real damage that's been done. Not only did the shadowspider spear its leg clean through the tapestry of the wing, but it looks like the wing itself must've been torn from its socket. It's no wonder the way it dangled from Ryven's back ever since. Upon further examination, I'm surprised to find that the tear in his wing isn't the only injury he suffered. Both wings are riddled with scratch marks and tears, divots that chink away at the black bones that give his wings their shape. I wonder how long it's been since he's been healed, considering some of these cuts look as if they're days older or more.

Leaning over him, I press my hand against his spine to brace him for the contact that's about to come. Fiery warmth exudes from his skin into my palm. I try not to let my traitorous thoughts drift to the taut curves of muscles beneath my fingertips, and instead I hover my hand over the place where his wing is connected to his shoulder.

"It's different for everyone," he says, sensing my readiness. "But druid magic comes from our beating hearts. Our lives bind us to the earth, they connect us to all that is living, and as such, our influence allows us to reach through that web of connections and trigger a power greater than ourselves."

My hand falters. It's more words than I've ever heard him speak, and they're spoken in a scholarly and distant sort of way that makes it sound as if he's reciting something he himself had been told when he first began learning about druid magic.

"I'm not sure I follow you," I say.

"It means, don't think of it as *your* magic. It's not something inside of you that you're giving away. The magic is already all around us. A druid's privilege is knowing how to sense and channel it when the time is right."

"Like with the lightning," I say, mostly to myself, as I recall the tempest that had rolled overhead during my escape from the Castle of Nigh. "The storm, it had already been there, but I beckoned the lightning down from the sky."

Ryven's head tilts back and forth. "Yes and no. The storm is always there, even when it isn't."

"You've lost me again."

The wry smile is audible in his tone. "Storms are nothing more than wind and rain. Wind is air. Rain is moisture. Both exist always, it's just a matter of sculpting them into the storm you desire."

It makes a small amount of sense, enough that my hand rises back to its place, not quite touching his wing, but readied.

"Healing," Ryven continues. "Above all of our powers, healing is most intricately connected to life. It is the birth of new flesh, the mending of bones over time. Fortunately, there is almost always life around us to draw from."

"Even here?" I ask, my skeptical gaze wandering to our dismal surroundings.

"Even here. Close your eyes and you can feel it."

Despite the healthy amount of doubt I have that anything he's saying could be true, or perhaps because of it and my desire to catch him in a lie, I find myself obliging him. My eyelids shut, closing me out of the dimness of the Shadowthorn and plunging me into my own darkness. The blight sickness is more difficult to ignore when I turn my focus inward. The fever tinging my cheeks makes me sway, and my outstretched hand grazes Ryven's gnarled wing. He flexes beneath me, but holds steady, unmoving, unflinching.

I withdraw my hand. "Sorry."

When he speaks again, his voice is harsher. Not angry, simply ragged. "There's a vibrancy, one that carries all around us. Some druids can sense it in color, others in smells or sounds. For me, it is a sense of feeling. A pulsing warmth that emits from every living thing."

My eyes flutter open. "I—I didn't feel anything," I splutter, trying to change the subject to anything other than the warmth between us emitting from *him*. I say the first thing that comes to mind, one blighted soul staring at the back of another. "A-am I going to grow wings?"

I can't see the smile tick up his face, but his clipped laughter is unrestrained. I sink back into my heels, my arms crossed.

"What's so funny? It's a reasonable question."

"Nothing," he says, voice heady with the fading tendrils of amusement. "Just, the thought of you with wings—"

"You think I couldn't handle them?" For some reason, this makes me even more irritated. Dimitri used to tease me all the time for my incoordination. "I'll have you know that I can be quite adept at figuring things out, despite people doubting me and laughing in my face."

He shifts enough so that our eyes can meet. His look is one of solemn, genuine candor. "I wasn't going to say that at all. I only laughed because I was thinking about our encounter in that village; I think you called it Ashenvale?" My nod is quick so that he might explain himself. He laughs again, this time both of his canines showing in what I think might be a genuine smile. "I saw the way you slew that shadowbeast. You were quick and lethal, just as you were with the shadowspider. Can you imagine how much deadlier you'd have been if you had wings?"

A small smile twitches in my lips, and he resumes his position with a satisfied, lazy grin. But he's not finished flattering me yet.

"Demons rue the day that Halira Devonshire grows wings."

All it takes is that one word, that single, dreadful word, to remind me that I have no space for laughter in my heart.

Demons. Demons are why I'm here. They're why I lived my adolescence in fear; why I fled my home; why my country needed people like me to become Crusaders; they're why I'm blighted. Demons are at fault for all of it. And I am in the presence of one. Where Ryven gets the nerve to treat me like a friend, to possibly ever think that we could be so casual, I'll never understand…and honestly, I'm afraid to ask. My hatred toward him, I need it. It's the only tangible target I have to direct my vengeance toward. Wanting to kill the Primordial Qaeus was one thing, but even it—*she*—didn't singlehandedly kill my parents. A demon did. The very demon before me.

But if I truly believed that, then why haven't I killed him already? Why am I sitting here in the dirt attempting to mend his broken wing?

I fight against my constricting throat and focus back on the conversation at hand. "Why *do* you have wings then? Most of the demons I've learned about don't have them."

He lowers his head. "When a druid…devolves—that is, when they become a demon—we're…different than the other ones. The creatures you call demons, they draw their magic from the Primordial Qaeus; they exist only as an extension of her will. Despite what some hateful few may say about us, we druids have our own souls, our own connection to magic, and when the blight takes hold, it isn't creating a creature from nothing. It mutilates what we were and transforms us into something…horrid."

He pauses just before I think his voice is about to waver, giving me enough time to make sense of this for myself. A staggering realization occurs to me then.

"Is that what makes the different monsters? Like the one I faced in Ashenvale? Like the shadowspider? Are they…were those creatures druids at one point in time?"

Ryven is silent for a long while before finally answering, "I suspect so."

I sink back into my heels, heavy and hopeless. That's the future that lays ahead of me—ahead of the both of us—if we don't find a cure. And for some reason unknown to me, that is more terrifying than any death I've ever imagined. Being eviscerated while in the line of duty in the Shadowthorn, defending my country, that sounds strangely akin to dying in my sleep when I think about the life I'd be subjected to as one of those behemoth monstrosities. How much of myself would be lost? As I ravaged villages and feasted on peasants, would I still remember the days before, back when I was among those fleeing from the terrors Qaeus has brought upon us?

It's that feeling alone, that heavy and sinking doom in my chest that finally gives me the courage to ask him what I've been wondering ever since our paths crossed in Ashenvale, and again when I opened my eyes and found myself in the medic tent.

"Why did you kill my parents? If you're not fully a demon yet, why were you there during the scourge on Gravenburg?"

Ryven's spine becomes so taut that I fear he might snap at the gentlest gust of wind. Slowly, he twists to face me, and I startle at the look in his dark eyes. I can't place it exactly, only that I recognize just how shattered he really is, and it serves to confound me all the more.

"I wondered when you would ask," he says softly. "It's a long story, one with a painful ending. Are you sure you're ready to hear it?"

"Yes," I say without hesitation. Wondering why my parents died is all I've thought about these past few months. Why them? Why wasn't I there to defend them? Why do demons even exist and why do the wreak such havoc on us? No matter how painful these answers may be, I need to know.

He swallows before starting. "To this day, most druids stay within the confines of the Eyve. Ever since the border fell, our people walled themselves off from the rest of the realm, just as our oppressors had forced onto us. But by the time the wall fell, our ancestors had made their homes in the Eyve. Very few saw any reason to leave.

"But I grew bored with hearing the stories my people told about the hateful Arcathainians, the even more wicked mages. We seemed just as fearful as the Arcathainians and mages had been of us when they trapped us with the Primordial."

It's a sentiment I can understand, one I've been grappling with myself lately.

"My best friend was tired of it too," Ryven continues. "And so, as naïve people do, we left in hopes of finding the leaders of

Arcathain and brokering peace between our people. We thought they would listen since we possess the magic to prevent demons from encroaching into our territory—magic that we were sure we could get our people to agree to sharing. We thought we had it all figured out. The leaders of Arcathain would rejoice at our aid and recompense our people for what they'd done to us all those years ago."

I avert my doubtful gaze. The *leaders* he speaks of are the Magistrate and his Senate, a devout bunch of crotchety elitists who only trust themselves, let alone the druids they don't even know exist.

He laughs, a breathy sound. "I know. We never had a chance. Even before..."

Something shifts in the air around us, becoming thicker and bitter as the conversation veers to that place we're both scared to venture. "Before what?"

The dark brown pools of his eyes flick to mine, a profound sadness making them appear like deep wells of regret. "Before...everything changed for Ahl'Ro and I... You see, most of our people stay within the borders of the wall. There is very little that we need from the outside world. And so, although we were aware of the dangers the Shadowthorn can present, we were woefully unprepared.

"We'd almost made it to where the Shadowthorn meets Arcathain when we were ambushed by a pack of demons while we slept. Ahl'Ro was bitten before we could fight them off. Not just one bite, but dozens. I had to pry the creatures off him, his flesh tearing in the wake of their razor teeth, and all I could do was hope that once they were all dead, I would still be able to heal him."

"Were you?" I ask, my voice cracking.

A dark shadow crosses him. "I healed his wounds. But for the sake of everyone, sometimes I wish I hadn't." My brow furrows, but he continues before I can press him on why. "I was also bitten. Right on the forearm." He holds it out now for effect, rotating the horrific thing as if the midnight skin should catch light—as if something that dark and wicked could—but all it does is remind us both of the terrible fate that awaits us. "When my efforts to heal Ahl'Ro did nothing to curb the fever spiraling through him, we abandoned our cause to return home, to seek the aid and wisdom of the Elders. We didn't make it more than a few days back before Ahl'Ro began…changing."

My eyes rest firmly on the spiked skin of his demonic arm, as if the more my heart climbs up my throat, the more I'm trying to remind myself what Ryven is. A demon. A killer. But the churning of my gut is something not so easily ignored, and I can sense where this story is heading already with surmounting dread.

"It happened more quickly for him," Ryven says, his voice like the dead of night, ominous and grave. "I think because… because he was bitten so many times, because the demon toxin had been pumped into his bloodstream more than it had mine, his turning was more rapid.

"Soon, there was little of *him* left. He fled before the final stages of the turn, I think to protect me by putting some distance between us, but I couldn't leave him like that. I couldn't abandon him to wreak havoc on the very realm he'd set out to change. You didn't know him, but…at his core, Ahl'Ro was virtuous. He was…he was…"

When he struggles to find the right words to honor his friend, I supply them for him. "He was the kind of gentle soul who would leave the comforts of his home and traverse the dangers of the Shadowthorn, in an attempt to advocate for peace between our two peoples."

Appreciation shines in his half-tugged smile. But then another shadow consumes it. "I wasn't about to let him become everything he stood against. I started following his tracks. For months I searched for him. For days, maybe weeks I killed any demon I came upon in the hopes that one of them would be him and I could put him out of his misery. But when druids turn, they're different than the others. I knew he was still out there, hunting, killing."

His dark eyes glaze as his mind wanders back to those days, to what surely must've been some of the darkest moments of his entire life.

"Eventually, I found his trail again. I followed him to your village. I thought it was ready. I'd eviscerated dozens of demons by then. I thought this would be the same. But by the time I'd arrived…it was already too late, and…"

He hangs his head even lower, sorrow wrenching through him like a hot blade. "I—I wasn't thinking straight. Seeing him like that, with blood staining his—" His chest rises and falls in rapid succession. "His teeth. I couldn't stand it; I couldn't face it. I left him and ran back toward the Shadowthorn, toward the Eyve, hoping that I'd be able to wipe the image of him like *that* from my mind.

"But before I could reach the border, I heard footsteps behind me. I turned and saw *you* running straight for the cottage."

Heat, erratic and gurgling, rises up inside me, and I know once it reaches the top, once my anger and resentment and empathy and sorrow fill me so thoroughly, the walls of my being will crack, and I will explode.

"I didn't know what I was doing," he says. "But I ran back into the cottage, and when I saw him lunge for you, when I saw you trying to fight back, I remembered myself. Remembered the promise I made him." His dark, bottomless eyes hold my gaze, two vast wells that I lean into when it becomes too much for me to contain what's overflowing inside me. "So, you see, although it wasn't me who shed your parents' blood, I am responsible for their deaths all the same."

The floundering thing beneath my breast doesn't even feel like a pounding heart anymore. It feels like a wild thing with its own mind. The way it thrashes, the ballooned squishy organ thumping against my ribcage feels unnatural, unsustainable, as if it's nothing more than a bubble of water on the brink of popping.

Ryven's given me my answer.

My parents' deaths were perhaps worse than I feared. They weren't simply one of the hundreds who are slaughtered along the border of the Shadowthorn every day. They were the victims of a single blighted druid who had ventured far from the heart of Qaeus' lands in an effort to protect his friend. They were one in a thousand. It didn't have to be them; my home didn't have to be the cottage that Ahl'Ro stumbled upon during the last moments of his transformation. But it was—they were. And now, here Ryven and I are, battered and blighted, mere days or weeks or months away from losing everything.

"I am so sorry for your loss," he says, each word heavy and lingering in the air between us before he utters the next. For all his faults, for everything I've ever accused him of, there is no doubting his remorse. The longer he speaks, the older he looks, aging nearly a decade right before my eyes. "If I had known, if I had acted sooner—or if I'd never healed him and just let him bleed out from the bites—your family would still be alive. You wouldn't be in this mess…"

By the time he finishes, my cheeks are wet, drenched with the sorrow I've kept locked away and buried deep inside the gaping hole in my chest for months now. As he watches the tears fall, I think I see his hand twitch, gravitating toward me as if he is about to wipe away all traces of my heartbreak. But then he thinks better of it, balling his fingers into a fist and breaking our gaze and I can't tell if I'm glad or disappointed.

I *am* grateful for everything he's shared though—for *all* of it. I hadn't known it then, but I'd been wrong about thinking I needed the anger and hatred. Those things had only left me lost and cold in a world that is already too volatile. But this? Understanding, closure, peace? These are the things I really needed; the only way I was ever going to be able to move forward again.

It is the greatest, most painful gift anyone has ever given me.

I test my voice, despite feeling as if someone has poured an entire beach's worth of sand down my throat. "Is this why you didn't want to return to the Forgotten Forest of Eyve?"

Unease settles into his gaze as he meets mine. He watches me with the wide-eyed fear of a deer that's spotted its hunter moments before they released their arrow. Finally, he nods, the motion sticky, and for the briefest of moments, I think he's going to share more than that, to elaborate or explain why. But his jaw remains firmly clamped and a thoughtful silence resumes.

I don't want to press him, not after all that he's shared with me already, so instead I return to our original topic of conversation.

I grasp his good shoulder, spinning him so his back is to me again. "Are you going to teach me how to heal you, or not?"

The sound that escapes him is a pitiful excuse of a laugh, but I allow it, considering the circumstances. "I already did," he says. "As I said, close your eyes and focus on the life around you. It might be a sound, a scent, a vibration—"

With my eyes closed, I realize the only sound, scent, and vibration I can sense is him. The deep rumble of his voice that penetrates my skin and trickles all the way down, deep into my abdomen; the aroma of cedarwood and frankincense that reminds me of late night strolls through the woods before they were overrun by the Blight. The longer my eyes remain closed, the more overwhelmed by him I become.

When the strange ache in my chest has ballooned until I am

stretch so taut that I'm struggling to breathe, I force my eyes wide. "I can't do this! There is no life here. The Blight has taken everything!"

My outburst doesn't faze him at all. He doesn't even flinch, his voice remaining as calm and soothing as a gentle wind blowing through the leaves on a warm, summer day. "I already told you these lands aren't blighted in the ways that the Arcathainians have led you to believe. How else would tangled trees have sprouted amid your open fields of barley? How else would you explain entire villages disappearing beneath the unruly underbrush and leaving behind only ruins of a forgotten civilization buried beneath acres of bramble and vines?"

My brow furrows. "I…suppose I never thought about it. I never went this far into the Shadowthorn. But Ashenvale was still—"

"There was new growth there. You were a little preoccupied to notice."

I'm not sure if he means it as a slight—after all, what idiot would insult the only person around who's able and willing to mend his wing—but I take it as one, the toxin coursing through me turning my veins to frayed nerves. "I wasn't doing what I was told like some dog. In fact, the exact opposite."

"Oh yeah?" He twists around. "You weren't ordered to return to that village just to pilfer the bodies of the dead?"

I scoff. "That's not—I was, but only until I…"

He snorts as if he's already proven his point.

A quiet fury in me rises. This man—this *half-demon*—doesn't know me. Not ever in my life have I been one to blindly follow authority or even expectation. I was often found doing the exact opposite of what I was told in my youth: flouting my responsibilities when it came to maintaining the household and my mother's beehives. Even as I've grown, I'm still as reckless and rule-averse as ever. Did I not spend the months I was at Nigh wandering into the Blighted zone of the castle, sneaking into the catacombs to visit Dimitri, and spending countless hours in the library trying to learn more about demons and magic when I should've been training with my axe instead?

He has no right to presume he knows me.

"When I stumbled upon that shadowcreature in Ashenvale, I was no longer following orders," I tell him, defending myself with my head held high. "I'd just discovered that me and some of the others had unwittingly been sent on a fool's errand, and rather than wasting my time completing the meaningless task I'd been given that would ensure I never became a true Crusader, I left rank to confront Alphonse and demand he grant me the same opportunity he was granting his favored few. It was because I went against orders that I found my friends in danger. So do not pretend to know me or my loyalties. I listen to my own imploring impulses, not those of anyone else."

With a haughty huff, I pull away from him, my hands leaving his wing still mauled. With a huff of his own, he twists back to face the firepit and grabs the beets with his bad arm, his knife with the other.

As I plop down at the base of a tree, I'm prepared to sit in silence for the rest of the evening, if we must. It's not like I don't have a lot to preoccupy my mind anyway, nor would the rest be useful. Although most of the time the fever does nothing more than warm my skin, the moments when the hallucinations cease me and when my body fails me have become almost crippling. And since it's been a while since one of those bouts attacked, one is likely just over the horizon and now would be as good a time as any to close my eyes and rest.

But before Ryven has a chance to start peeling the unappetizing forage in his hand, his head snaps up.

Seeing his dark eyes widen erase all notions of rest from my thoughts.

I sit up, alert and already feeling woozy. "What is it? What's wrong?"

"Your cousin," he says. "He has been gone too long."

THE LABYRINTH

THE LABYRINTH, SHADOWTHORN

Squatting over the black soil, Ryven drags his good hand through the tarnished leaves. "No signs of a scuffle. He wasn't taken by demons."

With a sigh of relief, my shoulders relax as much as they're able. The fever has spiked again, our frantic search for my missing cousin leaving my mind swimming in a vortex of dizzying nausea.

But I push through it. "Do you think he's still looking for somewhere to…relieve himself?" Each word I utter is a struggle, and it takes everything in me not to find the nearest tree to lean upon for support.

From where he's crouched, Ryven glances up at me with a knowing look, one that suggests I should sit down before I fall over. I'm grateful when he keeps those thoughts to himself though because it means I don't have to waste any more of my energy arguing with him about how I will not sit and wait while he investigates Alphonse's disappearance.

Ryven returns his attention to our surroundings, his eyes roving over every seemingly meaningless detail of the land knowing that somewhere there might be a clue.

"No," he says at last, standing tall beside me. He points back the way we came, to the tracks we followed that led us here. "His trail suggests he took a straight path, likely trying to avoid taking any unnecessary turns that might've left him lost. But here"—he points at the ground at our feet—"his direction changes. Sharply."

I frown. "Okay, but if demons didn't take him, and if he wasn't running or fleeing from danger, then what happened?"

"Fiends," Ryven answers, the single word spoken like a bad omen. His fists clench then, a low, nearly inaudible growl boiling inside him until it bursts free from his lungs. He charges a tree, his fist swinging into it so hard that the girth of the trunk indents from the devastating blow. "I should've known better!"

"Known better about what?" I ask, unsure if I should be impressed by his power or terrified by it. "It couldn't have been fiends. He's protected by the necro-ink. I saw him applying more just before he left."

His sneer is contemptuous. "You don't give those creatures enough credit."

I'm taken aback by the vague suggestion that I fear isn't vague at all. I don't think he means it's only me who has under-estimated the fiends that prowl in the Shadowthorn. They are nothing more but pesky imps in bedtime stories, the mostly harmless if not trickster creatures that are outwitted by the heroes of the stories.

We're taught to never trust them, for they are masters of disguise and deception, but what if they are more; what if they always have been? What if the few defenses we had against them aren't as effective as we've been led to believe? Could they be immune to necro-ink? Or are they simply more intelli-gent, and capable of strategizing ways around it? Either way, the Crusaders back home might not be as prepared in facing them as they believed they were. Crusaders like Dimitri might find themselves captured and lured to their deaths…just as Dimitri's father had been, and so many countless others…

With both hands pressed against the tree, Ryven deflates, head sagging between his arms, and there's something just concerning enough about his reaction that I'm able to pull my thoughts away from my friend.

"There's a nest of them nearby," Ryven says. "They congregate at the Labyrinth."

"What's the Labyrinth?"

"That's what Ahl'Ro and I called it. It's a dense thicket, a maze of underbrush unlike anything you've ever seen, and the horrors that dwell there are disturbing beyond imagination."

Now that he's calmed a little, I caution a step closer. I lean around him to try to get a look at his face. "And what would happen to Alphonse if he was brought there by fiends?"

It's a stupid question, one I already know the answer to.

Ryven pushes away from the tree. "That depends. Death by sinking pits? Mangled by depraved shadowmonkeys? Swallowed by the giant wyrm?"

"Piss on a mage…"

"The Labyrinth has no shortage of monsters. If they've taken him there, then—"

"Then we have to go find him," I shout. "We have to save him."

Ryven's neck twists slowly, his dark eyes assessing me and the way I'm slouched. I force my spine to straighten, to exude the strength that's left me almost entirely, but despite my failure to do so, I realize he's not looking upon me with concern or pity. Disbelief is reflected in his expression, even if it is removed from his tone.

"You'd rather rescue the man who abandoned you to your demise, than continue on your quest to the Eyve to intercept your sister and aunt?"

Biting my lip, I turn toward the path we'd been following.

Kalli and Imryll could be two days ahead of us by now, what with my frequent need for rest and our traveling by foot instead of riding horseback. The longer we tarry, the less time either Ryven or I have. If my fevers have been any indication, the demon toxin will only continue to ravage my body and mind, long after the initial stages of blight sickness have passed.

But I can't stop myself from thinking about what it would be like to lose oneself to the fiends. I wonder how much awareness a person still has while under their spell of deception. When Dimitri's father was lured away from the village, did he remember he was leaving behind his wife, a daughter and a son? Was he afraid as they marched him to whatever death awaited, or was he blissfully catatonic to all rational thought and fear?

"We're not going to catch up with Kalli and my aunt any time soon," I say over my shoulder, my voice as quiet as the Shadowthorn. "At best, we can hope that it'll take the Elders some time to give them the information they've requested."

He snorts. "That's very likely."

"That might give us time before they leave again, but even if it didn't, I can't just leave Alphonse like this." And that's the truth. It physically hurts to think about abandoning him now, even though he's more than earned it. I would be justified to turn my back on him and let him pay for his many crimes against me.

But that is not who I am. I do not relish in his suffering, nor anyone else's. It seems to be in my nature to risk my own life for the sake of others. Perhaps it's part of my druid ancestry and the supposed connection I have with the living world. Maybe it wasn't only my parents' deaths that led to the Shadow Crusade. Maybe it's this compulsion to defend others.

I'm well aware that not everyone shares the same conviction though, and Ryven is still staring at me. "That is my decision. If you don't want to come, then—"

"It's not that," he says, shaking his head, and the dark mess jostles between his horns. "I didn't think *you'd* want to. I know he's family, but..." A rueful smile cocks up one side of his face. "I shouldn't have expected anything less from Halira Devonshire, the girl who threw herself in front of a behemoth shadowcreature to save a friend, and then threw herself before another to save an enemy." With a tilt of his head, he says, "Come on. The Labyrinth isn't far."

Ryven stops abruptly, the spider-leg-branches thick around us and making it nearly impossible to see much of anything. He pulls back the low-hanging branches aside.

"Behold, the Labyrinth."

I push forward, shocked in my disbelief that we could've arrived so soon. But as I emerge from the clearing, my breath catches at the sight. The massive stone structure is nearly entirely overrun by the thickest bramble I've ever seen. The outside walls are tall enough that to fall from the top would end in a tangle of limp bones and cracked skulls. Death would be all but inevitable. Depictions of the Primordial Qaeus vary, but I'd imagine that even she could seek refuge inside the tall walls.

"May bravery fill our hearts and protect our lives," I mutter, wondering just how likely it is that we will enter and ever come out alive.

But as I scour the perimeter for an entrance, I find none

amid the twisting, thorned vines that wrap in and out of each other like netting. It strikes me, however, how perfectly mani-cured the structure is in some respects. In its entirety, it's not an oblong shape, but rectangular, even if the branches sticking up from every wall give it a jagged edge. But I think, some-where beneath it all, this place might've once been built by mankind, taken over by the shadows.

My head swivels for a better look around. "I don't see him."

"He's already inside. Look—" Leaning in closer, his breath grazing my cheek, Ryven's hand stretches ahead to indicate a soft patch of mud near a dark shadow in the bramble. I squint across the field, my sight nothing compared to the eyes of a half-demon, someone much farther in their transition than I, and realize that the shadow just might be an opening, a way inside. "Fresh footsteps," he says. "They look human."

"Not sure how you can tell from here," I mutter. "But I believe you." He angles an eyebrow at me, and I roll my eyes. "So how do we save him? If he's already inside, does that mean he's…dead?"

"Maybe." Catching my scornful look, he amends. "It's possi-ble, but unlikely. He wasn't gone *that* long. The fiends, they enjoy playing with their food as much as field cats." We break our gaze as he stretches his finger out again, pointing back to the same hollow between the tangled vines. "There's our way inside to find out. We're lucky it's not nightfall yet. That's when the place really comes alive. You have your shadowsteel ready?"

I nod, my dagger already in hand. The battle-axe has proven too heavy to carry around when the fever has its teeth in me. The moment I regain any semblance of strength again, I'll draw it, if only to feel the security and power it always provides. Until then, I have Tor to guide and watch over me.

Ryven whips out his short sword, a weapon barely longer than my dagger, but one that looks lethal in his grasp. Not that he needs it. Judging from the state of the demon that had been discarded in my home, and the indentation in the tree he punched earlier, I'm fairly certain that he has brute strength on his side. If it's a symptom of the blighted infestation of his blood though, then the demons that dwell inside the Labyrinth will have it too.

"Let's go."

He slinks forward, like a thief prowling across an open courtyard to breech a dark castle and commence the slaughter. I follow closely behind him, my drowsy eyes fixating on his shadowsteel blade, and I wonder how he obtained such a thing if he lived in the Forgotten Forest of Eyve his whole life. My drifting thoughts take me deeper, and there's a lot I still don't know about him. Like how he came to join my uncle. And what he'd been doing in the catacombs at Nigh during that demon attack.

Suddenly, I'm not so confident in my newfound trust of him. The story he gave me about Ahl'Ro seemed truthful, the weight of it bearing down on the both of us and leaving us brittle and raw in the end. But for all I know, it could've been a rouse, a false act of honesty meant to gain my trust so that he could lead me here to what seems to be one of the most dangerous places in the Shadowthorn.

My blood boils at the thought. I'm too angered by the possibility of being duped to remember that the demon toxin infiltrating my body feasts on paranoia as much as it does rage.

My grip tightens on my dagger and I vow to be on my toes as we venture to the other side of these walls.

The corridors of the Labyrinth are just as organic and strangely manicured as the outside. It's as if every wall is covered in thick claws of death, the thorns hiding in the shadows to leap out and slice anyone reckless enough to stumble into them. I get the sense that this place is as much alive as every shadowcreature I've ever encountered, like the vines squirm where they rest, the walls ever-shifting and changing. But that could just be the fever talking.

Ryven doesn't make mention of it, nor does he caution me to keep my distance. It makes me all the more paranoid about him and his intentions, and makes me question why he didn't insist I stay behind. Anyone in their right mind would've; they would've seen the way I sway, the glossiness in my eyes, and for my own protection they would've insisted I remain far, far away from this place.

It's what Dimitri would've done.

My ears ring from the constant ruffling of leaves, the grating of thorns against the buried stone. The chirping of insects, more than anything, fill these rotten walls. Centipedes weave in and out of the underbrush, cicadas chirp from atop the strangled trees. Somewhere in the distance, the shadow-monkeys fill these walls with their rambunctious howling and I grow warier with every step.

This is a mistake. This place is death. If Alphonse is here, he is lost already and I won't be far behind him.

Ryven glances over his shoulder at me. My brow furrows at the worried look he casts me. It seems far too genuine for someone leading me into a trap, but that's a possibility I can't afford to consider. I have to remain vigilant. I can trust no one.

Whatever dwells inside the Labyrinth, I can sense it with every fiber of my being. I have no doubt that pandemonium would unleash upon us if we were to utter a sound, and so, I am careful to be void of any. I belabor every step, submitting completely to the lethargy that's been trying to claim me for an hour now, all in the effort to keep my strides as muffled as possible. There is no avoiding stepping on the crisp, blackened vines that have slithered across the floor though. They crunch beneath me no matter how lightly I step, and each time I swear the walls shake.

A few corridors in, I realize that I have lost my bearings.

There are too many twists and turns to keep track of, and Ryven weaves us through them all as if he has this place memorized, as if this place could be his home as much as it is the horrors he's mentioned living here.

If I were to flee now, I would be lost forever.

Around the next bend of gnarled branches, I have to clamp my hand over my mouth to prevent myself from gasping. Just down the corridor, we finally spy Alphonse, being marched by a half dozen fiends that prance around him and bounce off the walls with impish delight.

I release my hand and start to charge forward. We've done it. We've found my cruel cousin before they could deliver him to an even crueler fate.

But Ryven clutches my arm. I glare at him, the dagger shaking in my hand, ready to strike should I need to.

But he just shakes his head, a silent imploration for us to maintain our cover.

I mouth the words, "Why? He's right there."

By way of response, he bobs his chiseled jaw back down the corridor. I turn around, just as Alphonse and his party of fiends turn down another hallway and disappear from sight. I roll my eyes, frustrated to have so much distance between us, but then my eye catches on the wall at the end of this corridor. Leaning forward, I notice the wall isn't covered by branches and vines like the rest of this place. It almost looks like a hollow, at first, but the darkness is so black it almost seems like a living thing. A warm, gentle breeze washes over us, a putrid stench engulfing the corridor in its wake. It comes again, and again, a rhythm that can only mean one thing.

Something is breathing inside there.

Something that we don't want to awaken.

I tiptoe backward, my back smacking into Ryven as his hands steady my arms before I can fall. My scowl returns as I yank myself away from him. He doesn't seem to notice, his concerned gaze drifting to my hairline and to the beads of sweat that have dampened my hair.

With a purse of his lips, he pulls his attention away and waves me down a different path. We veer left and right, up and down, but it's not long before we're climbing out of the thick underbrush and landing in another wide corridor of black ivy.

My heart thrums when I see that we are not alone. Somehow, in our twisting and turning, we've managed to place ourselves in the path of Alphonse and his fiends. Frantic that we've been spotted, I reach up in a desperate hope to reassure myself that I'm painted in necro-ink—a habit that's still engrained in me from my Crusader training, even though I haven't worn any in days. Unsurprisingly, my fingers only graze over clammy skin.

Ryven takes my wrist, gently lowering my arm back to my side. One glance at his calm expression tells me that we are in no danger, though I don't understand how that can be possible when we are not only lost somewhere in the heart of the Labyrinth, but a small gaggle of fiends are approaching.

The mischievous things continue to advance on us, Alphonse following close behind them with dutiful, if not slightly lumbering strides.

When the group of them are close enough that I can see the black divots of the fiends' eyes, make out their busy, flipping tails and long claws, I realize that Ryven was right not be alarmed. They're not lunging for us. They hardly even seem to notice us. Instead, they continue walking right on by as if we weren't even here, or at the very least, like we aren't anything that might be appetizing. They already have a meal in mind.

As I turn my quizzical gaze to Ryven, he motions to his arm, to the black scales and quills growing out from his pitch-black skin. Understanding hits me. It's not that their hunger has already been satiated with the prospect of the meal that will be Alphonse, it's the demon blood. It must protect us somehow. I recall our encounter in Ashenvale, how the shadowwolves hadn't attacked Ryven at first, not until they were certain he was an enemy. Even when I encountered the shadowspider just a few days ago, it had given pause before attempting to devour me. The creature had run its bristled fangs over me, smelling, determining if I was a threat or something akin to it. Ryven had even said something about how if I hadn't attacked it, it wouldn't have bothered with me.

I wonder if it's like this for all of the Primordial's spawn, or just those who lack the intelligence to decipher beings apart by sight. They are the ponderings that I'll reserve for another time.

Alphonse is the last to pass us, a single lupine fiend curled over his shoulders protectively. The necro-ink has been wiped almost entirely from his forehead; there's hardly any trace of it along his chin or beneath his eyes, which is shocking since I know for certain he'd applied some not moments before his disappearance. Where the paint had been, the skin is now raw, like the creatures had scrubbed it off him themselves.

He keeps marching, not even glancing at me, with no vestige of recognition anywhere behind his dulled eyes.

My lips move, but I take every precaution to ensure no sound comes out, not so much as a smacking of lips or my teeth clacking. "What now?"

Ryven, however, doesn't even risk that much. He urges me along with another nod, the two of us falling in between the fiends as if we belonged among them. I ignore the horrendous thought that maybe we do, blighted as we are. We draw the attention of a few, but it's always short-lived, the sprite-like creatures flashing toothy grins at us one moment, and then bounding up the wall the next.

Still, my heart races being so near them. I feel like a fly hovering around the rear side of a horse, just a tail-flick away from being noticed and swatted.

The more we walk, the more anxiously Ryven moves, as well. His head tilts to the sky frequently, presumably trying to assess whether the sun has fallen through the thicket that weaves overhead. I can't tell if he's nervous because it hasn't, or if his intentions really have been pure, and he's as afraid about being stuck here after dark as I am. Regardless, I don't want to waste any more time trying to find out, let alone waiting to see what awakens in this forsaken place once the moon rises.

Glancing around at the fiends, I count only seven of them, which is really more of a nuisance than anything considering the creatures don't typically attack outright. We could grab Alphonse, drag him away from the fiends' influence, and escape before anything worse awakens and comes for us. But though the fiends might not attack us, I have no doubt that they wouldn't shriek their heads off just to rouse those who slumber here. We might not have to fight them to secure my cousin, but what atrocities would they beckon in retaliation?

Stifling a disgruntled sigh, I keep up the pace, every now and then glancing up ahead to determine where we are going and wondering when Ryven will deem it the right time to make our move. If he ever will.

Finally, after crawling beneath a canopy of low-hanging thorns and shimmying between fallen trees, we arrive at a great courtyard. A few ruins and rocks are scattered throughout, but otherwise, the gray place is barren, the earth trampled and flattened. It's like the black bramble has actively avoided this section of the Labyrinth. Or perhaps it can't grow here at all.

Once the three of us enter, the fiends scatter, climbing up the ivy that clings to the walls and bounding atop the branches that jut from the corridors leading into large chamber. They spring up and down with excitement, apish in their manner, but bearing more likeness to squirrels and raccoons than to the shadowmonkeys I heard howling earlier.

Alphonse continues marching into the place that appears to be an old courtyard, Ryven and I close at his side.

Now that we are no longer surrounded by a thicket too dense to glimpse anything through, and only once I'm certain that all of the fiends have left us, do I whisper across my cousin to the half-demon. "What's happening?"

Almost as if in response, Alphonse stops abruptly in the center of the courtyard. His eyes remain glazed and distant, and he stares out at nothing like a lifeless husk of himself. The influence that the fiends have over his senses remains ironclad, despite the distance put between him and the little monsters. I'm not surprised though. If I remember correctly from my training with the Shadow Crusade, fiends can continue to hold onto a mind as long as the person is still in view. Perhaps that's why they've clambered up to the canopy, to ensure they keep him in sight while waiting for whatever demise is about to befall him.

"Put the necro-ink on him," Ryven mutters, his gravelly voice so low that I almost don't hear him over the rumbling ground.

Moving slowly so as not to arouse suspicion from our onlookers, I come around and take Alphonse's necro-ink vial in my palm. My hands tremble as I remove the delicate lid. They quake even harder when I press the first stroke to his forehead.

When the cross is in place, I pull back, assessing. Alphonse doesn't move, doesn't change. He remains as lifeless as he was the moment we arrived.

"Are you sure this will work?" I ask, terrified that it might already be too late for him. I've never heard of necro-ink being used to remove a person from a fugue after fiends have already entranced them.

With his back to me, Ryven nods, keeping a wary gaze on our surroundings. It's not until I've finished painting the two necro-ink lines below both of Alphonse's eyes that I realize Ryven isn't just watching *all* of the courtyard. His gaze is fixated on one of the dozens of openings in particular that leads into this room.

"Ryven?" I ask, my finger dragging down my cousin's chin for the final mark. When I'm finished, I recap the vial and let it hang from Alphonse's neck before inching closer to the half-demon. "What are you looking for? What lives here?"

A shake of his head, one that barely moves the thick black hair atop it, is the only answer he gives to that question. "Is he awake yet?" he whispers.

I glance back to my cousin, finding him exactly where I left him. "No. Should I put the necro-ink on myself as well?"

"There's no need," he whispers. "You're part demon now. Their tricks won't work on their own."

There's a sharp pinch in my chest at his words, but I bite back my revulsion and worry at my lip instead. "What do we do if the necro-ink doesn't work?"

He pulls his gaze away from the tall, hazy opening long enough for his eyes to bore into mine. "Then we leave him and save ourselves, or we drag him out of here with all demon-kind nipping at our heels."

My stomach sours at the mental image that conjures. Dozens upon dozens of demented creatures lunging from the shadows. The vines writhing and blocking off our escape. The teeth. The claws. The carnage. It's not a death I'd look forward to, to say the least.

But more than that, more than the fear of what I'm sure will be a most brutal end, the saccharine squelch in my stomach is one of dawning guilt. We have made it this far and Ryven is still proclaiming that he plans on helping us, helping *me*. And I have spent every second of this rescue mission doubting him. It's in this moment, when almost all other hope feels lost, that I finally succumb to the realization that maybe, *maybe* he doesn't mean me any harm.

Of one country, of one blood.

I may not be a Crusader any longer, but each day that I spend in the Shadowthorn, I understand the sentiment behind that mantra more and more.

As if he can hear the conversation in my head, Ryven flashes me a crooked grin. His lips part to say something that I'm sure will be devilishly dangerous about the odds we're about to face, but before he can utter a single syllable, there's a loud rasp behind us. A gasp of choking air.

The two of us whirl, knees bent, shadowsteel drawn. I brace myself for the creature that's snuck up on us, only to find Alphonse heaved over and coughing.

"What is that awful stench?" he barks between choking sounds.

Ryven's jaw flexes as he returns his diligent attention to the ominous courtyard, and I dive for Alphonse, my hand smacking against his mouth. Even muffled, he insists on hollering, long after his eyes are able to focus on me and discern that I am no threat, nor do I look like someone who has the patience for his jerking. But his arrogance can't handle being restrained, especially not by me.

A dragon-like shriek cuts through the air, and Alphonse finally stills. The terrifying sound is followed by another, one of a slightly younger tone that sounds almost childlike, and a third that is even more grumbling than the first two. The fiends screech and jeer with delight.

"What is that?" I yell over them, forfeiting the silence because, let's face it, there is no longer any such thing.

The Labyrinth comes alive. The fiends jump on the branches, frenzied by the awakening of the monstrosities we were hoping to evade, and perhaps even by the sudden realization that Ryven and I have duped them. The ground quakes as more roars and screeches fill the Labyrinth halls.

I'm frozen in place. As is Alphonse beneath my grasp. Kalli's cautionary voice fills my thoughts of a time that feels so long ago.

"If the demons reach the borders, we hide."

That had been our plan. It had been the explicit instructions of our parents, even more so after Tor's death. Our mother always thought it best to hide and leave the fleeing to the idiots and the fighting to the Crusaders.

But I am neither now. My choices are mine, and mine alone.

At the same moment I choose to stand, escape the only viable option in my mind, Ryven whips around and dashes for us.

"Run!" he shouts, snatching my hand in his and bolting.

I barely have a second to register what's happening, but Alphonse is lucky I have the wherewithal to snatch his hand in mine before my feet are scrambling after the half-demon.

"What's happening?" Alphonse splutters, barely keeping up behind us.

"They've awoken the lunar hydra," Ryven calls over his shoulder.

"What in the eyve is a *lunar hydra?*"

"It doesn't matter!" I yell at my cousin. "Can't you tell by its thundering footsteps that whatever it is, it's not friendly!"

The three of us bolt across the barren courtyard, far larger than I thought it was when we first arrived, and scramble around the scattered stone ruins. Ryven jerks us behind an especially wide pillar, three stories tall, and my back slams against the gray surface. All of us heaving and wide-eyed, we crouch as low as we can. And listen.

On the other side of the courtyard, footsteps boom into the expansive room, stopping right as they reach the threshold.

The fiends grow wild at the spectacle unfolding before them. This is the most tantalizing display they've ever seen, three dinners, instead of one. The spry creatures leap through the branches, cackling and pointing, giving away our location before we've even had a chance to hope that it might conceal us long enough for one of us to form a plan.

The footsteps start again, pebbles quaking on the craggy ground at my feet. Ryven's hold, still firm on my wrist, tugs, and before I know it, the three-person-chain that is us bursts from our cover.

Foolishly, I glance over my shoulder to catch a glimpse of the creatures that might reside in such a dreary, forsaken place. My lungs catch on fire. My heart skitters to a halt and plummets into the depths of my stomach when I behold the behemoth behind me. It is the largest creature I've ever laid eyes on, triple the size of the shadowspider, and far surpassing even the size I imagined the Primordial being. The beast glistens with dazzling, jewel-like scales, its great legs nubby. But it's the sight of three necks protruding from its shoulders that turns my skin to ice.

Ryven veers left, jerking me with him, and the creature vanishes from sight.

"This way!" he shouts, throwing caution to the wind as the rest of the Labyrinth livens around us. Everything quakes, as if there are a dozen or more of those things residing here.

"Do you know where you're going?" I ask, seconds before my foot snags on a clawed root.

When I fall, it's hard and fast, and my firm grip on Alphonse's arm brings him down with me. Ryven stumbles forward a few steps, our grasp on each other suddenly lost and his momentum carrying him farther. He looks back over his shoulder at the same moment I look up at him. Fear, unadulterated and profound, is reflected in his gaze, the kind that I feel thrashing inside me and telling me to get up.

But, at the same moment our gazes snag on each other, another hateful beast lumbers into view behind him. The two horns atop its head are as sharp and sparse as the teeth gleaming in its crescent maw. It beholds Ryven, its head cocking and twisting, but its nostrils flare like it knows he's not entirely the demon that his blood masks him to be.

Just as the demon's attention begins to shift, its nose twitching and following a seemingly far more decadent scent, I realize it's not Ryven's human blood that it's scenting.

Alphonse scrambles off me, yanking on my belt to pull me up with him. "We have to go," he says in a harsh and rasping tone.

And the creature's neck snaps. A wicked grin peels back to reveal rows of finer teeth, all along its gums, ones that it will use to tear Alphonse apart, if not me as well for being seen with him.

When the demon lunges, Ryven shouts. "Hey!" He bangs on the Labyrinth walls, the thorny bramble slicing open his fist and spraying blood all over the shriveled vines. "Over here! If you want a good feast, it's me you want!"

For a moment, the demon doesn't falter. It devours us with its hungry eyes, long claws clacking against each other like it can already feel the sensation of tearing into our flesh. But begrudgingly, almost against its own volition, it twists away from us, snarling at Ryven's continuing clamor.

"Go," Ryven growls, tilting his head only slightly to direct his words to us. As he begins to move closer to the corridor beside him, he stumbles over the uneven terrain. The way his good wing flails out with every hitch in stride makes me wonder if he'd have an easier time staying balanced if I'd been able to heal the other one earlier. "Take the channel to your left. The trick of any maze is to pick one direction and continue heading that way."

The shadowcreature lunges, landing so close to him that it

almost knocks him off the ground. Ryven spins around just in time and bolts, yelling back after us only once, "Go!"

Alphonse shoves me out of the way to race toward the other corridor, the one Ryven had indicated. Meanwhile, I'm stunned into silence and immobility. If I'd had any lingering doubts about the half-demon, they're obliterated now. He saved us. He sacrificed himself just so the two of us might get away.

I can't let him do that.

But just as I'm about to veer down the corridor he'd taken, Alphonse's hand wraps around my wrist. "Come on!"

It's surprisingly hard to fight someone as they run. To plant my feet would only make me fall and Alphonse would either fall with me again or he'd drag me through the thicket, bloodied and screaming the entire way. So despite my protests, and me tugging on my arm to try to turn back around, before I know it, the entrance behind us becomes a small window, and the thundering feet of the hydra somewhere around the corner gives me no choice but to follow him.

And so, we run.

My feet hammer against the vine-entrenched stone ground nearly as fast as a horse can gallop, and the idea suddenly occurs to me that maybe I can. If I can figure out how my aunt can effortlessly will herself into a raven or a horse, then perhaps Alphonse and I can gallop out of this mess before we have to face any of the horrors rising from the shadows.

But it's a foolish notion, one that quickly dissipates as a claw snatches at us from somewhere in the vines beside us. Down the next corner, it's a foaming maw that chomps at our heels as we pass. Even if I did know how my aunt or any druid for that matter turned into an animal, I wouldn't be able to focus long enough to try, let alone would this be the right time and place. We have to keep moving. Stopping will mean our deaths.

We barrel through thornbushes. We crash into piles of

stones. Our bones are bruised, our skin bleeding, my head swimming more than it ever has, and yet we still race on.

The Labyrinth becomes one living mass of evil, rather than a home to shelter any of the monsters individually. They *are* the Labyrinth. The walls squirm every time we barely escape the clutches of a demon; the maze shrieks every time I slice my axe through one of the behemoths that gets too close. And there are many. Ryven was not exaggerating when he said that there were unspeakable horrors here. Alphonse and I come across a few, but I can hear the untold others howling in the distance.

I wonder, are those howls of rage or of triumph? Has Ryven made it out safely or is he being torn to shreds and devoured as Alphonse and I make a break for it?

"I think I see the exit!" Alphonse exclaims, more to himself than to me, but fortunately he's close enough that I hear him. The prospect livens his steps and he tears farther ahead.

"Wait!" I plead despite myself, knowing full well that he will do no such thing.

But something doesn't feel right about this. Leaving Ryven behind, it's not fair. He didn't have to come here. In fact, he hasn't had to do any of this. If he'd wanted to, he could've left me and Alphonse to be eaten by the shadowspider and been done with us. He could've returned to the Wardens immediately afterward, and avoided the trek through the Shadowthorn to the homeland he was avoiding.

When I realize the nightmarish sounds have faded, the cycling of my legs slows, until my feet pound to a stop. Chest heaving, I take one glance over my shoulder. All of the evil that had been chasing after us is gone. Sure, the walls are still covered in thick, angry vines that look hungry enough to slice through anyone that touches them, but I see no signs of the demons nor the behemoths who I know were hot on our heels.

In fact, the entire Labyrinth has gone silent.

Dread grips my heart like the icy hand of death.

I pivot back toward the entrance—toward our escape and our salvation—just as Alphonse is about to reach it. "Alphonse, stop!"

The ground before him implodes without warning. Alphonse is flung back from the impact, his head slamming into the thornbushes like a crack of a whip. I would run to him and make sure he hadn't just cracked his skull if it weren't for the writhing, hideous creature that erupts with the soil. Its slimy, ribbed body is repulsive by all measures, but it's the creature's gaping mouth, and the bones lodged between its teeth, that give me alarm as the creature crashes to the ground. My knees tremble. The Labyrinth falls silent, as if the whole realm were holding its breath.

A raindrop splashes on my cheek, the first thing to break the silence. But as more begin to fall, the pitter patter of an early spring drizzle filling the corridor with a somber melody that would've been soothing under different circumstances, fear turns my bones turn to ice. I stiffen where I stand, heart hammering against my fragile ribs. Despite the weight of the axe in my hand, something tells me it will do nothing against the wyrm's mighty girth. When we were children, we were told that worms could actually survive many injuries, including decapitations. I don't pretend to know if the same would be true for a shadowwyrm, but I imagine even if it weren't, it would take me an entire hour to hack through the wyrm's thick neck. The creature fills the entire hallway, the bramble smashed to dust beneath its mighty weight like autumn leaves crunched beneath boots.

Fortunate for my cousin, the wyrm is so large that its head has already passed the corridor he flew down, ensuring that the wyrm can't see him and therefore will not strike.

I, however, do not share that same fortune. With the direction it's facing, there is only one way for the wyrm to go, and I'm standing in its path.

As if the creature has deduced the same, it opens its mouth wide and slithers after me. Only, slithering isn't quite the appropriate word. Snakes can slither through grass with decent speed, but even their skittering is nothing compared to the great shadowwyrm. Every muscle in its rutted body propels it toward me with terrifying and slippery alacrity.

There is no time to run. The corridor behind me is too long, with no corners or safe havens for me to dive into without fear of becoming squashed by the wyrm's passing body.

I wipe away the wetness from my face as if I'm seeing things wrong, but still I find nowhere to go.

I've never been more envious of Ryven's wings. At least he could go *up*—if he were healed. And without wings of my own, my only option is to climb, which I'm far slower at than running.

Then, a thought strikes me. There is nowhere to run ahead or backward, and I am unable to go up, but perhaps this crea-ture can go down, back to where it came from.

The thought is foreign in my mind, like someone speaking a foreign language has placed it there. But the moment the general idea comes through, I have no choice but to put it into action.

"The magic is all around you," I tell myself, channeling Ryven's brief teachings from earlier.

I close my eyes and reach for the life I've felt thrumming around me ever since stepping foot into this place. The breath of the Labyrinth has been palpable from the start, and though I might not have understood it then, sheer desperation is making it clear now.

The air is cool, the beating heart of this dark place, black and unruly, but I am the voice that it must obey. I am a druid. I am of the elements, of life. At first, I'm not sure if the shadowwyrm counts as something that's alive. After all, the Primordial creating the Shadowthorn, and legends say that the monsters inside are nothing more than death incarnate.

But as the wyrm shoots forward like a shark diving for a kill, I feel the vibrations of life around me, and pull. A strange warmth trickles over my skin, a fiery blaze that flares in my chest before plummeting into my abdomen. It feels like nothing and everything, like I am apart from it, and simultaneously connected to it. To this place, to the creatures inside it that I am now sure are in fact living, to this wyrm, to this moment in time.

"Please let this work," I mutter to no one but the vines. Rainwater trickles into my mouth. "I will not be eaten here."

I don't know what I expected to happen; I think part of me was focusing on making the ground cave in beneath he wyrm's body before it could reach me, even though I know the creature would likely just burrow up again.

But instead of any earth-shattering quakes, the wyrm suddenly glides to a halt. It's rancid breath breezes over me like a steaming heap of onion stew. If I could breathe, if I had control over any muscle in my body, I would shield myself from the stench that blankets over me. But I'm too terrified, too struck with awe to do anything.

The shadowcreature's breaths are as ragged as mine, and I get the impression that it came a long way to reach me, summoned by the other demon's calls, no doubt.

And yet, it waits.

The blubbery beast has no eyes, no distinct pair of nostrils that indent the long and squirming tip of its head, and so I'm not sure how it assesses me, but I know it does. Its scrutiny bears heavy on my skin. It *wants* to strike. It craves the taste of my blood regardless of the blighted toxin.

It dawns on me that I have no way of knowing for certain.

It wouldn't be too difficult to guess it, considering not moments ago the wyrm was charging at me and practically dousing me in saliva as it prepared to eat me. But the idea of its internal struggle now, to lunge or to flee, that I should have no knowledge of. And yet, I do. I know it like I know the changing of the seasons

But something I did, something about the magic I drew upon, has stayed its hand—or rather, its teeth.

Almost begrudgingly, the shadowwyrm retreats back through the crater it created.

Not a moment later, I collapse to my knees in a puddle that's already formed beneath me. Exhaustion seeps into my bones much like the rain seeping into my clothes. Every inch of me aches as if I'd been pulverized by Güthric's meaty fists. The relentless pounding in my skull only grows louder, but even it is almost overshadowed by the grating pain that screams down my spine. Even my feet ache, the soles convinced they've been flayed right from under me.

In this briefest moment of respite, the fever grips me anew. Even if the shadowwyrm is gone, I know I can't stay here. It was the reason the other monsters left, but without it to frighten them away, the others will soon return.

I tell my body it needs to move. I tell my legs to straighten beneath me and carry me to Alphonse so that I can drag him out of here if I have to. Once we're free of this place, once the fever stops making the ground swim beneath me, then we can figure out how to find Ryven and get him out of here as well. But for now, I have to—

My straining muscles finally fail me, and I plummet face-first into the rainwater and thorns, succumbing to the darkness around me.

FRACTURED

OUTSIDE THE LABYRINTH, SHADOWTHORN

When my eyes finally peel open, it's to the black, crooked fissures cut into the sky by the branches of the forest rather than the dense thicket of the Labyrinth. I struggle against the weight of my exhausted body to push up onto my elbows, but my head is heavier than I remember it being, the sloshing thing dragging me backward to the scratchy scrap of fabric I'm lying on.

I blink the rest of my blurred surroundings into focus. There's a fire just outside of my vision, a warm glow radiating off it and keeping my toes as toasty as if they were bare and sunbathing. The rest of me is admittedly still damp, but I'm grateful that I find no signs of rain in the clouds overhead, at least not as far as I'm able to tell through the gray atmosphere that always clings to the Shadowthorn.

My axe is not too far away me, resting unsheathed, along with my dagger, on the ground beside me. Some clothes are hanging to dry atop a makeshift clothesline—which is really just a few sticks spiked into the ground with another stick on top of them.

This time, instead of trying to stand, I swivel my head toward the fire.

At the glimpse of dark hair, hope swells in my chest. Ryven's escaped, unscathed and somehow still breathing. I suppose we'll have our own tales to tell of how we narrowly escaped every vicious demon the Labyrinth had thrown at us. Of course, none of his feats will be nearly as impressive as my sudden memory of single-handedly thwarting a giant wyrm. If he's lucky, I may even thank him for being the reason I thought to try to use my druid powers on it in the first place. Without his lessons, I'm not sure I would've thought about trying to call upon the *life* around me, nor would I have even known to call it that or recognize it.

Before I can follow any of my excited thoughts though, the man by the fire shifts on his heels, a long sweep of hair falling over his shoulder. It's longer than Ryven's by at least double.

As the man glances over his shoulder, his long, sharp nose comes into view first, and for some reason I'm more surprised to see Alphonse than I was when I thought he was Ryven. I didn't even know Alphonse knew how to make a fire, let alone did I think he'd bother with hanging what I presume to be our waterlogged leather armor out to dry.

But most of all, I'm surprised by the care with which he's handled me. I don't know what happened in the Labyrinth, but I'm starting to think that this time around, Alphonse might've been the one to drag *me* to safety.

Alarm buzzes in me renewed. I push myself to one elbow, bracing myself against the rotating world. "Ryven. Did he make it out? Did you see him come out of the Labyrinth?" The spinning has lessened since I was last conscious, but it's still enough to disorient me.

Alphonse heaves a peevish sigh. "You're welcome, cousin, for saving your wretched life."

I roll my eyes, but the motion is a dizzying mistake I regret almost instantly.

"And yes, the back of my head is feeling much better now, thank you for asking."

Before he can continue chastising me for my lack of manners, I buckle over the edge of the fabric I'm lying on and spill the contents of my stomach to the ground.

"Repulsive," Alphonse sneers.

I continue retching.

"Did you see him?" I manage once I'm done, wiping my mouth with the back of my sleeve. The cut that Alphonse so graciously gave me just a few days ago is already pink and shimmery with freshly healed skin.

"No, I did not." His jaw is set when he twists around to face the fire, poking it with a charred stick. "Though, I can't say I searched much. You're lucky I even brought *you* with me."

My eyes well with hot tears, which doesn't help as I try searching the distance for any signs of Ryven. I don't have my bearings though. I have no way of knowing if the Labyrinth is behind us, before us, or how far we've traveled since leaving. Knowing Alphonse's predisposition toward shirking any unnecessary physical exertion, I have the suspicion we're not far.

But just as I'm starting to convince myself we should go back for him, the severity of Alphonse's words hit me.

"Why did you?" My words are like anchors in the silence, plunging deep into the dark waters with an audible plop.

Though his back is already turned to me, Alphonse leans more heavily toward the fire, avoiding my gaze. Moments pass without a sound, and I don't know why I expected anything else from him. We have never been ones to communicate, let alone share our thoughts or feelings on matters such as life and death, selflessness and heroism.

Just as I'm about to give up entirely, he shifts, his shadowed face revealed, backlit by the fire.

"Despite what you may think of me, I do not enjoy being a monster."

His voice is low, ruinous. It gives me pause as I sit there, teetering between bolting and staying. Never have I seen this man admit he has any faults. Never have I seen him express remorse or an inkling that his heart is not as mangled as the beasts we've been taught to hate all our lives. He's vicious and cruel and cold.

But with his jaw set like that, with the way his brow quivers as his gaze burns into the ground, I see what I've always seen, what I've always convinced myself to ignore: someone wounded, someone just as lost as I am.

This single act, this one omission of years of his undying hatred for me, is not enough to erase all the years of pain. But…it is a start.

I tamper the frenetic desperation that has been charged inside me and scoot closer to the fire.

"Thank you," I say, eyes flitting to his. "For saving me. I know you didn't have to."

His thin lips press tighter. "And you didn't have to save me. Besides, I wasn't about to spend the rest of my life alone and defenseless in the middle of the Shadowthorn."

A crooked smile inches up my face. "Right. Who would want that?"

As I hold my hands out over the flames, my thoughts return to the man we left behind. "We have to go back for him."

His head lolls back, eyes rolling with him. "I knew you'd say that. You're aware that it's very likely he's already dead, correct?"

"It doesn't matter," I growl. "He didn't have to come in there with me to save you. He could've left me, or insisted we leave you to the fiends—and worse, might I remind you—but he didn't. He chose to come."

"That's all very chivalrous of him, but you still haven't quite pleaded your case. I am *not* going back in that nightmarish place. I value my life far more than the way you'll look at me if your newest lover should perish."

My brow furrows. "He's not my—"

Silencing me with his upheld hand, I'm reminded of the time we spent in Nigh. He was my general, our leader, the man I was meant to follow and obey. Not that I ever did any of those things quite to a tee, but I'd tried in those last months, for Dimitri's sake. Some habits don't fade so easily.

"Need I remind you that your quest is to go to the Forgotten Forest of Eyve to find the cure and be freed of the wretched toxin in your veins. We know the direction we need to head. This half-demon abomination isn't our problem."

My hands tighten to fists and I growl, jumping to my feet. "Fine, if you won't help me, then I'll go myself."

"And, pray tell, what is this genius, heroic plan of yours?" he asks, standing to block me from my trajectory to retrieve my weapons. "You barely escaped the first time you entered that forsaken place, and that was *with* two others to aid you, one of whom dragged your unconscious form out from the under-brush and back into the—I never thought I'd say this—the slightly less dangerous part of the Shadowthorn. You can't go back in there, Halira. It'll be your death."

"I can't just leave him either," I counter.

He flings his hands into the air. "And what if he's dead already? Hmm? You know, as well as I, that the odds of him surviving—of *any* of us surviving that place were stacked against us. If he's dead already—which I'm telling you, he most assuredly is—then you racing back inside will be for nothing, other than to bring about your own demise and undo the good deed I performed by saving you."

My resolve falters for a moment, but so he can't see it, I still shove him aside. My thoughts war as I bend over to retrieve my shadowsteel axe. I know everything he's saying is right. I know how reckless of a plan this is, and though we were just as reckless when Ryven and I headed into the Labyrinth to find Alphonse, we at least had a vague assurance that he was probably still alive.

"Of one country, of one blood," I utter, the words emboldening me and I hope they'll do the same for him. My chances of surviving another trek inside are momentously improved if Alphonse is with me.

His hand startles me as it clasps my shoulder. "A brave sentiment, but a foolish one engrained in the mind of every Crusader so that they will have some falsehood of comradery and allegiance to clutch onto as they stare down the eyes of death."

Shock spins me around to face him, finding his apologetically honest expression.

"It's a fool's mantra, and you, Halira, are no fool. At least, that's what you've always insisted."

A small smile tugs at my lips. "Then what would you have me do? Abandon him like you tried to abandon me with the shadowspider?"

Air gushes from his hanging jaw. "I just rescued you. I could've left you in that place, but I didn't." When the hard set in my expression doesn't falter, he rolls his eyes. "You take it too personally. It's never been about letting you die, but about my own survival. We will not survive another venture through there. We barely made it out alive this time! Do you really think he'd want you to go back there for him? After the sacrifice he made so that we could escape? He is not as selfish as I am. He did what he had to so that we could survive. Don't let the man's dying choice be one he made in vain."

Now it's my jaw that tightens. My chest constricts with a

feeling I've been familiar with my entire life, something twisting and heavy. Shame. In Gravenburg, I could never live up to the expectations of society; I could never just do what I was told. And I know how it wore on my parents, on my sister, how they wanted better for me but couldn't quite do much about it other than chastise and scold me—always with love— whenever they had the chance.

Why can't you tend to the beehives without making a fuss?

Why can't you be more ambitious like your sister?

Why must you accompany Dimitri on those filthy hunting trips?

Why can't you be an obedient daughter like all the others in this town?

I've grown accustomed to letting people down, especially those I care about most. I've built shields to defend against the ache of it. But this…this is different.

In Ryven's time of need, I failed him. He'd been there for me the day my parents were slaughtered. He'd shielded me in the catacombs even when I still believed him to be evil. He'd fought at my side in Ashenvale, in the shadowspider's pit, and in the Labyrinth, and the one time he needed to rely on me, I couldn't return the favor.

Clearing my throat, I swallow the sobs threatening to rise inside me. "We don't know if he's dead," I argue, making Alphonse throw his arms in the air once more. "But you're right. If he didn't escape last night, then he's…gone."

When Alphonse doesn't correct my assumption of how much time has passed, based hastily on the frigid air and low-hanging sun that remind me of early morning, I'm quick to form a plan.

"I'm relieved to see you *can* be reasoned with," Alphonse replies. "If it's any consolation—"

"We have should check the surrounding area, see if we can find any indications that he might've escaped. We won't go back inside, but we can at least sweep the perimeter."

Alphonse stares me down for a moment, before finally sighing. "If it's the only thing that will appease your doubt, then lead the way." Seeing my confusion, he adds, "Oh, right. You were unconscious. I suppose that means I'll take the lead then."

Leaving the modest camp as it is, Alphonse guides us toward the low-hanging sun that is barely more than a blink of light beyond the gray Shadowthorn atmosphere. Just as expected, it's not long before we spy the tangled fortress once more. In the light of day, it's resumed its eerie silence, but the sinking pit in my stomach tells me that's not necessarily a good thing.

I duck back behind the bushes, finding Alphonse cautiously awaiting my word. "I can't see anything from this far away. We'll have to get closer. And we should split up."

"You want us to separate?" he scoffs, incredulous. "Do you not recall what put us in this mess to begin with? Those fiends waited until one of us was alone and then they attacked! The horde of them pinned me down as the others scrubbed my face clean. They'll do it again, too, if I'm left alone—"

"Don't be such a mage. Now you know what they're capable of and you can fend them off. Besides, we'll cover more ground this way."

He crosses his arms. "It doesn't matter how much ground we cover if one of us is captured again."

Biting my lip, I consider his suggestion. It's true, we are in no real rush to finish sweeping the grounds. In fact, the longer it takes, the more of a chance we give Ryven in escaping and flagging us down.

"Fine. We stay together, but only if you can promise to keep your mouth shut."

He feigns like he's wounded. "When have you ever known me to talk incessantly?"

"You're doing it now," I growl, pivoting around to shove back through the bushes.

But rather than coming out the other end into the open clearing, my face slams into something solid, something warm, something glistening with sweat and demon blood.

My hands shove back, hard and fast, just as I register the creamy skin and corded muscles that make the thing before me decidedly not demon. At least, not fully.

Wide-eyed and hopeful, my gaze wanders up his broad shoulders and thick neck to find his eyes. His dark, russet gaze meets mine, as decadent as hazelnuts and steamed chocolate in the cold winter nights.

Without thought, without any restraint or care in the world, I fling my arms around Ryven's neck.

"You're alive!" I squeal against his skin, the demon tendrils of black brushing against my bottom lip. "I can't believe you made it."

Slowly, his arms reach around my back, grateful and relieved. "I wasn't sure you did either, until I saw you peek out through here."

"You saw that?"

"I've been searching the perimeter to see if you escaped, but the Labyrinth is massive, and without knowing which exit you fled from, it was taking longer than I would've liked. Then it rained through the night, a true downpour, washing away any tracks I might've found."

It's no wonder I'd awoken damp and drying beside a fire. I take a moment to slide an appreciative glance at Alphonse who, it would seem, not only dragged me out of the Labyrinth before I could be swallowed by the next atrocity, but then took the time to build us a fire, dry my cloak, and set my weapons out to dry.

Ryven, however, appeared to have done none of those things for himself. His trousers are still drenched through. Suddenly aware of our bodies pressed against each other, I release him, shuffling back to a more appropriate distance beside my cousin. Alphonse eyes me sidelong, a hint of mischief dancing being those condescending eyes and I scowl at him.

Ryven's hair is tousled, forced to dry by the wind in his face as he spent the night running through the grounds in a frenzy toward freedom, searching for us. Hadn't he even stopped to sleep? Had he, like I had, believed the worst?

"Well," I say, tucking the unruly mess of my white hair behind my ear. "Now that we've found you, we should take you back to the camp Alphonse made."

Ryven's eyebrow shoots up. "*He* made camp?"

Grimacing, I shrug. "It's not much, so don't get your hopes up."

"I beg your pardon—" Alphonse starts, but I ignore him.

In fact, Ryven does too. The two of us can't break our gaze away from one another, like we're afraid that if we so much as blink, the other will disappear again.

"I don't need much," he says gruffly. "But if I could trouble you for a fire, I'd be eternally grateful."

I bite down on the smile threatening my lips, but only manage to heat my cheeks instead. "Then you're in luck. Alphonse here made a fire." My eyes flick to the fabric plastered against his thighs. "And you look like you could use it."

The three of us made sure to spend the next few days as avoidant of trouble as possible. When deciding to take the short route through a particularly dark and spooky section of the Shadowthorn or to go around it, the vote had been unanimous to opt for the longer, scenic route. The boys took shifts at night to stand guard, since my fever and hallucinations prevented me from being reliable for such a task. Plus, Ryven had insisted that I, over both of them, could use the rest.

I wasn't one to argue against having a lessened workload, especially not when it impacted my sleep, but I did feel a little guilty every time I caught one of them yawning as we dragged our feet through the blighted forest.

"We're not too far now," Ryven says, scanning the trees ahead of us as if they look any different than the thousands of others we've passed in the week since we left the Wardens.

Alphonse adjusts the bag that's slipping down his arm, heaving it back atop his shoulder, a gray, tattered sack that we pillaged a few days back from an abandoned town. The cast iron skillet inside clangs against some of the other essentials we were able to scrounge over the course of our journey. It had felt...strange, knowing that we were taking things that had once belonged to people. If we had left them there, no one would've returned for them—no one lived anywhere near those places to ever put things like the skillet to use—but for some reason that was also the very reason it felt wrong. Stealing from the dead was almost worse than stealing from the living. The living could at least buy another skillet; they could continue cooking meals for their families and they'd always have a story to tell about how one year their iron skillet went missing. But the dead had no such opportunities. Long gone were their days slaving over the fires.

Stranger still was that some of the villages we wandered through seemed too well-stocked to have been swallowed by the Shadowthorn years ago. But, if I had to venture a guess, it's likely that the Crusaders were forced to stop visiting those towns once the demons started terrorizing ones closer inland.

"How can you possibly tell?" Alphonse groans. "Everything looks the same here."

I incline my head. "He's not wrong."

A soft laugh ripples from Ryven up ahead. "Because I can feel it. The magic in the air is thickening. It's the border. Its power is palpable, even from this distance. Can't either of you feel it?"

Alphonse's face twists with cynical incredulity, while I, on the other hand, focus on my surroundings just like I did in the Labyrinth. My eyes flutter shut. I inhale the saccharine scent of the Shadowthorn and let the breath of the realm speak to me. Everything has a song to whisper, a vibration that murmurs around us. The trees creak, ever so softly, even without the presence of any breeze. The soil beneath our feet thrums with our footsteps, making it sound like the beating of a heart. And somewhere buried beneath the sounds of life all around us, I hear the border Ryven's talking about.

The magic sizzles in the air, electric and powerful. It is the crackling of wood thrown into a fire, the charge of lightning where it strikes down a tree.

Before I can exclaim that I think I can hear it, I slam nose-first into Alphonse back.

"Forgot how to walk?" he asks, eyebrow crooked.

I rub my tender nose.

"Here it is," I hear Ryven say, that same spark of magic and wonder dancing in his voice. "Welcome to the Eyve, home of the druids, home to your ancestors."

Looking past my throbbing nose and the fingers still clutching it, a wall of verdant ivy climbs into the sky. The black vines and branches of the Shadowthorn seem to shirk away from the vivid liveliness of the wall before us, their shadows dying at the touch of the golden branches of the magnolias on the other side, the lavender petals of the wisteria cascading down in thick bundles of serenity and calm.

Blinking at Ryven, I stagger forward, my jaw dragging on the ground behind me. The glimmer in his eyes makes leaving the darkness behind me and behold the vibrancy before us all the more enchanting. It's the first time I've seen color in weeks —*truly* seen it, the way it's meant to be seen. Not shrouded in haze and shadowed by sickly branches, but gilded and dazzling in sunlight.

Even before I'd entered the Shadowthorn, it's been years since I've seen anything quite so beautiful. Gravenburg had been a dull and dreary place, long before the Shadowthorn encroached on our borders. The blacksmith fumes and butcher's market made the Wallows especially dreadful and disgusting.

The Castle of Nigh had been gloomy too. The stone masonry had made it impossible for any light to seep into the halls, and the castle itself had been so tall that, even when we were outside, we were often cast in its shadow.

"I always thought this place would look...different," I breath as I approach one of the fluffy trees and stroke the soft, fuchsia petals.

I guess because I knew that the druids had been shut out from the rest of the realm without any choice in the matter, I'd always assumed they'd live in squalor. I always thought the Forgotten Forest of Eyve would be in ruins, more decrepit and filthier than the grimiest gutters of Gravenburg.

But this? This enchanting place is thriving when the rest of the realm is crumbling.

I'm still gawking at the beauty of the verdant foliage before us, when Alphonse staggers forward.

With an I-told-you-so scowl etched into his pale face, he holds his arms out wide. "*This* is it? *This* is Eyve?"

Frowning and alarmed, I look back at Ryven hoping he might share my confusion. He crosses his arms, clearly wondering the same. This place is beautiful, breathtaking. Anyone who would be unimpressed might be absolutely delirious.

Or perhaps it's me who's delirious. Maybe what I'm seeing isn't vibrancy at all. What if the hallucinations have taken root again?

Alphonse spins around to us, his arms still extended wide. "Where are the druids then? Have they all gone? You've prattled on about your homeland for days now; I'd expected it to be more than a wall and a few pretty trees."

Finally, Ryven dips his head before the relentless smirk can break free. "It's what lays beyond the wall, Alphonse. What you see here is just the tendrils of magic that have slipped past our borders and protected the earth from the Blight."

Almost immediately, Alphonse drops his arms, holding his chin up indignantly. "Well, you didn't say *that*."

Worry niggles inside me, and my neck cranes back to gaze up the length of the massive vined wall. "I...hope you don't mean for us to climb this thing?"

A snort comes from Ryven. "As much as I would love to watch the two of you try to scale an ancient wall covered in vines that tear away from the bricks as easily as autumn leaves fall from trees, there is an entrance."

Alphonse rolls his eyes theatrically. "Well go on, then. Lead the way, half-demon."

With a tilt of his head, dark shaggy hair swaying across his eyes, Ryven guides us around the wall. From time to time, I catch myself reaching out to the jade leaves that climb up the stones, the power of the magic calling to me. Before I can lay a finger on any of them though, caution draws my finger back. For years, I've been taught that magic is evil. It's what cost my father his parents, and what's left our people—or at least, who I thought my people were—terrified and doomed.

After everything I've seen these past few days, everything I've done, I can no longer say with certainty that magic is evil, but I've felt the power of it, and I understand the cautious fear. I was able to deter a giant, writhing wyrm with a simple command of thought. And I'm entirely untrained. It's no wonder the humans have been led to fear magic-users. If I can control a wyrm, could I control a human mind too?

The thought sends a shiver through me, and I ignore every one of the impulses that follows to reach for the magic around us.

After a while, rubble begins appearing on the ground. It takes me a moment to notice it, since so many of the rocks and boulders have already been covered in a lush blanket of grass or moss, but the fractured stone peeks through enough of them for me to wonder. I pull my gaze up from my feet, to find that we've reached an opening in the wall.

It's nothing so perfectly designed as a door, but rather a gaping hole, jagged and wide, that looks like something massive barreled through the stones.

The cool claws of fear grip my heart as I realize what

must've caused such damage. I've heard stories of Qaeus' enormity, but never had I imagined something could be so colossal, so vast. I shudder at the thought of charging into the Shadowthorn without having the slightest clue what we were up against. Crusaders can't kill such a being. Not alone anyway.

Ryven steps over the shattered stones, Alphonse and I close behind.

On the other side, I'm startled when we are immediately greeted by two terrified faces.

"V-visitors," the girl stammers, fiddling with one of three braids she has fastened in her flaxen hair.

"From the outside," the man says, more astonishment shining in his eyes than fear. His gaze drifts back to Ryven, catching on his black arm. Not a hint of emotion seeps into his expression though. No horror or disgust or dread. He simply swallows the distance between them and clamps a large, ebony hand on Ryven's human shoulder. "I was afraid we'd seen the last of you."

Ryven's grin comes pained. He focuses on the ground instead of meeting the man's eyes, and I know exactly where he's drifted to. He wasn't ready to return yet. He's only here because of my insistence that I reunite with my sister and help her find the cure for the evil that blights us.

The man gives his shoulder another pat, before shoving past him. He narrows his eyes on us.

"Names." Gone is the warmth he exuded toward Ryven. In its place, he's become the stone-cold sentinel that he needs to be. "All who enter or leave must be logged."

"Halira Devonshire," I say promptly, extending my hand.

The man glances to it, one thick eyebrow raised.

Self-consciously, I pull it back in.

When my cousin doesn't respond, I elbow him sharply in the ribs. Alphonse winces before straightening, looking down the length of his nose as he says with haughty arrogance,

"Alphonse Reid Graham the first, son of Esmond Thomas Graham, Magistrate and prestigious sovereign of—"

"Alphonse?" the girl chirps, wriggling out of Ryven's embrace. "Isn't that—"

"The smarmy twat that arrested Imryll's nieces?" the man finishes for her. He eyes Alphonse with domineering scrutiny. "You tell me."

Alphonse's hands fly up in defense. Slowly, he starts backing away. "Now wait just one minute. Where I come from, magic-users are illegal. I only did what was expected of me—"

The foreboding man sneers, approaching on heavy, thunderous feet.

"H-Halira? Ryven?" Alphonse pleas, looking to both of us. His back bumps against the stony wall. "Surely, there's something you can say on my behalf to reassure this strapping man here that I am no foe."

Rolling my eyes, I step between the two of them. "Please, my cousin might be a greater nuisance than the fiends of the Shadowthorn, but..." Biting my lip, I consider the implications about what I'm about to do, the dark history I'm letting wash beneath the bridge between us. "He's come all this way. Whatever wrongs he's done to me in the past, well...I've f-forgiven."

There. I've said it. The past is now officially in the past where it belongs, and I can't begin to even describe the weight that lifts from my shoulders.

"You may have forgiven him, but Imryll hasn't," the man says, shoving past me. "She spent the entire length of her stay here talking about what she would do to this man if she ever got him away from the protection of the Wardens."

Part of me perks up at the mention of my aunt's name and I have to fight off the urge to ask of her.

My pleading gaze whips to Ryven as the sentinel grabs Alphonse's shoulder and rips him away from the wall.

"Is this really necessary?" Ryven asks at last.

"I'm afraid it is. At least until Imryll returns."

"Returns?" I ask, my heart plummeting once more. "She's… not here?"

"Nope. Left about as fast as she came. Spoke to the Elders, rested for the eve, and then was gone."

The girl runs up to the man with a pair of shackles jingling in her grasp. Alphonse doesn't struggle as they bind him, though he continues staring between me and Ryven like there's something we can do about it. I try telling him with my eyes that now is not the time and that we will figure out how to help him when we can, but he only grows more indignant.

When he starts spitting hateful names at me, I shut him out. "Where did she go?"

The man shrugs. "How would I know? That one comes and goes like a cloud passing in the sky." Once the shackles click in place, the sentinel grabs Alphonse's arm and starts leading him down a path. "If you need anything from this one, he'll be in the dungeon until Imryll can tell me what to do with him."

"You can't let him do this!" Alphonse cries. "I—I am the Magistrate's son!"

He yells the entire distance, until the two of them disappear behind a door carved out of a tree trunk, and even then, I can still hear his muffled shouts.

Ryven appears beside me.

I smack him hard against the chest. "What was that? You didn't say anything about one of us potentially getting arrested when we crossed into your territory."

He rubs his pec. "I didn't know we would be. How was I supposed to know your aunt would've blathered on enough about your cousin that the sentinel would not only recognize him by name, but that the story of his treachery would've turned my people against him so thoroughly that they would arrest him on sight?"

I square my shoulders at him. "And there was nothing you could've done?"

"What? You want me to fight one of the Eyve's deadliest guards as my *I'm back* announcement? I'm sure that would've gone over well." He crosses his arms. "Besides, your cousin deserves to spend a few hours in a cell. He did the same to you, didn't he?"

With a sigh, I finally acquiesce. "Fine. What do we do now then? My aunt has already left. The guard didn't even mention Kalli…"

"Hey," he says softly, firm grip upon my shoulders. "We have no reason to believe they're no longer together. Your sister is fine. All we have to do is meet with the Elders. They'll be able to tell us where your aunt and sister went."

Nodding, I try forcing a hopeful smile, but it doesn't quite reach the edges of my lips. "Are the Elders close?"

Ryven winces. "Not exactly."

We wave our farewell to the spritely girl, and Ryven leads me down another path that winds between the towering oaks. I've never seen trees of this size. They could be thousands of years old, given how wide they've grown, how sturdy they are where they've planted their roots.

But once we make it through the dense trees, another wonder comes into view. Ryven holds out his arm to the village tucked inside the colossal tree's roots. A waterfall cascades from high overhead, the streams trickling through every level of the enchanted village. Fireflies dance in the high-arching canopy, their glow radiant against the verdant leaves, glowing like a thousand flickering candles.

Yet again I'm reminded that these were the people who were shunned from Arcathain. When the Arcathainians couldn't kill Qaeus, these were the people misfortunate enough to have been boarded up with the Primordial and left for dead. For generations, Arcathainians had just presumed them all dead. Even after the wall finally fell, my mother venturing into the broader continent, very few Arcathainians hazarded a journey to the Forgotten Forest of Eyve; none had wanted to see the carnage their ancestors were responsible for.

How little we understood about them. Not only do they have their own special kind of magic different from the mages that separates them from Arcathainians, but they are not suffering as I'd have imagined.

The druids are thriving.

Their home is everything I would want for Arcathain. The luscious woodland, the quaint cottages speckled with verdant moss and bright red mushrooms, the nooks and crannies that the tree roots offer where they drape over the village and give the children places to run and hide and laugh.

After seeing nothing but darkness for so long, the striking colors of the livened forest are almost assaulting against my eyes. It's been so long since I've seen so much joy, so much peace, that it's almost staggering to behold now. It feels foreign, and unnatural, even though I know it's not. I've always known that life could be better than slaving away in the slums as impending doom approaches, but I'd been led to believe it couldn't. I'd been told to accept my miserable fate and that that's just how things were.

But this place…these smiling people…they're proof that a better existence is possible.

"What do you think?" Ryven asks, and I think I notice a slight worried hitch in his voice.

"It's…it's…enormous. I never dreamed that the Forgotten Forest of Eyve was so massive, so vibrant and flourishing."

A crooked smirk. "Our people have lived here a long time."

My enthusiasm dulls at the seemingly effortless way he loops me in with him and the others. I have not lived here among them. I might be druid by blood, but I am Arcathainian, and it was my people who secluded his from the rest of the realm. Although they don't seem to have suffered for it, I can't help but feel guilty for the part my ancestors played in removing them from the rest of humanity.

"Yeah, well," I say, clearing my throat. "It's impressive. It's nothing like any place in Arcathain, and certainly nothing like the dreary streets of Gravenburg."

"Oh, I remember." He chuckles. "Seeing the way the humans live, so removed from nature, so confined by gray slabs of concrete and stone, it's no wonder most of the druids have opted to remain here."

I snort. "That, and I'm sure having a magical barrier that protects them from Qaeus' tyranny doesn't hurt."

Ryven halts abruptly. He scans our surroundings, grabbing my arm and pulling me to the side of the path so that no others are near enough to overhear us. "Be careful with the tone you take in regard to Qaeus. She is…revered, in a way, by our people."

"Revered?" His words remind me of what my uncle told us while we were with the Wardens and I scowl all the more, snatching my arm from his grasp. "She unleashed a horde of demons on all of Arcathain, demons who have killed thousands of people and desecrated dozens of towns and villages."

Ryven rubs the back of his neck, still keeping a wary eye on the people going about their day behind me. "I know. I know. I learned a lot when I left the confines of the Eyve, and you're right. Qaeus might not as benevolent as my people had led me to believe, but…while you're here, it'll be in your best interest to pretend that you share their preconceived notions of the Primordial."

Defiantly, I cross my arms.

It spurs one of his crooked grins. "If it helps, try to see it from their perspective. Qaeus could've killed them when she was locked away with us, but she didn't. According to the histories passed down from generation to generation, the years living here with Qaeus were some of the most peaceful to ever befall the druids. There was no Blight, no demons.

"The druids believe that the Primordial begrudges Arcathainians for slaying its brethren, and that now she is just doing what is her right: avenging her fallen."

"It's her right to murder innocent people?" I balk, spinning away, my mind racing. I pace in the small distance between us, not wanting to venture too far in this unknown realm. "The ancestors killed the Primordials. Not me. Not my parents. Not my brother."

"I'm not saying I believe it's the truth anymore. I'm just trying to explain it to you. As far as the druids can see, the humans are the evil ones. They killed three of the four ancient beings who had governed over the realms for as far back as written history dates. Then, when there was only one remaining, they imprisoned her with peaceful people who had done nothing to deserve being sequestered, other than angering the very mages whose magic erected the barrier."

Biting the inside of my lip, I fight the urge to see any logic or reason in what he's saying. The Primordials are wicked, that's what I've always been told. It is our duty to slay them, not celebrate them. But every truth I thought I knew has been flipped upside down. The mages aren't the only ones with magic, and perhaps magic might not even be as evil as I mistook it to be. Some people can survive the bite of demons. Even this place—the Forgotten Forest of Eyve—has a farse; this supposedly abandoned and ravaged land is thriving far better than any Arcathainian village I've ever visited.

Who am I to say that the druids are evil for worshipping the beast that didn't kill them but towered over them like the sun? Who am I to argue that Arcathainians can't be cruel?

He presses his lips into a thin line. Watching me through a hard set in his brow, the twitch of a smile that bleeds through his expression is forced. "Let's just not talk about it anymore.

As long as we're here, maybe it's best that conversations of Qaeus become off-limits. That way you don't find yourself in a position that might end unfavorably, and we don't have to debate the morality and ethics on a subject that no one has been able to agree upon for hundreds of years."

A fragile smirk works its way into my expression. "Deal. As long as you take us to the Elders before I begin to wonder if you're stalling."

The gentle smile he'd flashed me falls right off his face.

"What?" I ask, doubt threatening to consume me as I recognize the shame in his expression. "*Have* you been stalling?"

"It's...complicated." He stares at the ground, resolutely silent. Finally, he looks up at me through thick lashes. "You remember me telling you about what happened with Ahl'Ro?"

"Of course."

He sighs. "When we were back with the Wardens, do you remember your uncle mentioning that I've been avoiding the Eyve?"

I nod again. He told me about losing his friend, and the blame he'd cast upon himself for it. I just assumed that guilt had prevented him from returning, that with Ahl'Ro gone, Ryven didn't believe he was worthy of the cure that might await him here.

A muscle feathers in his jaw. "It's...difficult being back here without him..."

"Oh," is all I can bring myself to say. I don't know how to comfort him in this. The loss of a friend like the one he had in Ahl'Ro could be as painful as the loss of a brother, I'd imagine. Thinking back to when we heard the news of Tor's death, nothing anyone said had comforted me. I'd appreciated their silence more than anything, and so patient silence is what I give Ryven now.

He shakes his head, clearing away the muddied thoughts. "It's more than that. Before Ahl'Ro and I left, we were warned about the dangers outside. Our friends, our family, the Elders, they urged us to remain here. But we didn't listen. We couldn't. Our dreams had already become too grand for us to…"

His gaze wanders somewhere distant, somewhere I recognize, but cannot follow. I had no part in the fond memories of his youth, of the friend he lost. Still, I recognize the pain of shame all too well. Shame is the ballad that has been my life: for how I was never good enough, never the right kind of way, never what my parents hoped I'd be.

There's regret in those eyes too, for the days he and his friend had planned on sharing but will never be able to get back. I've felt that kind of grief as well. My brother Tor and I had been as Ryven describes. Spending most of our upbringing in squalor had no hindrance on the dreams we had for our adult lives. When we were young, long before the Shadowthorn had reached our backdoor and become a real thing, we planned on joining the Shadow Crusade together; we would defend Arcathain against the demons that plagued our lands, and be the ones to take down Qaeus. We'd play in the yard with sticks and jab at one of the butcher's cattle pretending it was the Primordial, and when it would finally grow weary of our prodding and run from us, we celebrated our victory in scaring away the great, scary beast. We envisioned ourselves as glorified heroes. Our names, our family would go down in history.

But then, Tor was gone, and so were my naïve dreams of heroism.

"It's not your fault," I say at last, battling the lump in my throat that has ballooned just as much from Ryven's pain as it has mine. "It's okay to dream. It's practically a rite of passage for people our age and younger."

He scowls at me as if to suggest how ridiculous I sound.

"It's true though," I argue, reaching for his bared, broad shoulder and giving him a jostle so that he knows I'm being serious. Reluctantly, he allows himself to sway from my force. "Your friend had wanted the adventure as much as you did. You can't blame yourself for being the one who survived."

"But I do. I do blame myself. If I had woken a moment sooner, if I had been able to deflect just one more of the demons, prevent one more bite from landing its mark, I might've earned him a little more time. Instead, he turned too quickly."

"And it didn't feel right to come back to ask for a cure when your best friend had died without one," I supply. His shocked gaze flashes to mine ever so briefly, before he hangs his head low. But then I do something that truly surprises us both. Some instinctual swell of emotion emboldens me to reach out for his chin and tilt his head until I can see his eyes once more. "But do your people really need to lose *two* of their own? One is already too many."

He holds my gaze, the weight of his sorrowful eyes crashing into me with agonizing force. His pain has burrow so deeply it has become a tarry pit inside him, and I can see him drowning in it. But I hold firm. I do not shirk away from the darkness reflected behind those russet eyes. I do not abandon him to his dismal thoughts.

With nothing more than a mere look, I tell him that he is not alone. He is not the first person to lose someone they care for dearly, which isn't much of a consolation in and of itself, but it means that we've all been there. We lose, we grieve, our hearts begin to repair, and we come out of the other side stronger. It means he will do the same, as have I. And it doesn't mean that we ever stop thinking about them, but they become part of us, a chink in our armor that we carry with us for the rest of our lives so that they might live a little longer.

Slowly, his head begins to nod, and I pat his shoulder. But realizing that I'm *still* touching him—touching his bared, taut skin—I snap my arm back to my side, playing it off as if I had an impossible itch to scratch on the top of my thigh.

"So," I say, my voice caught in a higher note than I'd like it to be. "If you're ready, should we visit the Elders now?"

He winces, a completely not reassuring gesture. His head cranes back, eyes drifting all the way up the massive tree that serves as the focal point of their woodland village.

Following his meaning, I splutter, "They're all the way up *there*? At the top?"

"Should anyone want their sage wisdom, they must earn it by climbing the great tree. The Elders' home is carved inside it, just at the top of the waterfall."

"It would take another day to climb all the way up there. Maybe two."

He chuckles, but the sound is quick to become melancholic. He returns his gaze to mine, eyes distant once more. "It would be quicker if I could fly."

My cheeks burn crimson. "I—I know. I'm sorry. I wish I could but—"

"That's not what I'm suggesting. We're among the druids now. There are many healers here."

"Oh," I say, perking up, suddenly eyeing each person that passes us with renewed thrill and wonder. "Great. Let's ask someone."

He falls silent again.

"Let me venture a guess: it's not that simple?"

Swallowing hard, he runs his hand through his dark hair, fingers sliding around the horns as if he's already grown accustomed to them in the few short months since he's been part demon.

"Most druids can use all magic, but each one has their specialties. Your aunt, for example, I believe she is quite adept at shapeshifting—that is, taking the form of an animal. Before the demon blood cut off my connection to my powers, I was most skilled with plant-based spells. I could snare anything in a root trap, make herbs and gardens sprout from freshly planted seeds to full-grown bushes before your eyes." Seemingly out of nowhere, a thoughtful expression crosses him. "What have you done with your magic so far?"

It doesn't take me long to form an answer. Despite my newfound understanding of the druid power I possess, the magic itself has been a lurking part of my life for as long as I can remember.

"Well, you saw me strike Alphonse with lightning."

Ryven's crooked grin kicks up in response. "That I did."

"Well, it wasn't the first time I'd impacted the weather. Sometimes during the winter and rainy seasons, it's like I could shield myself from the weather."

A thoughtful hand drifts to his chin. "You stopped it from raining and snowing?"

"Not exactly. It's like I could put myself in a little protective bubble so that I wouldn't get soaked to the bone."

"Maybe you have a connection to the winds and air, then."

I nod, even though I have no understanding of what that would mean exactly. "There's more too. During my time at Nigh, I think I…summoned mice."

His dark brow crooks. "*Summoned* them?"

Frowning, I shrug. "I think so. They weren't in the library when I first arrived, but then I was getting so frustrated that it was taking me so long to find anything about what was happening to me. I wished I could find the answers easier, and then the mice appeared."

"Interesting."

"It's also not the only time that happened to me."

"You've beckoned mice to your aid more than once?"

My eyes narrow. "No. But, animals have always acted… strangely around me. Dim—" Dimitri's name falls short on my lips, as if uttering it is a violation of some kind. "My friend would tell me that I always scared the game away when I joined him on his hunts, as if the animals were warned we were coming."

"Dim-your-friend might've been right." To my mortification, Ryven doesn't bother at all to hold back his teasing grin. But the longer he muses, eventually his delight in my discomfort settles. "Some druids are adept at shapeshifting, like Ahl'Ro was and like your aunt, but others simply commune with them."

"So, which is it? Do I control the air and wind, or do I commune with animals?"

A smile forms. "First, not you nor any druid *controls* the elements. Second, you might have a strong connection to both. As I said, most druids learn how to do a bit of everything, but we have strong affiliations toward one, sometimes two."

My hand presses against the sudden tightening in my chest. I don't even understand one aspect of my magic, let alone can I fathom unraveling two. But, I take solace in realizing that at least some of what he's saying is beginning to make sense. The shadowwyrm, for example. If I have an affiliation toward communing with animals and beasts, then it's no wonder I was able to intervene when I had.

Desperate to talk about something other than myself, I redirect the conversation back to the topic Ryven has so elegantly dodged.

"You were talking about healers? And the complications of finding one here?"

He deflates a little, but I swear I see a gleam of approval in his eyes. "Ahl'Ro's brother, Ceph, is one of the finest healers the Eyve has ever seen. Their father, too."

It's then that I finally understand his reservations. "You've finally come home and it's time you tell your friend's family what happened to him," I say, breathless.

His head hangs, the weight of the world upon his druid-demon shoulders. "They deserve to know…and by now I'm sure they've heard of my return. It is only a matter of time now."

"Really?" I frown, looking about us. "Word travels that fast here?"

He holds out his black arm, flexing the fingers that almost look like claws in the firefly glow. "We're not that small of a community, but this has been drawing some attention. It's unlikely many other young, strapping men have left the confines of the Eyve in the past few months, and therefore even more unlikely that any others will be walking around with demon arms. Word will have traveled that a blighted druid has crossed the border. They'll know it can only be one of two people."

My chest tightens at the thought. The rumor will be that it's a young man and woman, not the two young men who left together. His family will hope for the best and prepare for the worst, but nothing will prepare them for the news that they've lost their son, their brother.

Nothing had prepared me or my parents. Despite the dangerous life Tor had chosen as a Crusader, despite knowing that death could find him at any moment, hearing the news had felt like the black hand of a clawed demon had speared through my chest, grasped my beating heart, and yanked it from my torn ribcage.

It's written all over his face that he knows all too well how this reunion will go. Sure, they'll be relieved to see him, but learning they've lost a family member will be devastating, and it will far outweigh relief they have that Ryven has returned.

I'm tempted to grab his hand and offer what little comfort a gentle squeeze can provide. But before the impulse takes hold, Ryven turns away from me, facing down one of the paths.

"That's their home, right there." He gestures with a jerk of his head to a small hut carved into the side of the thick, tan tree bark. "It feels like years have passed since I've stepped foot inside, and yet it feels like no time at all."

I give him a gentle shove on his back, savoring the fleeting breath of warmth that graces my fingertips. "Come on. This won't get any easier."

"You...don't have to come, if you don't want to."

I pause, confusion and something akin to offense jerking me in place.

"I know you will forever see Ahl'Ro as the demon who killed your parents. I don't expect you to accept that he was also a person, someone with a father, a brother, with friends. I'd understand if it would be too much to meet his family. I can do this alone if you don't want to come with."

I consider him for a moment. Every time he's spoken of Ahl'Ro, his love of his friend has been so apparent that I'd nearly forgotten he was the same man—after the demon toxin had taken hold, of course—that was responsible for my parents' deaths. It does not take long for the reminder to awaken the thrashing grief and rage that's always waiting just barely beneath the surface.

It would be tempting to stay here and admire the beauty of this place, to keep the memory of the demon in my mind, and to hold on to the hatred I have for that creature responsible for taking away my parents.

But as much as I'd like to lie to myself, I know that Ryven is offering a sense of closure that no one else can. Meeting the demon's—*Ahl'Ro's*—family, just might be the closest thing I'll ever get to finding peace with the circumstances I find myself in. After all, I'm not the only one who lost someone that day.

I'm also not the only one who wants to avoid revisiting that horrible day. I'm not the only one who it would be easier for to walk away and never look Ahl'Ro's father or brother in the eyes. Ryven has been avoiding coming back here for months now, afraid to face his past and the possibility of a future that he would have to live without his friend.

I abandoned him in the Labyrinth, but I'm not leaving him now.

"Like I said," I say, bumping him with my shoulder, a smile on my face. "This isn't getting any easier."

We approach the home together, and I stand by his side as he knocks on the rounded door. There's so much life buzzing around us—quite literally, with the fireflies that fly amid the leaves—that I almost can't hear anything coming from inside.

The two of us exchange a look, one that suggests it's possible that they might not be home.

But then someone grabs the doorknob from the other side. The wooden latches creak. The door opens.

A man appears from inside the dark home. His sky-blue eyes glisten with fatherly love as he takes in the sight of Ryven. Something sad fills them a moment later as he looks between us, noticing who's missing among us. Understanding dawns on him like a veil, profound sadness etching into the grooves of his already sorrow-worn face.

With a simple blink, the veil lifts, leaving only the slightest glint in his eyes as he looks upon Ryven again. A fragile smile breaks through his expression as he holds his arms wide. "Well don't just stand there. Come here and give this old man a hug."

Ryven become even more firm in his hunched shoulders and scowl, avoiding the man's bright and inviting gaze just as much as he's ignoring his invitation for an embrace.

The noise that escapes the father is similar to a snarl but more playful, as he grabs Ryven in an enveloping hug and rocks him back and forth.

"I wasn't sure I'd be seeing you again," the man says with a laugh, one that cycles through every spectrum of emotion.

Blinking, Ryven staggers back. He shakes his head in small, rapid motions. He had expected questions, for there to be blame, but all I am witnessing—all *he* is greeted with—is love. The unconditional kind that hurts just as much as hate.

Before Ryven can find whatever words he's searching for, the man holds out his hands, not a callous in sight. "Easy now, Ry. Don't hurt yourself thinking too hard." If he expects a laugh, he doesn't skip a beat when none comes. "Why don't you come inside? I'll put the kettle on."

Ryven shoots him an incredulous glare.

The man's answering smile is rueful, hardened by a lifetime of tragedy but somehow also brighter for it. "I have soup. And difficult conversations are always best with soup."

We're led to a table in the main room and offered a chair as the blond man zips over to the kitchen. The scent of rosemary and thyme remind me of home, and the meals my mother would make, making me even more at home in this quaint cottage.

When the man finally returns, he's somehow managed to stack his arm with three small bowls, while clutching two mugs of tea and the teakettle in his hands. He sets the table, refusing our help when we offer it, and hands us each a mug.

"There's more in the kettle, if you'd like."

"Thank you…"

"Jiordan," he supplies.

"Thank you, Jiordan." I reach for my mug and let the heat warm my fingers. Spending weeks outside had left a bone-deep chill, but hopefully this would remedy it.

Ryven doesn't move for his mug, nor does he start

guzzling the creamy pea soup that's been placed before him. He spoons at it mindlessly, and I can do nothing but watch. This isn't my news to deliver. The only part of Ahl'Ro's story that I was present for was the brutal end. Sneaking glances at his father now, I can't imagine ever telling him what his son did, even if he was a demon. This man is too warm, too bright for such devastating and horrific news. No, it's best that he keeps the memory of his son as he had him, not as a vicious, bloodthirsty demon, but as the wide-eyed boy who Ryven describes, the young man who wanted to chart the realm and bring peace back to the continent, the shapeshifter, the idealist.

To my surprise, it's neither Ryven nor I that break the silence.

"We feared the worst when you didn't return," Jiordan says, clasping his hands over the table. "I'd tell you that we warned the two of you not to leave, but I can see you already bear more of the burden than you should."

"You were right to warn us." Ryven's voice is low and guttural, the kind of sound that tears through a person and leaves them shredded and raw. It resembles a noise closer to that which a demon would make than any human, but the emotion storming in his tone is nothing a mere demon could replicate. "We shouldn't have left. I should've told him it was foolish and reckless—"

Jiordan reaches over to grab Ryven's fisted hands. "You couldn't have done anything. That boy was intent on leaving this place the moment he was born. You remember the horse that almost galloped out of the Eyve with Ahl'Ro still bundled atop it?"

A begrudging, sorrowful chuckle escapes the Ryven.

"And then again when he was five, he almost wandered right out the front gate while the sentinel was distracted by his own small daughter." Jiordan starts counting on his fingers, almost comically. "Then again when he was eight, and four-teen, twice when he was sixteen."

The laughter becomes contagious, impossible to contain, and soon it's not only Ryven who's grinning despite himself and their dreary circumstances, but all of us.

"He sounds like he was a handful," I say, lips pressed against my mug as I attempt to control my grinning long enough to take another drink.

"Oh, that he was," Jiordan agrees. A new silence descends at his use of the past tense, a silence that's more stifling than the ones that preceded. Jiordan folds his hands before him and nods to Ryven's blackened arm. "Is that what happened to Ahl'Ro?"

Ryven's shoulders tense. The subtle jerk of his head is the best answer he can provide.

Jiordan's gaze drifts to the table and it's the first time he's let the smile drop from his face. It's not until now that I've real-ized just how much of a mask it truly is. Not only for him and the grief that is etched into his weary eyes, but also for Ryven, a young man whom he clearly loves like a son and hates to see tormenting himself.

A long silence stretches. It's not until the tea cools that Jiordan asks, "How long do you have?"

Ryven watches him with confusion, and I have to admit, I feel some of it myself. Jiordan knows his son is dead, he's so much as said it, and yet he still has not once asked Ryven *how* it happened. Not exactly; not in any way that would provide him with any real closure.

Perhaps it's more than that for him. Perhaps having Ryven returned safely is better than he had hoped for. When we first sat down, he said he'd thought both of them had died. So in some ways, maybe he's just grateful that one of them lived.

"I'm not sure," Ryven finally answers. "I was hoping the Elders could provide us that answer."

With a long sigh, Jiordan leans back in his chair, a dubious raise of his eyebrows preceding him folding his thin arms. "I wouldn't doubt they'll be able to tell you that and more." Then, considering a moment, he adds, "Can I ask what brought you *here*, though? Don't get me wrong, I am grateful to see you again, but it's clear to me that you would've avoided this reunion at all costs if you had the choice."

A muscle feathers in Ryven's jaw and his head dips low again.

"He was injured," I say, trying to spare him from finding any more courage than he already has. "His wing was—"

"Yes, of course!" Jiordan exclaims. "I noticed you'd sprouted wings since last I saw you. I wasn't sure if it was some in between animal form you'd learned in your travels or—"

"It's…part of the demon toxin," I say quietly, my apologetic eyes flicking to Ryven. "It gave him wings, and having access to them now would help us save another day's journey, if possible."

Jiordan strokes his smooth, hairless chin. "I see. You came because you seek Ceph's assistance."

"Is he here?" Ryven asks, barely looking up from his clenched fists.

"I'm afraid he isn't. Lately, he's been spending his days apprenticing with the herbalist. I could send for him, but truth be told, if you don't intend on staying long, I'd rather not interrupt him for such a brief and tragic reunion. The past few months have been hard for him…"

"I understand," Ryven says, abruptly standing from his chair. "We won't bother you any longer."

Jiordan stands too. "Withering willows, Ryven! I wasn't kicking you out. You don't need Ceph to heal you. I can examine the wing for you. But—" He pauses for dramatic effect.

Ryven's brow furrows again. Never in anger or challenge,

but it's like he can't comprehend the level of compassion this man is showing him. I find it staggering too. I'm not sure I've ever known someone to be so inviting and selfless. It makes me wonder all the more what Ahl'Ro had *truly* been like, and whether he took after his father's compassionate heart. Then again, I suppose I don't have to wonder. Ryven has already told me just how wonderful his best friend was, and how much it destroyed him having to watch him become something so evil and opposite of himself.

Jiordan finally continues, a teasing grin twitching the edges of his thin mouth. "Once you're finished with the Elders, I expect you to return." Ryven's scowl deepens, but the man carries on matter-of-factly. "By then, I'll have spoken to Ceph and prepared him for you and the conversation he'll want to have. You'll also be in a better position to talk about it after you've met with the Elders and found the guidance you seek from them."

Ryven's fists flex once more, but he says, "Fine. I will return once we're finished with the Elders."

My heart cracks a little in that moment. Although I'm sure Ryven has considered numerous times when this day might come, I'm not sure he could've ever truly prepared for it. Fortunately, Ahl'Ro's father has made it easier on him than he could've ever imagined, but I get the impression that the conversation with Ceph will be different. It seems he will be more inclined to ask questions, and might even ask for details that Jiordan has graciously forgone. Perhaps he knows the truth: there is no peace in answers, only more pain. Ryven won't be able to spare Ceph that pain once he starts asking. The day will be replayed for all of us, the atrocities cascading anew and tearing through us with familiar hurt, though for different reasons. I mourn the loss of my parents, Ceph will mourn the loss of his brother—both the time that he lost his humanity and the moment he was slain—and Ryven will mourn the loss of his friend, his brother, and his innocence.

Part of me hopes that once we reach the Elders, we won't ever leave. I dread returning here, and I can see in Ryven's eyes that he does too.

Only, buried deep beneath all that fear flooding his russet eyes, I see the truth. He wants nothing more than for this place to feel like home again, and the truth is that this is the first step he must take if it will ever be so.

"Very good," Jiordan says, clapping Ryven's good shoulder.

The sheer strength of the blow, however, is strong enough to make the half-demon fall forward over his elbows, the force inadvertently jostling his bad arm and making him hiss through his teeth with renewed pain.

Jiordan draws his hand back sheepishly. "Sorry. I guess we better see to that wing of yours before your good cheer rubs off on me again and I break your other one."

THE DRUID ELDERS

FORGOTTEN FOREST OF EYVE

For what feels like hours, Ryven's ear-splitting cries tear out from the back room, flooding the cottage with a heavy, noxious plume of despair. Every time another cry breaks from his clenched teeth, I flinch and curl further into myself. On more than one occasion, I've thought about offering to help, or at least to sit beside him and hold his hand when the pain becomes too unbearable to stomach, but I remember Jiordan had cautioned against it, claiming it would be easier for him to focus on the injury if it was only the two of them in the room. So, I remain where I am, as the shadows cross the room with the setting sun.

Ryven had assured me that it would be better this way. A wounded animal preferred solitude, not an audience.

But my stomach knots every time I hear the pain wrenching from his lungs and know that I cannot go to him. My knuckles whiten where I grasp my mug. The tea turned cold hours ago, but it's all I have for comfort.

I wonder whether this is actually saving us time. If the Elders know how to cure us, then soon Ryven won't even need to worry about whether his wing is broken because they'll be gone. Or at least, I hope they will. But what if the scars of our blighted souls remains? What if those wings have made a permanent home in Ryven's broad shoulders, forever hanging over him like a dark omen of what had been?

Tentatively, I unlatch the leather bodice that cradles my ribs. My fingers trace over the puncture wounds where the demon's teeth had sunk into me, before I let the garment fall to the seat behind me. I lift the black undershirt to reveal pale flesh. I've been too frightened to look until now. Walking around with a half-demon whose entire arm has deformed with malevolent darkness has made me worried to check my own malformities.

But there is no turning back now. With my stomach revealed to the empty room, I force my gaze down to my navel. I expect to find bristles like the ones that jut from Ryven's shoulder. Or obsidian scales like the ones coating the hydra's skin. Or jagged layers of charred flesh that cracks and peels, marking me as an abomination more akin to the demons I've trained to hunt, than the people I strove to protect.

What I find is so much worse.

Jagged marks cover half of my abdomen, six of them. The demon teeth didn't just puncture my skin and sink into me, they tore my flesh, the two on the end leaving the largest and most ragged of the scars. The canines. It's there that the blackness is starting, almost imperceptible now, but I can see the blighted blood veining away from the wounds like little dark worms of death.

The lethal sharpness of those teeth is still seared into my skin. As the demon bit into me and tore me away from the others, my blood ran as hot as fire across my skin. The holes burn anew, my vision flashing white and black and then white again, as the memory consumes me and becomes more like a living entity. I stare down into the horror of those markings, wondering at the miracle of my survival and the life I could've lost if my heritage hadn't been what it is.

The longer I stare at my scars, at the wounds that still won't heal even after Imryll's touch and a week of travel, the sting of them clamps down on me again and again, until I finally shove my shirt back down and cast my blinking gaze at the nearest wall.

Just when I'm about to scream, just when the pain and fear is at its peak, I realize Ryven's screaming has stopped.

Wiping the tears from my eyes, I look across the room to find him standing in the doorway, his head bowed, a look of sorrow weighing his expression. He smiles at me, a small quirk of his lips that says that he knows it's horrible, but that I'm not alone. Whatever pain I'm suffering, whatever fears and doubts, he's been there too.

I make quick work of fastening my bodice back in place as Ryven says his farewells with Ahl'Ro's father. Our departure happens quickly after that, and I'm only mildly surprised that Jiordan doesn't try getting us to stay. But then I remember the promise Ryven made to him. This is not their farewell. Ryven needed his wing healed so that we could make for a faster trip to the Elders. He expects a return, though, I wonder if it's what Ryven intends.

Once we're outside in the cool evening air, Ryven holds out his arm to me. I marvel at how easily he uses it now, as if he'd never even been injured to begin with.

"Are you ready?" he asks.

My eyebrows shoot up to my forehead. "You don't want to test it first?"

With a crooked grin, Ryven pops his wings out wide in a show of their magnificence. It earns him some frightful glances of those walking around us, and I notice the way his gusto deflates a little under their scrutiny, but he keeps his eyes trained on me.

I flash him what I hope is a reassuring smile. "They're just jealous that when they want to visit the Elders, they have to spend half a day walking up these steep paths."

He lowers his head to hide a smile that I realize too late is at my expense. "They could take the form of a bird, you know?" Before I can flush too brightly, he adds with sincerity, "Thank you, though."

There is no other warning before he scoops me into his arms, my hands clasping instinctively around his neck, and the two of us leap into the air.

The quietness of the peaceful village is swept away by the powerful whooshing of Ryven's wings, but there's something equally soothing about it, rhythmic, calming. Even as the people below shrink to the size of beans and then to ants, I feel my grip loosening. Any fears I might've once had of being flown high above the trees dissipate as the fireflies dance around us, warmth exuding from their small, vibrant bodies. I let go of his neck with one of my hands to reach out to the curious creatures, running my fingers through their masses as Ryven continues to ascend.

When I look back to Ryven, he's watching me with a sense of approval, of pride. I am the first outsider he's brought here. When him and Ahl'Ro had left, they've hoped to return with others, to share in the beauty of this place and in turn find peace with the rest of the continent. I am only one person, but I see the pride in his eyes now, the small sense of fulfillment. My wonder is exactly what they'd hoped to find in the outside world. This is his home, the only place he'd known growing up. And what he's seen of the outside world can't compare to the beauty the druids have managed to preserve here.

The flight ends abruptly with me staring over Ryven's arms down at the winding paths, through the canopies, and to the people who I suspect are still staring up at us. Ryven lowers my legs to the ground, but from this high up, with the rushing river behind us, I sway from the excitement of it all.

"Whoa," Ryven says, bracing my arms. "Are you okay?"

"Yeah, I'm fine. I just never thought I'd be…flying."

He smirks. "Yeah, well, you better get used to it. Once we get you healed and you start calling on your druid power more, you'll be able to summon wings whenever you'd like. You'll be able to swim as a fish or a turtle. You'll be able to burrow as a rabbit—"

I almost snort. "*Burrow*? That was the next wonderous thing you could associate with being an animal?"

His chuckle comes bright, the straight set of his teeth more visible than I've ever seen them before. My stomach dips, and though I try not to stare, my traitorous eyes can't stop taking in the beauty of him.

"Come on," he says, an airy laugh still drifting on his words. "Let's not keep the Elders waiting any longer than we already have."

Gesturing with one corded arm, Ryven presses his other hand to the center of my back and nudges me toward the great oak in front of us. It is the largest tree I've ever seen. The bark that trails up in jagged paths is as thick as my hand, the rivulets between wide enough for two or more fingers to fit between. This tree must be thousands of years old, even though it's verdant leaves and healthy roots make it seem as youthful as a sapling.

But despite its magnificence, despite the hundreds of branches that hang low and provide us with enchanting shade, it is the door my eye is drawn to. The frame is just as round and deeply set as any other door we've passed in our time here, but it's the detailed artwork that sets this one apart from all the others. Carved into the red oak are two trees. The carving itself shows their branches bare, their roots prominent, but it's the green iridescent painting behind the branches that give it the impression of life.

Ryven strides forward, momentarily blocking my view and drawing me out from my admiring trance. He grabs the walnut doorknob and twists.

When he motions for me to go, I gape at him with my arms crossed. "You want me to go first?" I scoff. "I might be a druid by blood, but I'm still an outsider here. I don't know your Elders. You should enter first."

His hooked brow battles his crooked smile. "You traveled through the Shadowthorn in the middle of a blight-fever, you killed a shadowspider, you entered and survived the Labyrinth, and you're telling me that it's the Elders who scare you?"

My arms untangle themselves. "I didn't say I was scared."

"You came all this way to find your sister, find the cure. You've made it. This is the finish line. I can cross it first if you'd like, I just thought—"

"Okay, fine," I groan, before trudging into the hollow of the tree.

I don't make it much farther than the doorway before awe consumes me once more. My eyes widen, my head reclining to take in the expansive, gutted space. Jiordan's home, although also wedged into the side of a tree, had still mostly resembled the homes I was accustomed to. The walls were constructed from boards, not the smooth flesh of the inside of a tree. There had been a single window offering some light to the half of the cottage without the hearth. It was decorated as if it was inhabited by a family: with a table for eating, chairs for sitting, and a few comforts like blankets and a rather worn rug.

But this place is no home, at least, not by conventional standards. The way the ceiling seems to stretch on forever reminds me more of the library at Nigh than anyone's personal residence. A staircase winds around the outer edges, scaling up the smoothed walls to reach a variety of hollows and crannies dug into the thick branches.

But once my eyes are done stretching up as far as they will go, Ryven taps the middle of my back, and I return my gaze to the floor before us. If the height of this place is reminiscent of a library, the bottom floor would be the storage closet. Every inch of space is cluttered. To walk through it would be more like walking through a maze, given that the tables and basins and other random pieces of furniture are scattered throughout in seemingly no logical order.

I find no sign of the Elders as we enter. Not at first. Instead, I walk among the clutter, eyeing each station with fascination and curiosity. The more I meander, the clearer it becomes that this place is actually more organized than I originally gave it credit. Although the room itself is overflowing with things, the tables and structures are very obviously organized, each one with their own purpose to serve. One table we pass is tiered with its own built-in shelves; a collection of multicolored vials stacked neatly on each shelf with no space unused. A wide bookshelf—placed awkwardly in the center of the room—has a collection of gold trinkets atop its surface that appear strange and randomly placed to me, but the books below are alphabetized by author. There is a particularly tall stack of cauldrons and pots beside another workspace, a collection of bundles of fabric forming another of the winding paths.

My eye catches on one of the black fabrics, distinct against the rest of the pastel colors, and I reach a hand out to caress the leather that is so familiar to me and my fellow Crusaders.

"Make yourselves at home," an elderly woman's voice calls from somewhere beyond.

Startling backward, I bump into Ryven, the two of us staggering in the claustrophobic strew before he steadies us both, just moments before either of us can knock over an intricate system of jars and flame and bubbling fluids.

We pull ourselves together, peeking around another tall stack of books until three older women come into view. They stand hip to hip as if they are one, but they are so uniquely different among themselves.

The Elder in the center is tallest and carries herself with the most authority. She also appears to be the oldest, her tawny skin leathery and ashen where it creases around her hazel eyes. In fact, her color and texture almost remind me of the oak we've stepped into, her skin akin to its rough tree bark, her clothes every shade of green found atop its canopy.

On her left is a short, twitchy woman who hardly looks the definition of an *Elder*. She hides behind a veil of blonde, matted hair, her skittish gaze cycling between the two of us, the woman beside her, and a crack in the floor where a mouse has just scurried. Her mouth puckers, a squeak whispering between her lips as she tries calling the creature back to her. It's then, as she's bent down with her arm outstretched, that I noticed the empty nest weaved into the hair at the top of her head.

As the mouse finally scurries back to her, I draw my confused expression away and to the third and final Elder. She watches us with a serene expression, and despite standing still in an enclosed space with no signs of wind anywhere, I notice her hair blowing at the nape of her neck, watch the flowing gown of her skirt ripple around her legs like a breeze blowing over a moonlit lake.

"I'll do the talking," Ryven whispers into my hair, his breath like a caress to my skittering heart. Then he pulls away, his voice reverential. "Greetings Elder Henness, Elder Nebadri, and Elder Irene. I am Ryven, son of Jeck and Maude, attuned to the voice of the plants and trees, and I—"

"We know who you are," says the Elder in the middle, the one he looked to when he said the name Henness. In a regal fashion, she pats the white, wispy cloud of hair that frames her face.

"We were told you were coming," the serene one, Irene, adds.

Ryven clears his throat. "Then, you also know why we have come to you?"

Elder Henness gives a careless wave of her hand. "The breezes and animals only know so much."

"Of course. Forgive me," he splutters, and I'm surprised by how easily he's coming undone before them. He's intimidated by them, and even as I try to think about what it would be like to, say, face the Magistrate, I find myself unable to relate, possibly because even if the Magistrate holds a title of power, he is still just my uncle in my eyes. Ryven continues. "You are so knowledgeable in ways beyond my understanding, that I forget that there are secrets even you three are not attuned to."

Elder Henness arches an eyebrow, the hood lifting from where it wrinkled over her eye. "He comes before us, sisters, and now he insults us."

Ryven's eyes burst wide. "I—I would never—"

Laughter bubbles from Elder Nebadri's lips, a cackle that simultaneously grates against my spine, and is somehow child-like and therefore endearing. Even Irene's lips quirk. They're toying with him, but more importantly, they're wasting our time.

Disregarding Ryven's instructions, I step forward, drawing every eye in the room. "We came to you with questions. It's been a long journey from Arcathain to the Forgotten Forest of Eyve, so if you're done making jokes, perhaps you would care to answer us."

Ryven stiffens, and the smiles fall from their faces. Elder Henness hadn't been smiling though, but something shifts in her expression as it settles over me, a curious squint to her clouded eyes. But something sharper, too.

"We were never forgotten," Elder Henness says, her tone as sharp as a guillotine. "We were abandoned."

I swallow, taking a step back beside Ryven. I avoid meeting the wide-eyed glare he casts at me. Perhaps he'd been right about me keeping my mouth shut. Despite being of druid blood, I don't know these people or their customs. I could say something wrong and offend them. What if they refused to help us then?

Stroking the mouse in the palm of her hand, Elder Nebadri giggles, her voice shrill and rapid. "She bears semblance to the other girl—the one who came the other day—she was from Arcathain—but not really—she had druid blood, so she was from the Eyve, but also not from it. Do you have druid blood— the animals say you don't smell like druid blood—you smell like dead blood—"

"Silence, Elder Nebadri." Henness whacks Nebadri in the arm.

I'm about to scold Elder Henness for her abuse of her sister, when I realize what Nebadri must've meant by *semblance to the other girl*. "M-my sister? Did you see my sister?" I nearly choke on the words, staggering forward again. "Kalli. She was on her way here with my aunt, Imryll. I lost them, but...t-they made it? They came?"

Irene holds up her gentle hand. Her petite nose twitches, and she inhales the scent of the room that seems to have suddenly become strange and interesting to her. Whatever it is, one glance to Ryven confirms that he doesn't smell it either.

"Elder Nebadri," Irene says, voice ethereal. "I fear you may be correct. I, too, smell death." She steps forward and into the glow of a nearby lantern. The other two follow. "Your arm, Ryven," Irene says. She extends her hand, and a gust of wind whips around the two of us. She scents the air again. "It is infested with blighted blood."

Elder Henness peers even closer. She reaches behind her

neck, beneath the collar of her green garb, and plucks a tuft of moss seemingly from her spine. Before Ryven can respond or do much of anything, she drags the moss across the demon skin and tucks it quickly into her mouth. I grimace as she swallows it, repulsed by the idea of chewing moss of any kind, let alone moss that's been dragged across blighted skin as if it were a chutney dip.

But as the Elder Henness masticates, my attention is pulled to Elder Nebadri. With the mouse still in hand, she steps forward. The poor creature curls into a ball, quivering with fear as she takes another step, holding it out farther. The closer it comes to Ryven, the more the mouse quakes and squeaks, as if even it can sense the danger lurking inside him, the death they're speaking of.

Elder Henness reaches between us for a jar on the table at our backs and spits the green, gritty saliva into it.

"Elder Henness," Irene says, eyes pleading. "Is he—"

"You have been blighted, our son. You come to us because your time is nearing its end and so you seek the cure."

I have to bite my lips to prevent my face from betraying my frustration. If they had simply let us speak, we would've been able to tell them as much. It wouldn't have taken eating moss.

"Yes," he says. "If there is one."

Elder Henness inclines her head and I swear the tree we're standing in groans. "There is one," she says after a time. Then, turning to me, she adds, "It is the same cure your sister and aunt now seek."

I suppress the urge to roll my eyes again and try to force my teeth from unclenching. "Yes. It's why they traveled all this way. How long ago were they here? Have they gone already?"

Elder Henness watches me from behind a cocked brow. "For one who's traveled so far, you ask pointless questions."

Ryven grabs my arm before I can decide to march forward and give her a piece of my mind. His touch is far gentler than the outrage simmering in me, and with nothing but his eyes, he asks that I let him handle it. Seeing how adept the Elders have been at ruffling my feathers, I concede.

"What information did you give Halira's family about how to cure a druid once they've been infected?"

Henness' hazel eyes narrow on him, as if she's considering whether or not she will tell us. "Elder Irene, do you care to share with them what you shared with the others?"

Irene steps forward, white, silken skirts dragging along the smooth ground beneath her. She fingers the air as she speaks, as if searching through the invisible waves for the answers we've requested. "A being touched by the Blight must reunite with a Primordial's core, so that the darkness may return. But to do so without protection would mean death."

"What does that even mean?" I ask, glaring from the Elders to Ryven.

His gaze sharpens while he strokes his rough chin. "*Reunite with a Primordial's core...* I think that's what Adrien spoke of. He believed that one of the blighted could channel the demon toxin back into the Primordial—that is, if they could get close enough." He returns his attention to Elder Irene. "You said that this blighted person would need protection if they wanted to survive. Halira's sister and aunt, you told them to search for this protection you speak of?"

Irene nods, a long and graceful motion.

"What is it?"

"The breath of life," she says simply.

When she doesn't elaborate, nor does anyone else in the room upon seeing my confused expression, I roll my eyes and finally ask, "For those of us who didn't grow up with druids, what is the *breath of life?*"

Ryven shakes his head. "The breath of life is not of the druids," he tells me, and I already dislike the wariness in his tone. "It's an ancient and powerful item, one that is as old as the

Primordials, as far as we know. I've only heard mention of it in fairy tales, I didn't even know it was real."

"What does it do?" I ask.

The glance he shoots me is dubious. "It's said to grant anyone who absorbs it a second life."

My brow furrows. Surprise, shock, and disbelief suck the breath right out of my lungs and leave my knees wobbly. "A…a second…did you say a second life? As in—"

"It's said to protect the person from death." He pauses, turning his attention back to the Elders as his thumb brushes over his lip. "But what I don't understand is why someone who's blighted would need it. Aren't demons immortal?"

"They are," Elder Henness replies. "But you would no longer be a demon, Ryven. Once you are rejoined with the Primordial's heart, all traces of demon blood would be leeched from you. You would be your druid self again: human, mortal. However, the demon's blood has already settled in the both of you, I'm afraid. It is attached to your soul now and, should the Primordial jettison the demon blood from your bodies, it is likely that it would take your life, as well."

Elder Irene adds, "The breath of life would ensure your… rebirth after the absorption."

Once again, my stomach fills with lead. I knew curing ourselves wouldn't be an easy task, but I never imagined it could be anything like what Elder Henness is describing. I'm not even sure I fully understand it. While in possession of the breath of life, we will have to approach the Primordial's heart and allow it to absorb the blighted blood inside us? It seems too whimsical of a plan to work. What if the process doesn't start? What if the Primordial kills us anyways, breath of life or not?

I try not to think about those things right now though. Kalli and Imryll have already been here, which means they're still ahead of us.

To my dismay, Ryven voices a question I hadn't yet considered. "But how do we get close enough to the heart for any of this to work? I've seen it. The Primordial, or whatever is left of her, is surrounded by an impassable boundary of some kind."

"Ahh," Elder Irene coos, her hand floating up. "You speak of the protection barrier around the Primordial's heart."

"Yes." He nods. "How do we get through it?"

If she was the kind of person to shrug, I imagine she would've done so. Instead, her gaze cuts to the side, her sleek brow rising. "Like calls to like because trust resides in the familiar."

These riddles have been so far from my area of expertise that I twist to Ryven almost instantly. His brow is already furrowed, assessment brewing behind his dark eyes. He reminds me of Kalli, in that way. Where I grow weary of word play and strategy, the two of them seem to be invigorated by it.

At last, he says, "Nothing is like the Primordials but other Primordials, and therefore they only trust each other?" The Elders give him an approving look. "So, in order to enter, we need to have a Primordial with us. Does that mean another still lives?"

Nebadri cackles. "There are no other living Primordials, you toad—how could there be, when all but one were slaughtered—slaughtered—slaughtered—" Blinking furiously, as if the slaughter of each of them is flashing before her eyes, Nebadri curls into herself and steps behind the others to seek refuge.

Neither Elder Henness or Irene seem fazed by her outburst, so I toss notions of worry out of my mind and ask the next obvious question.

"What of the dead Primordials then. Where are they? And could we cross the boundary with something like, I don't know, their remains or something?" All shadowsteel weapons are made from pieces of the Primordials, imbued with mage magic to make them lethal to the creatures.

Elder Irene speaks. "It would take more than simple bones to convince the spell around Qaeus' heart. It would take a Primordial's power."

Sudden realization crashes through me, an electric sensation that begins in my stomach and rises up my chest. My hand drifts idly over my shoulder to the weapon I have strapped there.

"A Primordial's power," Irene continues as my fingers trace over the skull of Khunas embedded in my axe. "Does not perish with the being itself—it is too great to be diminished so easily. It is passed on."

"Where?" Ryven asks, eyeing me and my raised arm as if he's afraid I'm about to draw my weapon.

"To what?" I add, numbly.

Elder Henness and Irene share another knowing glance. The corners of Henness' lips pull tight. "To the Primordial that killed it."

Ryven frowns. "But the Primordials were killed by the Arcathainians, not by each other."

But he cannot yet see what I have figured out. After all my scouring of the library at Nigh, everything I've read about the Primordials and the weapons we used to defeat them, the pieces of this puzzle fit together more effortlessly for me than they do him. Arcathainians might've wielded the shadowsteel weapons that killed the Primordials Khaymus, Khunas, and Qhistus, but the blades themselves?

Every wrinkled, faded page of the Primordials' written history flips before my eyes now, and I trace over every word I can possibly remember. In one of the horrific battles fought by the Crusaders of old, Khaymus and Qhistus arrived on the battlefield together. Our ancestors had to face both of the Primordials at once, but fortunately, it wasn't long before the beasts turned on one another. It gave the mortals enough time to flee and regroup.

But before all could, the Primordial Khaymus struck the Primordial Qhistus in the back, knocking one of its protruding spines off. A few unnamed Crusaders dragged the remnant off the battlefield and brought it back to camp where the mages were able to study the Primordial's bodies for the first time in history.

They soon discovered that only Primordial bone was strong enough to lance through another Primordial, and so they used the spike from the Primordial Qhistus and created the first shadowsteel weapons: a spear, a magic-infused combustible projectile, and an axe.

My axe.

But if the power of a Primordial goes to the Primordial that killed it, and each of the Primordial weapons were created from Khunas, that would mean…

"The power of the slain Primordials are in the shadowsteel weapons that killed them."

The words leave my lips in a foggy, wintery haze, ominous and chilling. Ryven is rigid as he jerks toward me. He considers me for a moment, eyes wide and unbelieving, before finally turning back to the Elders.

His attention snaps so fast back to the Elders, that he forgets where my hand lingers.

"Where are the shadowsteel weapons that contain the power of a Primordial?" he asks.

He is the only one in the room who isn't watching me. I can feel their attention burn into me like I'm standing bare before a bonfire.

"Before today," Elder Henness begins. "We knew of only one location of a Primordial weapon, the one residing in Illashore, said to be lost deep within the Pits of Bagamore."

"And the others?" Ryven asks impatiently.

"There is only one other. The third was destroyed the moment it slew the Primordial Quistus—"

"Where is the other then? The one that remains." Ryven's voice grows louder, a demonic growl low in the back of his throat as his patience wears thin.

Elder Henness straightens, eyeing him with a challenging glare that makes his head bow like a succumbing wolf to its alpha. Only once she is satisfied that he will not shout again does she finally speak. "It appears you already possess the other."

Ryven's head jerks up, and confusion wrinkles his expression as he eyes the three women before us. Realization settles in though when he sees all three of them—even Nebadri who has returned to stand beside the others—with their gazes trained on me.

Slowly, Ryven attention drags to mine. His gaze wanders up my arm, to the intricate carving in the steel, to stare at the shrunken skull of the Primordial Khunas beneath my fingers.

"Your…axe?" His breath hitches with something profound. "Your axe is one of the weapons that killed a Primordial?"

My lips are a taut line when I nod.

"And you knew?"

"I wasn't certain," I counter. "I read about the weapons while I was training to be a Crusader. It's the only ones I've seen with something like this on it. I didn't know it was one of the answers we searched for. I had no way of knowing we'd need it to get close enough to Qaeus' heart."

His gaze hardens again. When he rubs the back of his neck, dark hair falls over his eyes. He addresses the Elders. "What needs to be done with the shadowsteel weapons?"

"Simply sever the boundary, and Qaeus will let you enter," Elder Irene replies.

"Good. Done," I say, surprised by the seemingly easy addition to our already complicated task. "We have the axe to get through to Qaeus. Now all we need to know is where to find the breath of life so that we can return to the Wardens and intercept my sister before she sets out on this task on her own."

Elder Henness angles an eye. "Why would they return to the Wardens when they have also been told the location of the objects they desire?"

"Because that was the plan," I say slowly. "They needed the objects for me. They came to you to learn how to get close to the heart and how to cure me—*us*. Afterward, they were going to return to the Wardens." The more I describe it, the more I start to feel like I'm trying to convince myself. I search their dubious gazes, seeking Ryven last. "That was the plan. That's what they'd do, right?"

The half-demon angles his head, his sympathetic eyes fixed on me, even though his words are for the Elders. "Where is the breath of life located?"

From the corner of my eye, I see Elder Henness shrug. "Nowhere my trees can reach."

"Nor my winds, I'm afraid," adds Elder Irene.

"But you told Kalli and Imryll where to find it, correct?" he presses further.

"One of us did," Henness responds.

It takes Elder Nebadri a second too long to realize we're waiting on her. "Oh!" she chirps. "My fishes have seen it—they have. They told me all about the way it shimmers like a rainbow, even from the deepest depths of the sea. They say it's made from pure life essence, and so it contains its own energy and light, just like the sun—"

"What sea?" Ryven's growl is less riddled with impatience, than it is fear, as if there is a certain sea that he would rather not venture to.

Henness pats Nebadri on the shoulder to calm her chattering. "My sister says it resides in the Dark Sea."

Ryven curses under his breath.

"What?" I ask. "What is it?"

He will barely meet my gaze. "That's where they went then. To the Dark Sea to secure the breath of life."

I'm shaking my head. "No. They were going to return to me at the Warden's camp. Kalli promised."

His lips part, a tight breath of air inhaled between them before it hisses out. "And I'm sure she meant it when she made that promise, Halira. But the Dark Sea is just northeast of here. It wouldn't make sense to return to the Warden's camp first. Doubling back would've cost you precious time, and although I don't know your sister well, she doesn't seem like the type to waste time. Especially where her sister's life is concerned."

Biting my lower lip, I consider him, begrudgingly. "You're right. If she knew the breath of life was near, she'd go there first." A second, more frightening thought occurs to me. "She might've even convinced my aunt to accompany her to Illashore for the weapon before they'd returned for me."

Their abandonment and betrayal stings deeper now than it did when they'd first left the Wardens without me. I had begged to come with them, pleaded, but Kalli had assured me that they'd return as soon as they found their answers, as soon as I was clear of the blight-fever. I know it's foolish to hold it against her, but knowing that she didn't hesitate to continue their search without me, riles the demon toxin in my blood.

Ryven cups my shoulder, his touch bringing me back to the present and having a comforting effect. "You can't blame them for wanting to buy you as much time as they can. Once someone is blighted, there's no telling how long it'll take before…"

He doesn't finish the thought, and I don't make him. We both know what happens once the demon toxin has taken over completely. We've both seen it firsthand, him as he watched his friend devour innocents, and I as my parents were devoured by that same man.

"I just wish they'd let me come with. I made it this far, didn't I? Just as I said I would."

A roguish grin tempts the edges of his lips. "People really should stop doubting you, shouldn't they."

I meet his sincere eyes and warmth balloons beneath my chest. In the short time we've spent together, I've overcome more hardship than I have in my entire life. Losing my parents, my home, being betrayed by one best friend and abandoned by another, fighting giant spiders and outrunning three-headed hydras—but as I reflect on Ryven's involvement in each encounter, and as I think over the many battles we've shared, I can't recall a single time that he has ever doubted me. He, of all people, who has no reason to believe in me because he knows me least of all. We didn't spend our childhoods together like Dimitri and I, or my sister, and my mother and father. Ryven has no real way of knowing just how stubborn I can be when my mind is set. And yet...

Was it not Dimitri who doubted I was going to make the cut as a Crusader?

Was it not my mother and father who feared I'd ever find my true calling?

Was it not my sister who distrusted my ability to hold onto our family secret, and as a result, she kept it to herself?

Ryven just might be the only person who has *ever* believed in me, and the very realization has my chest coiling tighter.

Before the stinging in my eyes can liquefy, I shake away whatever pleasant ache has latched onto my heart and force myself to stand taller. "Well, they'll find out soon enough just how tenacious I can be. We'll meet them at the Dark Sea."

Though he nods his agreement, I notice the wince he's trying to conceal when he drags his hand through his dark locks.

"What? What is it now?" My hands plant firmly on my hips. "What's wrong with going to the Dark Sea?"

When it becomes clear he's unsuccessfully played his concern off, his grimace deepens. He angles his head. "You really don't know anything about this side of the continent, do you?"

"No. No one even knew the druids existed, let alone what lay beyond the crumbled wall of the Forgotten—" remembering Henness' chastisement earlier, I correct myself— "The Eyve. Why do you ask?"

With a long, drawn out sigh, Ryven rolls his neck. He starts scratching his thumb on the table beside him. "The Dark Sea is where the sirens live. Do you know of them?"

Frowning, I think back to the library at Nigh again. "I've read about them, but I'm sure there is plenty missing from our forgotten history books. Long ago, they were hunted to extinction."

"Almost." His eyes flick to mine. "They were hated by both the mages *and* the humans. Killing them was one of the only things that the humans and mages ever agreed upon. The mages imbued some of the humans' fish traps, and they lured them to their deaths by the hundreds until only a few clans remained. The sirens went deep into hiding after that. They found refuge in the Eyve, just before the mages locked all of us over here."

"Okay. So you're saying there are sirens in the Dark Sea? Is that a problem?"

He scoffs, but it's not meant to demean my question or my lack of knowledge; it's more like he wants to highlight the severity of the nature of this mission. "That's an understatement. We have been able to live here with them because they mostly keep to the sea and we let them. Our people value all living things, and even the sirens should be allowed to exist. But I'd be lying if I said they were a benevolent race. They prey on wanderers, on the lost, and especially on those who dare attempt to steal their treasures."

My eyes flash. "My sister could be in danger then." As an afterthought, I add, "Imryll too."

"They could be," he says regrettably. "And, if we go, we will be putting ourselves at risk as well."

I whip around to face the Elders who have been waiting patiently. "Are my sister and aunt in danger?"

Elder Irene considers us for a moment before swirling her hand in the air. A gust of wind blows about the windowless tree, a cyclone that moves with every twist and sway of her wrist.

Elder Irene listens as the zephyr tells her all that it has seen. Ultimately, she frowns. "My winds cannot find them."

Wide-eyed, I glance back to Ryven, flipping my moonbeam hair out of my way. "The wind can't find them because they're already underwater. We have to go."

He glances warily to the other Elders, seeking confirmation.

Elder Henness shakes her head, but the smaller Elder Nebadri squeals like a mouse.

"My-fishes-saw-them-sometime-this-morning—they-took-a-nice-swim-together—oh-how-they-do-love-their-swimming."

I step forward. "Have they found the breath of life yet? Do they possess it?"

Elder Nebadri frowns, seeming wounded. "Not-enough—not-enough—not-enough."

Elder Henness plants a firm, grounding hand on her sister's shoulder. She whispers assurances into Elder Nebadri's ear, and Ryven and I turn away from them to a more private conversation.

"Do you know how to get to the Dark Sea?"

His head swivels, frowning. "I can get us there. And now that my wing is healed, the journey won't take long, either."

"That's great news. If they're already underwater, then we don't have time to waste. Let's go—"

But just as I spin on my heels to traverse the cluttered path back toward the front entrance, the ground bucks beneath me. The glass jars on the table clink against each other, as a mighty earthquake rumbles through the Forgotten Forest of Eyve. Then, a blood-curdling shriek pierces the world outside.

I gape back at Ryven, heart pounding in my chest, but to my surprise, I don't see fear gripping him the same way it does me. He watches me with an apologetic expression, one I'm starting to associate with my lack of knowledge and understanding about the way of the druids.

"Is…this normal?" I let go of the wobbly stack of books I've foolishly clung onto, long enough to gesture to the quaking ground.

Another rumble makes my knees weak, and despite trying to compensate by holding my arms out, the earthquake wins and I stumble backward. Ryven hooks my arms before I can fall completely, my back pressed firmly against his warm, bared chest.

After pushing myself back out of his arms, I cling to the table beside him. "What's happening?"

Elder Nebadri giggles, a fluttering, tweeting bird landing in the nest in her hair. "The-birds-tell-me-the-hydra-has-awak-ened—and-he's-very-very-very-displeased—very-very."

Horror tears through me, but not as sharp and swift as the guilt. *We* are responsible for upsetting the hydra. *We* were the ones who ventured into the Labyrinth to save Alphonse and thereby prevented the creature from what I suspect would've been a quick snack.

It must've followed us here. But how? In all of my studies in the library at Nigh, there was no mention of demons with the ability to track like that. Sure, they could smell blood in the open air if they were close enough, but their noses weren't as keen as a wolf tracking prey. Besides, even if they did have profound senses of smell, demons were mostly distractable creatures. Once they found prey, they'd hunt it, but once they lost sight, they'd move on to the next movement that caught their eyes.

Another gentle breeze wafts through the room.

"It appears the blind wyrm has arisen as well," Elder Irene says.

Another lump of guilt catches in my throat. We woke that shadowcreature as well. In our haste to escape, did we lead every horrific beast in that dreadful place to these peaceful people?

"And the shadowbat," Irene adds, almost lazily, as if none of this is anything to be alarmed about.

Elder Henness is equally as unperturbed. "Just the three tonight then?"

Elder Irene shrugs. "At least two others aren't far off."

I scowl across the room. "What's happening?"

"After dark," Ryven begins, "the Shadowthorn surrounding the Eyve becomes a breeding ground of evil. The demons are drawn to the magic shielded here. They flock to us like moths drawn to flame."

"We didn't see any of them the last night we spent out there."

"I took us the long way around. I made sure we weren't in their path when they crept out of the Labyrinth."

"The Labyrinth?" I balk. "That's where they live?" He

manages a nod before another question flies from my lips. "Why didn't they leave the night we were there then? It's like we had to fight through every single demon in all the Shadowthorn just to escape that place." I suppress a shudder when I remember just how we all almost died.

"Because we brought dinner to *them* that night. They had no reason to leave the maze when three humans were within its borders."

I almost correct him and say *two half-demons and a druid*, but the realization that I'm calling myself a *half*-demon sours my stomach to the point that I don't want to speak.

"Besides," he adds. "I'd guess they were drawn to that." He gestures over my shoulder to the weapon strapped at my back.

"My axe? Why would they be interested in it?"

"It beholds the power of a Primordial. I think it's exactly the sort of thing that could draw demons toward it."

"So…you're saying this thing acts as a beacon whenever I'm in the Shadowthorn." I throw my arms in the air. "That's great. I wish I had known that before I selected the blighted thing."

He smiles sympathetically. "I could be wrong here, but it seems like it was a good thing you did, otherwise we'd need to figure out a way to Illashore."

I roll my eyes, but I do nothing to hide the amusement tugging at my lips.

Another howl sounds from somewhere in the distance, and my head whips toward the door.

"You endured this every night?" Turning back to him, I notice that, in my horror, I've inadvertently taken a step toward him. Moving back would only draw more attention to it, so I hold my ground. "How have you survived living here all this time with those beasts outside?"

A small chuckle. "The gates close once the moon rises, but that's mostly to protect our own. No one leaves or enters. And without druid blood, the demons are stuck out there."

"You're sure of it?"

His brow arches in a dubious display of arrogance. "I've lived here my entire life."

"I know. It's just...Alphonse. He's still at the gate, in the dungeons. He won't like being held prisoner, and if he's anything like me—which I loathe to admit he might be—he will try to escape, and if he gets out and goes back into the Shadowthorn—"

Ryven clasps my shoulder. "He won't. I can promise you that. The druid dungeons have to hold other druids. Their magic is powerful, and he will not evade it. And if he did, the magic guarding the boundary is ancient and far stronger than anything I've ever seen. He will not be able to cross it. Our people do not leave after dark. They cannot."

My brow furrows with sudden understanding. "That means we're not leaving yet either."

"I'm afraid not," he says, shaking his head. He takes my hand, startling me to my core, before glancing over his shoulder and back to the Elders. "Thank you, Elders. You have been most helpful."

"And you have been most welcome," Elder Henness croaks.

Beside her, Elder Nebadri gasps. She clutches her lips as she bounces up and down, frantic and wild. "They're-forgetting-something—aren't-they?   There-is-something-they-haven't-asked—but-if-they-don't-ask-then-we-have-nothing-to-tell—but-I-want-to-tell—can-we-tell?"

"Tell us what?" I ask, ripping my arm out of Ryven's. The tree hut is by no means cold, but whatever chill had been lingering in the air assaults my hand in his absence, making me regret it all the more. "What haven't we asked?"

Beside me, Ryven is brushing the back of his thumb over his lip again. Deep in concentration, he paces the small pathway, swerving around the obstacles that the random shelves and trinkets present whenever he encounters them. It's amazing to me that his great wings, though tucked against his back, aren't more cumbersome. Even though he's only had them for a few months—maybe less, depending on how long it took for them to grow—he treats them as if they're an extension of him that he's always possessed.

Suddenly, his eyes widen. "I've never seen you take the form of an animal."

Scowling, I cross my arms and use them as a shield to counter the insinuation. "Some of us weren't raised here," I snap. But then, trying to hold on to some of my dignity, I deflect. "I've never seen you take the form of an animal either."

"The Blight has corrupted my power. Remember? I can no longer transform. I couldn't even heal myself. But you were only just infected a week ago, which means you should still be able to access most of your strengths."

I look away, trying to hide the shame in my face. It's ironic, really, to grow up being told to hate magic, only then to discover you possess some, but you don't know how to wield it.

"I...my aunt can turn herself into a raven. Are you saying I should be able to do the same thing?"

The room releases its collective breath.

Ryven runs a hand between his horns, through his dark, disheveled hair again. The longer he's silent, the more I start to wonder what all of this is about. What good would turning into a bird do me when he can fly us to the Dark Sea anyway?

Seeing my confusion and shame, he offers me a gentle smile. "It's all right. Like I said, I can't take an animal form anymore either."

"I don't understand though. What does this—"

Before I can finish, his attention is already fixated on the three women behind us. "Elders, might I request your knowledge once more." Their faces brighten, almost knowingly, but they make him ask his question anyway. "How might we enter the Dark Sea if neither of us can take the form of an animal with gills? Is there a way?"

Elder Nebadri all but collapses with relief to hear him finally ask the question that should've been so obvious to the both of us from the start, but I had been too focused on my sister and the peril she might be facing. Ryven, I imagine, still isn't used to not being able to use his druid powers the way he once could.

Elder Nebadri squeals. "There-are-water-dwellers-who-could-help—if-you-could-get-one-to-offer-you-their-gills-then-you'd-practically-be-a-water-dweller-yourself."

Elder Irene examines the back of her hand, or at least, to an onlooker that's what it would seem, but even though I've only known her for a brief time, I can tell she's not examining herself at all, but instead the invisible air that's wrapped around everything and everyone. The two of them have a silent conversation before she inclines her head.

"If you can obtain the gills of a water-dweller, the air will relinquish hold of your lungs for a day. But only a day. No longer."

Again, Elder Nebadri squeals, but just when she opens her mouth, prepared to launch into her excited instructions, Elder Henness holds up her hand.

"Perhaps it's best if I tell them."

Entirely unfazed, the shorter woman giggles, nodding vigorously as she begins stroking the mouse in her hand again.

Elder Henness clasps her hands before her. "If the air grants you permission, then, should you bathe in the rivers of Ushines beneath the glow of the Star, there is an eel that dwells there who will grant you the gills you need to dive into the Dark Sea."

Exasperated, I throw my head back and groan. "Another place to search for? Ugh, I'm so sick of going from one place to another. Where are the rivers of Ushines located? How long will it take us to get there?"

Ryven shakes his head, stifling a laugh. "Well, fortunately, this place isn't far. You remember the river I showed you when we arrived, the one flowing through the Eyve?"

"Oh." Awkwardly, I start fidgeting with my feet. "So it's not another long journey."

This time, he can't help himself. "Not at all."

His laughter heats the depths of my stomach. I shift uncomfortably, trying to get the treacherous sensation to go away.

"Besides," he adds with a crooked grin. "We could both use a bath."

My jaw falls open. "What? In the middle of the town?"

Chuckling, he turns to the Elders and gives them his thanks once more before leading the two of us back out of the tree hut and into the starlit night.

If the Forgotten Forest of Eyve had been enchanting in daylight, it was ravishing when the moon was high overhead, and the stars twinkled above like distant, dazzling diamonds. The rushing waterfall almost seemed to fall silent in the peaceful calm of the night. The monstrous howling of the behemoth shadowcreatures was nothing more than a fading nightmare.

Ryven stood beside me, his head tilted back to mimic my own. "Never seen the stars before?"

I punch him in his demon arm. "Very funny." Then, returning to my awed gaze of the night sky above, I add with a longing sort of quiet, "It's just been awhile since they've seemed so…clear. So close."

It's a long time before I feel his gaze has turned on me. When I do, it's everything I can do to not stare up into those dark, russet eyes. But they bore into the side of my face, hot and inviting, not too dissimilar to the dazzling stars overhead. I turn my attention to something else—*anything* else—and find my ears pricking to the coursing river flowing before us.

"H-has the Ushines River always granted people gills?"

He nearly chokes on a laugh, and I realize just how foolish the question truly is. If the rivers that flowed through this serene village—the same village he's spent his entire life—had been known for doing such a thing, he wouldn't have needed to ask the Elders how to dive into the Dark Sea.

When he's finally contained himself, he watches me sidelong. "No. They haven't. And it's *rivers*. There are many that run through the village."

Absentmindedly, I nod, my attention drawn to the raging body of water now. I consider what it will be like to bathe in such a ferocious stream, whether the eel will come and give us what we request.

"Besides," he says, demeanor darkening. "I never had need of something like the magic the Elders plan to share with us. Before I was blighted, I could just turn into a sea turtle or a manatee whenever I entered the water. But, without the ability to change ourselves, it seems like the Elders had to work together and, with their elements, to offer us this alternative option."

Amazement becomes me. A *sea turtle*. A *manatee*. Creatures I've only ever seen in drawings and paintings, and heard mention of in stories.

Part of me knows that I should be repulsed by his blatant use of magic, or at the very least outraged by it, but all I can think about is how freeing it felt for him to fly us through the treetops, how impossibly astounding it would be to change form and suddenly be able to do things that I've never been able to do before like scaling cliffsides, breathing beneath water, racing across a plain with alarming speed.

But one look at him and the regret reflected in his eyes, and my eager excitement fizzles. As much as I'd love to ask him to talk me through trying to learn, it would only serve to remind him of what he's lost. It would also likely take more time than we have right now.

"You ready?" I ask, trying to pull him out of the dark vortex he's trapped himself inside.

His eyes flutter, but they finally meet mine and he nods before walking toward the edge of the cliff and peering down.

"We're not just bathing here?" I gesture to the river at his back. "This *is* part of the Ushines, isn't it?"

"It is. But the water here is frigid and full of rapids."

"And the water down there is in the middle of the town," I counter. "I'd rather not bathe on display for everyone."

He bows his head with a soft chuckle. "There's another place. Quieter and warmer. Trust me."

It's those words alone that awaken the skeptic in me, and mostly because I know I *do* trust him already. I shouldn't. We hardly know each other, and the circumstances which brought us together are not the kind of origin story you want to retell whenever someone asks how you met. But that's just it, isn't it? There is an inexplicable connection between us, one that began dark and raw, that has strengthened its hold the more time we spend together. Every time I look into his eyes, I see my strength reflected there. Maybe it's selfish to find comfort in that, to use someone to make me feel better about myself, but no one has ever made me feel strong, capable, resilient. And, I think he feels the same. The guilt he feels for his friend's death, I think he sees in my eyes that it isn't his fault, because I know my own parents' deaths weren't mine.

But I've waited too long to respond to him, so he spins around, ready for a debate. "Halira, we're stuck here all night, until the beasts out in the Shadowthorn go back into hiding. There is no need to rush through a cold and miserable bath when you could use the relaxation. Besides, I thought you might want a little more privacy than what even this place can offer."

He gestures to the coursing river. Although it's wide, there is no cover for either of us to bathe alone. Not to mention, with how fast the waters are flowing, it would be too dangerous to even try.

"But"—he sighs dramatically, dragging a hand through his thick locks—"if you don't mind us bathing together, then—"

I charge him, my fist landing square in his shoulder. He guffaws, sagging into the blow and cradling his arm for a moment. But then, something wicked flashes behind his dark eyes.

"Ryven, don't—"

His teeth flash in a winning grin that turns my stomach upside down just as he lunges for me. He swoops me into his arms and leaps backward, diving over the edge of the cliff.

"Ryven!"

My shriek is shrill, desperate, excited. The air hisses past my ears, and I squeeze onto his neck as tight as I can. I can feel his shoulders hitching with laughter, can barely hear the hearty rumble of it over the whizzing wind.

The ground approaches quickly, and I squeeze my eyes tight, even though I know he won't let us fall.

At the last second, he pops his wings out and the air catches in their sheen skin. We float for a moment, suspended just above the path and a few dozen onlookers, and for the first time neither of us seem to notice them. His grin is infectious, stretched from ear to ear and dimpling one side of his face.

I roll my eyes at him and give way to my begrudging smile.

We soar back into the trees, leaving the shocked and curious druids to marvel at us below. His flying is more leisurely than I remember. The longer the warm breeze drifts across my skin, the more I relax into Ryven's hold, sinking into the sculpted muscle of him. I wonder if he's always been like that, or if it's another side effect from the demon blood. When a mental image of him as a child swollen with rock-hard biceps appears in my mind, I chuckle.

His eyes narrow on me, that same hint of mischief still lingering in their depths. "What's so funny?"

"Oh, nothing. Just trying to figure out what you must've been like as a child."

"Oh?" He raises an eyebrow. "And how do you imagine I was?"

Flicking the white hair already cascading over my shoulders like a flag in the wind, I resituate in his arms, inadvertently pulling myself closer to him, to the heat his core has to offer.

"Well, like most people, I imagine you were exactly as you are now. Impossibly reckless"—I shoot him a scathing look for the near plummet to our collective deaths, and then resume my nonchalant façade—"selfless to a fault. Unbearably stoic."

"Like most people?" he quotes back to me.

Sighing, I roll my eyes. "I'm not saying most people are like that. I was saying that we don't change. Not much, anyway. We are who we are, and always will be."

The moonlight shines through his dark wings every time they beat, giving them a shimmering glow that makes me want to reach out and touch their silken sleekness. Obviously, I refrain.

He grows quiet for a moment, and despite trying to get lost in the beauty this new realm and experience has to offer, my attention is divided to the wounded half-demon that I've come to call friend.

"You don't think people are capable of change?" he asks at last, voice low, rising from the darkest pits of his belly.

"I haven't seen much proof that they can."

A sad smile ticks at the edges of his mouth. "You're wrong."

We land then before he can clarify, and I soon forget the conversation entirely as I become yet again entranced by the secluded meadow. I'd expected more roaring rapids, even though I'm now reminding myself that Ryven said he chose this place specifically because there weren't any. Still. They'd call this the rivers of Ushines, but this nook, this offshoot of water that's cradled between trees and swaddled in the stars could easily be mistaken for a moonlit lake. It rests in the valley before us, the calm waters a far cry from the rapids we've left behind. This place feels like it's been untouched for years. Even the fireflies appear to leave this area of the Eyve alone.

I relish in the solitude of it, the relaxing nature of the place that I haven't known since…for longer than I can remember. For years, I've been surrounded by the Shadowthorn, looking over my shoulder at every turn, fearing that that moment might finally be the day a demon took me.

But there is nothing to fear here. Nothing except…

The Elders had been quite clear about *both* of us needing to bathe in this place.

An electric warmth skitters through me at the idea of having to strip bare in Ryven's presence. The feeling amplifies, a surge of shameless allure twisting deep inside me as I think about the two of us dipping into these warm waters together. I curse my erratic heart and reassure myself that this ache in my chest is just a matter of loneliness. It has been a week or more since I fled Nigh, leaving yet another home behind, once again fully aware that there is no returning. To make matters worse, this time I didn't have Dimitri to hold onto for support. I had Ryven.

But was I really so desperate for connection that my sinful heart would settle for the single man in my life yet again? Was that all my attraction to him was? After all, Ryven was a beautiful man. Ruggedly gorgeous, as a matter of fact. It had taken me awhile to notice, since all I saw when I looked at him was his monstruous arm and his great, leathery wings. The longer I spend with him, however, the less I seem to notice his demonic attributes. The more I learn about him, about the goals he dreamed of achieving, and the guilt that eats away at him, the more I've started to just see him for who he is, not *what* he is.

He is a good friend, and a strong fighter. He is the kind of man who has made mistakes and isn't afraid to admit them. He's the kind of person who believes in the abilities of others and will stand by their decisions to pursue what they believe is right.

When I discovered my druid nature, he is one of the only people to embrace it. Fox exploited my secret. Dimitri ran from me. Kalli didn't even want to admit that my suspicions were right. But Ryven, he has done nothing but tried helping me reach my full potential, helping me blossom into my full identity.

And I'm not even sure he realizes he's doing it.

"I know what I said earlier." Ryven's deep voice jostles me from my thoughts. My cheeks burn only because I feel like I've been caught red-handed thinking about him right in front of him. But surely, he doesn't know that. "But I wanted you to see this place before you made up your mind. We don't have to bathe at the same time. In fact, I can leave you here if it's privacy you want. But I don't think bathing in the frigid river by the Elders' home is going to be as soothing as you need after the journey and the blight sickness you've endured."

I consider him quietly, my wandering thoughts struggling not to venture back to the lake and what might happen if both of our naked bodies were to submerge there. It's not until I register the words *leave you here* that my breath truly knots in my lungs. Being alone is the last thing I want right now. It's the last thing I've ever wanted.

He wets his lips, a worried edge in his brow. "If you disagree, I will take you back to town. Just say the word."

With my gaze fixed on the black waters, I wonder just how much darker the Dark Sea will be when we arrive.

"Is it safe?" I ask.

He appears beside me, inclining his head. "Of course it's safe. Only the druids can enter the Eyve, remember? There are no monsters to fear here."

"Except those lurking below, the ones the Elders have sent to give us their gills." I swallow hard, eyes sharpening on every ripple in the pool beneath the moon. "How does that work anyway? If only druids can come here, how are Nebadri's animals here?"

He gives a halfhearted shrug. "My guess is that they were here before the barrier was put up. They've lived here as long as we have. The boundary only prevents those from crossing over. It doesn't stop those from being here."

My eyebrow lifts. "And the birds that seem to come and go as they please? The ones that told Nebadri we were coming?"

He frowns, considering for a moment, but ultimately his confusion is short-lived. "I hardly think that when our people built the boundary to block out the humans and demons, that they were concerned about an uprise from the sparrows."

I grin despite myself, possibly even harder considering he said *our* people.

When the moment passes, Ryven's head dips low again. "I'll leave you to it then."

"Wait!"

The word blurts from my lungs before I can stop it, just like my hand that reaches for him of its own volition. I'd been anticipating for him to walk away at least a few paces before my outcry was answered, but he stopped so suddenly, so readily, that it's as if he knew my plea was coming. Or had hoped it would be. Since he's barely moved, I miscalculate my reach. My fingers graze his bare chest, taut and stubbled. Heat ignites my still-warm cheeks as my gaze drifts to the point of our connection. I remember him being farther away, but my arm is bent, my breath bouncing off his chest and clouding around my own face.

Swallowing the lump in my throat, I bow my head, hoping to hide my embarrassment behind the waterfall of my hair. I take a cautionary step back, if only so his cedar scent won't be so all-consuming.

"Please don't go," I say softly, steeling my voice against my quaking nerves. "I don't...I don't want to be alone."

Ryven doesn't budge, doesn't flinch. He watches me, his gaze burning holes in the top of my already inflamed skull, and the longer he doesn't say anything, the more terrified I become of meeting those russet eyes.

Finally, he puts me out of my misery. "Then you never shall be."

There is so much emotion edged into those simple words despite how fervently he tries concealing it. I'm grateful for the effort he takes. It means I can go on pretending his efforts work. It helps cool the flames that have started to burn deep, deep in my belly.

But when I finally bring my eyes to him, the inferno inside me roars. The headiness of his gaze is too intense, too deeply and profoundly raw that I have to look away.

I muster as much nonchalance as I can. "So...are you just going to watch?"

The rhetorical question was a mistake. I become molten at such a debauched suggestion, and the wry smile that twists the side of his mouth isn't helping.

Thankfully, rather than calling me on my bluff, he pivots so that his back is to me and the water.

Though getting undressed with him so near is still as unsettling as it is tantalizing, suddenly the idea of submerging my head under water and disappearing is all too enticing.

Toeing off my boots, I appraise the dark pool again. I can't remember the last time I soaked in a bath. Even when I was living at the Castle of Nigh, most of my bathing had been done in frantic splashes of cold water that were more meant to wake me up on the early mornings, than they were to cleanse me, let alone offer any relaxation. Bathing in the Shadowthorn had been an…arguable option. But here, within the safe confines of the Eyve, I can float without a care, taking my time and soaking in the moonlight.

Almost without thinking, so lulled by the idea of the relaxation awaiting me, I unbuckle my belt and set Tor's sheathed dagger on the ground. My axe follows next, then my leather armor, skirt, boots and socks. I hesitate when all that's left between me and the rest of the world are my undergarments, but the thought of soaking them in the pool along with me, and then throwing the rest of my dry clothes atop them, is enough to embolden me.

Naked as the day I came into this realm, I clutch my exposed chest and tiptoe into the black abyss before me. I brace myself for the bite of night and the chill that has surely seeped into the waters, but I'm surprised when I instead find myself surrounded by warmth.

I let the weight of my body drag me down until I'm submerged all the way to my neck.

Glancing over my shoulder, I watch his silhouette like a hawk, curious if I'll catch him sneaking a glimpse. But Ryven doesn't move. He stands like one of the Magistrate's soldiers, all wide-stanced and tight-shouldered. It's easy to imagine him among the ranks of the Crusaders; he certainly is built for it, his brawny arms so bulky that I'm not even sure he could fit them into clothes if he tried. I can envision him leading a unit to battle, strategizing the plan of attack and defending his members with undying determination.

All this imagining makes me realize just how little I know about it. I'm concocting his entire life in my mind, rather than simply taking the time to ask him.

I twist around so that both of our backs face each other, and drag a hand over my arm to scrub away the grime of traipsing through the Shadowthorn for a week from my skin. "Tell me something about yourself."

"Excuse me?"

"I hardly know anything about you other than you're a druid with plant-based magic and wings."

He chuckles.

"I'm being serious."

"What do you want to know?"

I tilt my head back, dipping my tangled hair into the liquid warmth and running my fingers through the silken tendrils that float around my head. "I don't know. Tell me about your family."

"They're dead."

With another choke of air, I rise. "All of them?"

"Yep."

"Ryven, I'm so sorry."

"Don't be. It happened a long time ago, and I'm not the only one to lose their parents."

Tentatively, I ring my hair out, even though with my length the ends will just go back in the water once I release them. "What happened to them?"

"They both died to illness when I was young." He sounds so scripted when he speaks, like he's either practiced telling his history a hundred times, or he's actually had to recite it that many times to others. The loss of my parents is still too raw for me to feel anything but shattered when I talk about it, and so I decide I'm not going to press him any further on the matter. But he continues of his own accord. "Jiordan took me in and raised me as his own. They have been my family ever since."

I nod, but we fall back into an uncomfortable silence that begs to be filled. I want to comfort him, but I also want to respect his boundaries in how much he's willing to share. He's clearly kept his answers short intentionally, and it would be rude of me to drag that conversation on any further.

It would be ruder, still, to just leave him with old wounds freshly reopened though.

I change the subject. "How did you cross paths with my uncle?"

A chuckle blows past his lips, easier than I expect it to. "By mistake," he says. "It wasn't long after…I killed Ahl'Ro. I didn't know what to do with myself. The change in my arm happened quickly, and I knew no one would offer me shelter in Arcathain, and I couldn't bring myself to face Jiordan yet, so I kept to the Shadowthorn. That's how I learned the demons left other demons alone. I think part of me was begging for them to come for me, to finish what they'd started. But each time I crossed their path, they showed no interest in me."

My heart aches for him, for this man I barely know. He'd spent weeks alone in the Shadowthorn, just praying for death to find him, but even that was kept from him. The thought occurs to me that he could've ended it himself if he wanted to, but it churns my stomach so greatly that I can't even bring myself to ask. Not to mention, the whole point of these questions wasn't to reopen old wounds, but that's all I seem to be doing.

"I stayed in one of the abandoned villages," Ryven continues. "The town sign said *Beyrn*, if you know the place."

"I do. I think that's where my friend Güthric is from."

"The big guy?"

"Yes," I say, laughing. "The big guy. He doesn't talk about—well, much, honestly—but his accent is similar to the Beyrn's harsh tongue. I just know he came from one of the recently overrun villages, and Beyrn was one of the last before Ashenvale."

"It was definitely overrun," Ryven agrees. "Not by demons—they hardly went there anymore—but the Shadowthorn had claimed it. Therefore, it made for a perfect camp. Until your uncle showed up."

"What happened?" I ask, tantalized to hear yet another of Uncle Adrien's adventures, even if it is told by someone else. That almost makes it more exciting.

Ryven groans thoughtfully for a moment. "I don't know. That's pretty much the story. He came through the town searching for supplies. He found me. He convinced me to come with him."

From where I wade in the lukewarm lake, I deflate. "That's it? That's the story?"

He laughs again, and my stomach dips at the honeyed sound. "If you have a problem with my storytelling abilities, then I suggest you ask him for his rendition the next time you see him."

My smile falters. There might not be a next time. Depending on how things go with the sirens, how long it takes us to reach Qaeus' heart, I could be fully actualized in demon form by then.

"You didn't ask them about your demise," I say, shifting the conversation back to our earlier visit with the Elders, confident he will be able to follow.

Ryven resituates himself, back straightening. "There was no need to mention it."

I bite my lip, unsure if it's my place to pry. "You told Jiordan that you were going to ask how long you had left."

His voice is so low, I almost don't hear him when he says, "I already know the answer, at least as much as I'd like to know."

I twist around, frigid concerning suddenly trickling through me and making my skin prickle. "And what do you know?"

He doesn't answer for a long while, and as he gathers his thoughts, I continue bathing. Cupping my hands together, I scoop the lake into my palms and splash it against my face, relishing the sensation of cleansing myself of the darkness that I'd been surrounded by all that time. Of course, no matter how long I bathe, nothing will remove the darkness rooted within. Only the Primordial's heart can do that.

"I think I have another week or two left."

The small rivulets of water dribbling down my face gets sucked into my mouth when I gasp. "A week?" I stand taller, my shoulders and the flesh of my breasts peeking out from the water, but I hardly notice. I'm too distracted. Too concerned. Too busy choking on water. "That's not long at all."

He doesn't move. Doesn't speak. The longer he stands there irritatingly stoic and stiff, the more my mind reels.

"But…don't you want to know? The Elders, they could've told you how much longer you had, couldn't they?"

He shrugs. "Maybe. But I'm not sure it's something worth knowing."

"Why not?"

He moves as if he's about to turn around to face me as he speaks but catches himself just before he can glimpse my exposed flesh. Realizing I'm more exposed than I should be, I slouch back down beneath the lake's surface.

"Would you want to know the day you were going to die?" he asks.

I fall silent as I think—as I *truly* consider what it would be like to know the very breath that would be my last. Living in the Wallows, every day that the Shadowthorn approached our borders, death felt more like a certainty. I didn't know when I would succumb, only that if my family and I stayed there, we would. Then, joining the Shadow Crusade, my life became even more forfeit. I knew that committing myself to a path of demon-slaying meant always straddling life and death. I knew that someone entering the Blighted territories of Qaeus could only evade such an outcome for so long.

But even now as my body is ravaged by demon toxin, as

death has lingered over me like a dark storm cloud, I've still been able to hope. I can choose to believe that we will find the cure in time, just like I could choose to believe that I could be among the Crusaders to slay Qaeus, or that the Shadowthorn's expansion might be halted before it consumed my home.

That hope, that desire to believe that an outcome other than death is conceivable, wouldn't be possible if I knew the exact moment I was meant to die.

How meaningless would it feel to exist? How frightening would it be to finally face the moment that you'd been dreading for as long as you'd known?

Ryven angles his head over his shoulder so that he can just see me from his peripherals. "Is everything...is everything all right?"

"Yes. I'm fine." I clear my throat to prevent my heart from leaping out of it. My head eases backward, my gaze drifting up to the tapestry of stars above. "It's quite beautiful here, you know?"

"I'd say I told you so, but..."

Scoffing, I muster as much strength as I have in shoving a tidal wave toward him. Of course, my meager, magicless hands only manage to create a small splash of water that doesn't even reach the shore, let alone his smug backside.

"Watch it," he warns, tone teasing.

"Serves you right," I say, resettling in the moonlit water. "You don't see me gloating."

"Gloating about what?"

"About how utterly blissful it is to be soaking in a lukewarm bath after days of travel. You really are missing out, you know."

I can hear the crook of his smile in his voice. "I'll get my turn. For now, you just focus on yourself and relaxing."

My heart skips. Then guilt gets the best of me. He's traveled just as long as I have, worked just as tirelessly, if not harder. Just earlier today he spent hours in excruciating pain while

Jiordan repaired his wing. Surely, it isn't fair for me to keep him from the relaxation he's earned. For a splinter of moment, I actually consider throwing all chagrin to the wind and inviting him to join me. The lake or lake or whatever you want to call it is small, but it's plenty big enough for two people to wade through without worrying about the embarrassment of naked limbs bumping against one another.

But the thought of him stripping off his black leather pants both thrills me and terrifies me. It's been one week since Dimitri left me. *One week*. I should be more heartbroken about him than I am, and I definitely shouldn't be throwing myself at the next person who shows me any vestige of kindness.

I throw my head back in a show of how much I don't care about either of them.

"Or is it too difficult to relax when you know a creature lurks just beneath you and could spring at any moment?"

My head snaps back up and I shred through the water in mad dash back to the shore. How could I be so careless? So forgetful? Somewhere between getting worked up over thoughts about being naked near a handsome man and how desperately my body needed to float in a relaxing bath, it had completely slipped my mind the other reason we came here. This is where the Elders said we would receive our gills. This is where the creature lives. In this water. And I am just casually floating around like I'm just daring the beast to gobble me up.

Ryven's bursts of laughter are the only thing that could make me still before reaching the shore. He hunches over, hands to knees, as bellow after bellow rock him.

If I would've been anywhere else but in the lake that the Elders themselves proclaimed to house the creature, his laughter might be enough of a relief to ease my nerves—still maddening, but comforting. But I'm too jostled for it to work on me now.

"What? Why are you laughing? Is the creature they spoke of really here?"

Ryven finally brings himself upright. "Not for a few more hours," he says with a final sigh of laughter.

Scowling, I fix my glare on his back, cursing my eyes for snagging on the bulge of muscle between his wings. "What do you mean? The Elders said to bathe beneath the glow of the stars so that—"

"*Star*," Ryven corrects. "Elder Henness said the *Star*."

"Star, stars—what's the difference? It has to be one of those dazzling lights up there." I gesture to the night sky, but my arm retreats back into the warm water once it realizes how much chillier it is out of the water.

"Well," Ryven says. "This *star* won't be back until the morning."

"What does that even—" Then, the realization illuminates before me like the blazing sun. "Oh," I say, elongating the syllable. My glare returns with full force. "Then, what am I doing in here?"

His head dips with another warm laugh. "It's like I said, you needed it. We've come a long way and we still have farther to go. Besides, you think I want to travel beside a walking, breathing person who smells more like a dead skunk?"

I cross my arms. "I change my mind. You can leave after all. Who needs company that just insults you?"

He shakes his head, his fading laughter warming my stomach and reawakening that ache that had been buried inside me.

"Oh, I don't think you mean that at all, Halira," he says, voice rich and bemused. "And for that reason alone"—abruptly, he squats to the ground, sitting so that one elbow is propped on either knee—"I'm staying right here."

The next morning, I awaken to the gentle lapping of water at the bay, to the distant drilling of a wood-pecker high up in a tree. Blearily, I blink my eyes open and find myself staring out across a crystal blue lake.

My mouth unhinges in a great yawn. I hardly remember even falling asleep. Ryven and I had stayed up for hours, long after either of us had bathed, talking about the constellations, our battles in the Shadowthorn, his friend Ahl'Ro and their childhood. I'd opened up about mine, as well, told him about Dimitri and growing up in one of the poorest parts of Graven-burg. Of course, then I had to explain what poverty was and why it existed, since the druids here apparently don't have such a thing.

"We are a community," he'd told me. "We take care of each other. How could I gorge myself in good conscience knowing that my neighbors starved?"

I hadn't had an answer for him, only that some people make that decision quite easily.

Propping myself on my elbow, I glance about the meadow in search of the half-demon now. I don't have to look far. It would appear he fell asleep opposite me, so that the two of us were sleeping head-to-head.

Considering how chilled the night had turned, especially with my wet hair to ensure my coldness, it would've been wise for us to sleep closer, to conserve our body heat and warm each other.

But, I'd rather not let my traitorous thoughts venture down that path.

Instead, I give Ryven's shoulder a firm shove. "Hey, wake up."

He bolts awake, half-crazed and delirious.

"Sorry, I—I didn't mean to scare you."

Heaving a heavy sigh, he hangs his head low. "It's all right. I'm not used to sleeping in the Eyve anymore. I forgot there is no danger lurking here."

"There'll be danger enough from me if we don't get going."

His smile is lazy, but he starts to push himself off the ground. Rising on strong, muscled legs, Ryven stretches his arms wide, and it's everything I can do to avert my gaze from the taut grooves of his chiseled stomach.

"We've already wasted too much time. Kalli and Imryll could be—"

"They'll be all right," he says firmly. "Your aunt is a smart woman. I get the impression that your sister is as well. Neither would risk a reckless attempt at the breath of life unless they were certain they could obtain it with their lives intact."

Nodding, I concede to the fact that he's right. Kalli has never been the type to make rash decisions, and she certainly wouldn't put herself in the position of dying before being able to return to me the things I needed to be cured.

"The sun is up," Ryven says. "If you're ready, we can do this now."

"Do what…"

But the words die on my tongue. He wasn't planning on

waiting for a response; he already knew my answer would be yes. Still, I hadn't expected he'd strip himself naked again so quickly, so…without any hint of modesty.

He marches toward the lake, and my eyes stray down the backside of him.

"You coming?" he asks.

Curse him for that wicked, knowing grin I hear in his voice.

So that I'm not bested by the likes of this arrogant man, I hold nothing back. I remove my multitude of garments as quickly as he removed his trousers, and I, too, stomp toward the lake.

To his credit, not once does he glance back at me, giving me a modicum of privacy as I wade into the Ushines waters. Meanwhile, I have difficulty getting my eyes to cooperate as they drift of their own accord down the wings flat against his muscular back to the curve of flesh and muscle that makes sparks a knotted heat deep in my belly.

Blinking so hard that it actually hurts, I manage to pull my gaze away and grasp at the first thought that comes to mind.

This lake. It's rather beautiful. We'd talked about it, last night. How some of the higher channels of water feed straight into it, but that it has nowhere else to go and so the water is able to stay warmer here.

Once I'm buried up to my shoulders again, Ryven finally looks over his shoulder, crooking an eyebrow at me. For a moment, I fear he's caught me staring, even though I'm positive I wasn't when he turned around. To my relief it's not what he says when he opens his mouth.

"When you're ready, all you have to do is dive below."

I frown. "I thought you said you haven't done this before."

"I haven't. But I know of the eel that lives here. It huddles in the depths of the lake, so we won't find it up here."

"I thought the whole point of this was that neither of us can breathe underwater. How are we expected to swim to the bottom of the lake while we still don't have gills?"

The only answer I get is a flash of his crooked, dimpled smile.

Then, he inhales a great breath and dives below the surface.

"Ryven?" My eyes flare wide, and I scoop the water away as if I'd be able to get a clearer view. "Piss on a mage. Ryven! You can't just—"

I take a deep breath before plunging after him. From above, the water was clear and crisp, and I felt as if I could see all the way down to the mushy land beneath. But the moment I submerge myself under, the magnitude of the depths of this lake becomes clear. I can only see so far. In Ryven's wake of bubbles, my vision becomes obscured, and the deeper we dive, the harder it is for the sun to illuminate the pit.

My arms propel me in great, mighty strokes, my legs beating frantically behind me. Once I veer so that I'm no longer directly behind Ryven, away from the onslaught of the misting, disturbed ripples of water he leaves in his wake, I can finally make him out ahead of me. His pale skin gleams almost silver, but only one of his arms is visible, the demon one so dark that it gets lost in the darkness around us as it strokes.

I'd almost forgotten that he was naked, and as the sun above dances on his bare skin, I find myself staring, yet again, at his voluptuous backside. My gods, was he sculpted to perfection from clay? It shouldn't be legal. And the ache that's building all the way down to my core shouldn't be either.

I focus my thoughts elsewhere: on my sister; on coming to her aid in the Dark Sea; of obtaining the breath of life; of curing myself and Ryven—which in turn brings my thoughts back to him and his glistening, firm flesh.

My momentary distraction is graciously interrupted though when a massive bubble the size of a cottage coalesces from the blackness below us. It wobbles and warps its way upward, bursting when Ryven swims through it, but the severity of its presence doesn't fade with it. No, a bubble like that can only mean one thing: something enormous lies in wait below us.

My limbs still. The air caught in my lungs becomes solid, sinking to the pit of my stomach and threatening to take me with it. I can't do this. I can't breathe.

Panic tears at my chest like a lose boar rampaging through the trees. I can't see the creature move, but I feel it. All around us. The shift in the water is palpable, both dragging and thrusting, as something mammoth presses up against it.

I float myself back upright and start tearing to the surface, but I can't peel my gaze away from what's beneath, what's coming.

The bottom of the chasm becomes iridescent as golden scales flick into view. They shimmer every color of a burning fire, if one could be trapped beneath rippling waters.

I still when the creature's black eyes pop wide. It slithers up from the depths, its gaping, grinning maw opening and closing. Ryven looks up to me with a rueful grin just before the eel can swallow him whole.

I scream, the panic in my voice muffled by the water rushing into my mouth and lungs. I want to save him. I want to pull him from the eel's corpse once I slice it open with my axe. Only, my weapons are back on land, and I fear Ryven might already be gone…

My limbs burst to life once more. They flail and cycle and claw their way back toward the surface, toward hope and defense, toward my shadowsteel, but the surface proves to be a destination that, no matter how long I watch it and how much I stride for it, never seems to get any closer.

The water yanks on my limbs, making me heavier than I should be. It drags me backward, surging with impossible suction as I'm caught like a leaf in the drainage. One glance behind me is all I need to know why. The eel's grinning mouth is wide open now. It's guzzling the water and everything nearby. Against its torrent, nothing can outlast it, outswim it.

Despite the burning of my arms and the kicking of my legs, I'm dragged slowly at first, down and down and down until the creature's mouth closes around me.

Then there is nothing but darkness, nothing but the burning of my lungs as the breath that they clung onto is finally spent.

A heavy weariness consumes me. It tells me that nothing will be more divine than a long, long slumber, and I am inclined to believe it. After all, what else is there to do in the darkness but succumb to it?

But just as my eyes flutter, something soft nuzzles my hand. Warm fingers lace themselves into mine, squeezing tightly. I blink back into consciousness to find Ryven floating in front of me, watching me with hopeful, unrelenting eyes. If I could smile at the sight of him, I would. Knowing he's still alive is a relief I didn't know how badly I wanted.

I can't tell if I've enough strength for him to feel it, but I squeeze his hand in return, a silent admission of my gratitude. At least neither of us will die alone.

And just before I can succumb to that plight, just before the water has its way with my human lungs, something strange and unfamiliar occurs.

I notice the acrid stench of rotten fish first. It hits me like a palpable wave of putrescence that awakens me to a fit of squirming and shielding my nose.

My eyes widen with realization. If I can smell, that means I can breathe.

As if the half-demon can hear my thoughts, he nods, the movement languid in the water surrounding him. His dark hair floats in a halo around his horns. He shreds water to keep afloat, as do I. Our limbs, our bodies, are just mere inches apart. And with his eyes trained on mine, I'm finally able to find the restraint to keep my curious gaze from wondering down the length of him. Not that it does any good. This close, I can see every inch of him, and I flush when I realize he must be able to see all of my curves as well.

Just as mortification is settling in, I realize that neither of us should be able to see each other at all. When the eel had first swallowed us, everything had been utter darkness. Blacker than any black, like the night sky swept clean of the stars. I'd never beheld such darkness. With no flame to light the eel's mouth, with no cracks for the sunshine to reach through, everything in here should still be obscured.

My keen sense of sight from the depths of a lake, however, is the least of my growing interests. With a shuddering breath, I realize I am breathing in water. It doesn't fill my lungs like I'd expect it to. In fact, the coolness of the liquid seems to pool somewhere along the edges of my throat, but I am breathing. In and out through my…my neck.

From where we float inside the eel's mouth, the water suddenly shifts again. The creature we're inside ascends with such fierceness that I worry for any human or animal who might be near the lake, for a tidal wave is most certainly about to befall the nearby area.

I can only tell we've broken the lake's surface because of a suspended moment where we are light, and my chest bubbles with adrenaline. Then the moment passes. We crash back down with a hollow, grand splash.

I can hardly tell which way is up or down anymore from all the sloshing, not until the eel's mouth cracks open.

Ryven offers me his hand, and I take it, the two of us swimming to the freedom of open air and land. Naked and sodden, we drag ourselves to the shore. I watch over my shoulder as the shimmering eel presses its eyes shut before sinking back below the water.

By the time I pull my attention away, Ryven is standing

before me, shielding his eyes with one hand while my clothes are outstretched in the other. I make quick work of pulling them back on, relishing the crisp, fresh air.

"Why aren't we gasping for air—I mean water?" Almost of its own accord, my hand reaches up to the soft of my neck. I flinch at the velvet ruffles I find there, the ones that confirm that I do, in fact, possess gills.

Ryven stares at my neck, refraining from searching his own. "Many sea animals can live without water for hours, some can even manage it for days."

"So which ones are we?"

A sheepish shrug. "I guess we'll find out."

Securing my belt and dagger back around my waist, I heave a conceding sigh.

Yet again, Ryven offers me his upturned hand. "Are you ready to see the Dark Sea?"

"How long will it take?" I ask, stroking my neck and the parched sensation that's already lingering just beneath the surface. "Are there other bodies of water along the way, just in case?"

"We'll be fine. We'll make it. The Elders wouldn't have made a deal with the eel if it wouldn't have met our needs for such a journey. We can go back to town though and grab some water-skins if you'd like."

I gnaw on my lip. "No. I don't want to waste the time."

"Very well," Ryven says, swooping me into his mighty arms again.

As we take to the sky, my thoughts surprise me by flitting briefly to Alphonse. We'd left him to rot in that dungeon and hadn't even bothered giving him an update on our progress or what we'd be doing next. I know I shouldn't feel guilty about it. He'd have done the same to me, if not worse, back at Nigh.

"I know enough about self-loathing to recognize that look,"

Ryven says, even as his eyes are trained ahead rather than on me. "What is it?"

I scowl at his uncanny ability to read my thoughts, but I have no reason to hide this from him. "I forgot about Alphonse. We should've at least told him what we were doing."

He considers the options a moment. "You said it yourself, there wasn't enough time. Besides, there's nothing we can do for him until your aunt's return. The sentinel made that much clear."

Nodding, I let my concern for my cousin dissipate as we rise into the clouds.

A silence falls between the two of us, the mission that lay ahead plummeting Ryven and I both into our own personal reflections. Every time fear grasps my heart, I busy my mind with the task at hand: go to the Dark Sea, find the breath of life, find my sister and aunt, and leave. I can't allow my mind to drift to the dangers that might befall us, to the possibility that Kalli might already be dead, to the challenge of locating an ancient magic that's been kept from the rest of the realm for ages.

After a long while, Ryven resituates me in his arms. I wonder how long he can carry someone like this. I'm no plump, prized heifer, but I'm certainly no malnourished calf either. Surely, he'll have to tire of carrying me eventually.

Just as I'm about to offer to walk for a ways, the clouds part, an ominous, gray body of water appearing below amid the desolate sands. Ryven lands us farther away than I expected, and the mere unsettling sight of this place tempers my eagerness to find my family and this cure.

"What is it?" I whisper, noticing his twitchy ears. "Is it the sirens? Do you hear them?"

He hushes me with a finger to his mouth before crouching low to the ground. I follow suit, inching beside him and keeping my back turned toward him. I draw my shadowsteel axe, the grip warming in my hands as we scan our desolate surroundings.

A pebble skitters over the wasteland, catching both of our flashing eyes. But the moment we behold it, its obvious duplicity strikes me with unrelenting fury.

I whirl back around just as the demon lunges from behind the boulders. I swing my axe at it, but the shadowcreature's mighty claw bats it away and barrels into the both of us. Jaws snapping at our ears, I hold the beast back with nothing but the pole of my axe and sheer willpower.

"How did it recognize us?" I grunt out.

Faster than lightning, Ryven reaches down and plucks the dagger from my waist, striking the small blade straight into the demon's throat. Black blood spills down its chest. I can feel the warmth of it sliding into my gills, and I splutter, repulsed and frightened, shoving the creature off me to spit everything in my mouth out.

I know I'm already blighted, but if what Ryven said about Ahl'Ro's rapid demise being related to how much demon toxin he had in him, then I don't necessarily want to risk ingesting any demon blood.

"I-I'm sorry," Ryven stammers, rushing to my side. "I wasn't thinking—"

"It's fine." I wipe my mouth with the back of my sleeve, grateful that black can't stain black. "You saved our lives. There's nothing to be sorry for."

The muscles in his square jaw tighten. "I should've pushed the demon off you first. I should've know that—"

"Ryven," I growl more emphatically. Demanding his gaze, I hold him there. "You have to stop blaming yourself for everything. That demon came out of nowhere. You responded quickly, as did I, and you made the right choice. I'm already blighted anyways, and if all goes as planned, we'll soon have the cure in our grasp."

Brow furrowing, Ryven turns away.

Spitting the rest of the tarry toxin from my mouth to the ground, I stare at the dead beast. "How did it recognize us?"

"I don't know," he says stiffly, angrily. "Maybe it has to do with Elder Nebadri's eel."

For the first time, I notice his fingers flexing around the hilt of the dagger. His gaze is sharp on the oily blood smeared across his hand, and I remember something my uncle Adrien told me about the druids and their view of the shadow-creatures.

Gently, I slide the dagger out from his hand, securing it back into my sheath. "Druids don't kill other living beings."

There's a tick in his jaw, a flash of pain crosses his expression, but he blinks it away, face softening as his gaze focuses on mine. "They don't, but that's because they grew up in the safety of the Eyve. I know the value of my life, of those I care about, and I've learned that some lives *do* matter more than others. At least to me."

Crimson awareness rushes to heat my face. I resist the urge to pull away, letting our gazes bury into one another and the magnitude of the moment devour me. Ryven killed to protect me, just as he did in my parents' cottage when Ahl'Ro's demon moved to attack me. He cares about me and my life. And, I've been remiss to admit it, but I'm beginning the think I feel the same.

With a bow of his head, Ryven breaks our eye contact. "Are you ready to face the sirens of the Dark Sea?"

My mouth is already dry, but it becomes a desert at the mention of those dark creatures and what they might be capable of. I know very little about them, other than the supposed atrocities they once inflicted on humankind. I've read about their sharp-as-glass teeth, the grace with which they move in the water, and the way they were known for luring humans to their deaths.

Anyone else would've begged me to reconsider, but not the half-demon beside me. He believes in me. He always has.

"Why?"

My question makes him frown, drawing his gaze back to mine.

"Why do you believe in me so fervently?"

He raises his brow at me in amusement. "I'm fairly certain we've had this conversation before."

"I know," I admit, my fingers fidgeting with one another as we stand before the Dark Sea and whatever horrors await us below. "But, suppose we hadn't. What would you say?"

He takes a slow, calculated step forward. Then another. Each time he moves, I expect it to be his last, surprised when he doesn't stop until he is right in front of me. I angle my eyes up to meet his as he gently tucks my silver hair behind my ear.

"I'd remind you that you've faced worse already and survived. I'd tell you that in the few short months I've known you, you've survived at least two demon scourges. In the past week alone you've faced some of the most vicious and horrific beasts among the shadowcreatures, all while hallucinating from fever. You've pushed yourself through the Shadowthorn, met with the druid Elders, and been swallowed and spat back out by an ancient eel."

The last part makes me chuckle, my chin tucking toward my chest.

Ryven catches it though, forcing my gaze back to his intoxicating, russet eyes. His breathing is ragged for someone who hasn't been running, for someone standing stiller than death.

He swallows hard, the lump in his throat bobbing. "I'd remind you that it's not you who has anything to fear from the sirens, but the other way around. I mean, who wouldn't fear the woman boldly venturing into siren-infested waters, without so much as a plan or any magic to speak of?"

"Hey," I balk, tearing my face out of his soft grip. "I have magic…somewhere."

He smiles, eyes shimmering as he watches me, undeterred. "There is nothing you can't do once you set your mind to it, Halira. This blight, this sickness, it doesn't stand a chance against you."

A rueful smile of my own greets him. "It doesn't stand a chance against *us*. Remember, we're both beating this thing."

To my dismay, his expression grows grim. A dark shadow washes over him, and he turns his back to me to look out over the ominous, still sea.

"We'll see."

The words sound strangled, drowned in sorrow and self-pity, but I can hardly blame him. I've been blighted for a week. He's been this way for months. He had to watch his friend turn and then he had to kill him with his own bare hands. It's no wonder he's doubtful. There have been no signs of light to offer him through these dark times.

I step forward and rest my hand upon his shoulder. "You'll see," I tell him. "Once we have the breath of life in our possession, you'll never doubt me again."

Before he can wallow in self-pity and doubt, I flick my hair over my shoulder and stride into the gray abyss. The water rushes in through my gills with cool relief. I hadn't realized just how parched I'd become since our time in the Ushines River. Relishing every drink of it, without another look back, I dive into the Dark Sea.

INTO THE DEPTHS

DARK SEA, FORGOTTEN FOREST OF EYVE

It's not until I'm completely submerged, and my garments are so soddened they feel like I'm wearing lead that I realize my mistake. I should've undressed first. There was a reason we'd done so back at the lake, many reasons, first of all being that it is extremely cumbersome to swim in wet leathers.

I can't bemoan it too much though. For as uncomfortable as it is to have the leather swelling and grinding against my skin, the idea of facing the cannibalistic sirens while naked is too chilling a thought to even consider.

Somewhere behind me, a large mass plummets into the dark waters, and shortly after, Ryven appears by my side. He, too, is still dressed, although for him that's still significantly less fabric than what I'm working with.

Languidly, he jerks his head and guides the two of us farther into the sea.

To my great disappointment, the Dark Sea is hardly discernable from any other underwater experience I've had. Although my eyesight has improved and I can see more clearly through the murkiness, there isn't much magnificence or awe to behold. I'd hoped for an underwater metropolis, for spires carved from golden coral, windows created from iridescent seashells, seahorse sentinels, and bioluminescent sea slugs giving everything a radiating glow.

Instead, the sea is aptly named.

There is nothing but gray water. The mud that's settled along the seafloor is thick and slimy, and more closely resembles the fetid blood that drips from demon victims than it does sand.

If this is where a once mighty race has retreated, I'd expected to see signs of their life, but there are none. The Dark Sea is a void of both light and sound. An eerie quiet has made its home here, but I know better than to think we are alone.

The deeper we swim, the darker the waters become, if that's even possible. The sun can't reach this far below the surface, and my eyes struggle to distinguish between one strand of seaweed and the dark nothingness before us. But we keep swimming, keep diving, keep looking. All the while I wonder where my aunt and sister are in this great abyss. In my haste to reunite with them, I hadn't spent much time on the surface looking for signs of them. For all I know, they've already retrieved what they came here for and have already started heading back for the Forgotten Forest of Eyve.

Though, somewhere deep down I know that's not the case. Ryven and I would've seen them as we flew overhead if it were.

My fingers have pruned, the skin on their tips unaccustomed to such prolonged stints in water, for even though my lungs were altered, my skin was not. Neither were my muscle. My lungs burn from the effort it's taken to get us this far. I'm not sure they'll be able to make the journey back once we have what we came for. It seems like the sort of thing that will prove to bite me in the end, but I can't think about that now.

I focus on the mucky water all around us. We keep each other close as we continue our exploration, weaving in and out of patches of seaweed, hovering over the coral, until finally, something catches our attention.

We can't see it at first. There's nothing in the surrounding abyss when the bright ringing begins to hum throughout the sea. It's more than that though. This tune is ethereal, tragic, poignant. It calls to us through the dark expanse, a beautiful rhythm that coaxes us through the waters, urging us on, and we oblige it.

I've heard the stories of the sirens, how they lured humans with their silken songs, but those were just tales told to keep small children who couldn't swim away from the docks and shores. These sirens cannot lure me with their song. I can choose not to follow. I can choose to turn back. It's just...I don't want to. Wherever they're leading us, it will be deeper into their lair, closer to the treasures that they keep hidden among themselves.

And so, I listen. I drift to the melody like I'm tethered to it. We follow the song, until finally it becomes more than a mere harmonious call, but a light, vibrant and blinding. I'm drawn farther still; that light, that glistening beam of glorious beauty, and it's just beyond my reach.

Ryven sees it too. I watch with twisting jealousy as he begins tearing through the water at a hastened pace—his stupid, unnaturally strong arms and the blighted blood that gives him an advantage that I don't have. Yet. He'll make it there before I do; he'll get to stroke the ball of sun and claim it as his own personal gemstone. I won't let him.

I, too, swim harder. My muscles are tender and fraying, but what's another yard of swimming if it means I could possess such a lustrous wonder. I reach for Ryven's ankle, grasping and yanking him back. My grip is slippery and his legs powerful, but I squeeze tight and pull again. The motion isn't much, but it's enough to throw him off, to interrupt his rhythmic, powerful strokes.

Fury flickers behind his dark eyes as I spear past him, my arm outstretched. The illuminating orb is just at my fingertips, just within my grasp.

And I am only dimly aware of the maw full of sharp teeth that appears from below me. A creature of nightmares emerges before me, but I feel nothing but joy, nothing but contentment, as my hand closes around the floating ball of light.

When I try to bring it to my chest though, I frown at the resistance I find. This beautiful object, this vibrant gemstone, is caught. I tug again but it doesn't give.

Only once I'm in a state of frustration, ripped away from the bliss that had been oh so close, do I become aware of the danger closing in on me. An anglerfish draws nearer, and I release the radiant lure like it's burned my skin just to touch it.

I flail backward, colliding into Ryven who is still too drawn by the light's glow to have realized what I have, that this monstruous fish means to devour us. I grab his arm before he can blow past me, but the fish's hunger is already set, its jaw already cracked wide, its teeth all but closed around us.

I curse myself for letting it come to this. We'd come here knowing exactly what could await us, and yet we'd swam right into one of the siren's traps anyway. Maybe the anglerfish won't eat us. Maybe once it's tongue grazes Ryven's arm, it'll soon realize it doesn't have an appetite for tainted druids.

Or perhaps it'll realize the opposite.

We can't risk dying this way. Not only do our lives obviously depend on it, but I still haven't found Kalli and Imryll. Even Alphonse relies on our safe return.

With nothing left to lose, I draw my axe. My Crusader training has taught me to kill anything that would cause me harm, but my brief time with the druids has taught me something else. This isn't the war, this is merely a battle, a precursor to the sirens we still have yet to see, and I believe we are close.

But killing this creature, their protector, will not endear them to us.

Instead, I cram my weapon between the creature's teeth and let its mouth war with the blade. The axe is just tall enough to leave us an opening, and I grab Ryven's belt to pull him out with me, but fortunately the melodic hold has faded now that he's inside the creature's mouth, and so he swims on his own accord.

We rush from the anglerfish's teeth, heaving and horrified, but the excitement doesn't stop there. I'd expected—I'd hoped—we'd emerge to greet the sirens, but to my confusion, after hours of swimming in a vast, seemingly empty sea, we come face-to-face with a single majestic turtle and its jellyfish companion.

My head cocks, the sight of these two oceanic creatures floating together side-by-side is so jarring I can't make sense of it at first. It must be another trick, another means of preventing us from finding the breath of life. Or perhaps neither are tricks at all, but tests meant to ensure that the powerful magic only falls into the hands of the worthy.

I have nothing to go on but the knowing feeling in my gut as I reach out a tentative hand. The sea turtle whacks it away with one of its flippers and swims straight up toward the surface. My hand lingers in the water, my eyes watching the beautiful creature ascend and disappear, unaware of the jellyfish as it approaches. Ryven snatches my hand before the thing can get too close, and, as if by way of protesting, it floats over to him instead, reaches a long, slender frill at him, and zaps him before following after the sea turtle.

Bewildered, I turn to Ryven, but he just shakes his head and follows after them, as if he knows something I don't.

I have no choice but to ascend with them.

Ryven breaches the surface first, I'm not too long after him.

"What is it? Why have we come up for air?"

He doesn't answer me, but his knowing eyes flick to something behind me.

My heart cleaves in two when I turn around to find silver, corded braids emerging from the water.

"Kalli!" I exclaim, throwing my arms around my sister's neck. "I've been looking for you!"

She shoves me away, scowling. "You shouldn't be. You're supposed to be back with the Wardens. What are you doing here?"

My aunt surfaces next, smoothing her sleek, silver hair down the back of her head.

I glance between the two of them, suddenly realizing.

"You—it was you two!" My glare fixates on my lying, deceitful sister. "You can take the form of an animal and you never told me!"

"You didn't need to know," Kalli says coolly.

I balk, my jaw practically breaking away from my skull. I channel every flare of rage I have into my glare and wade closer so she can see it. "I asked you at Nigh if you knew anything about us. I told you that strange things were happening to me, and you couldn't even bother to tell me that you had gone through them too—"

"I had no choice," she snaps, her voice more sharpened by emotion than usual. But she recovers quickly, holding her chin high and flicking her braids back behind her to float in the gray water like sea serpents. "It hardly matters now though, does it?"

Petulance gets the better of me and I snort.

My sister ignores it. "I take it you've come to retrieve the breath of life?"

"I came to find you," I snarl. "The druid Elders told us you'd come here and told us what you'd find."

"Did they also give you the ability to breathe underwater?" my aunt Imryll asks, eyeing us skeptically.

It takes me a moment to realize her question is genuine. She truly is perplexed by how we were able to be below for so long.

"Elder Irene requested that the winds cease their reign over our lungs for the day," Ryven tells her.

"A day?" Imryll's eyebrow quirks up as she assesses the location of the sun in the sky. "Then I suppose we must make haste. The afternoon hours will fade quickly now."

"Have you found the breath of life already?" I ask them.

"We believe we have," Kalli replies. "But it will require some strategy."

"The anglerfish you encountered, the one that almost ate you, is a rare and powerful creature. Judging from the length of its teeth, I'd venture to guess it's been alive for thousands of years. It likely lived during the time when sirens were spread throughout every body of water, not just the Dark Sea."

Growing impatient with Imryll's story, I snap, "And?"

"It's loyal," Kalli answers. "And likely highly trusted. The sort of guardian you'd asked to, say, protect a powerful and rare magic that only the sirens behold."

"The anglerfish is guarding it," Ryven adds.

"Yes," Imryll snaps. "But it requires an offering: a life for a life."

Frustrations simmers inside me. "Why didn't the Elders tell us this?"

Ryven shakes his head. "We didn't ask. Their collective knowledge is too vast to be able to tell when to share and what without prompting. It's why questioning them is such a challenge. You never know if you'll get the information you seek."

"But if we need an offering, what are we going to do?" I ask, more to myself than anything.

My sister answers. "We don't know. We've been trying to figure that out ourselves. We've tried offering clams and oysters. We've brought the creature sea slugs and guppies.

Though it will eat anything brought to it, the creature's price has not yet been met."

Imryll is reverent when she speaks. "It is a creature of great fortitude. It will want something larger than guppies. I've already told you."

Kalli's face purples. "Yeah, well, at least I'm trying. We're running out of ideas."

"We don't need ideas, dear niece. We need courage and sacrifice."

"Then sacrifice yourself, already. I have no intention of dying an early death."

"Not even for your sister?"

My glare burns hot into my aunt's face. "No one is dying for anyone. Especially not you," I say, returning my gaze to my sister. "We'll think of something."

"Well, we better hurry," Ryven says. "You and I won't be able to breathe underwater for much longer."

"You shouldn't be breathing underwater anyway," Kalli says under her breath.

But I mostly ignore her. My thoughts have already started drifting to our dwindling options. The breath of life is just below us; all we have to do is convince the anglerfish we are worthy. But the only proof it will accept is that of a life, a large one.

Well, if it's a body the anglerfish wants, a body it shall get.

"Do you think the life needs to be human?"

Imryll's cunning eyes falls upon me. "Not necessarily, but it needs to be a creature of greater worth than that which feeds off scum."

Kalli flashes another seething glare at our aunt.

I wriggle my eyebrows. "Do you think the life we give needs to be alive upon arrival, or can we produce a death instead?"

Everyone's confused eyes turn to me.

A DEAL WITH A QUEEN

DARK SEA, FORGOTTEN FOREST OF EYVE

"This is a foolish idea," Kalli groans, lugging one of the demon's legs in her hands. "A foolish, *foolish* idea."

It took us two hours to swim back to shore. The sun has moved just past high noon and it'll still take us two hours to return to the anglerfish. How events unfold from there will determine whether we have enough time with our gills left.

"You're just jealous you didn't think of it," I grunt, heaving with every effort it takes to drag the demon's body into the Dark Sea.

Kalli rolls her gray eyes but continues lugging the dead demon with me, Imryll, and Ryven, until the creature is at the lapping waters' edge. Her raven circles us overhead, and until it showed itself, I'd almost forgotten it even existed.

The four of us dip our toes back into the sea, not so much as bothering to remove our boots. The time for keeping our garments dry has long since passed. At least, not the garments we care about. Imryll and Kalli have dawned tattered gowns that appear to be used for those who shift to and from their animal form. The two women tug the white garments off and fold them in neat piles before submerging themselves entirely, leaving Ryven and I to drag the body.

If I thought I was exhausted the first time we made this journey, I was mistaken. For a solid hour, a cramp has lanced through my calf, another piercing my ribs. I feel the weight of the Dark Sea around me like a warm blanket threatening to strangle my limbs and pull me down into its depths. I want nothing more than to close my eyes and simply rest, and I can tell Ryven wants the same.

But we've come too far to stop now. We are almost there, and if we can just push ourselves a little harder…

The tantalizing, toxic melody ripples through the sea. This time, we take heed when following it, keeping our eyes fixed elsewhere, long after a light starts to shine from ahead.

I can feel the presence of the anglerfish as it inches forward. Despite knowing what can happen if I become entranced again, I can't help but look into its open maw, searching for the shadowsteel axe that is integral to our plan. Without it, we would need to find a new way to breach the boundary around Qaeus, and the only alternative is to possess another Primordial weapon. Without the axe, we'd have to go to Illashore—a land no human nor druid has ventured—find the Pits of Bagamore, retrieve the spear that slew Khaymus, and return to Qaeus in time before the Blight consumes either me or Ryven. I'm not well-traveled, but I am fairly certain we don't have enough time for all of that. At least Ryven doesn't. We need that axe.

And as luck would have it, I find no signs of it in the anglerfish's mouth. The blade that had been crammed between its teeth, is gone. A terrible sense of defeat fills me like lead, attempting to drag me down into oblivion where I care about nothing and no one. If the axe is gone, Ryven and I are as good as dead. Actually, worse than dead. Soon, he'll finish the transformation he's already nearly completed, and I won't be too far behind him. Will I have months like he had? Weeks? A few more days?

My gaze snags on Ryven's. He's already watching me, dubious adrenaline making his already large eyes seem bigger, his expression seeming to ask me *what do we do now?* There's no defeat there, no sense of helplessness. Ryven still plans to fight for the future he wants, and really what choice does he have? What choice do either of us have? To concede to failure? To our demises?

That's never been me. I will fight until my last breath. If we have to travel all the way to Illashore, then so be it.

Before the lure of the anglerfish's light can summon me again, Ryven and I nod to each other. We release the demon's arms slung over our shoulders and begin wading back out of the anglerfish's reach. My sister and aunt circle around us, prepared to strike if need be.

The anglerfish opens wide and swallows the demon whole. The four of us wade in the cool black, watching the anglerfish crunch through the demon bones and tear through black sinewy flesh. Compared to the anglerfish, the demon is but a snack, and it makes quick work of devouring it.

When the demon is no more, the anglerfish watches us with its glazed, white eyes, and I hold my breath. I'm beginning to doubt whether this will work, whether serving up an already dead demon will be sufficient enough a trade, but we have no other choice. What else could we have done? Offering up ourselves instead was out of the question, and offering some innocent human was even further from the things I'd consider doing.

The light over the anglerfish's head flickers, the bright glow dimming along with the serene melody still wafting around us. Finally, the light fades completely. The waters return to absolute darkness, but thanks to whatever magic the eel shared with us, I can still see enough of the shadows to tell that the anglerfish is retreating. It clears a path for us into a cave.

I glance to my jellyfish-sister, to Ryven, then finally to the turtle that is my aunt. When I read nothing in any of their body language or expressions that suggest this is a bad idea, I glide forward and enter the small cave.

I don't have far to go. The cavern is shallow, more like a shelf than anything, and a pedestal rests against the back wall. The day is full of surprises, because I had expected the breath of life to be some mystical, enchanted flower or reed, or even a luminescent conch shell, given the location where it's been hidden. But, resting atop the pedestal is a glass jar barely bigger than my thumb, topped with a cork.

Again, I hesitate, glancing back to my friends. Something doesn't feel right. We'd been warned about the sirens before coming here, but then where were they? If they were the ones guarding the breath of life, why had we so far only encountered an anglerfish?

Then again, it was centuries ago when the sirens were banished. I'd heard no mention of them in history books since, and even Ryven talked about them as if no one had seen them for decades. It's possible that after the humans and mages killed so many of them, their species didn't make it.

Shaking away my doubts, I push forward. The stone pedestal stands before me, a testament of time and durability, a structure far older than any of us, and one that would survive long after us. My pruned fingers reach up and fold over the smooth jar.

As if in response, the water sizzles with the screeches of the enraged, the violated, the vengeful. A cacophony of ear-piercing shrieks surrounds us as I press the bottle to my chest and swim back to my friends.

An army of sirens emerges from the darkness, teeth sharp, eyes dead. I watch them with a mixture of awe and horror as the creatures close in around us, clawing and howling like ravenous demons. They aren't demons though, I realize. Not entirely anyway. They are made in the image of humans, if our flesh was sickly, hollowed, and covered with scales instead of baby-soft hairs. They are every shade of iridescence, from teal to periwinkle to fuchsia. They look like skeletal monsters who have draped themselves in glittering, shimmering fabrics in an attempt to conceal their hideousness. It only serves to magnify it.

The four of us get into formation, whether by instinct or teaching, as we watch the sirens surround us. I break my gaze to look up toward the surface, unsurprised to find the anglerfish floating there, ready, waiting.

When I return my gaze back to the sirens, an impending sense of doom sinking into the pit of my stomach, a single finned woman floats forward from the mass. Her scaly flesh is aquamarine and coated in barnacles that cover half of her forehead, cheek, and trail down to her collarbone. They crop one of her black eyes, and even with my advanced sight, I can't tell whether they've been gouged out, leaving nothing but black emptiness behind, or if her entire eye is black.

Aside from the ferocious air of death about her, she otherwise carries herself with regal grace. The crown atop her head, made from clam shells and pearls, matches her aquamarine scales and the ruffling fins that ripple from her ears, elbows, and legs.

The siren holds out her webbed hand toward me, and I clutch the bottle tighter. We've come all this way, and I'm not giving up now.

The mass of sirens screech in unison, their unease riling up one another until they're in a frenzy once again.

The siren before me holds up her other hand to silence them. They obey her, their queen, but the ravenous disdain does not leave their black eyes.

The queen tilts her regal head, seaweed hair shifting around her petrifying face. "You dare enter the domain of the sirens, and attempt to cheat *us* what we are owed? If it is the breath of life you desire, then it must be paid for. For your crime, the price is doubled. Two lives for the one the breath of life would grant you."

I frown, concern swelling inside my chest. What does she mean *for the one the breath of life will grant you*? Surely, she isn't implying that the breath of life can only be used a single time. The Elders never mentioned—

But I hardly have time to dwell on it. Without any warning, the siren queen presses her cracked lips together and inhales sharply. A shrill whistling vortex forms from her mouth, the waters churning and bubbling with the screeching raucous.

The other sirens join her, small vortexes of boiling water jetting into their mouths.

My body has never been more alert, more fueled with fear. I am out of my element here. Literally. I've never trained to fight underwater, and even if I had, I lost my axe when the anglerfish tried to swallow us. I still have my dagger, but my movements are too languid down here, buried beneath the pressure of the waves, and the sirens have already proven how easily they would be able to outmaneuver me.

The sirens have the advantage. They could kill us with teeth or claws. The queen herself could spear me with her very crown.

But instead, they keep singing.

Why?

Suddenly, my back turns cold. I glance over my shoulder to find that half of our party is missing. The turtle and jellyfish are no longer anywhere to be found.

Until I look up.

My heart catches in my chest. Not only have Kalli and Imryll turned back into humans, bubbles rising from their drowning throats, but they are dazedly swimming away, toward the anglerfish awaiting them with its jaw opened wide.

I scream, the sound strangled and warbled but entirely raw and unhinged. I swim through the bubbles that burst from my throat, arm outstretched for my sister, but I know I'll be too late. She's already too far away, and the anglerfish is drifting nearer to her. It made quick work of the demon. How fast will it be able to tear through soft, human flesh?

We need to think of a way out of this, something that the sirens would want, something they'd find valuable. Frantic and desperate, I search Ryven for any ideas he might have, but his eyes are just as wide as mine. He shakes his head, hand resting over the sword hilt at his waist. In this moment, I admire his willingness to fight for the death for this, recognizing that were it not for me, he wouldn't even be in this mess. All this time, he'd never even hoped he could be cured; he hadn't even planned on returning to Eyve, let alone diving in siren-infested waters to cure himself. He'd been content in just living out the rest of his time as he was.

But I wasn't. I don't want to become one of the very monsters I was trained to kill. I don't want more people to die because I'm pillaging villages. I don't want to become the creatures of children's nightmares, like these sirens would be if any Arcathainians still remembered their existence.

The thought occurs to me then, and I'm almost too frazzled to grasp it. But I focus as best as I can on the existence of the sirens, on their history in this realm, and how they came to be here, alone and forgotten.

And I realize, I *do* know what they want.

My mouth springs open, another cloud of bubbles bursting from my lips as I beg the siren queen to listen. But I curse myself, for my voice is useless here. The eel might've given me gills, but it did not change my vocal cords.

Helplessly, I look back up to my sister, a halo of teeth stretching wide overhead.

The siren song stops.

Awareness returns to Kalli and my aunt, the two of them clutching their throats before quickly turning back into their water animal forms.

Blinking away my confusion and relief, I stare back down at the siren queen. A bubble the size of her head warbles in the water before her, and with a flick of her wrist, she sends it sliding across the gap between us. It crashes into my face and I expect the mass to pop. Instead, it forms around me, my own personal pocket of air.

"Speak," the siren queen says, voice like a harbinger of death.

Before she can change her mind, I spit out the same thing I tried saying earlier. "I—I imagine it's been a long time since you've fed."

Her head twitches. "We feed daily."

"Fed *well*," I amend, watching her webbed fingers tread through the water as she considers it. "What if I can offer you something better than the two lives you demand?"

A shrill wave of whispers washes over the crowd like a steam from a hissing pot.

The queen holds up her hand and again commands silence. "We are listening, human."

I swallow hard, resisting the urge to glance between any of my friends for fear of the doubt I'll see reflected there. Looking to them now would only make me appear weak anyway, a trait I can't risk showing to the queen.

Looking down my nose, I examine my wrinkled fingers and the bottle closed between them. "What if I could offer you your freedom from this place?"

Another roar of hissing rises up from the others.

"You offer what is not yours to give," the siren queen sneers, her black eyes growing darker still.

I ignore her outrage. "We came for the breath of life so that we could slay the Primordial Qaeus."

"The Primordial is your enemy, not ours. Let her hunt down the land walkers like they hunted us, and we would be eternally grateful."

"Yes, but the humans want the Primordial dead. Anyone who aids in that process would be revered as heroes." I pause long enough to watch her barnacle eyebrow arch, her dark eyes consider the magnitude of what I'm offering. "If you let us go, if you allow us to take the breath of life and slay Qaeus, *you* will be those revered heroes. The humans will have no choice but to allow you back into their waters."

Her horrific face contorts. "Lies! Trickeries! I have dealt with humans before, and I will not be made a fool again. Once you leave with our first queen's dying breath, you will never return and your promise will be null in your eyes."

"No, that's not true."

The siren queen snarls again, spinning away from me in a rage, but it gives me time to think on what she said. *The first queen's dying breath.* I look down to the small bottle clutched in my hand. Inside, an opalescent shimmer swirls about the container, bright and enchanting. Beyond magic, I hadn't considered it to be anything more, but I understand now why this magical item has been guarded here for so long. The vial contains the last living breath of the original siren queen, the one the humans and mages viciously slaughtered, flayed, and used as a sail to chase the last colony of sirens away. It's no wonder they've protected it all this time. It's no wonder they feed any human who attempts to steal it to their anglerfish. It is the only thing they have left from their original queen, the only power she bestowed them upon dying.

With the current siren queen still pacing, her patience

fleeting by the moment, I do the first reckless thing that comes to mind. I draw my dagger from its sheath.

The sirens recoil, baring their teeth at me, but before the queen can charge me, I hold the dagger out, hilt first.

"This belonged to my brother," I tell the swarm of glutinous merpeople. "Qaeus' demons killed him and took him away from me. This dagger is all I have of his, of any of my family. Take *it* in exchange for the breath of life, one remnant of a shattered family to another."

Murmurs ripple through the crowd like hissing snakes, but the siren queen's abyss eyes remain glued to me.

My next words are for her alone. "There is no item in the world that matters more to me, and I think you can relate. I will return for this dagger, I promise you, and when I do, I will lead your people across the border of the Forgotten Forest of Eyve and back into the open waters of Arcathain."

I regret glancing at my sister. Even as a jellyfish, her disapproval is palpable. She is still of the mindset that magic is evil, and I have no doubt that after seeing these sirens, she believes it even more fervently, even as she herself unfolds the secrets of her own power. But I, for one, grow weary of the divides that separate us all. Demons hunt the humans, the humans plan to attack the mages, they condemned the druids who now condemn them—the cycle will never end as long as we continue to keep ourselves divided.

Truth be told, it's far less heroic than that.

But Ryven watches with proud understanding. He comprehends the truth that I am also coming to recognize—all life is precious, especially if it means protecting the ones you love today, so that they might fight tomorrow. In that, I'm sure, my sister *will* understand. After all, she is driven by logic, not the heart; she always has been, and this is the most logical decision I have ever made.

After a long, painful silence that hinges on one vengeful

people being able to come together with another, the siren queen finally speaks. "A bargain struck, but you will need not only the breath of life to slay the Primordial, but also this."

She signals to her people behind me, and they part as another scaled and finned woman to swim forward, a shadow-steel battle-axe in her hand. The siren shoves it against my chest, and I nod my thanks, even if the cordiality isn't recip-rocated.

"Now, land walkers, if that is all, then be gone, but take nothing more from these waters again until you fulfill your duty."

With a flick of her webbed fingers, the sirens disperse, leaving us floating once again in an aptly named watery lagoon.

Ryven and I breach the surface first, lungs aching for a breath of the air they've started missing. The sun has still not quite set, so we should've had a few hours more with the gills, but I suspect the magic is fading because our task is complete.

Spending half a day dragging my waterlogged body through a thick sea of darkness has left me spent. As we rock with the waves, drifting somewhere at sea, I struggle to keep my head above water.

A dolphin's nose peeks up from under my armpit, and if I wasn't so delirious, it might've startled me. But I'm too weary to question it, and I've seen too much magic in the past few days not to know that this creature is either my aunt, my sister, or one of Elder Nebadri's creatures sent to help me. I lean against the dolphin's dorsal fin and let it carry me to shore.

An hour or more later, Imryll is dragging me out from the lapping waves while I cough up the salty sea I've swallowed. Ryven and my sister aren't too far behind. My sister, though, infuriatingly bears no show of the exhaustion the half-demon and I feel.

She chucks his spent body on the ground and storms through the black sands toward me. "What did you just do?" Every word is enunciated with lethal precision, an architect of fury and judgment, making me flinch with every syllable. "Do you even know the evil you just unleashed on Arcathain? On our people?"

Her raven lands on her shoulder, but Kalli doesn't even seem to notice. Her sharp gaze is fixed on me and only me, and it will not waver.

My breaths are still ragged, every word uttered, labored. "They're...not our people..."

The raven squawks, a sound that is disturbingly human and conveys the bird's disapproval with eerily perfection.

Kalli scoffs as well, lips pulling back in disgust. "Are you so quick to forget the country we were born in? The people who raised you? Are you so quick to condemn them to a lifetime of fear and torture? Not only do they have the demons and a Primordial to contend with, as well as whatever impending war the Magistrate is set on commencing with the mages, but now you've unleashed a bloodthirsty legion of sirens on Arcathain? Have you gone mad?"

I refrain from reminding her that they're hardly a legion. They were thirty bodies maximum, a pitiful population that clearly still hasn't recovered from the damage our ancestors wrought them, and maybe never will.

Coughing on the shore, Ryven splutters in between hitches, "She saved your life."

Kalli's fists turn solid. "If it means dooming our people, then she should've let me die."

"And which people are those?" Ryven asks. On wobbly limbs, he pushes himself up to stare her down, his black wings spread out to help him maintain his balance. "The humans who shunned and shackled you the instant they thought you possessed an ounce of magic, or the druids who were persecuted by those very same people and have been living in peace with the sirens for centuries?"

My sister's smoldering gaze turns explosive. From where I'm hunched over on the beach, hands buried in sand, I reach up for her, barely seizing her wrist before she can barrel toward him.

"Ryven is right, Kalli. I know it's not the easiest thing to accept, but I did what was best for *all* people. We need to kill Qaeus. We can't do that without the breath of life, and the sirens weren't going to let us leave with it without some kind of compensation, and I wasn't about to just let you die!"

The tendons in her wrist flex, her gaze cooling back to its usual irritated chill.

"The sirens have suffered long enough, just as we have—the druids, Arcathainians, *everyone*. It's time to put an end to it all."

Kalli stares me down for a moment longer before begrudgingly turning to Ryven. "I assume you came here by flight?"

He flicks his wings out wider, giving them a sardonic look.

"Delightful." Kalli rolls her eyes before saying to me, "Then I'll see you back in the Eyve."

Before my eyes, my sister disappears in a tuft of ivory feathers, wide wings yawning behind her as the snowy owl she's become flaps into the sky. I am transfixed. She turns so seamlessly, without hesitation or any effort, and it brings out every terrible sisterly emotion inside me. Jealousy. Indignation. Shame.

But most of all, it is a maddening reminder that Kalli lied to me when we were in Nigh. When I bared my soul to her, confessed about the strange events occurring around me, she'd told me to ignore them. She said nothing good would come of digging deeper into the unknown, and led me to believe that she really had no idea of the magic I spoke of—which, is clearly inaccurate judging by the expertness with which she can shift into animals. Kalli has seemingly known about her powers for a long, long time.

A black raven dives through the trees behind her, my aunt catching up with her star pupil, and the bitterness bites down harder.

Instead of letting it fester into cool, unadulterated rage, I do what any sister would do. I remind myself Kalli's shoes are no more impressive than mine. Let my aunt and her flaunt their flagrant uses of druid magic. Neither of them can say they've flown in the arms of a half-demon.

I'm shivering when Ryven and I return back to the confines of the Eyve. Our waterlogged clothes made for poor insulation to the cool night air as we flew back.

The sun sets only moments after we cross the border, and we find ourselves trapped in the enchanted forest-village for the night once again. I can think of worse places to be. Right outside these borders, for example. The terrors of the Shadowthorn gurgle and moan in their nightly awakening, diminishing the serenity I felt in the Eyve upon our first arrival, back when it was still daylight.

Ryven sets me on the path, and we walk in silence, the exhaustion of the day weighing heavy on us both, or perhaps it's the exhaustion of what still lies ahead. How is it that we can have accomplished so much and still feel so far from our destination?

Still, he doesn't have to tell me where we are going for me to figure it out; I know even before the smoky scent of charcoal tickles my nose, before my aunt's voice reaches me as she instructs Kalli on stoking the fire, before Imryll's hut comes into view and I can see Kalli adding more lumber to the flames, while our aunt wraps eggplants up in giant fig leaves and sets them on a rack by the fire to roast.

Instinct carries me forward, my weary soul drawn to being reunited with what little family I have left, but I stop short when I sense a chilling absence at my side.

"You're not coming with me?"

Ryven halts too, glancing over his shoulder from where he's already started back down the path. "There are...I have other matters I must attend."

My expression softens, remembering the promise he'd made to Jiordan about returning once we'd finished with the Elders. That was over a day ago now. The poor man and his son didn't deserve to be forced to wait any longer.

"I wish you the best." The words sound stiff, even to me, despite trying to make them sound as light and genuine as possible.

"And to you."

A heavy hush falls between us, like the blanketing of snow-fall in the middle of winter. The longer it settles, the more our words to each other begin to feel more like farewells than I want them to be. This isn't goodbye. Our task is yet to be completed.

I summon a doleful grin. "You should count your blessings. I'd rather spend more time with Ahl'Ro's cheerful, kind father than the two harpies over there whom I call family."

The sentiment brings the slightest quirk of a smile to his morose face. "Well, when you've had your fill of cantankerous family, your company would be more than welcomed to visit with my...less cantankerous one. Although, I will warn you, Jiordan may be a beam of sunshine, but Ceph, I fear, did not inherit the family charm."

"I doubt he's any icier than Kalli. I'm sure I can handle him."

His grin broadens. "I have no doubt that you can."

By the time we break away, headed in our separate directions, my aunt has disappeared somewhere back inside, but I've already drawn the attention of Kalli. She stands with her hands on her hips, orange flames blazing behind her and casting ominous, haughty shadows across her face as she watches me approach.

"What's the matter? Fire-roasted dinner too civilized for the barbarian?"

In an instant, my blissful grin crumbles to ashes, replaced only with seething rage. "What is wrong with you?" I snap from the middle of the path, still too far away to feel any of the fire's heat, much less have this conversation in private. "He's blighted, not barbaric! As am I, need I remind you. Furthermore, Ryven's the one who saved me when the two of you abandoned me in the middle of the Shadowthorn—"

"Abandoned you?" she balks. "We left you in the care of uncle Adrien, where you were meant to remain until we could return to you with more information about how to heal your condition."

"Like you really expected me to just stay there? Do you even know me at all?"

Her lips purse into a thin line.

Our aunt reappears in the doorway with a curious bundle of linens and a look that says she's not to be crossed. "That's enough. I can empathize with sisterly squabbles as much as anyone, but tonight is not the night. Tonight, we celebrate our victories, for they were hard-fought and well deserved."

Kalli and I share a begrudging look with each other, but ultimately, I think we're both too tired to continue fighting anyway. The swimming from earlier has left my bones weary beyond belief, and I can only imagine it is the same for Kalli and Imryll who had been at the Dark Sea longer than Ryven and I. There's no telling how much they exerted themselves the last few days.

"Here," Imryll says, shoving the folded garments at me. The drab fabric scratches my hands when I grasp them. "You may change inside, and we'll dry your old clothes by the fire."

Considering my lips have been numb for over an hour, I don't argue. With no lantern to guide my way, I enter the hut, leaving the door open to use the light from the fire outside, and hurriedly clamber into the dry clothes. When I return moments later, Kalli is sitting on a nearby stump. Imryll hands her a freshly charred eggplant before gesturing to me to do the same. I oblige. I've never much cared for eggplant, but anything is better than the food I've been eating in the Shadowthorn.

"So, you and our mother didn't get along either?" I ask, sinking my teeth into the herbed, tender flesh beneath the charred rind and thinking about what she'd said earlier about empathizing with sisterly squabbles.

Imryll barks one loud, resonating laugh. "Does oil *get along* with water?" Sighing, she takes a seat on another carved stump. "No, Evelyne and I were not the kind of sisters who grew up doting on one another. Where I was interested in honing my magic as a shifter and becoming an adept druid, Evelyne gravitated toward…more frivolous joys: sewing, cooking—"

"Candle making," I add, a solemn smile riding out with the memory.

"Oh, yes, how she loved her precious bees. Neither of you were raised among us, so you wouldn't know, but tending to animals, caring for and communicating with them, is heralded as a virtue, one of our people's greatest prides. But Evelyn wouldn't practice beekeeping like a druid; she refused. She all but shunned her druid callings. With her hives, she chose not to communicate with them, nor would she use the energy from the earth to make flowers bloom and provide her bees the pollen they needed. She wanted them to thrive naturally, believing that our power was a mistake, one that too many were abusing."

She heaves a long, heavy sigh as she returns to the food cooking by the fire. "We were often at odds with each other, long before the wall fell. But when it did, the divide between us became a chasm.

"Our parents had heard of the old world, and they ventured into Arcathain with wanderlust in their eyes, eager to see the places from their great-grandparents' stories. Traveling with five children made it difficult to get very far though, so we set up a new life in Harwood—"

"*Five?*" Kalli angles a brow at her. "Are there other mystery aunt and uncles that we don't know about?"

"All dead that I know of," comes Imryll's emotionless response. "It was in Harwood that your mother was finally among people whom she could relate. They feared magic just as she thought they should; they believed it vile and wicked and unnatural, further reaffirming her own bullheaded beliefs. Eveyln stopped practicing her druid magic altogether. And once the Primordial Qaeus crossed into Arcathain and unleashed the Blight upon the people, darkness spreading, demons prowling through the population, it was the last bit of evidence that my sister needed. Magic was evil in her eyes and the Primordial needed to be stopped. It didn't mean I loved her any less."

Hearing about this side of our mother, of the druid life she had forsaken, it feels like it's not even the same person. It's strange learning our parents could've kept such profound secrets from us. She must've known that one day Kalli and I would discover our heritage, that our magic would awaken and we'd have no idea what to do with it, let alone how to use it, conceal it.

"Did you know your grandmother was an Elder?" My heart skitters at her words, but I hardly have time to process them before Imryll answer herself. "Of course you didn't. Evelyne kept everything about our people from you and now I'm the only one left to tell you any of it."

"An Elder," I finally manage. "Like...one of the women who live in the great big tree in the center of the village?"

"Do you know of any other Elders?" Imryll's superior gaze cuts to mine as she removes the rest of the eggplants from the fire. She walks them over to a wooden table that looks like it duals as the place she washes her laundry. "Your mother was next in the line of succession."

The news shocks me so thoroughly that I inhale my bite in my throat and start to choke.

As I'm busy coughing myself to tears, Kalli finishes chewing before she finally says, "You mean to tell me, our mother would've been one of your Elders?"

Imryll nods. "The honor is passed down through the blood-line to the eldest daughter. The was born a matter of minutes before me, so the title was hers."

I blanch again, but the lodge in my throat is finally cleared so I splutter, "You're twins?"

"Now that she's dead," Kalli interjects. "Our grandmother's title would fall to you then."

Imryll casts her eyes down, a sad smile splayed on her lips. "I'm afraid that's not how it works. Whether Evelyne accepted the title or not, whether she served in the capacity of an Elder, matters not. She was the eldest. The role was hers and would never be filled by any other. Except—"

"Except Kalli." The words leave my lips on a breath, and I whip around to face my sister.

Her gray eyes look almost onyx in the firelight, her skin ashen as stone. The expression she wears is one I don't think I've ever seen on her. It's rife with anger, that I can detect, but some twists it even darker, something bitter about the glint in her eyes. If my aunt is trying to slyly suggest Kalli step into the role, she's been utterly tactless.

"But that's neither here, nor there," Imryll says, catching my surprise with the genuine nature of her tone. "The Eyve has functioned with three Elders for decades now. No one hardly remembers a time when we were governed with all four."

Still sensing the waves of raw and tense emotion rippling off from my sister, I attempt to veer the conversation back to safer topics. "What else can you tell us about the secret life our mother lead before we were born?"

Imryll thinks for a moment, then a grin curls up her lips. "Did you know she founded the Wardens of Qaeus?"

I shake my head, thoroughly immersed once more.

"She wanted to learn as much as she could from the Primordial to aid in her slaughter. However, then she met your father. They were young and reckless, and it was only inevitable that a baby would soon follow. Upon your birth, Kalli, Evelyne lost all will to fight. She had a new purpose: to protect her family. She couldn't bring herself to put you in harm's way, whether by Primordial, by demon, or by the druids whom she believed would come for you.

"She left the Wardens of Qaeus without a leader, which was for the best since they were in need of better leadership, someone who understood that not *all* magic was evil, and that the Primordial needed protection, not obliteration."

Kalli crooks an eyebrow at our aunt. "So you resumed the role?"

Imryll waves her off. "Only for a time. Arcathain was never my home. After our parents died, as Harwood was swept away into the Shadowthorn, I returned to the homeland I still remembered so fondly. I'd almost forgotten what it was like to not fear for your life every time you left your home, to live protected from demons and away from the humans who would have me hanged if they ever caught a glimpse of the power I beheld. There was peace in the Eyve, there still is, and I wanted you all to know it, to share it with me. I tried for years convincing Evelyne to return, to bring her family back home so that you all might live long and happy lives. No matter how close the Shadowthorn crept toward that pit you called home, no matter how many times I pleaded with her to return home, Evelyne always refused my invitations."

Using a long stick she pulls from the ground behind her, Imryll pokes at the fire, stirring the ashes and giving new life to the flames.

"The two of you still have a home here, should you like it."

She falls quiet then, allowing silence to provide us ample opportunity to consider what she's offering. Once we're done curing me of the blight sickness, Kalli and I only have two options: return to the Wardens of Qaeus and live the rest of our days in the Shadowthorn fighting for scraps and barely surviving, or we can embrace our heritage and live here.

It's not much of a choice, really, like being offered to walk over the edge of a cliff or to take the bridge across. But even if it wasn't so dire, after all I've experienced and learned this past week, I believe I'd be tempted by the offer.

Still, until I'm cured, I can't risk having such dreams. It's as Ryven said—once someone is blighted, they have no way of knowing how much time they have left. It's best not to think about the possibilities of a joyous life, until I'm sure I'll have a life to live. After all, it's easier to face death when you feel no hope, rather than having all of that hope ripped from your chest.

My expression must be as ghastly as I feel because it draws Kalli's concerned scrutiny. "Why do you look so somber? You now possess the breath of life *and* a weapon that's slain a Primordial. If anyone has death to fear, it's that half-demon you keep for company."

My eyebrows draw together. "What do you mean?"

Sounding moderately irritated that she even has to explain, she responds. "The original siren queen only had one dying breath, as do we all, and the vial contains it."

I wait for her to elaborate, but she appears to need more prompting. "And?"

"Isn't it obvious? One dying breath of a siren. One vial of mystical protection from death." She watches me, waiting for some sign that I've caught on, but I either can't make sense of what she's saying, or I don't want to. I shake my head and Kalli growls. "The Elders said in order to be cured, the person cleaving the Primordial's heart must possess the breath of life, but there is only one. Only one of you can be cured, Halira."

Slowly, I rise from my seat, turning to Imryll. "Is that true?"

But I already know the answer. I knew it, or at least I was beginning to suspect it, when we were still in the Dark Sea and the siren queen said *two lives for the one the breath of life will grant.*

Imryll inclines her head, silver hair tumbling over her shoulder and reflecting the fire's glow. "I believe your sister is correct."

"You both knew," I say, staring between them, my hand closing unconsciously around the vial hanging from my neck.

"What does it matter?" Kalli yells. "It wouldn't change anything. The both of you would still be blighted and there'd still be but one way to cure you."

Fear cascades over me in sickening waves that turn my stomach watery. The cool slickness washes down my back, icing my spine as the worst of my fears are realized. Not *realized*, accepted. I've spent all this time convincing myself that we actually stood a chance—the both of us—but deep down, I knew very well that wasn't possible. There is only one Primordial left, one heart. Though there are two weapons that have slain the beasts, we possess only one, and therefore it would be impossible for Ryven and I both to strike the heart at the same time.

I should've known, but I hadn't wanted to consider it, hadn't wanted to face the truth.

Only one of us will walk away from this alive.

My sister calls my name—chastises it—as I peel out of my aunt's yard and race down the path. This realization, this acceptance, it's not between me and my sister, nor does it have anything to do with my aunt. This impacts Ryven and me alone, and as much as I loathe to admit it, I need him right now. I can't face this decision alone. Kalli may think it's one that's already been made, but she's wrong. It's not so easy to accept life knowing it will condemn another. This choice has to be made by the both of us, and only us.

It's a short race to Ryven's home, but by the time I arrive, I am slick with sweat. My damp hair clings to the base of my neck like a hot rag. The clothes Imryll lent me, already thin and worn, are so soaked through that I can see the outline of my body beneath the draped fabric.

Sitting outside around their own bonfire, Ryven, Jiordan, and a young man I presume to be Ceph share in quiet conversation.

Until I catch Ryven's eye.

He stands abruptly, the teasing smirk he flashed at Ceph at the joke Jiordan cracked falling from his face in an instant.

"Halira," he says, speaking my name as if it were a dream. Or perhaps a nightmare. He bounds over the dancing flames to reach me. "What is it? Is everyone all right?"

Behind him, Ceph and Jiordan have stood readied as well.

"I'm fine. Everything's fine," I say loud enough so they can hear. "But...I need to talk to you about..."

My words trail off. I can't bring myself to classify such a topic. *About one of our impending deaths?* Or how about *which one of us is going to die so that the other one will live?*

Jiordan throws his hands into the air. Without a word, he heads toward his front door, smacking his son in the chest when he doesn't immediately appear to be following suit.

Ceph rolls his narrowed eyes, mumbling something sarcastic under his breath about the joys of unexpected company.

"Sorry—" I mutter.

"Don't be. You were invited and he is well aware. It's like I told you earlier, he just lacks tact." Ryven shoots Ceph a caustic glare, one he returns with another eye roll before disappearing into the hut. "Tell me, what's wrong? You're shaking."

He reaches out, taking my trembling hands into his own, and oh, how I relish their heat. They are a cozy kind of warmth, like hopping beneath a mountain of blankets after standing outside in the cold. Too long, and I'll overheat, but for the first few moments, it is bliss that I want to melt into.

But heat is a sign of life, and life is a reminder of the death one of us must face.

I snatch my hands away. Having this conversation will be easier if I'm not simultaneously cozying up to the fire inside him.

"It's about the breath of life. There's something we didn't know."

His gaze falters almost imperceptibly, but I catch it all the same, eyes narrowing on him with harrowing understanding.

I take a step back. "You knew?"

His mouth forms a thin line. "Not until they handed it over, but I suspected."

"You did? But…how?"

A wry smile answers me. "It didn't take long to do the math. There was only one vial in the Dark Sea, one mention of the breath of life, one Primordial heart."

I stare at my hands, to the vial I'm clutching subconsciously.

"How long?" I blurt, a lump forming in my throat that I can't explain. "How long have you known?"

"Suspected," he clarifies with the raise of an eyebrow. "And since I became blighted and met your uncle Adrien. When he told me he believed there might be a remedy, I figured there was only one, otherwise we'd have heard of it before. People would've looked for it."

For months then; he's known for *months*. I should be furious, outraged. He's kept this from me all this time, and yet…all I feel is rapt appreciation. He knew that only one of us would see our way through this and he accompanied me anyway; he helped me when he could've instead let me die; he followed me into the Labyrinth to save my cousin, instead of marching forward on his own.

"You should take it," I say at last, yanking on the vial and snapping the leather cord around my neck. I offer it to him. "You've been blighted longer than I have, and there's time for me to find another way—"

He steps forward, close enough that I can smell the sea salt in his hair amid his usual scent of cedar. He grabs my hand and closes my fingers around the vial. "I will not take this from you, just as you will not take my chance at redemption away from me."

"Redemption? But for what…" Solemn realization hits me but a moment too late.

"Ahl'Ro is no longer here to atone for what he's done…for taking your family away from you… He was my responsibility though. I was supposed to watch over him and prevent him from causing anyone harm. Your parents' deaths, they're on my hands as much as they are on his. The cure is yours and it is my sworn duty to ensure you obtain it. It's the only way I can cleanse Ahl'Ro's name, and my conscience."

"You have nothing to atone for. Need I remind you, you saved me that day."

"I condemned you to the Shadow Crusade, a life where you were sworn to risk yourself every day to fight a futile battle with the demons, only to then be forced on the run."

"That wasn't your—"

"If I had stopped him sooner, if I had killed him before he'd turned, you wouldn't be here."

"You tried." My voice warbles, drowning in the tears I'm struggling to hold back.

He shakes his head. "Your sister and you would be safe in Arcathain, living out your long and contented lives."

And for some reason, it's that thought that makes me lose my restraint. I spent most of my time at the Castle of Nigh foolishly believing the same thing, but it's far from the truth. I had never been content a day in my life living in the Wallows of Gravenburg, the bleakest of pits, long before the Shadowthorn was at our borders. I had no purpose, no calling, and the only friend I thought I had, the only person who'd known me as long as any family ever could, abandoned me the moment he discovered my druid bloodline.

"You're wrong," I tell him, fists clenching at my sides as I steel myself for what needs to be said. "My life would've been short and harsh. If my parents weren't slaughtered in that demon scourge, they would've been in the next one, or the one after that, and I might've been home with them, utterly useless with a blade. You didn't rob me of my happiness, neither of you did."

Dark eyes set, he shakes his head. "It doesn't matter. I won't allow you to suffer any longer. The breath of life is yours. I want you to have it. Truthfully, I never thought I'd beat this curse anyway. Besides, you have family, a sister, an aunt, an uncle."

"What about you? What about them?" I gesture to the candlelit window in the hut beside us, to the father and son inside.

"They…already understand." His words come limpid, if not slightly abashed.

Understanding grows heavier in my chest, cleaving my heart in two. "They already know?"

"I told them just before you arrived."

Pacing the area, I turn my back to him to blink away my disgruntled tears with whatever privacy I can muster. "You knew I would come here and try to convince you to take it."

The fabric of his clothes ruffle and I can all but see him shrug. "You're not difficult to read, Halira. You might've felt like you had no strong convictions before all of this, that you had no purpose, but you are selfless without question. You'd put yourself before the sharp teeth of sirens just to protect your loved ones. You stormed back to the Labyrinth to save a man—practically a stranger—who was already condemned to death. You charged a behemoth monstrosity in an overrun town just on the off-chance that you might protect a friend long enough for him to escape."

My smile comes against my own volition, sad and contrite.

Ryven strides toward me. His hands find mine again, and my heart skitters to a halt. He gestures to the quiet hut beside us.

"My sacrifice will mean that Jiordan and Ceph, that my best friend will not carry the burden of his deeds with him to the afterlife. By making this right, I grant him and his family peace. That is *my* purpose, to see you through this so that I can make things right again."

Something dark and dense plummets from my chest to my stomach. "Is…that the only reason you're here then?"

I can't believe I'm so bold to ask him such a thing, but I can't stop myself. After everything we've been through, after all I've seen him risk for me, for this cure, I have to know.

His lips quirk and the knots in my stomach pull taut. He reaches up to brush my sea-crusted hair behind my ear. "Not since the day I saw you charge that demon in the catacombs. Your drive to protect the ones you love—even the ones who you barely know—is more than admirable, it's…it's…it subdues me. I searched for you to right the wrong that Ahl'Ro and I had caused you, but that's not why I've continued to follow you. You're like a hellebore—"

"A what?"

"A hellebore. Don't you have flowers where you're from?"

Grimacing, I recall the damp, stony streets and the thin, overcrowded roads. "Not really." And then realizing what he's saying, I cross my arms. "Are you calling me a flower?"

He chuckles. "The hellebore is the most tenacious and fierce flower you'll ever find. It blooms all through the snow of winter, even as the other buds wither and die. It stands against the harshest weather and defies all expectations of what *should* be.

"Just like the hellebore, you remind me what it means to fight for what's right, something that I'd almost forgotten when I lost Ahl'Ro."

My stubborn eyes soften, finally blinking up to meet his through my lashes. Like the pull of magnets, we draw nearer, the gravity between us too strong to fight any longer. I stare at his lips, at the chiseled jawline that has never looked quite so inviting, and a delicious stirring wells inside my belly. It burrows through my depths, both satiating and igniting a hunger I never even knew was alive in me. It's unlike anything I've ever felt before.

But it's that realization that brings about my guilt. I shouldn't be feeling anything for this man—this half-demon. I should be too devastated about losing Dimitri to even think about anyone else, let alone to marvel at the tick in their jaw, to wonder what their plump lips might taste like. If I had ever truly loved Dimitri, wouldn't it be impossible to rush so quickly in the arms of the next man who showed me even the slightest interest?

Through heavy lashes, I watch the shape of his mouth draw, and I'm not sure if he's the one leaning in or if it's me. His warm breath caresses my lips, and my stomach tugs, and I almost plummet with it.

My heart is racing. I thought I'd loved someone before—I thought *he'd* loved me, as well—only to find in the end that we'd both been wrong. At least, I think we were. Why else would this aching heat be building inside me every time I'm near this half-demon man? Why else would Dimitri have left me?

There might be a connection between Ryven and I now as we fight toward this common goal, but how long will that last? How long before one of us inevitably changes our minds, or learns something about one another that makes us decide that we were wrong?

Before our lips can brush, I turn away, severing whatever magnetic strings keep trying to pull us together, thereby ravaging my heart.

"I should get back to my sister and aunt," I say hoarsely. I left them abruptly and they'll be wondering how I'm doing and where I've gone."

Out of the corner of my eye, I see Ryven's hand reach out for me. It lingers there, suspended between want and duty, before he finally withdraws it.

"Rest well then, Halira. I will find you tomorrow to begin the final leg of our journey."

Before the bitter tears can work their way down my cheeks, I run away from the man who has made me feel more in one week than anyone has in my entire life.

When I open my eyes, my surroundings are so cheerful and calming that I rise without any care in the world. I relish the soft warmth of the blankets atop my skin. I admire the sun shining through the hollowed-out window in the tree bark wall beside me. But as I glance around the room, the memories come.

I tossed and turned all night long, never too far away from consciousness, even when I did finally submit. Something nagged at me though, a tiny, niggling thought that I could not rid myself of, no matter how hard I tried. At first, I'd mistaken it for confusion of the heart; I'd reasoned that my betrayal of Dimitri by my ever-growing feelings for Ryven had left me too addled for the quiet content that sleep requires.

But it was something more than that. Something that, even now, hours later, I still can't quite grasp.

It leaves my stomach unsettled, threatening to twist every time I even think about trying to get comfortable. Unable to go back to sleep—and desperate for some time alone before Kalli, Imryll, or Ryven awaken and want to talk about what needs to happen next—I retrieve my dried clothes from the rack outside, and get dressed. The sheath on my hip is noticeably light without Tor's dagger in it, the air seeming to pierce my skin as if there was a hole in my armor beneath. I know I don't need my axe as long as I'm inside the Eyve—not with the demons kept at bay by the barrier—but I secure it in its place on my back all the same, if only to feel some semblance of security.

Then, I wander out into the village.

In the early morning hours, few grace the streets with their presence just yet. Even most of the songbirds are still lost in slumber. I envy them all.

It's not long as I walk the climbing paths though, trailing my hand over the rope railing just to get a feel for the place, that I realize just how easily I could find myself living here. It's like my whole life I knew there was a part of me missing and I finally know where that part has been hiding.

As I climb and descend the walkways—making sure to stay away from the river or any body of water for that matter, for fear of growing gills or seeing the sirens too soon—I eventually find my way back toward the entrance, the same one Ryven and I came through.

Only, it wasn't just us who entered that day, and for all my desire to have some time alone, I realize we've left Alphonse on his own for far too long.

After a brief conversation with the sentinel, he grants me access to the dungeon, personally guiding me into the tree hollow and down into the cell block. It would seem my family ties to Imryll make me trustworthy, despite the sentinel hardly knowing me.

"I'll be up top, should you need me."

I give the man a swift, appreciative nod before turning toward the dark cell. Beyond the rails, there is only shadow and obscurity. The stone floor seemingly disappears into the abyss. Inching forward, I narrow my eyes through the slits and catch a hint of hazel eyes glowering back at me.

"Come to gloat?"

I stagger back, startled by the sudden rasp seemingly coming from nowhere. Beneath the harshness of the parched vocal cords, I hear it though, the familiar, adenoidal, aristocratic tautness.

"Alphonse," I say, guilt getting the best of me and softening my heart. "I'm not here to gloat. I—"

He strides forward into the torchlight. He's only been here a couple of days, I remind myself. The harsh angles of his cheekbones and chin, his thin frame, that's just a part of who he is—how he's always been. But the greasy shine to his hair, the shadows cast over his eyes, those are new.

"What is it then? Come to marvel at how the mighty have fallen? Or did you just come here to watch me rot?"

My hands ball into fists as I try to remain calm. "Neither. None of it. I came to see how you were doing."

Derision pulls back his lips in a sneer. "Oh, I'm doing splendid, as you can most certainly tell. Finest arrangements in all of Arcathain." His lips purse, opening slightly as if by surprise. "How could I forget. We're in the land of savages now, not Arcathain. Were it our homeland, the moment my father received word that his son had been imprisoned without having been read his rights or the charges, he would have all of the guards' heads, yours too for leaving me in this squalor like some filthy peasant."

All traces of the guilt and sorrow I felt for him fade away in an instant. "Get over yourself, Alphonse! What else should we have done? They had a bounty on your head before we even crossed the border. There was nothing we could do. Even if we *had* known, would you have preferred to have waited for us in the Shadowthorn? I'm sure you've heard the terrors that awaken out there after dark. You wouldn't have stood a chance."

More to himself than anything, he mutters, "I am the Magistrate's son…"

"Yeah, well, not here, you're not. So, I suggest you get used to it."

"*Get used to it?*" His eyes snap back to mine, greasy hair sliding around his face like wet snakes. "Haven't you spoken to your aunt about my being here? Shouldn't she be releasing me?"

I open my mouth but look away. "I…it's not so simple."

"Is it not?" he asks, coming even closer, face almost pressed against the bars. "It takes five minutes to have a conversation. We've been here days. Are you really so incapable that you couldn't even handle that—"

"She wasn't here when we arrived!"

My words echo throughout the dim hall, and this time it's Alphonse who steps backward, panic bright in his eyes.

"Well, where is she? When will she return?" Then, realizing the implications of my delayed arrival, he extends a pointed finger at me. "On second thought, I've been down here for days and you're only just now telling me this? What have you been doing all this time? Frolicking about the Forgotten Forest of Eyve with the other druids?"

I inhale deeply. "We weren't here either."

Finally, he stops speaking, stops scowling, at least, not with so much contempt. Alphonse assesses me through weary eyes, the flames from the torchlight casting the gaunt grooves of his face in greater shadow.

"You spoke with the Elders," he says at last. "They sent you after the cure."

My only response is a single curt nod. I don't want to think about the past day of events. I specifically left my aunt's home this morning to avoid having to think about it, about how I've been forced into the position of stealing Ryven's last chance at survival.

"Well?" Alphonse asks. "Are you cured, then?"

"No yet." My words come low and guttural, as harsh as I feel ragged.

His brow bunches. "Well, why not? Did you fail in whatever errand the druid Elders sent you on? Is that why you entered the dungeons with such a long face?"

"What? No. The Elders sent us to retrieve the breath of life."

One of his brows climbs his pale forehead. "The what?"

"Never mind that. It doesn't matter. What matters is that we succeeded." Reaching up to my neck, I wrap my fingers over the cool vial and hold it out for him to see. "We obtained it. The breath of life is ours."

"Then…" He draws out the syllable as if he's still thinking, trying to piece together what it all means. Until his expression turns sardonic. "That must mean you simply don't know how to enjoy a good victory."

"It's no victory when it can only save one of us…"

He tosses his head back. "Ahh, I see. And let me guess, you're trying to come to terms with which one of you deserves it more?"

"Ryven's already decided," I say, leaning my head against one of the iron bars when the rest of me becomes too heavy. "He won't take it. He's leaving the cure to me."

After a long stretch of silence, Alphonse snorts.

I twist my head toward him. "What?"

"Oh, it's nothing. I'm simply having déjà vu."

"Yes, because I've found myself in this exact predicament so many times: blighted, on the run, and with someone else's life in my hands."

"That's just it," Alphonse says, pushing off the bars and striding closer. "It's not in your hands at all. You are just as I remember you: the sniveling, weak cousin I never wanted. You were the one willing to let anyone walk all over you."

My jaw clenches.

"The one who passed through life without direction or cause."

"Stop it."

"The one who never dared fight back or take a stance on anything."

"I said stop!"

"No!" he shouts, his stagnant breath reaching my face. "Here I was, thinking you'd finally grown a backbone, that training with the Shadow Crusade might've done you some good, but the moment you face authority—the moment someone else tells you what to do—it's back to your old ways."

My jaw falls from my face. "You don't know what I've done. I faced a siren queen to retrieve this thing."

"Doesn't sound too challenging to me," he mutters.

"I saved you from the lunar hydra."

"I didn't need your saving."

"I traveled across the Shadowthorn—"

"So have countless others." He shrugs.

Breathless and seething, my rage becomes too great for me to contain. I scream, fire practically erupting from my lungs. I wish it would. I wish I'd incinerate his stupid, smug, condescending face right here, right now, and never have to endure another senseless conversation with him ever again.

When the air has all but left my lungs, he wipes his eye with a single finger. "Are you quite finished?"

My chest is still heaving, my thoughts still too covered in flames for me to dare reach for them.

"Wonderful. If you're done yelling at the person trying to

help you, then might I suggest clearing the hatred from your ears and listening. I'm saying that the Halira you were becoming refused to accept defeat. When faced with an impossible challenge, she did not cower and back down, but she charged headfirst. In Ashenvale, you did not run from the beast that had cornered Crusaders Maxwell and Saimenimus; you determined a strategy that would work and then you brought your foe down. When your training proved difficult, you dedicated yourself to the library's arsenal of knowledge to give you a leg up." Noticing my wary scowl, he clarifies. "I was instructed to keep a weathered eye on you, and so I did. I had spies watching you at every turn."

I crook a displeased eyebrow at him. "Spies like Fox."

Contemplative, he frowns. "Actually, no. Her duplicity was an unexpected turn of events. She volunteered for the honor."

Although I'd already been aware of her betrayal, at least to some extent, hearing it now is like taking a new knife to the heart. Fox had been one of my closest friends and allies while I'd been at the Castle of Nigh. Between she and Dimitri, I'd felt like I had some semblance of a family again. Oh, how wrong I'd been about both of them.

"Why?" I growl the word more than ask it, well aware that we've veered so far from our initial topic, that I hardly even remember the original point anymore. But I don't care. I've been able to accept a lot about that dreadful day—my banishment, my powers, the loss of my best friend—but there was still one unanswered question that kept me up at night.

"Why?" I ask again, my voice as thick as stone.

Alphonse examines his cuticles, grimacing at the grime he finds there. He only glances at me once. "We were…involved. For a time, it was nothing more than that. A mere distraction from the grim and tireless days. But she soon discovered I had been keeping an eye on you. Prior to that, we'd been discussing ways to ensure that she remained at the castle with me after initiation, when she suggested that she be rewarded for providing me with the proof my father had been waiting for."

There's so much about what he's saying that catches me off guard, but I manage to stay focused on what matters. "Proof?"

"Your magic."

"Oh, right…" I turn away, but it's short-lived when another thought occurs to me. "How did he know though? *I* didn't even know. Not fully, anyway."

"He always suspected. He wouldn't say why."

Gnawing on my lip, I start flipping through the chapters of my life. My father never much cared for Esmond, as he never much cared for my mother. Perhaps he suspected her, as well. My parents kept my mother's upbringing in the Eyve secret—as did most druids, I'm guessing, judging from the lack of knowledge Arcathainians have about them—but maybe Esmond knew. Maybe it's why he gave Kalli her seat at the Senate, to keep an even closer eye on our family?

Alphonse sighs dramatically, tugging me away from my past. "Now that you've thoroughly made me lose my train of thought, can we get back to the matter at hand: your strategy."

"My what?"

He throws his head back and groans. "Must I spell everything out for you—never mind. Clearly, I must." He pinches the brim of his nose. "Well, let's start from the beginning. Two weeks ago, none of us knew that such a thing as a druid existed. We certainly didn't know that their blood contained a mild immunity to demon toxin, and up until a day ago, we hadn't been certain a cure was even possible."

"Your point?" I ask, even though I sense him reaching. Mostly, I just like seeing him scowl.

"All of those things, we believed them impossible. But it was you who proved them otherwise." He waves a hand toward the door and to the Eyve behind it. "These people, these *druids*, they say there's only one cure. However, who's to say they alone have all the answers?"

Frowning, I answer the question despite knowing it's rhetorical. "The Elders say so. They seem to be revered and wildly knowledgeable."

"Yes, well, and the Magistrate seemed to be all-powerful while we were in Arcathain, and yet here his bastard son is, trapped behind bars."

I begin biting my lip again, trying to distract myself from the treacherously hopeful thought he's planted in my head. But once the seed of doubt sprouts into wonder, there's no stopping it. Alphonse is right: I don't cow down when the people I care about are in danger. I am a fighter; I listen to my gut. And if there is even the slightest chance that Ryven could survive, then I *will* find it.

A smirk climbs up my face.

"What?" he asks, suddenly seeming worried. "What are you doing?

I laugh. "It's called a smile."

"Yes, but, why are doing it?"

Shaking my head, I sigh, surprised by the gratitude welling in my chest. "Because that was actually helpful, Alphonse, and I really appreciate it."

He's frozen for a moment, taken aback by my kindness as much as I am. But then he straightens, holding his head up high as if even he is no longer aware that he's standing behind bars clad in skunky clothes that haven't been washed in days.

"Yes, well, I've been known to have a good idea or two."

"I'll be sure to keep that in mind," I say, returning my thoughts to what I should do next. Where would I even begin? Arcathainians don't even know about druids, let alone have I ever heard whispers of a cure, so even if they weren't all the way on the other side of the Shadowthorn, talking to them would be useless. Ryven said the druids don't know much about the realm outside of the Eyve, but if the Elders were aware of a cure, maybe someone else was too. So much of common knowledge is passed down from family to family, or studied—

My eyes brighten. "The druids may have a library."

Confused skepticism wrinkles his brow. "Bully for them?"

"The answers you're saying I should seek, maybe I can find them there, buried in long forgotten histories like I did back at Nigh."

He shrugs, black leather creasing at his shoulders. "It's worth a try."

Wasting not another moment, I spin on my heels and spring up the stairs.

"Hey! When will you be back?" he shouts after me. The hint of concern in his tone is actually endearing.

"I don't know!" I yell over my shoulders, taking the steps in bounding strides. "A few hours."

"A few hours!" Behind me, he grips the bars and rattles them with all his might. It's not very effective, further proof of just how difficult it would've been to try to break him free. "And what am I supposed to do until then? You can't just leave me here again!"

"I won't! I'll tell my aunt to come see you."

And just like that, I race from the building, closing the door on his hollering and profanities.

"Great. You've riled him up," the sentinel says. When he notices my haste, he raises a bushy eyebrow at me. "Is everything all right? Is there anything I can do?"

"Yes, I'm fine." I don't plan on stopping, until his offer strikes me. "Actually, there is. Can you tell me where I might find your library?"

I slam another book shut, a plume of dust rising from its useless existence. Growling, I slide it across the table to crash into the others, grabbing the next on the pile I've hastily gathered of some of the more ancient-looking tomes.

The next book I flip through talks about the creation of the realm at the hands of the four original Enchantresses. Each possessed control over one element: earth, wind, water, and fire. Judging from the descriptions, I start to wonder if the Enchanters were druids, given that the powers mentioned are gifts I have witnessed Imryll and the Elders use: summoning vines and tree roots; communing with animals; controlling the wind and breezes.

I even start to wonder if the sirens were once druids, given that the book describes the Enchanter of water being able to adapt to an aquatic lifestyle; they could breathe underwater, control the tides, they even developed an agility while swimming that was akin to the grace of dolphins. Perhaps one day some of the water druids went into the sea and simply never returned to land.

But it's the Enchanter of fire that I find the most fascinating. Their power, though it included mighty blasts of flame and lava, wasn't limited to only those things. Theirs was a power of great destruction, chaos, and evil to balance out the life that the Enchanter of earth could create.

Skimming ahead, I find proof of my suspicions. The book says that the Enchanters are believed to have been the first Elders, and that as long as one from each line lives, they pass their magic on to every druid alive. The same chapter also details the ascension of the Elder bloodline and I learn that it's more than just a title; once a new Elder rises, they not only inherit a surplus of power in exchange for all other forms of their magic, but she would also inherit the wisdom of all the Elders who came before her.

Imagining Kalli with even an even sharper mind chills my bones, but fortunately I have other more pressing matters to consider. It isn't the first time I consider returning to the Elders now and demanding they tell me everything they know about blighted druids. I'm sure there is something they're leaving out, some possibility or fact that they didn't deign to tell Ryven and I because we hadn't asked the correct questions.

Without Ryven to fly me to the top of the canopy though, it would take more time than I want to waste. By now, Imryll and Kalli have surely noted my absence, maybe the half-demon as well. They'll be searching for me, intent on leaving as soon as they find me, and if any of them know me at all, the Elders will be the first place they visit. Considering how tucked away this keep is, it might be hours before any of them think to search for me here. Hopefully, that will be enough time for me to find another solution.

Before I can even get halfway through the book, I slam this one closed too. As interesting as it is to learn about the dawn of time, there are more important matters I must attend to, and if all goes as planned, I'll have time to read these books in greater detail later.

I flip through the next tome with hardly more than a glance after gleaning from the title that the book is about healing spells. The next two volumes I grab are equally disappointing, one of which details every single Elder to ever assume the role, the other outlining the history of tension between the druids and the mages, and the countless ways in which they'd wronged each other.

It's not the first time I've considered what the mages might know either, but the mere thought blisters my skin and boils me from the inside out. The mages can't be trusted. I might've been raised with the inaccurate belief that all magic is evil, but I know in my heart that the mages are. No being—magical or otherwise—would fracture a continent with no regard for the people who fell through the fault lines, no regard for those they left behind to be devoured by demons.

The next book I grab doesn't strike me as relevant, but the title is too vague to tell from first glance: *The Edge of Eyve: Beyond the Wall of the Shadowthorn.*

I skim through the chapter headings, quickly forming a sense that this ledger details the architectural advancement and growth of the Eyve after the wall was constructed. There are sections devoted to how the druids came to understand the spells the mages cast on the wall, how they broke through it with the Primordial's help, and the magical enchantment they placed on the wall once it fell to ensure no one without druid blood could enter.

And just when I think the musty pages beneath my scanning fingers will prove as meaningless as all the others, I see it.

"And though the wall had once stood as a symbol for hatred, isolation, and captivity, druidkind soon adapted the understanding that the wall was their own. The border may have kept them from the rest of the realm, but it kept the rest of the realm from the Eyve in kind. The structure itself had been designed and erected by the Arcathainians, and as such, it bore their dreary aesthetic. Gray stone and mortar had no place in the charming forests of the Eyve, but the druids knew better than to tear down the fortitude it provided. Instead, they made the stone into works of art, covering it in vibrant colors that would help them to admire and remember where they'd come from."

My head lifts from the pages, my eyes dancing. "They painted a mural on it."

I keep reading, devouring the pages as quickly as I turn them. The druids decided to use the wall to document some of their greatest achievements, as well as their failures. The volume at my fingertips doesn't even begin to elude to them all, but judging from what's left unspoken, I can tell that some of the histories and knowledge here will only be found on those walls.

Leaving the books where they lay, I peel out of the keep and head back toward the entrance—it seems as good a place as any to start. The entire way back I keep asking myself how I could've missed such a thing before. Large paintings that span an entire enclosure seem like the sort of thing that would not go unnoticed, but truthfully, I can hardly even remember the Arcathainian stonework, let alone the brush-strokes atop it.

When I reach the entrance again, I'm reminded why. There isn't much of the stone left to see, at least, not buried beneath the impenetrable heaps of ivy, wisteria, and honeysuckle. They scour the towering walls almost as high as the border itself.

"Back so soon?" the sentinel asks, his wide stature giving him the slightest hobble as he makes his way toward me. He crosses his arms. "Tell me, what is it that's forced your return? Surely, you haven't come to plead that man be released."

It takes me a moment to make sense of what he's saying. "Oh, Alphonse? No. You've made it clear that only Imryll can release him, and hopefully she will soon, now that she's returned." With a bob of my jaw, I point to the climbing vines ahead, and the wall I know is buried somewhere beneath. "I came for that."

His stoic face doesn't change much other than taking on a slightly more displeased look. "The wall."

"Yes. Can you...you are a druid, yes?" Realizing how stupid I sound, asking someone within the boundaries of the Eyve whether they're a druid or not, I shake my head before he can answer me. "Can you do things like commanding nature? You know, making the trees move, or—"

"Or manipulating the vines covering the wall?"

I grimace. "If it's not too much to ask. I'm told there's a mural beneath, one that might have answers that Ryven and I need to heal the darkness festering inside us." Seeing his unamused expression, I change tactics. This man has no relation to me and therefore no concern for my life or happiness. But I'm not the only one implicated in this. "Please, I know you care about Ryven; I could tell the day we met. The Elders said there is but one way to save him, but he won't allow himself the option. He believes he doesn't deserve it because it would take that chance away from me… Seeing what's beneath those vines, what the older generations of druidkind wrote on that wall, might be the only way to save him now. Will you help me?"

The stout man grunts, a sound of neither displeasure or content, but he flicks his thick wrist and I watch in awe as the vines start untangling themselves before my eyes. I step forward, slowly, almost as if I was moving by the will of the wind or some other unseen entity. The first scenes of the mural appear. They're not as vibrant as I'd expected, but then again I have no way of knowing how many hundreds of years old they are.

My fingers graze the designs, the images of people and elements and trees. Each one is carved into the stone, the grooves filled with something amber that has long since hardened.

Farther down the wall, the sentinel's magic continues to go about its work, peeling back in layer after layer to reveal dozens upon dozens of drawings. There are too many stories to count; recountings of the first winter solstice that the druids spent here; of the informal peace treaty they formed with the Primordial Qaeus; of the way in which the Eyve grew, thriving with each new hut they built.

Before the vines had been torn away, I would've never guessed, never even considered, that so much rich history would be hidden beneath. The overgrowth had been too thick, too pervasive.

"What have you done?"

Like a deer startling to the sound of a snapping twig, I spin around. Ryven stands behind me in the clearing, eyes wide as he takes in the magic at work and what the vines have kept concealed all this time.

My mouth moves, but no sound comes out. I can't figure out what it is I should say. He should already know what I'm doing: I'm looking for answers, for a way out of this mess that doesn't end with one of us dead. Or worse: wreaking havoc on unsuspecting innocents.

"What are you doing?"

There's tempered rage in the undertones of his voice, an anger I don't quite understand. Nor one I'm inclined to accept.

"I was trying to find answers. I searched the books in the keep, hoping to find someone's journal collection, a note, anything that might tell us something more! But none of them did, except the one that led me here."

"An answer to what?"

I watch him, incredulous. "The answer to saving us both. I'm not going to just let you sacrifice yourself, and I don't exactly want to die either."

Turning my back to him, I continue tracing my hands over the sketches, symbols, and markings, making the most sense of the simple drawings as I can. When my fingers graze over a dark shadow etched into the stone, the scribble wild and mad, the creature larger than I am standing, I recoil my hand to my chest. I've never seen a Primordial before, but I recognize it all the same. It exudes power, dominance, evil, even as a mere painting on a wall.

The picture shows a gathering of people circled together and clasping hands. I recognize them as druids by the markings that accompany them, a small ball riding atop a whisp that resembles wind. The Primordials stand in the center of their circle, all four taller than even the trees depicted in the scene.

Beneath them is a dark chasm that stretches down, deep into the ground. Tiny symbols are carved into the pit, runic figures for which I do not know the meaning, nor have I seen anywhere before.

Ryven comes closer, his mouth a taut line as he examines the wall before us. "That's the Pits of Bagamore."

It's a name I've only heard a few times in my life, a faraway place I don't know much about since our continent was shattered from Illashore, but I've heard mention of it recently, so it rings a striking bell. "Isn't that where the Elders said the other Primordial weapon was located?"

Mutely, he nods.

"What is this story?" I ask him, eyes roving the black smeared over the Primordials' bodies. "What are the druids doing here? Why were they at the Pits of Bagamore?"

"I don't know," he growls, his frustration palpable. "I've never been taught this story. These walls have been covered for generations. I don't think anyone's seen what's underneath in years, before today."

"But why? *This* looks important, like the sort of piece of history you wouldn't want disappearing."

He shakes his shaggy head of hair. "I know, but our people decided long ago to live like the past never happened. After we were shunned from the rest of the world, the Elders of the time eventually decided to shun the world from us. To our people, humans, mages, they practically don't even exist."

My curious gaze lingers on the Primordials' bodies a moment longer before I realize how much time I've already wasted, and what Ryven's presence here means. They're looking for me—they *found* me—which means I have even less time than I'd hoped for.

Shaking away any lingering curiosities, I storm away from this peculiar and alarming scene and continue my examination of the wall, searching for anything that might look half-demon.

"Stop," Ryven pleads, his voice fatigued and spent. "I understand why you've come here. I should've known you wouldn't have been able to drop this."

"Drop this? *This* isn't some petulant squabble. This is about your life—*our* lives. I'm not just going to let you die, and if you didn't know that about me already then—"

Sighing heavily, Ryven catches my arm, gently spinning me away from the wall to look at him. He clasps my shoulders when I start to twist away. "Please. The vines will still be there in a few minutes, just…let me say what I want to say."

Begrudgingly, I still, my heart betraying me with its frantic pounding that I am actually interested in hearing what he has to say.

"Speak then." I fix my words with the same cold ice I've heard Kalli use hundreds of times, the one that often forces people to put distance between them, rather than seeking her further.

Ryven does no such running though. If anything, he moves closer, his russet eyes set on mine, his dark horns gleaming in the early morning light. "I wanted to confess that…I thought about visiting your aunt's last night while you slept. I feared that if you didn't take the breath of life soon, you'd find a way to selflessly and recklessly force it upon me instead, and I didn't want to risk that. I didn't want to be the one to live while you died."

I fold my arms over my chest. Although the thought had crossed my mind to do just that—to slip him the breath of life in his breakfast or in a sip of water—ultimately, I couldn't bring myself to do it. Not because I was too selfish or too afraid of my own death, but because I could see the pain in his face when he found out, the pain I'd force him to live with.

"It occurred to me," he continues. "That if I could steal it from you in the middle of the night, what would stop me from taking it for myself? In fact, that should've been my first thought. My *only* thought. Any intelligent, dying creature *should* be concerned for their demise."

I don't know what he's saying, and I frown as he reaches up for the vial hanging from my neck. He twirls it between his fingers for a moment, before grabbing my hand and bringing it to clutch the jar.

"That's the thing, though. My survival means nothing if it dooms you. Penance be damned. Ahl'Ro's soul be damned. I lied last night. I'm not doing this for him, for his family. I'm doing this for you, because I want you to live."

My chest cracks in half with simultaneous heartbreak and yearning, two warring sides of a complex coin that I still struggle to come to terms with. With Dimitri, it had been different. My feelings for him had been spurred by the fear of our short existence and not being able to live our lives to the fullest. Being with him had stifled the loneliness, but it had never quite quenched the hollow pit in my stomach that had haunted me all my life, the senseless meaning of all of *this* that I could never quite appreciate enough.

But with Ryven, things aren't like that at all. He makes me feel alive in ways that Dimitri never could. Instead of second-guessing me or trying to mold me to the way of the world, Ryven sees me for who I am and he stokes the fire of my soul, trying to keep me burning as the darkness of the world attempts to snuff me out. I'm not drawn to him because of some reckless whim, or to satiate the pain of a short and lonely existence, but rather for the life that could come after all of this.

Where I once had accepted that Dimitri's and my life would come to an abrupt end, I ache at the thought that my time with Ryven could ever be cut short, that we could miss out on so many of the opportunities that could be in store for us, even if none of them are certain.

"And what about me?" I say, letting the vial fall from my hands, the leather cord catching it at my chest. "I want you to live too. We don't know if this is the only way, but there is still time to find an alternative for me—"

"And what if there's isn't? What if this is the only answer and your time is ticking? You can't ask me to willingly take away your only assured chance to live."

I cross my arms again. "And yet you can ask the same of me?"

He opens his mouth to protest, but no more than a hiss comes out. His expression grows grim. "I didn't want to tell you."

Concern tightens my chest. "Tell me what?"

Another sigh. Ryven tilts his head so low to the ground that I can hardly even see his face. "I fear that it is too late for me. The blight has taken root too deep in my blood to be stopped. I feel...different already. Ever since I lost touch with my magic."

"That's all the more reason for you to take the breath of life. I don't feel different yet. I still have time to find another way for me—"

"I'm not doing that to you!" he roars, baring his teeth in a blind rage. They seem more like fangs than I remember them being. Just as quickly as the rage comes, it disappears behind his hand as he rubs his face, ashamed. "Only one of us has a chance to survive this and it's not me. Please—" He takes the vial between his fingers once more. His thumb rests danger-ously on the edge of the cork, the bottle brushing my lip. "Breathe in the breath of life and do it before we leave the Eyve.

This treasure was being guarded for a reason, and you'll be safer with it inside you."

I shake my head. "No. Now more than ever, you should be the one to have it."

Growling, Ryven throws out his arms. He paces away on thunderous steps and hooks a hand on either hip. The look on his face worries me more than anything I've ever felt. The silent calculating occurring behind his dark eyes is dangerous, but just as I'm about to ask him what he's thinking, his wings burst wide from his back and carry him straight into the sky.

"Ryven, no!"

I know what he's doing before he's even disappeared; I understand the finality of his decision.

If I won't do what he's asking of me, then he's removing himself from the equation.

I will never see Ryven again.

"What's his problem?" Kalli's voice is harsher than usual against my tender heart.

I don't answer her; I don't even look her way. My eyes are fixed on the black dot in the sky that keeps growing smaller, desperate for him to turn around and return. I know there has to be a way to save us both, but I can't do anything for him if he's not here with me.

"He's gone," Imryll answers for me, void of any ounce of empathy or remorse. "It appears as though he's left the breath of life in Halira's hands."

Kalli scoffs, mumbling, "As if he had a choice."

Hot tears trickle down my cheeks, burning my skin. My aunt veers in the opposite direction, and I become faintly aware that she's headed for the dungeons. I'm sure Alphonse will be his version of elated to see her, but I can't be bothered to feel any joy for him about it. Part of me fears I won't ever feel joy again. How can I, knowing a man I've come to care for will soon be nothing more than a ravenous demon, while I'm left to live out the rest of my privileged days in the most enchanting place I've ever known?

The gust of wind that blows around us cools my tears, turning them into sticky scars of a cruel world and unfair decision. But what I mistake for a simple breeze is clearly something more. Kalli's spine straightens. Her lupine features become primal as she stretches to see over me and toward the break in the wall where Qaeus busted through.

"What is it?" I ask, but Kalli tempers my concern with a wave of her hand.

The sentinel charges the entrance, spear drawn, as Kalli slinks toward the wall, motioning for me to get down and do the same. I join her without question, hugging the freshly cleared wall and inching toward the entrance. Her gaze only falters once to the mural exposed beside us, but despite her intrigue, she remains focused on the presumed threat approaching from the Shadowthorn. Surely, it can't be too frightening though. The boundary of magic here prevents anyone without druid blood from crossing, so if there are demons—or even Qaeus herself—on the other side of this thick wall, it won't matter. They cannot get through.

Or at least, that's what I've been told.

Doubt sinks into my stomach as voices grow nearer from outside.

A man's—not a demon's—face is the first to come into focus. "Ah-ha! Here it is! I told you we'd find the border if we just kept heading east."

"You told us it was a shot in the dark," a smoky female voice answers.

"Yes, well, it was that too."

And with sudden recognition, now it's my back that straightens.

"Halira," Kalli warns, reaching for my wrist as I tiptoe past her.

I shrug out of her grip, rounding the corner with an expression of sheer awe when I lay eyes upon the group of familiar travelers waiting on the other side.

"It's Uncle Adrien," I say, smiling over my shoulder. "And he's brought friends."

UNEXPECTED VISITORS

THE WALL, SHADOWTHORN

"Ha!" Adrien exclaims, hobbling forward with one arm outstretched, and the other cradling his side. I scan his tunic for blood—red or black—but find none. "Well, I'll be blighted," he hisses with each step. "You're still alive."

Before I can warn him not to come any closer, let alone snap at him for thinking I wouldn't have made it, his nose smacks straight against the invisible barrier between us. He staggers backward, nursing another injury with a wry smile.

"Ow," he says, rubbing his tender nose.

As I cross the boundary to fling my arms around his neck, nearly toppling him over because of the leg he's trying not to put any weigh on, I spy Silver behind him, donned in a long, slate-gray dress, the collar rimmed with white wolf fur. She nods once, the gesture one of relief as much as it is one of greeting. Güthric stands beside her, his stance wide, weapon in hand, but his crooked, toothy grin ruins any hope for menace he might've been aiming for as he approached the druid world.

Sai is with them too, rolling his eyes at my uncle as he bounds for me.

"What are you guys doing here?" I ask my uncle.

Clasping my shoulders, he steps back. "Translation, anyone?"

Kalli steps out from where we'd been crouching on the other side of the wall. "She asked what you're doing here. You've come a long way, and I'd guess that there is an unpleasant reason why."

His expression wilts. He releases my shoulders to stand on his own, and quickly winces at the weight on his leg again. "I'm fine, I'm fine," he assures Sai who rushes to his aid. "I'm afraid we come bearing terrible news. The Wardens were attacked. The Crusaders came and destroyed everything. I have one of them to thank for this—" he gestures to the hip he keeps favoring.

"They what?" I breathe, still reeling from the news.

The Crusaders don't attack people. They're trained for fighting demons, for slaying Qaeus. What reason would they have to risk their lives by venturing into the Shadowthorn just to attack the Wardens?

Kalli, however, seems unfazed. "I'm not surprised. The Magistrate has his faults, and he may feel disdain for his bastard son, but family is family." She looks pointedly at me as she says, "And family would go to great lengths to their protect blood."

If I wasn't so moved by the sentiment, I might've scoffed at the suggestion that the Magistrate would risk so much for Alphonse. The idea that Esmond cares about anyone but himself is ludicrous, especially coming from Kalli, one of the two blood-relatives that he recently tried executing not that long ago.

But her skewed perceptions of the man who used to be her superior are the least startling thing about what she's suggesting.

"The Magistrate came for Alphonse?" I ask. "But...he thought he was dead. Not to mention, Esmond was heading back to the Capital."

Even if Adrien could understand me, he's too buried in his memories to hear me. As Imryll comes to his aid to assess his bum leg, he mutters, "Everything we built…everything your sister built…it's all gone."

I turn back to my sister. "It doesn't make sense. The Crusaders, the Magistrate, they thought Alphonse was dead. Why would they have come looking for a dead man?"

Unexpectedly, Alphonse's arrogant voice rises from the Eyve-side of the wall. "Even if he *did* believe I'd perished, my father would've sent a unit to retrieve my body. Valuable necro-ink cannot be sacrificed," he says dryly. "If he caught wind that his fugitive brother had somehow been involved in my end, well, it's unlikely his orders would've been anything but search and destroy once they found the Wardens faction."

Gritting his teeth so loudly I can hear it from across the clearing, Sai lunges for Alphonse's smug face. "This is all your fault!" He clips him across the shoulder, taking him down to the ground with a resounding thud. Gripping the collar of Alphonse's tunic with one hand, Sai's free fist collides with his face. "If you had just let them go! You didn't care about any of us! You could've just let the three of them go without hunting them down like a pack of demons!"

Adrien scrambles after him, hobbling out of Imryll's capable hands and catching Sai's arm mid-swing before pinning it behind his back. He drags Sai off my cousin, and the man mostly goes willingly.

Alphonse crawls out from under him like a frightened rat running away from a raging fire.

He pats his nose, finds blood dribbling down his lip, and wildfire ignites in his eyes. "I am your general! You will show me some respect—"

"You are *no one!*" Sai yells, his chest heaving from how long he's been holding that in. "You left me to die in Ashenvale. You left me and you never looked back."

I cringe at the memory, at the careless way Alphonse had swatted his hand in the air when asked if the Crusaders should retrieve his body.

"It's not worth the effort or time it would take, what with demons having already arrived."

Alphonse's lips purse into a thin line, his jaw swiveling as indignant thoughts tell him he was in the right.

"If it hadn't been for Adrien and his Wardens, I would've been demon food."

Adrien releases Sai once he's calmed down, patting his shoulder a few times before giving it a reassuring squeeze. "What's done is done. It took some convincing, but we finally got the Crusaders to believe that we did not have Alphonse's body."

"Then why are you here?" Imryll asks, her question sounding more like an interrogation than any act of concern or curiosity. "Why have you brought your humans here, knowing that they could not enter?"

"They left us no choice. They destroyed our home, and the bloodshed beckoned the demons to take care of the rest. This was the only place we could think to go."

"Were you followed?"

Adrien rolls his eyes at my aunt. "No, we weren't followed. What kind of fool do you take me for?"

She levels him with a look.

Sai looks between the two of them before donning a placating grin. "We weren't followed. Honest. Once the Crusaders were finished attacking, they left."

"They left?" This time it's Kalli that becomes interrogative, but she, more than anyone, has the right to be. She's worked under the Magistrate for years now. If anyone should be suspicious about his decisions or the way he delegates, it would be her, for she knows his tactics inside and out.

Sai shrugs, utterly unaware that my sister's alarm should be cause for his own. "Yeah, they just left. Their commander drew them back and they started marching deeper into the Shadowthorn. They practically trampled over us on their way out."

My watchful gaze turns back to my sister and to the clutched hand pressed to her bottom lip. "What do you think it means?"

"I don't know what it means," she snaps. "But an attacking and winning unit does not fall back. They strike harder. And if they came for Alphonse's body, why leave without it? They must've found something else to placate them."

Frowning, I examine my cousin from head to toe. He's still wearing the same black leathers he's always worn, the same boots. The only thing he didn't bring with him before following me into the Shadowthorn was—

"He had a sword on him the day we fled Arcathain. I think he left it at the Warden's camp. Maybe that's what they found?"

Kalli shakes her head. "No. The Crusaders took his sword back with them the day they thought he died. Even then, something isn't adding up. If they found something that proved he'd been with the Wardens, or perhaps even proved he was alive, why go deeper into the Shadowthorn? Again, why leave at all if they believed he was being kept there? They must've found something else, something that was more important or more valuable than retrieving him."

There's a mouselike quality to my uncle as Kalli speaks, and when she notices it too, it only worsens. His expression turns apologetic and he holds one finger up. "Actually, there might've been something. It's the same thing the Crusaders have always wanted."

With shattering realization, I answer for him. "To find and kill Qaeus."

"If you said what I think you likely did, then yes. They must've found our maps, but even with them, they wouldn't be able to find her. The area surrounding Qaeus' heart is dense, impenetrable. It took us months to create a map of the weak points of entry to get close enough just to see the heart behind the wards. Even then, the heart is well-guarded, by demons and magic alike. They won't be able to reach it. Not without great loss."

Imryll's disbelief is palpable, even before she charges into a sprint and leaps into the air. Black feathers sprout from her skin, her body contorting and shrinking to the size and shape of a raven in the same time it takes to blink. She circles overhead once, twice, before diving to the ground, shifting back into her human form at the same time she takes a knee by the pile of clothes left in the wake of her transition.

"What did you see?" Kalli asks.

My aunt slips into her silken gown, flicking her silver hair from beneath the collar before shooting a finger out at Adrien. "You fool! Did it not occur to you to check for a tail?"

"I—I—no. It couldn't be. We weren't followed. The Crusaders kept going south when we veered east. If they're going after Qaeus, they'd have no reason to follow—"

"I see no demon blood gleaming on your weapons," Imryll says pointedly, cinching the corset at her waist. "And yet, I spotted at least three fresh demon corpses not a mile from here."

Adrien exchanges a worried look with Sai, then the others. I scan the black forest before us, searching for any of the new dangers we know might be lurking there now. But I find no signs of movement, no distress or ruffling of the trees. There's little solace to be had in knowing that just behind me lies a magical barrier that only a few of us would be able to cross. If we are overwhelmed, I could simply slip back over the border, but none of the Crusaders would be able to follow, unless they had druid lineage as well—which I doubt they do.

I draw my battle-axe, fingers sliding into their position around the hilt and tightening around the grooves.

"Did you see them?" Kalli asks. "The Crusaders. Are they near or do we have time to prepare?"

"I saw no one. Only the demon bodies. They must be spread out and traveling beneath the cover of the trees."

Kalli nods, but the assumption doesn't sit well with me.

"That's not how Crusaders move through the Shadowthorn," I say, aware that only my family can understand what I'm saying right now, and two of three of them have little knowledge of the innerworkings of the Crusaders. "We're trained to stay together, to attack as one, not to branch out."

"It's not demons they're hunting today, Halira," my sister reminds.

"It doesn't matter. You don't know them like I do. *Of one country, of one blood.* They stand together. They fight together. They wouldn't spread out as you're suggesting. Most of them aren't even aware that druids exist, so they wouldn't know they're coming up on an entire community of people, so what reason would they have to remain stealthy?"

"Halira's right."

Alphonse startles everyone, me most of all, as he strides to my side. With his hands clasped behind his back, he gives me a respectful nod before turning his attention to the other members of our family. "To my knowledge, none within the Magistrate's employ know of the druids. If word reached him of your magic, they'd simply think you mages. That's what they believed Halira and Kalli to be.

"Furthermore, no Crusader would ever willingly break from their ranks. They are stronger as a unit. It's one of the reasons we train as a group and emphasize their unity within their divisions."

"Not to point out the obvious," Kalli says, glaring in my direction. "But my sister was one of your recruits, yes? Yet didn't she venture into the Shadowthorn alone hardly a week ago?"

"She did," Alphonse responds. He turns to me, something curious about his expression. "She left because she had set out on a mission, heedless and with blatant disregard of anything we ever tried teaching her." When he turns to me, I think I see the faintest amount of reverence twinkle behind his derisive glare.

Suddenly, with almost imperceptible speed, he shakes his head, frown deepening.

"What is it? What are you thinking?" I ask.

"It might be nothing, but…it's just—The entire *unit* might not disperse as you're suggesting, Imryll. But a rogue Crusader might, one a mission to do what they believed was right and necessary, like Halira did. Someone like that might venture off on their own."

Every Crusader's face is analyzed in my head. Maxwell would never be caught dead doing something so rash, not to mention in direct violation of any order to stay within the unit. As much as I'd like to believe Dimitri would follow me to such great lengths, he, too, doesn't have a single rebellious bone in his body. His mission is his duty to his country, his oath to the Crusaders. Eparah—it's been so long since I've thought about Eparah—given her role as a leader, she'd be unable to break away on her own. The entire unit would follow her if she chose to come after us, but I don't think she has the motive to.

There were others from different units as well, names and fractured faces, but none seem to fit the reckless diligence and drive Alphonse is describing.

Bones crack from Güthric's neck when he cocks his head back and forth. He squares off to the Shadowthorn, pounding his fist into his palm. "Whoever comes. We win. We are many. They are one."

Biting my lip, I look to my sister, my doubt reflected in her gray eyes. Again, I find myself thinking about every Crusader I've known, even the ones Tor trained with whom we met during his initiation. None are so terrifying that I'd be afraid to face them alone, especially not with so many other friends backing me now, but something doesn't sit right with me. This person, whoever they are, is reckless, and that alone makes them dangerous. I know I'm one to talk, but that's precisely why I'm well aware of the havoc one bullheaded fool can make.

Fortunately, I don't have to rack my brain for long, because just as I'm starting to recall someone who embodies the heedless characteristics Alphonse described, a battle cry screeches from the trees, and bright auburn hair flashes through the darkness.

$\mathcal{A}$ wild and rageful woman flings herself from the edge of the woods like a blazing ball of fire. Red hair flicks around her face like angry flames, her blue eyes set in coal. Saber drawn, Fox charges, snarling and roaring, her gaze set on me with deadly intent.

I barely have time to blink, barely have time to even register who she is, why she's here, and what she plans on doing before my old friend tackles me.

"You killed him!" she bellows, our bodies tumbling and crashing against each other as we squirm and twist and shove and kick. "He sheltered you, he trained you, and you killed him!"

After blocking her first few swings, her small fist finally collides with my jaw. The pain lances up to my ear, making it difficult to hear and easy for disorientation to settle in. It takes me a moment to realize Fox is straddling me. I'm pinned me to the ground, her lethal fingers grasping for my throat.

"I didn't...kill...anyone" I manage to rasp through her vise-like grip on my throat, completely forgetting that my words will hold no bearing over her because she can't understand me.

The person closest to us—Adrien—grabs her arms to yank her off me, but she swings her skull back. His nose cracks and he staggers to the ground with a painful thud that likely only make his hip worse. A fountain of red spews down his face as he curses.

"He…lives…" I croak, again not even thinking how futile it is. The pressure builds behind my cheeks, my eyes, my skull, and I'm desperate for it to end. For her to release me.

"I can't hear you," she spews, teeth clenched, nothing but dark hatred seething from her once bright eyes.

Kalli comes next, charging the woman atop me with wild resolve, like a cat thrown into a lake and scrambling for the nearest ledge. But despite her anger, she lacks the knowledge and skill. With her arms outstretched, she races toward Fox, and I'm unsure what she planned to do, but my old friend—my former roommate, my fellow Crusader—twists from where she sits, grabbing Kalli's arm and flinging her forward in one fluid motion. My sister thuds to her back on the ground beside me, the breath whooshing from her lungs.

Finally, Güthric lumbers toward us. His booming steps, slow and steady, give Fox pause. Unlike the others, he doesn't threaten her with violence, and he doesn't strike. He doesn't need to. Güthric stands over her, a heavy boulder beside a dainty flower, and crosses his arms, the warning all but spoken.

My vision is turning gray, the edges of my sight fizzing behind a sea of stars.

Finally realizing she's outnumbered and can't face Güthric even if she wanted to, Fox growls her irritation. The strangled noise becomes more desperate, clawing its way up her throat with the might of a mother lion as she finally releases me.

I gasp for the air I've been denied, swallowing it in lumps that feel jagged and awkward in my throat. Despite the pain, I swallow them like a glutton, tears streaming down my cheeks.

"How could you?" Fox says, lip quivering.

Güthric plucks her off me, and I roll to my side to get a better angle for the oxygen I need. My throat stings too much for me to try to speak, otherwise I'd tell her how absolutely irrational she is. She, of all people, trying to kill *me*? After what she's done?

"He's not dead, you fool," my sister spits, venom laced in her words. But it's her cool gray eyes, as sharp as shadowsteel, that are aimed to kill.

Fox squirms in Güthric's arms, even though she'd already conceded. She is a viper, primed and poisonous. Her snapping teeth don't aim anywhere but to unleash her enraged roars, but I'm sure they would tear through flesh if they sank into anything living.

"Foxglove."

Fox stills at the sound of her full name, her freckled skin paling at the voice I'm sure she never thought she'd hear again. Behind us, beyond the border of Eyve, backlit by fireflies and peaceful willow trees, Alphonse steps into the clearing.

"Alphonse?" Her voice cracks, but that's not for lack of strength. With a hefty swing of her feet, Fox kicks Güthric's legs out from under him, the man dropping her as he tumbles over. Her feet are moving before she even reaches the ground. "Alphonse!"

Alphonse steps through the gate before she can collide into the unseen barrier, thereby saving her from accidentally breaking her nose—a courtesy that I silently bemoan him for. But just as I'm about to vomit watching my friend-turned-enemy and my enemy-turned-friend smack into each other with a sickening embrace, she surprises us all with a swing of her opened hand.

The smack of it echoes like the crack of a whip across the clearing between the Shadowthorn and the Eyve.

Alphonse nurtures his reddening face, swiveling his sore jaw. "And here I thought you'd be thrilled to see me." He runs a hand through the dark locks that are disheveled by his standards after his extended stay in the dungeons.

"I thought you were dead," she snaps, her hands balled into fists at her side, ready to strike again but with more force. "What in the eyve are you doing here?"

"I was about to ask you the same," he retorts, tugging on his wrinkled leather tunic as though he is able to get out the creases. "No Crusader has ever come this far."

She scoffs, nodding to each of us in turn. "None except Silver, Güthric, Sai—who's also supposed to be dead, mind you."

"Well, when you put it like that…"

"What are you doing here, Alphy?"

I make a piss-pour attempt at stifling my laughter at the saccharine nickname, warranting a glare from my cousin. Fox, though, is unfazed. She's just waded through half the Shadowthorn on a solo mission to avenge his death, only to find him alive. Her focus is honed.

"Why are you with these…these traitors? You know what I went through to get here? I came all this way, fought every demon imaginable, just so I could avenge the man I thought was dead, only to find that he still breathes. So, tell me, what is this? Why are you here? Did you just decide to abandon your post the moment your father charged you with protecting the western shore?"

"No! I would never abandon the Shadow Crusade." I'm surprised to see him put so easily on the defense. Alphonse isn't one to cower normally. Either this journey has changed him, or this woman has.

"Then what are you doing here? How are you still alive?"

He drags his hand through his dark hair again, grimacing at the greasy slickness of it. "It's a long story, I'm afraid—"

"Piss on a mage, Alphonse. We thought you were dead! Dimitri's leading an attack on Qaeus as we speak, just to make sure our general's dying mission to end the reign of the Primordials doesn't die along with him."

Shocking realization ripples among us. About the attack, about the sudden shift in the Crusaders' plans. But it's my heart that plummets to the forest floor with a hollow thud.

"Dimitri? He's here?"

Fox glances over her shoulder. "Why do you sound like that?" The hatred is gone from her expression for a moment, replaced by confusion as she examines me from bottom to top. "You were supposed to be dead too, you know."

I meet her glare with one of my own. She has no right to be so furious with me. I've done nothing to her. The man she thought I killed is still alive. Meanwhile, she's the entire reason I was forced to flee into the Shadowthorn where I was bitten by a demon only minutes after crossing the threshold.

If either of us have a right to hate one another, it's me.

"That's what they told us, anyway," she continues. "But I...I couldn't believe it. Dimitri said the leader of that shithole in the Shadowthorn was your uncle, and he didn't seem upset enough to have lost a niece so recently. When we attacked them, he insisted Alphonse was still alive. I wasn't so certain about that, either. So, I followed him." Her fierce gaze returns to Alphonse. "But I swear I never dreamed I'd find you."

We get lost in her storytelling for as long as it lasts. But leave it to my sister to direct the conversation back to what matters most.

"Where did you say the Crusaders are headed?" Kalli asks, before realizing that she doesn't need to rely on Fox for the answer. She and the raven that is almost permanently perched on her shoulder turn their interrogative gazes on Adrien. "Where is the Primordial Qaeus?"

"I-it's less than a day's travel from here."

I turn my pleading gaze on my sister. "We have to do something. If anyone tries to kill the heart without the breath of life, they'll die."

"They'll die trying to get anywhere near it." Adrien pads his aching nose, wince at the blood he finds there. "The heart is guarded, remember?"

And only a Primordial blade will grant someone access to it. I say nothing of it though. The people in my company are too heroic for their own good. Most of them have been told that the only salvation our people will ever know is if the Primordial is killed. All but two of us trained as Crusaders for the chance to be the one to wield the blade and the killing blow. If they know my axe is how we will get close to Qaeus, there's no telling who just might try to seize the opportunity of cleaving the Primordial's heart in two.

If Qaeus is killed before her heart can siphon the blighted blood from me...I don't even want to consider the possibilities of what could happen. Most assume that once Qaeus is dead, the Blight will fade with her. What would that mean for all of her demons? All of the druids trapped inside the bodies of monsters?

I think about Dimitri, Maxwell, and even Eparah instead, and the stacked battle they're charging into. I've known Dimitri long enough to know that he would willingly be the first in line to lead the charge, not only to avenge his mother, his sister, his father, but maybe even me.

Adrien let him believe I was dying. According to Fox, he kept up the charade even after their attack. And now he's charged headfirst into the most dangerous mission he could've ever volunteered for.

If he wasn't in so much peril, I might actually be proud of him. Attacking the Primordial was undoubtedly *not* one of the Magistrate's direct orders, and as such, by following the maps that the Wardens had drawn to chart the path to Qaeus,

Dimitri just might be participating in his first act of true rebellion, ever.

Kalli clasps my shoulder. "Don't worry. We will intervene. No one will near the boundary."

Instinctively, I turn my silent, hopeful plea to Ryven, the man who's been at my side the entire time I've trekked through the Blight, only to remember he's no longer here. Gone. Not only has he chosen to force my hand, but he's also chosen to abandon me—abandon all of us—at what just might be our greatest time of need. We could've used his expertise, his knowledge of the Shadowthorn. I could've simply used his presence.

I stomach the urge to scream his name, to search the shadows in hopes of finding him nearby, waiting. But if he were anywhere near here still, he would've already shown himself. He would've been the first to stop Fox from striking. He might've even detected her before she charged in the first place.

"Now is the time." I hear Kalli's voice, but only faintly.

"Hmm?" I ask dazedly. Ryven's abandonment leaves my mind in a fog, but I know that is no place for me to be right now. Lives are at stake.

She flicks the bottle hanging from my chest. "It's time, Halira. If we're going to charge into battle with the Primordial, maybe even with the rogue Crusaders, you must first take the breath of life. We can't risk it being destroyed or lost or taken. It is the only protection you have."

"I—I...I can't. Ryven, he—"

"I know. I understand your apprehension, but I regret to remind you that none of that matters right now. He's gone. If he were here, we might have other options to consider, but he's not. You are the only one present who needs the breath of life, which means you are the only one among us who can face the heart and survive." While I'm still shaking my head, my hands trembling in hers, she adds, "Do you want to prevent your fellow Crusaders from getting themselves killed?"

Of one country, of one blood echoes from the dark outskirts of my mind in response.

"Of course."

"Then, take the breath of life. It is the only way."

Gnawing on the inside of my lip, I look down to the iridescent vial. I could stand here and argue. I could insist that the answers we may need might be just on the other side of that wall. But Qaeus' heart is still a few hours away, and the Crusaders have likely arrived there already if Fox has made it this far.

With no time to lose, I pop the cork out of the bottle and press the glass up to my lips. I prepare to drink the warm fluid I've imagined was in there since I first saw the vial in the Dark Sea. The contents had rocked and swayed with the grace of an ocean, and often were as blue as one as well.

But, instead of a refreshing sip of water, a tepid, stale wind blows into my mouth. I'd almost forgotten what the contents of this bottle were. They weren't some magical tincture concocted by the mages, or an elixir mixed by the most adept healers among the mages. It was the dying breath of the first siren queen, and it tasted exactly as I'd imagine a dying breath would. Stomach bile. Salt. Blood.

My head starts to spin as the putrid spell courses through my lungs and I feel the vitality, feel it shielding my heart from the demon poison inside me. I become emboldened by it, more than I ever have by anything.

The Crusaders, they were my friends, and they are now potentially facing death. Even if they'll surely hate me once they learn what I am, and even if they did abandon me first, I will not abandon them. I cannot.

"We have to stop them before they lose any more Crusaders."

Alphonse nods his agreement, turning to Adrien. "You said the Crusaders continued south. How far away is the Primordial's heart?"

"It's a little less than a half day's journey—" Adrien starts to repeat, but I barrel through him.

"Which direction do we head?"

My sister repeats the question for me.

"We passed it on our way here," Adrien replies. "Silver knows where to find it."

Silver nods to me before I even have to ask her to lead the way, and leaving Imryll with Adrien to tend to his wounds, and Sai behind for moral support, the rest of us embark on another trek through the Shadowthorn.

Ilead us through the blackened overgrowth at a steady jog. Alphonse, Silver, and Fox have no trouble keeping up, but Güthric's lumbering strides struggle to maintain a constant speed. His breathing is already labored before the border of Eyve is lost to the trees behind us.

Not that I ever look back to notice. My gaze is fixed. Engrossed. Unrelenting. Too much rides on our hasty travels for me to be able to focus on anything else but the path ahead. I have to stop the others from getting themselves hurt or killed. I have to save myself.

Only when I see a flicker of white feathers gliding down from the sky does my attention allow me to pull it away from the path before me. I glance up to the sky, an owl landing on my shoulder a few moments later. I halt the group by holding up my hand and behind me, I hear Alphonse whining to Fox about how he should be leading the charge. I have no doubt that once we arrive that he won't try stepping in. As long as he doesn't impede what I need to do, then he can do whatever his ego needs from him.

Retrieving the folded bundle of fabric from where I'd

pinched it beneath my underarm, I hold the garments out to the owl, and she flutters off my shoulder, snatching them in her talons before disappearing behind a nearby tree. A moment later, Kalli reappears, fully dressed down to her dutiful raven upon her shoulder.

"Based on Silver's descriptions, and from what I could see from above," she says, striding toward us. "It's not too far now. I was able to spy the dense area Adrien spoke of, the one that keeps the heart protected. He wasn't exaggerating: the shield around it is profound. Even the blighted trees were forced aside from where it formed."

I'm too impatient to hear about the trees, so I snap, "And? Did you see them? Did you see the Crusaders?" Hope and fear roil inside me, turning my stomach to a slimy, twisted thing.

Kalli nods. "I believe so. They are not too far from it now."

"They haven't arrived yet? I thought you said they charged past you? Shouldn't they have arrived already then?"

My question, directed at Silver, falls on confused ears. I suppose it's been a while since I've been in the company of non-druids that I'm having a difficult time reacclimating to their inability to understand me, a half-demon, one of the blighted.

If all goes according to plan, that won't be the case for much longer.

After my sister translates for me, Silver finally responds. "They're not as familiar with this part of the Shadowthorn as the Wardens are. The maps would've helped guide them, but they still had the shadowcreatures to contend with in an unfamiliar territory."

Alphonse snorts. "I'm surprised they made it here so quickly."

I level him with a glare but address my sister. "Did you see Dimitri? Was he with them?"

Her stoic expression is unflinching. "Yes. He was among the few leading the charge."

Of course he was. I expected no less, not from the man who would rather die of starvation before even considering stealing so much as a bread crumb.

Biting my lip, I start marching our party forward again, every step and bounding stride bringing us one step closer toward stopping the others from doing something they'll regret.

But despite our bounding strides and my desperation to save them before any more lives are lost, I'm not entirely convicted in my charge. I'm all too aware as we advance on the location of Qaeus' heart that, although I'm nearing my own salvation and hopefully the salvation of others, I'm also coming closer to facing Dimitri. It's an encounter I'm not ready for, maybe even less so than I am to face the heart.

The time we've spent apart has been short, about a week or so I'd venture to guess, but it still feels like decades. I no longer know how to act around him. I've never felt that way about him before. We'd been best friends for so long that being around each other had come naturally. Even as our relationship developed into something more, I always knew how to *be* when I was with him. But now things have changed again. I am no longer the lover he wanted, no longer the young woman whom he considered a friend. When I see him, am I allowed to be excited, to be nervous, or will his cold assessment of me crack me in two? After all, I am a druid, a creature of magic, and magic is something no Arcathainian can abide. To make matters worse, I'm part-demon right now too...Dimitri has trained for months to kill creatures like me. Will he turn on me like Fox did?

I have to believe that seeing me alive will temporarily stun his loathing of me...

My sister jogs alongside me, the thick ropes of her hair

beating against her back in time with our steps temporarily distracting me. I never thought I'd be charging Qaeus with my sister by my side. And despite my jealousies of her and how easily she's been taking to the sky, my heart swells knowing that in this endeavor, I am not alone.

Hours pass and the air begins to thicken. Darkness shrouds us like a blanket tossed over the sky. I've never seen such obscurity before, none that feuds in such a way with the light of day. It's as if the Primordial's heart is burning, emitting a black smoke so heavy that it has nowhere else to go but to sink to the forest floor and stifle the air around it. There is no burning stench though, only the scent of mist and trees, and the cloying undertone of death.

Our pace slows. We're getting close now. Not only do we have to be careful of our steps so that we don't inadvertently cross the unseen threshold guarding the heart, but also to keep our eyes open for the Crusaders. They will be on high alert today, this close to Qaeus, and I don't want to spook them before we have a chance to announce ourselves.

The farther we go into the gray mist, the louder the slow, steady thrumming of a beating heart amplifies around us. It's difficult to tell which way it's coming from since it seems to encapsulate the entire surrounding area, but I keep my eyes peeled. I search for any dark masses, for clearings through the grayness.

Every time we veer too close, I can practically feel the palpable boundary constricting, shoving us back to protect its source of power.

And then I see it. Through the dense fog, sheets of darkness ooze from a heavy void, and I can just barely make out the throbbing mass. A boulder of black: Qaeus' heart.

Kalli glides through down from above, her white feathers muted by the darkness, and lands on my shoulder. We go through the same motions we've done three or four times since departing the border of Eyve, until she's dressed and emerging from some corner of the Shadowthorn that she's deemed private.

"They're on the other side. We'll have to go around if we want to confront them."

Before I can respond, a scream pierces the air. I twist around, assessing the small unit we've formed, relieved to find that none of them are being attacked by a sudden onslaught of demons.

A sizzling wave of energy ripples off the heart, sending all of us staggering away from the shield.

"What was that?" I ask.

"I don't know," Kalli says, looking to Silver as if she might have more information.

Despite being unable to understand me, Silver can tell enough from our body language to guess what's been asked. She shakes her dark head of hair, her thoughtful eyes penetrating. "It wasn't nearby. It could've been the Crusaders. Adrien said that no one can go near the heart without...without consequence."

"Then they've already reached the boundary and they're attempting to break through." My voice wavers, dread threatening to seize me.

Fortunately, my sister has enough strength for the both of us. "Come on."

We race around the boundary, taking a wider berth so as not to accidentally cross over and experience whatever pain and agony had befallen the person who'd screamed. For as vast as the Shadowthorn is, the heart is small by comparison, and the shield surrounding it doesn't take too long to circle.

We find the other Crusaders in a matter of minutes. Two are huddled over a supine body on the ground. At first glance, I almost mistake it for a demon until I see the smoke rising from the fallen Crusader's charred skin. It takes me a moment longer to understand why the other Crusaders are even bothering with their fallen comrade, why they're going to such great lengths to gently trickle water over the smoking flesh, but then I see the ragged rise and fall of the person's chest.

Alive.

Alive, but wishing for death.

"Piss on a mage," I curse. "Where's Imryll when you need her?" I don't know why I ask such a rhetorical, pointless question. I know full well where she is and why she had to stay behind.

But Kalli draws her lips together with fierce determination. "I can help them."

My neck snaps toward her so abruptly that my silver hair cuts through the air like a sword. Again, I find myself having too many petty questions on my mind, and I can tell by the slight roll of her eyes that she can feel them too. Kalli braces herself for my immature chastisement, but I won't give it to her. Especially not now.

"Go," I say, my voice gentle but resolute. "If you can help them in any way, you must."

Kalli doesn't hesitate, sliding to the trio's side with bright magic already exuding from her outstretched fingers.

I return my attention farther ahead, closer toward the Primordial's heart. The Crusaders there still haven't noticed us. They're too preoccupied in their strategy to see the five of us approaching. But as they pull back from their huddle, swords and halberds readied in their grips, enough of them startle at the sight of us to draw the attention of the rest of the group.

"Alphonse." Captain Eparah straightens, blinking wildly at the dead man walking toward them.

The others notice him too, their acknowledgment coming first as stunned silence, before the real bravado of the Crusaders comes to life.

"*He's alive!*"

"Fox found him!"

"Welcome back, General."

To his credit, Alphonse takes most of the hoorahs in humble strides, or at least as humble as someone like him is capable.

"Halira."

I stop paying attention to him at the familiar sound of my name. I don't need to look to know who calls me. I wouldn't even need to recognize his voice. I can tell from the crack in his tone and the weight with which he speaks exactly who has noticed me while the rest are busy celebrating the return of their general.

Only Dimitri remains where the pack had once stood.

My heart drops at the banged-up sight of him. Black-crusted demon blood coats his forehead and cheeks in speckles. He's stopped shaving his beard, casting the lower half of his face in a rugged, dark sheen. Seeing him like this takes me back to Gravenburg, and the countless days I'd find him covered in deer urine from hunting and pig's guts from preparing the meat.

It used to churn my stomach. But now, I'm too relieved by the sight of him to care.

Too relieved, and frightened.

I've thought about this reunion the entire way here. I've wondered if he would strike me down the moment he laid eyes on me just because he believed it was the right thing to do. I've wondered if he would he have the stomach for it, or if he would call on someone else to restrain me so that I could be brought back to the Magistrate as their prisoner. I wouldn't go down without a fight, but could I really fight Dimitri?

My gaze flicks every so often to the broadsword hanging heavy in his hand, but mostly, I lock my gaze onto his, to the sage green eyes that remind me of the thriving forest that had once stood behind our homes, frosted by a winter's breath.

Dimitri takes a staggering step forward, my heart thudding

like the Primordial's thunderous gait in time with his. I force myself to hold my ground, although every one of my instincts suggests I should run. If I don't want to have to defend myself against my best friend, if I don't want to be forced to kill him, then I should leave. Now.

He dares another step, and this time, I do falter backward, ever so slightly.

With a single shake of his head, he drops his sword. I'm still staring at where it landed in the black dirt when he wraps me up in his arms.

"How is this possible?" He laughs into my hair, squeezing me tighter. "How are you alive? I saw that demon bite you. I saw the blood. Y-you should be dead. You *were* dying…"

I can't answer any of his questions; I can't bring myself to say anything. My tongue no longer knows the words. All I can do is pull my arms out from where he's pinned them and wrap them around his back in kind. The tears fall freely where I rest my forehead against his leather tunic, inhaling the earthy scent of him that has always been so familiar, so much like home.

Grabbing my shoulders, Dimitri pushes me back to get a better look. "A-am I dreaming? Are you really here?"

Nodding, a smile bursts from my lips. I never thought I'd see him again, and if that day did come, never in a million years would I have allowed myself to think that he would be so relieved to see me.

He surprises me further when his calloused hand finds the back of my neck, crushing our mouths against each other. My stomach shutters, my heart yanking me forward and shoving me away in equal parts rebellion and submission. I have mapped out the thin curve of his lips more times than I can count. I have relished in the salty taste of him after a hard day's training, every time wanting more and more, until whatever emptiness inside of me was full. Before we fled the Castle of Nigh, I would've plunged deep into the reprieve of him without any question, losing myself and leaving the madness of the world behind us.

But I'm not sure I want to lose myself anymore. Nor do I want to pretend the madness doesn't exist.

Gently, I shove him back. Hurt and confusion wrinkle his expression, but I try playing off my rejection with a cool smile. "Sorry, it's just…it's a lot. I didn't expect you to…"

His expression shifts from one of confusion to distrust. Possibly even horror. Dimitri takes a great step backward and I don't think I've ever seen his eyes bulge so wide. "Your voice. What is that? You sound like…like a…"

"A demon," Eparah answers on a breath. The rest of her unit arrives with her as she eyes me warily. "But…how is that possible. You're no fiend. Even if you were, we've been reapplying our necro-ink every hour, so we wouldn't fall victim to your trickery of voices."

A Crusader I don't recognize steps forward, a ruthless jagged scar across his lip. "I say we slice her open. If she's a demon, she'll bleed black, not red."

Dimitri takes steps between us, shoving the man's shoulder so hard that even the burly fellow staggers a step back. "No one touches her."

I open my mouth to defend myself, but stop myself when I realize nothing I can say will convince them of anything other than that I am the demon they fear me to be. My frightful gaze wanders back behind us to Kalli. Her eyes are closed, and she's lost somewhere deep in the magic that she's conjuring to save their fallen Crusader. Imryll is still back at the Eyve, if she'll even be returning to us once she's finished. I have no one to translate for me, and therefore no way of defending myself, let alone telling them what needs to be said.

The Crusaders grow restless. Not even Dimitri will deter them for long.

But to my surprise, Alphonse appears beside me. "Despite

her menacing vocal cords, and the demonic way in which she's led most of her life"—he pauses long enough to grin at my sullen glare—"Halira, here, is not a demon. She's been blighted."

Murmurs ripple through the crowd, the Crusaders' distrust loudly prevalent among them.

"Blighted how?"

"That's not how a demon bite works."

The man who suggested gutting me like a sow points an angry finger at Dimitri. "You said she was dead."

Dimitri watches me with his own suspicious eyes. "I said she'd been bitten. I assumed death would follow."

The Crusaders begin to argue again. Some say that regardless of whether I'm a demon, I still deserve death for my treason. Others suggest shackling me and returning me to the Magistrate to be prodded and tested.

"That's enough!" Eparah shouts before their concerned murmurs can become enraged outcries. "We won't find the answers by going at each other's throats."

"Show your general some respect," Dimitri says by way of support. "Please, General Alphonse, you were saying?"

It's as if the man never even left his post. Alphonse's hands return to the base of his back, and he holds his nose up with regal aristocracy. "Thank you, Crusader. As I was saying, Halira is blighted. Most Arcathainians, when they are bitten by a demon, it is true that they die. But Halira is…unique. Her blood is more resistant to the toxins present in the demon's fangs and claws, and so when she was bitten, her body waged war on the toxin. It's still fighting it."

"Unique how?" The disgruntled Crusader spits on the ground. "I've seen what a demon bite can do. If she was bitten the same day they stole you from your country, she would be long dead. Unless she wasn't bitten." He stares at me, a challenge in his hateful eyes.

Beside me, I catch Alphonse frowning as he considers going along with that lie. It would be far easier to gain their trust if we left out the demon and druid part all together. Perhaps we could tell them I've simply contracted a severe cold that's left my throat rasping and weak.

But such a lie wouldn't explain why I am the only one able to enter the foreboding boundary before us. It wouldn't explain why Dimitri swears he saw me bitten, nor would it explain why Alphonse had me arrested as a mage but is now standing by my side, defending me.

I'm done hiding who I am. Once these people return to Arcathain, I'll never see them again anyway. Who cares if they know what I am, what I'm capable of. I have a mission to complete.

Uncinching the corset around my waist, the others shuffle uncomfortably.

Alphonse leans over to me, a hand shielding his mouth as he whispers, "What are you doing?"

"I'm proving our point."

The corset falls to my feet, and I raise the blouse beneath it enough to reveal my belly. I don't look down; I already know what they'll see: the puncture wounds of a horrific bite, and the beginning tendrils of the blighted toxin spiderwebbing out from the scarred wounds.

Many of the Crusaders jump back with gasps of horror.

Dimitri, however, brings his hand to my belly. His fingers trace around the wounds like he's afraid to touch them—not for fear of catching whatever plagues me, but rather not daring to cause me the pain of a graze.

"Are you all right?" he asks.

Alphonse snorts. "Does she look alright?"

"I just mean… How is this possible?" Dimitri's sage green eyes snag on mine. "You were bitten but you survived. How?"

"Well, she's not exactly human," is Alphonse's vague and alarming response.

"*Demon!*" someone shouts from the crowd.

"*Mage!*" cries another.

With a roll of my eyes, I punch Alphonse in the arm. "Will you just let me do the talking?"

He looks at me with feigned hurt that I could insinuate his unhelpfulness.

Dimitri notices how vastly different Alphonse looks at me compared to everyone else. There is no hint of repulsion, let alone confusion in his expression.

"Can you…understand her?" he asks.

Alphonse's mask of poised indifference wavers. "Yes. Of course I can."

"But…why?"

I wave him off. "That doesn't matter right now. Alphonse, will you translate?"

My cousin nods, glancing uneasily at the Crusaders who are now watching him with suspicion.

We don't have time to talk through all of that though and hopefully they will drop their concerns once I start talking.

"I didn't know this until Alphonse imprisoned me," I begin. "And not even then. It wasn't until my aunt broke my sister and I from our cells that I learned that my ancestors were neither human nor mage. They were another race that Arcathain had forgotten about entirely."

I pause, giving Alphonse time to translate.

"I am of druid descent." A strange thrill spirals in my stomach when I say it. "I wish I knew more about what that means because I'm sure you have your questions, but seeing as I've only known for a few days, you'll understand why I have no answers for you."

Again I pause, allowing Alphonse the time he needs to recite my words with impressive accuracy. The Crusaders listen to their former leader with apt resolve, though a few still rile with disdain. They mutter among themselves how they've never heard of a druid; how it sounds a lot like magic, and magic belongs to the wicked mages; how they still don't understand why any of this is relevant.

"Tell me," Alphonse muses. "Would you prefer to stand here and continue speculating, or would you rather we tell you what we know?"

The Crusaders finally settle again, and I continue.

"What I know is my people were among those who were trapped in the Forgotten Forest of Eyve back when the mages and humans trapped Qaeus. And perhaps it's for that reason that they—*we*—have a partial immunity to demon bites. I don't actually know. But for whatever reason, having druid blood has been enough to protect me. For now."

When Alphonse is finished speaking for me, Dimitri levels me with a look of concern. "For now?"

I lower my gaze, preparing myself to speak the words that will inevitably remind me of Ryven, and the plight he still faces, the one we were supposed to face together.

My pause persists too long though, and Alphonse steps in to respond for me. "The demon blood will still kill her if she doesn't do what she came here to do."

"And what's that?"

"The same thing this heroic bunch of fools was attempting to achieve." Alphonse's arms sweep out from his leather-clad body, gesturing to the density surrounding the black Primordial heart. "She needs to near the heart."

"We've tried," says Eparah, her charcoal eyes drifting guiltily back to the Crusader splayed on the ground with the medics. "The Primordial has protected itself. No one can break through. Not even shadowsteel can penetrate whatever this dense fog is."

I draw my axe, startling many of the Crusaders into

drawing their weapons too. I hold out my other hand, placating them if only for a moment so that I can explain.

"Only certain weapons will be able to break through the shield around the Primordial."

Dimitri watches my axe curiously as Alphonse translates. "And what makes your weapon so special?"

For a moment, I consider whether that information is something I'm ready to share. To the Crusaders, there can be no greater thing to covet than a weapon that has already slain one of the Primordials.

Before I can deflect, Alphonse crosses his arms, his expression smug. "Halira's axe is the same weapon that destroyed the Primordial Khunas."

I glare at my cousin who seems so eager to give away all of our secrets. His expression falters, his hands upturning in an innocent shrug.

Our brief squabble gives the rest of the group enough time to reassess the situation. Though they've begun lowering their blades, many appear to believe they have some say in the matter of how we proceed.

"Then it's perfect timing we're here. To see our great general slice through the barrier and slay the last Primordial will be an honor."

Arrogance gets the better of him, and Alphonse beams amid their hurrahs and cheering.

My elbow finds the space between his ribs.

"Right," Alphonse groans. He addresses the group with his hands held high. "Yes, well, it will not be I, but Halira who enters the boundary of the Primordial."

More disagreement belches from the group. I don't remember them being so vocal and obstinate before. Then again, they have spent the last few days wandering the Shadowthorn, leaderless and dogged in their objective of avenging their fallen general. They're exhausted, and tired, and quite frankly, struggling with the idea of having a victorious kill so close, before having it yanked away from them. They want blood, and they want one of their own to draw it.

"It's the only way to cure her." I hadn't even noticed Silver's arrival until she speaks. Everyone turns to face her, as if she's addressing them all, but her attention is solely fixed on Dimitri. At first, I find it perplexing. With Alphonse presumed dead, the role of highest in command would naturally fall to Eparah, even if the Crusaders with her aren't exclusive to the unit she'd been assigned. But most of the Crusaders present are men, many of whom I recognize as the roommates Dimitri would sit with during mealtimes, the men who'd spar with him when he had free time and wasn't busy studying. These men know him and respect him, and Silver knows it. She knows they will listen to whatever he decides.

Judging from the momentary squint of his eyes, to the clear sheen that follows, it takes him but a moment to understand as well.

"Halira was one of us," he barks into the quiet as if anyone had still been arguing. "If she can defeat the blight ravaging her body, if the general wills it to be her to enter the tomb behind us, then it is our duty to allow it."

Some of the rowdier Crusaders take a bit longer to settle, including the one with the scarred lip, but most become submissive the moment Dimitri starts speaking. When he's made his point and all have agreed, they lower their gazes, stepping aside and providing me a direct path to the boundary surrounding Qaeus' heart.

Eparah is the last to step aside, but only because she's too lost in staring between Alphonse and me, two people whom she believed were dead but are still breathing. Her smile is as infectious as always, even if it is sadder than usual.

She clamps my shoulder as I pass by, and I flash her a rueful smile of my own.

Then, standing before the gray cloud of Primordial emissions, I brace myself for whatever is about to come next. I swing my axe overhead, my muscles quivering with the anticipation of the blow that will bounce up my elbow and ricochet into my shoulder. I pause for only a moment, wondering if I should turn back around and search for Ryven once more. Maybe he's changed his mind. Maybe he's come back. But it doesn't matter now. I've already taken the breath of life; I've already stolen his one assured chance at living out his days as a druid. The only chance he has now is if I can cure myself quickly enough and return to scanning the mural at Eyve for the answer I'm certain is there.

With newfound resolve, I swing the axe hard, shadowsteel cracking into the dense fog as if it were as solid as stone. The barrier rings like a thunderous gong before a tidal wave of power knocks every single one of us back.

FOR ARCATHAIN

THE HEART, SHADOWTHORN

The pounding of my skull is white hot, but even as I roll over from where I've landed in the dirt, I know the pain won't last long. I've endured worse blows to the head than this. More than anything, I'm simply dazed. I hadn't expected the barrier to respond like that to my axe. The Elders had said that like trusts like, which had made me think that my showing Qaeus—or her protective barrier—that I was like her, she would open to me with loving arms, not knock myself and everyone within a nearby radius to the ground.

I push myself onto my elbows, recognize the hilt of my axe still in my hand, and gape up at the gray void before me. A tear has appeared where I struck. It ripples as if the wind were blowing through the very fabric of the spell Qaeus has placed here.

"Are you all right?"

I look up to find Dimitri offering me his hand. I take it.

"Yeah, I'm fine," I say. Then, remembering he can't understand me, I nod for emphasis.

Around us, the others are still scattered throughout the black forest. Most stir, though others who were thrown into tree trunks or who landed in awkward positions remain where they lie. Silver is among those who haven't moved. Güthric flings his dazed body over, crawling and dragging the heavy weight of him just to reach her. The look on his face nearly cracks my heart in two.

I want to run to them. I want to summon the healing power that I know has to be buried somewhere inside me just like it was Kalli and help her.

But Dimitri's hand catches my elbow when I move to rush to their aid. "I'll see to them," he assures me. "But you have something more important to handle." He reaches out for me, tucking my moonbeam hair behind my ear. "Go. Heal yourself, and let the rest of us tend to the others."

Glancing over my shoulder, I see Güthric lift Silver's limp body into his arms. He bounds to my sister in only a few short strides and lowers Silver to the ground. Her gown pools beneath her and finally I glean the slightest rise and fall of her chest. Relief floods me. She's alive.

And thank the gods too because Dimitri is right. We each have a role to play, and mine isn't healing the others. It's healing myself so that I *might* someday be able to heal Ryven.

Without another thought, I clasp my hands tighter around my axe and charge through the rift.

The smog is thicker still inside the boundary. Its density makes it difficult to breathe, filling my lungs with irritating harshness. Raging, howling winds every shade of gray thrash inside the boundaries concaved walls. I have to shield my face from the slashing of the air, squinting and struggling against every step I take to march forward.

The cloud of darkness is too dense to see through, the winds too loud to hear anything other than their howling and wheezing. And so I turn to the only part of my druid power that I even remotely understand.

The sensation of feeling life.

Qaeus' beating heart has called to me since we neared the boundary, but its call is more charged here. The vibrations ripple through me in rhythmic waves, a certain electric current about them.

I may not be able to see, nor hear, but the beating of the heart, I can follow.

Keeping my face down, my grip on my shadowsteel axe ironclad, I press forward.

Every step is a battle, the war between me and the wind only growing more difficult with each one, but still I lift my feet. I move through the darkness. I follow the thrumming of Qaeus' heart.

It's here, in the grim cyclone, that the moment hits me profoundly. It was only a few months ago that my parents died in a demon scourge that wreaked havoc on our home, our neighbors, the refugees flooding our city. I swore then to avenge them, my brother, and every other Arcathainian who has lost their lives to the Shadowthorn and its creatures of darkness.

And here I am the only human—the only druid—to ever venture this close to Qaeus in centuries.

It dawns on me then, something I'm surprised I haven't even really considered before. The Primordial will be defense-less. If all that's left of her is her heart, and I have a shadowsteel weapon that can cleave straight through it, I can end the Blight plaguing us all here. Today. I, Halira Devonshire of the Wallows of Gravenburg, will go down in history as the girl who slayed the last living Primordial, ended the Shadowthorn, and rid demons from the land forever.

A small part of me wonders how the Magistrate would handle such news. Would I be pardoned for deserting my post, for being an alleged mage, or at the very least, for possessing magic? Perhaps I'd be welcome back to Arcathain, to the employ of my home country, and returned to Dimitri's side.

The thought twists a surprising and dull knife in my gut. And it's not because I worry that I'm getting ahead of myself and that none of those victories would be granted to me. It's the fear that they *might*.

All of the things I once loved—once *thought* I loved—the dreams that kept me going through even the worst, grueling days of my Crusader training, of grieving the loss of my mother and father and brother, none of those same hopes seem to fill my heart with the fulfillment they once did. And honestly, maybe they never had. I joined the Crusaders to find meaning and purpose, to fill a hole that had been cored in my chest, but I can't honestly say it was ever once filled during the months I spent behind the castle walls.

Despite everything I thought I knew and wanted, I don't think I actually want to return to Arcathain.

Something had always been missing from my life there. For a time, that void had been filled by the Shadow Crusade. I believed that slaying demons was my newfound life's purpose. But once the Shadowthorn is disrupted, once the Crusaders disband back into the ranks of the Magistrate's army, what would become of my life then? Waging a new war with the mages? Moving across the country to reside in the Capital, a place in Arcathain that is the farthest from the Eyve?

The Eyve.

It is where my heart has belonged since the moment I stepped over the threshold. All those years I spent wondering why I never felt like I belonged in Gravenburg, why I never felt like I knew how to just *live* there, I understood upon my arrival to the druid homeland. It was where I was meant to be. With my aunt, with the people I never had the chance to know but find myself wanting to, honing my druid powers.

And with any luck, with Ryven once he resurfaces, once he comes back after he finds out I've cured myself. After all, he'd have no more reason to stay away then. He left so that I'd take the breath of life. Now that I have, he's probably already at the wall examining the mural and waiting for me to return.

When I'd thought of returning to Arcathain, I felt numb and dead. But the moment the idea of a life in the Eyve sprang to life, I am revitalized.

My decision's made up then and there.

First, I will touch the heart and let it siphon the blight from me, the breath of life protecting me from death until it's done.

Next, I will strike Qaeus' heart with my axe. I will put an end to the suffering of Arcathainians, because I truly want a better future for the country that had been my home and the people I love who reside there. Then, after Qaeus is gone, the Shadowthorn disintegrated, I will return to the Eyve. I *will* find a way to save Ryven. Because, although even without him life in the Eyve sounds more appealing than returning to the country I never belonged, I'd be lying to myself if I didn't admit that when I think of my future, I see Ryven in it.

The winds shove and push with all their might, but my renewed vigor is unstoppable. With monumental effort, I finally reach the heart. It thrums before me, a dark and oily thing. The membranous veins pulse with thick, black blood. The ground beneath it is saturated, a shade of black darker than anything else I've encountered in my time in the Shadowthorn. It is onyx dipped in a void of chaos. It is demon's blood and liquid obsidian. It is toxin. It is death.

If I wasn't seeing the Primordial's exposed, beating heart with my own eyes, I wouldn't believe it possible. How can such a grotesque thing even exist? How can this single living thing have caused so much suffering?

Life pulses from the slick membrane holding the organ together. The loud beats spark something innate inside me, my magic stirring in response. For the first time in my entire life, I feel pity for the creature before me. It must be my druid blood, my affiliation toward beasts and creatures, because I suddenly find myself wondering why such a being should have to die. It is the last of its kind, after all, and it's hardly in any condition to fight back or cause harm to—

Shaking my head, I pull myself out of whatever trance I'd just fallen into. Those thoughts do not belong to me; they can't. Qaeus is evil incarnate. The Primordial is solely responsible for the damage that's been done to Arcathain, for the demons that bleed across our borders, for Tor's death, for my parents', for Ahl'Ro's.

Demon trickery—no…Primordial trickery. I don't know how it's possible for an organ removed from a living creature to have sentience, but this one must. It's how it has erected the boundary around itself, and it's why I thought for a fraction of a second that I didn't want to slice this heart the moment I had the chance.

I will not be played by a Primordial, let alone this malevolent chunk of its being.

Before whatever vile magic is at play here can strike me again, I do as the Elders instructed. I reach my hands out and touch Qaeus' beating heart.

Nothing happens.

I peer through my squinting eyes at the mass beneath my grip. The heart pulses in rhythmic beats, but nothing significant changes.

Perhaps it's already done? It takes me only a moment to check the black wound on my abdomen, verifying that I am still blighted.

I touch the heart again, this time squeezing tighter. The heart pounds against my palms, but it doesn't appear distressed or even notice that I have it in my clutches. No changes in the air or vibrations surrounding us. No strange sensations spiking through my body. I remain exactly as I was when I first entered the boundary.

My druid powers become louder though. With the Primordial's heart in my hands, it is a direct line of communication, an amplifier of the power I could channel if only I tugged on the chords. It is life. It is breath. It is blood.

Blood.

It's what pounds through the vessel. It's what surges through my veins. The blood of a demon; the blood of a druid. It's how this all began and how it will all end as well.

I dig my nails into the spongy wetness until black blood, warm and sticky, pools around my fingertips. The second it's exposed, energy thrums around me; through me. It crashes into me, chilling compared to the warm blood my fingers are dipped in, as if I'm standing before a cascade of icy ocean waves. The current wrenches through my body, surging through every fiber of my being before pulling back with the force of an earthquake.

The draw jerks me forward, my face slamming into the Primordial's slimy heart. The pounding grows louder, thudding more violently the longer I'm entrenched, but I couldn't let go even if I wanted to. Whatever magic was inside the Primordial's heart, whatever magic is laced inside me now, digging its claws into my very depths, it has me by the throat. My soul is in its dark grasp. My life.

Darkness leeches down my arms and out through my fingers, draining back into the heart. The dull ache that lingering in my belly eases as the blight is drawn out of me.

But the Primordial's heart draws from more than just the demon toxin. As my knees grow weak, I can feel my own blood, my own life force draining as well. Not only does the heart claim the demon inside me, but also the druid, the human, the mortal.

This was the price, the risk that had to be taken. I'd known that. And yet, I hadn't imagined it would be like this. It feels as if my veins are being ripped out from my skin. Like my insides are being sucked out of me until I am nothing more than a skin shell, hollowed and decrepit.

I fall to my knees, my hands still stuck in the fleshy organ despite my efforts to pull them away. The heart draws and draws until I am spent. I have nothing left to give but my last few breaths. They come ragged in my lungs, a grim rasp for air, for life, for another chance.

The last rasp ends, a wheeze of air that chokes my throat and blackens my vision. Everything fades to darkness. My awareness of the forest. My awareness of myself. I die.

But then, it comes.

Like a comet falling from the sky I crash back into my body with a whoosh of air. My eyes fly open. I feel life rising beneath my ribcage, a warm and salty breath that tastes like the tempestuous sea and mysterious darkness. It rises up my throat, bursts from my lips with a macabre three-note tune that's sung in a voice that isn't my own.

The breath of life, the first siren queen's dying breath, has been spent.

The Primordial heart releases me, and I clamber to ground beside it, silver hair matted to my cheeks and forehead by sweat and tears and something stickier. I lay there, exhausted and useless, my eyelids heavy but determined to stay open, to gaze upon the second life I've been granted.

I roll onto my back, my head tilting to the side, and my gaze falls to my discarded axe. For a few moments I simply stare at it in disbelief. Once I'd made it to the heart, I hadn't even thought about the axe, hadn't even noticed I'd apparently dropped it somewhere along the way. More Primordial trickery, I'm sure. Even the heart likely senses the danger such a blade can cause it. Shadowsteel was made to kill the Primordials, and this axe has already successfully ended one of them. It's no surprise that the heart made me drop it when it was infiltrating my thoughts.

On my next delirious blink though, something worrying catches my eye.

I lift my head upright, still too weary to bring the rest of my body with it, and gaze more intently at the axe. The shadow-steel seems duller than I remember. Even amid the gray smog around us, there is less of a gleam, no shine. It looks more like unpolished coal than magically imbued steel.

Rolling myself over onto my stomach, I drag my body through the blackened grass. The axe isn't that far; I managed to carry it all the way through the thrashing winds only to drop it a few paces away. My fingers grasp the leather hilt and the power of the slain Primordial pulses through me.

My knees are no longer weak. My bones no longer brittle with death.

I rise to my feet and face the heart.

The winds go still. Qaeus' heart drums with erratic speed, the black valves hastening in tempo like the climax of a lively song.

I take a step forward, my chest so tight that I almost can't breathe.

Thump-thump.

For centuries our people have fought the Primordials.

Thump-thump.

For centuries we have sent Crusaders into the Shadowthorn, only for the Primordial's reign to thrive.

Thump-thump.

My grip tightens, and I raise my axe. I will bring my people and our ancestors the justice they deserve.

Thump-thump. Thump-thump. Thump-thump.

Then, something changes in the beating of the heart. One of the throbbing veins starts to pulse irregularly. Unease drips in my gut like oil to water. The vein bulges, the thin skin stretching and expanding as something dark claws from underneath it, until I fear the skin will—

Burst.

Something black and sinuous juts from the tear, startling me so fiercely that I drop my axe. It clatters to the ground, black blood spilling atop it, as bony claws reach from the hole in the thrashing heart. The limb extends, as jagged as the barest tree branches in winter. The joint of the wrist cracks with jerky convulsions until the elbow pops and the rest of the monstrous arm stretches out before me.

I stagger backward, tripping over nothing but adrenaline before falling to the ground. I gape in stunned silence, my own heart battling the Primordial's in speed and volume. It rackets from my ribcage up into my throat when the heart's hand snakes down to the slick earth. The fingers drag over the curve of the axe like a mother caressing a babe's cheek.

My chest tightens. Dread unravels inside me, the kind of icy fear that fills my lungs until I am drowning. I cannot move. I cannot breathe. I can barely think anything beyond an acknowledgement that something has gone very, very wrong.

The dark hand forms a fist and, without warning, slams into the shadowsteel blade. The axe shatters as if it were nothing more than a replica, a child's plaything made from twigs and twine. The fist rises to reveal steel that has crumbled to broken shards and dust, and my panic coils tighter.

As the black ink spilling from the heart slows to a trickle, the rhythm quiets too.

Thump...thump.

From where I sit, half-perched and ready to crawl backward if I need to, I can see the muscles quivering with each mighty pound.

Thump...thump.

But rather than giving off the impression that the heart is by any means weakening—

Thump...thump.

I sense nothing but ominous chaos on the other side of these events.

Thump...thump...

thump...

...

And with a shuddering surge of power, the heart beats to an eerie, palpable stop.

AWAKEN

THE HEART, SHADOWTHORN

My heart rackets against my rattled bones. I'm not foolish enough to think that this is anything but a bad sign. The very air is wrong. The winds have died, even if the thick grayness remains. The lack of sound should be a sign that the heart is dead—that *Qaeus* is dead—and were I anything but a druid, I might believe it.

But my power is linked to the vibrations of life, and despite the heartbeat having ceased, I can still sense its life. In fact, it feels more powerful than ever. Raw and unbound, like a newborn demon bursting from the Shadowthorn to have its first feast.

I look back to the remnants of my shadowsteel axe, a weapon that had once felt electric in my hands but is now nothing more than ashes.

My eyes widen with horror and understanding at the same moment the ground begins to quake. If I weren't already lying flat on it, I'd fall over again. The rumbling is mightier than any magical blast I've endured today already. The winds whip anew, as sharp as razor blades.

I bury my face in the dirt to shield myself, but it still cuts through my leather, along the back of my neck, my hands. I grit my teeth, bearing through it, praying that it will stop, praying that I'm wrong about the axe and the power that had been inside it.

But the Elders had been quite clear. The Primordials do not die. Their souls are redirected to the Primordial who slew them. That was why my axe had been so powerful; it had absorbed the life of Khunas upon her death.

But there is no more blade to contain such a force anymore.

Gritting my teeth, I crush myself into the dirt as hard as I can. I smell the rotten stench of it seeping up my nostrils; I feel the charred flakiness of it pressing into my eyelashes, against my lips. No matter how unbearable and nauseating it becomes, I keep my head down; I know doing anything else would mean the death of me. I'm not even sure I'll survive this storm where I'm huddled now.

But then, something changes.

The dirt no longer reeks of death, but instead carries the fresh scent of damp soil. It becomes softer against my skin, more malleable. I open my eyes as the blackness seeps out of it. Risking being eviscerated, my curious gaze follows the inky darkness seeping out of the land as it returns to its host: the heart. Darkness lifts from the entire area, the air becoming less dense, less gray and less dim. Even the winds seem to fade away. Life is breathed back into my surroundings, not returning everything to its once vibrant state, but simply returning to it its livelihood. The land will not be renewed overnight; the Blight has lingered too long, corrupted it too deeply. It will take time for the earth to heal...and maybe the druids can help with that...

But the Shadowthorn is receding.

The air, although changed, still feels muggy, marred, and dangerous. The Blight on the lands may have been lifted, but

I'm not so certain it's to birth a new era of peace and prosperity.

With bulging, terrified eyes, I watch as the Primordial's heart writhes. Its membranous walls move as if there are a thousand hands pushing and clawing against the flesh from the inside, just as the hand had done earlier. The organ grows. It shifts and molds, looking less and less like a heart and more and more like a living thing as new limbs and pieces pierce through its diaphanous walls, riding waves of tarry blood.

Adrenaline sinks its teeth into me. Something primal in me stirs as I watch the awakening of the Primordial.

I scramble backward on hands and feet, my rear bumping against the uneven ground beneath me. I'm still too weak to stand, but I couldn't tear my eyes away even if I wanted to.

The heart bulges. Each section stretches and shifts and twitches until it starts resembling a creature. A creature of nightmares. Something more horrific than any of the shadow-creatures I've laid eyes on. It is grotesque and slippery and enormous.

I did not save Arcathain from the Blight; I condemned them to a fate much worse.

The Primordial Qaeus rises.

But this time she is fortified by the soul of another. Twice as strong. Twice as deadly.

And Arcathain is in dire trouble.

With no shadowsteel weapon to speak of, I break out in run on my unsteady limbs, but my feet slip and slide out from under me, drawing the undivided attention of the Primordial Qaeus herself. Her black and empty eyes fall to me like voids sucking me into their vortex. The Primordial leans down from where she towers, taking me into her squelching, sinuous, hideous hand as if I am a daisy she's plucked from a field.

Once again, my muscles tense, but this time my choice to still is my own. There is nowhere to go as she hoists me higher.

The other Crusaders cry out for me below, suddenly able to see me now that the barrier has fallen. But I can't hardly hear any of them. Numbing fear washes over me until I can't feel anything. Not my weak legs, nor my impossibly small human hands.

Qaeus brings me up to her void-like eyes, and I hope to whatever gods that are out there—and maybe that's just the Primordial—that she will show me mercy for being the one to free her.

"Please don't kill me," I beg, teeth chattering in my skull. "I freed you. I gave you Khunas."

To my stupefying amazement, Qaeus seems to answer my pleas. Not with words or anything so direct, but I swear the Primordial nods her understanding.

I can do nothing but blink up at her, at the face as dark and obscure as a night absent of stars.

Slowly, she raises her other arm up to me, one thick finger extended. It's both longer and larger than my entire body, and I quiver as it draws nearer. But when it presses its slick skin to the top of my head, something passes between us. Not another case of blight sickness, but something sacred, lost, profound.

Images flash before me, assaulting my entire being with undeserved knowledge and meaning. Faces and locations. Tools and conversations. Memories long since lost to time. Stories that haven't yet been discovered and possibly never will. They go so quickly I can't grasp any of them. I reach, and reach, but they slip through my fingers like I'm grasping at water.

Finally, the memories slow, and I realize the Primordial has been searching, looking for the thing she wants to share with me. I don't know whether to feel honored or dread, but both well up in equal measures.

The Pits of Bagamore come into view. I recognize them only by the depictions in the mural of the tarry pits surrounded by pink rock. The black abyss bubbles and boils until something breaches the surface. It drags itself out from the depths and I recognize it almost instantly.

The Primordial Qaeus.

Three others rise from the shallows with it: Khunas, Khaymus, and Quistus.

All this time we've been led to believe that the Primordials have been alive since the dawn of time. But they are not the ancient beings we thought they were. Something about the memory is too recent to have come from a time so long ago. The Primordials were born.

In fact, they were created.

And all Qaeus wants—all any of them ever wanted—is to be destroyed.

Their power is too great—*her* power. She cannot contain it. For years she tried, but with every century that passed, the magic grows wilder inside her. The Blight, the demons, they were only the beginning. Now that she has arisen, and with the soul of Khunas inside her, her reign of terror will be far, far worse than anything in written history.

The docile version of Qaeus twitches, her head cocking to one side, as if she's asking if I will be the one to do it, if I will end her suffering.

But it takes only a moment for wicked malevolence to flash behind her black eyes, replacing any ounce of kindness she had exhibited. The Primordial who'd awakened is gone. The magic is in control now, and it is dark and malicious.

The Primordial bellows a bloodthirsty cry. Its damp breath gusts over my face. I don't have time to think, to plan, to fear. All I know is if I stay in the palm of her hand, I will be crushed.

When her fingers twitch beneath me, I bound from the edge of her upturned palm, my arms spread. Wind blows through my white hair.

"Halira!" I hear Kalli and Dimitri cry as one, but they're too far down for me to see them yet.

The ground is approaching rapidly. I've never noticed how very hard and unwelcoming it looks. From this distance, I know that crashing into it will be the death of me, but I've come too far, fought too hard to die so easily.

If I can summon storms, if my one of my innate powers is channeling the air, then I must call upon it now. I think of wings. I think of wind. I think of light, buoyant things like clouds and autumn leaves and snowflakes.

I'm hoping for a gale strong enough to ease my landing when I remember the power my aunt and sister possess of animal transformation.

Unexpectedly, the two ideas become one, and instead of calling sprouting wings or summoning a current to carry me to the ground, I feel a door open inside me, and I unleash something more.

My mass disappears. The weight of me is gone. I become nothing, suspended where I fall, but this is different than when I died. The nothingness I'd felt then had been black and endless. But my consciousness does not disappear. I seep out into the world, into the whooshing air. I am nowhere and nothing, and yet, I am everything I touch.

With a thought, I blow through the sky. I whirl through the trees, rustling the dead branches in my wake—that are now brown, instead of black—and I spiral toward the ground.

When I land, I am nothing more than a pocket of air, a resting breeze come to settle at the basin of the sky.

But the moment the words *ground* and *solid* and *land* come into my mind, I expand into them. I feel myself fill out again, becoming solid once more where I lie crumpled on the ground.

My sister gasps as I appear, flinging herself at me where I rest, a tangled mess of limbs.

"Halira!" she yells, cupping my face in her hands. "What just happened? Are you okay?"

Blinking away my shock, I try focusing on her steel-gray eyes, on the fine hairs that fan from her tightly woven locks, on anything that will keep my mind from unspooling and my head floating back into the clouds.

The ground thunders beneath us. Qaeus is on the move and that is enough to snap me out of it and keep me in my skin.

"We have to go," I say, glancing from Kalli to Dimitri as he arrives beside her. "We have to get as far away from here as possible."

"Are you kidding?" he guffaws, pointing out at the creature. "This is the moment we've been waiting for. We've finally found the Primordial. We can kill it and end its tyranny—"

"No, you can't." I push myself up, slowly, but with Kalli's help I manage to stand. "I will explain later, but we have to move. Now. That thing isn't just Qaeus anymore."

Dimitri frowns. Alphonse appears as well, Fox not too far behind him.

"Where's your axe?" my cousin asks. "Where's your Primordial weapon?"

My head jerks in rapid motions. "It's…it's gone."

The magnitude of that statement hits them with about as much force as it collides into me. That axe had been the weapon I chose as a Crusader. It had protected me this past week or so in the Shadowthorn. It had granted me entrance across the Primordial's protective boundary so that I could cure myself. To be without it and my dagger feels…unnatural.

Dimitri stands with his fists clenched, looking over his shoulder at the Primordial who is taking lumbering strides toward us. But whereas the rest of us quake with fear, he is unflinching. As he watches Qaeus, he doesn't see an impossible fight; he sees the promise he made to avenge his family.

Alphonse notices him too, and for all his terrible qualities, in this moment, his decency shines.

Alphonse dawns the mask of a general and clamps Dimitri's shoulder. "You heard her, Crusader. Live to die another day. Retreat!"

THE ANSWERS THEY SEEK

THE WALL, SHADOWTHORN

Once we're far enough away that the trees no longer rustle from the force of Qaeus' mighty footsteps, we finally slow to catch our breaths.

"Why isn't she following us?" Captain Eparah pants, her thick, black hair falling around her face where she leans over her knees. "We were right in front of her. We would've been an easy meal."

I'm too winded to bother telling them what I suspect, that the real Qaeus—the decent one who shone through just before the evil took hold—gained control of its body long enough for us to escape undetected. These people have spent their entire lives hating the Primordial. I don't have enough fight left in me today to try to convince them that the creature is actually benevolent.

Besides, they don't need to know anyway. The Crusaders' mission has been and always will be to slay the Primordials, which is exactly what Qaeus wants. They will continue to try, in vain, to bring her down, while I search for real answers.

But first, I need to find Ryven and figure out a way to save him before it's too late.

By now, anyone within a ten-mile radius has likely felt Qaeus' return. Come to think of it, anyone within or near the Shadowthorn has seen the darkness withdraw from the land. If Ryven is anywhere nearby, he knows I've done what the Elders asked, and hopefully he'll be returning to the Eyve soon to congratulate me and resume our search to save him as well.

Unless…unless he's already succumbed.

"Don't think about that," Kalli says beside me, her voice cool but more soothing than usual.

I scowl at her. "Think about what?"

"The half-demon. The one who left."

"That's like me telling you not to think about the enormous Primordial we just awoken."

Kalli's lips purse into a thin line. She inhales through her nose, her shoulders taut. "It will be headed for Arcathain. The people in the border towns will be utterly defenseless. If it destroyed your axe, then every other shadowsteel weapon is useless. How will Arcathain defend itself?"

"Don't think about that," I echo her words at her. It comes off more condescending than I mean. "For now, I mean. Let us reach safety first and then figure out the rest."

We begin walking again, and it takes me a few strides to realize that where I'm leading them is futile. Most of the people with us won't be able to enter the Eyve, and camping outside its borders would be a death sentence once nightfall comes.

But I don't know where else to guide them. With Qaeus somewhere between us and Arcathain, with the Wardens' camp destroyed, there is only one safe haven to turn to. Besides, I have no time to waste in returning. Every second Ryven spends with demon toxin coursing through him is another second he's drawn closer to the Blight.

Fox appears beside me, a hopeful look about her. I nod to my sister, who slows her pace to fall behind with the others, leaving the two of us mostly alone to chat.

"So... You're speaking human again, I see?"

"It appears so."

She winces as if my vitriolic tone actually strikes her. "I'm sorry about attacking you... And about..."

"Turning me into the Magistrate, even though you said my secret was safe with you?"

She rubs her forehead, hiding half of her face and none of her shame. "Yeah, that. I just...I didn't want to die in the Shadowthorn. If you recall, I didn't join the Shadow Crusade of my own volition like you. I never wanted to be a soldier. And I certainly didn't want to die for the country that did piss-all for me.

"Then I met Alphonse, and then I *really* didn't want to die. I told myself that you'd be found out eventually anyway, and that if I waited any longer, some petrified fool would accuse me, your closest friend, of being a mage too."

I stop midstride, whirling on her so quickly that the others behind us startle. "You almost got me killed. What's worse: you almost got my sister killed! She's the only family I have left."

Fox's hands shoot into the air. "Hey, I had nothing to do with her. Alphonse said the Magistrate had been watching her already. They were all but a moment away from convicting the both of you before I came along. I just...I did what I had to do to look out for myself. I'm sure you can understand."

Untampered rage flares inside me.

"You would've," she insists. "You've been doing it for days now. You fled your post, never considering what your abandonment might cost your friends. Did you know the Magistrate threatened to hang Dimitri? Me as well, if we didn't comply."

"Comply with what?"

"Why do you think we're in the Shadowthorn? The Magistrate demanded that Dimitri lead the mission back to where the fight happened and that we can't return until we find the Wardens. He made me come, knowing I'd been your friend, even though I told them about you. But if you ask me, he just didn't think I was good enough for his son. Even a bastard."

"Excuse you!" Alphonse cries behind us.

Fox waves him off with one of her roguish grins.

We fall into a comfortable silence, like nothing has changed between us. I want to stay in this place. I want to be able to forgive her. And at least for right now, I don't have the energy to do anything but.

"I'm not a mage, you know."

"Yeah, I heard you say that—well, I heard Alphonse say it for you. Druids, huh?"

I shrug. "Apparently."

"What does that mean exactly? You can use magic. I've seen it."

"I don't know enough to understand it yet, and the demon toxin prevented me from being able to explore my powers, but I think our magic is different than that of the mages. It seems more rooted to the earth and living things...I think."

She considers me for a moment. "Then, where does the mage's magic come from?"

Frowning as I think on it, I let the topic fade away, turning back to the issue of our friendship, or lack thereof.

"You know, you tried to kill me first. And you—you had no right to be angry with me after what you did to me."

"I know," she says hurriedly, hanging her head low. "I thought he was dead though... I thought... What would you do if you lost someone you loved?"

The bitter sting of heartbreak cracks my chest open again. Ryven's disappearance, his impending doom, it's all too much to bear. Thinking about what might be happening to him, what will happen if we don't find a solution and quick, it's like having my heart wrenched from my chest and torn to shreds.

"Oh, right. Dimitri," she says, misinterpreting my expression.

Guilt fills the cracks of my shattered heart. It should be Dimitri I'm thinking of. After all, we spent most of our lives together, whereas Ryven, I've only known him—*truly* known him—for a few days.

I can feel my cheeks brightening with embarrassment, my heart quickening as confusion rolls through me.

In the end, I decide to say nothing, letting our conversation fade and her making sense of my silence in whatever way she sees fit.

"Let's stop here for a moment," Alphonse calls from the back of the group. "Tend to the wounded and discuss our plan of action."

If it weren't for Silver, the singed Crusader, and a handful of others who still needed treatment, I have no doubt that Kalli and her raven would be among those of us gathering to develop a plan. Her goals and vision are not too dissimilar from Dimitri's though, and so when he joins Alphonse, Eparah, and myself, I'm sure Kalli's opinions will be represented.

"Now that Qaeus is loose, we need to send word back to Nigh, to *all* of Arcathain."

"They might mistake the retreat of the Shadowthorn as a sign of the Primordial's defeat," Eparah adds.

"Precisely. Especially when my father recently pulled every Crusader from the border towns. They'll have no reason to believe the threat has worsened. The Magistrate may have abandoned the castle, but once he knows that the Primordial is heading toward them, he will have no choice but to turn back around with the full force of his military and strike. Whatever war he wants to wage with the mages can wait."

At the mention of our neighbors on Illashore, my hope for Ryven grows greater. If the druids don't know how to cure his blighted heart, perhaps the mages do. After all, they possess the only other remaining Primordial weapon, and the Pits of Bagamore—the very place that birthed the Primordials and the demons they possess—resides somewhere in their territory as well.

But first, I need to find Ryven. The Elders can help me with that. Elder Irene can use her winds to whisper of his location, or Elder Nebadri can commune with her animals. Either way, my time with the Crusaders ends here.

While the three of them fall deep into their discussion, I slip away. It will be easier like this, not having to say goodbye again.

"And just where do you think you're going?" Alphonse voice is haughty, the same domineering tone he used in every one of our skirmishes.

I feel Dimitri's eyes fall to the back of my neck. He jogs toward me, spinning me around to face him. "You're just going to leave? Just like that?"

My lips purse. "I thought it would be easier on everyone—"

"Not on me, it wouldn't be." He scoffs, clasping his hands atop his head as he starts to pace. "Look, I know I left you before but...that was—I didn't know what—I shouldn't have. I've spent the past week agonizing over that decision. Even though I thought you were dead, I shouldn't have left you. I shouldn't have told you I was leaving before then, when I witnessed your...magic."

He steps closer, taking my hands into his. Despite having held them dozens of times, they no longer feel familiar. Their callouses are too rough, the shape of his fingers all wrong as they try to enmesh with mine.

"I know that now. I should've stayed by your side. I should've been with you for all of this."

"I...I..."

Words fail me. The sentiment, though touching and every-thing I had wanted to hear from him on that dreadful day, can't seem to reach me any longer. The fact of the matter is that he *did* abandon me. In one of my greatest times of need, no doubt.

With a timid, pained smile, I slip my hands from his. "I can't go back to Arcathain. I'm a wanted fugitive. The Magistrate would have me hanged."

The lie comes easy, probably because it's not entirely a lie, but it's not the full truth either. I can't bring myself to tell him that I can no longer see myself with him. I shouldn't have been with him to begin with. It was never an act of love, but one of convenience, desire.

Shaking his head, the fierceness in Dimitri's eyes grows. Then he grabs my arm again and drags me back to the group.

"Hey!" I yell, squirming from his grip. "What do you think you're—"

He jabs a finger at Alphonse. "You'll tell the Magistrate she's innocent."

"I'll do what?"

"He believes she's a mage. You'll make him believe otherwise."

Alphonse's eyebrows crinkle in a dubious expression. "As much as I'd like to fool myself into believing that man would ever take my word on such a matter, it would never work with this. He's been watching Halira's family for years. He knows about their magic, even if he presumes them mages."

"That's exactly what I tried telling him." I aim my irritated glare at Dimitri. "It's why I'm not coming with you."

Fox scoffs from behind Alphonse, shoving her way into the circle. "You're joking. For months all you could talk about was slaying that creature, and now that we've found it, you're simply giving up?"

"I'm not giving up. Your plan is futile. The being cannot be defeated by your shadowsteel weapons. It is a being of an ancient magic, and as such, only magic can destroy it."

Curious, Alphonse frowns. "And how do you propose we go about this?"

"I don't propose anything. I'm no longer a Crusader, nor am I an Arcathainian. If you want to attack the Primordial, you're the general, so attack it. But don't expect to be called heroes, and certainly don't expect to walk away with your lives."

"What is this?" Dimitri demands. "You're behaving more like your sister, cruel and cold."

Rage flashes behind my eyes. "I just want to return to the Eyve to speak with the Elders, but you dragged me back here against my will, so excuse me for being irate."

My chest is heaving when I'm finished, Dimitri and I both glaring at each other, less than a breath away from one another.

"The Elders!" Alphonse exclaims. "That is precisely the kind of suggestion we needed."

"Who are the Elders?" asks Eparah.

"Well, I was too busy being imprisoned to have met them firsthand, but they appear to be revered for their wisdom. They were the ones who told Halira how to cure herself."

Fox scoffs. "Isn't that why Qaeus was awakened? Because Halira did what those people told her to do?"

Concern starts to grow in my belly. Imryll had said that the druids never wanted to harm Qaeus. They even managed to live peacefully with her for a time. Could it be possible that waking the Primordial was an intentional side effect, or perhaps even the ulterior motive they had for sending me to her?

"No," I blurt before I even know I'm speaking. "I mean, yes, but they didn't know that was going to happen. Or at least, I didn't ask them. They're very...particular about what they're asked. They know too much to be able to determine what information to provide or not. If they knew, I don't think they withheld that information from us on purpose."

"That only reinforces my point," Alphonse says. "They are

precisely the kind of people who would be privy to such information as how to defeat the Primordial. We should ask them, explicitly this time."

I consider his suggestion a moment before my shoulders give a noncommittal bob. "If they know anything, it could be worth a try. But I can't say for certain that they do, nor that they'll offer the information willingly. Their people—*my* people—lived with Qaeus for generations. They believe her to be benevolent, or at the very least, they don't want to see her slain."

"Then we won't tell them that's our plan," Dimitri interjects. "But surely, they can empathize with an entire country being at risk as long as that *thing* runs rampant. I saw the look in its eyes, Halira. If you hadn't jumped when you did, it was going to kill you."

"It would've killed the rest of us as well, had we stayed," Eparah adds.

"Exactly." Dimitri pounds one fist into the palm of his other hand. "We tell the Elders we need to know how to keep it from harming Arcathainians. How to trap it or tame it—whatever they know how to do."

The others nod in agreement.

"Only druids can enter the Eyve. If you come with me now, you'll be left outside the borders. Night won't come for a few more hours, but once it does...you don't want to be caught outside the Eyve at night."

Alphonse pats my shoulder. "Let us first speak with the Elders. Determining where to set up camp can come later."

"It's a half day's journey from the main entrance to the top of the canopy. At least, on legs. Unless you've suddenly learned how to sprout wings and fly?"

Alphonse stiffens, his nostrils flaring at the implication. To his relief and my chagrin, the rest of the group seems to think nothing of it though. Or at least, none of them mention it.

They're used to our bickering and teasing, and hopefully they think it's nothing more than a casual jest. Then again, Dimitri has already aroused their suspicions. But if they do have those questions, I guess maybe they'll come later. Especially if his powers ever manifest.

"Didn't you turn yourself into wind?" Dimitri asks, a muscle feathering in his jaw in his discomfort. "It shouldn't take you half a day to…breeze through the distance."

Alphonse's grin turns saccharine, feline. "Precisely. Halira will speak to them on our behalf. Now, let's move. Time is of the essence, as I'm sure you already know."

I narrow my eyes at him one final time before storming off toward the Eyve.

I leave everyone at the gates of the Eyve. Kalli offers to come with me, but this is a conversation I think will best be had alone.

Becoming the wind again comes naturally now that the demon toxin has left me. Or perhaps it's only easy because of the sheer drive I have to make it so. I will not waste a second. The sun hangs too low in the sky, the horrors of the Shadowthorn will awaken soon, and my friends—and at least one frenemy—are waiting outside the border like freshly baked pies ready to be eaten.

Not to mention the matter of Ryven's rapidly approaching fate.

I don't bother shifting back into my human form until after I've blown through the front door.

"Ah, she has discovered her nature," Elder Henness says from behind a steaming mug of tea.

"That can only mean she was successful," Elder Irene adds.

Elder Nebadri is resting on the couch beside them, an entire family of squirrels cuddled up with her.

"If by successful, you mean that I am no longer blighted,

then yes. But you failed to mention some fairly important details." The snarl in my tone runs wild and free like the beast it's become. I don't try stopping it. These three women just might've been the downfall of all of Arcathain. Let them feel my wrath on behalf of the Broken Realms.

Elder Henness shows no signs of remorse as she clasps her hands. "We shared with you what you needed to know, but you are on a course that we will not interfere with."

"So you knew!" My voice rises with the heat inside me. "You knew I'd unleash the Primordial on Arcathain, and you didn't even think to warn me?"

Her supercilious nature deflates. She frowns. The leathery skin of her forehead creases with the rising of her brows. "Qaeus is free? Nothing we told you to do should've awaken her from her slumber."

My eyes roll in my skull. "You just said—"

Henness cuts my words off with a sharp quickness. "I said we knew you are on a path that should not be interrupted; I did not say that we know where that path will lead. We told you nothing of how to awaken the Primordial Qaeus where she slumbered. She was safe where she rested, as was the rest of the realm—"

"Safe!" Anger flashes before my eyes, a shade of red so dark that it reminds me of death. "Arcathainians haven't been safe since Qaeus broke free from the Eyve! People die every day from the demons she's unleashed across our lands. Families have been forced to flee their homes. The towns become overrun with refugees. And the constant fear of when they'll be forced to run again wears heavy on everyone."

Elder Henness doesn't flinch away from my heated gaze. Her voice has the edge of a sharpened sword when she tells me, "They were safer than they are now. You Arcathainians are all the same: hearts full of vengeance and hatred. We did not tell you to strike Qaeus' heart with your axe. The Primordial has sought its fallen brethren for centuries, and you just reunited her with one of them."

My brow twitches. "Khunas."

I'd felt it. The moment the Primordial Khunas' power had fled the axe, the atmosphere had become a charged nightmare of rage and destruction. I knew something had happened, even if I didn't quite understand it. I didn't want to. But now that the Elder has said it, I recall some of the excerpts I read in the library of Nigh, ones that told about how the Primordials absorbed the souls of the fallen.

Bewildered, I look from one to the next them.

"I wasn't warned about this! About what would happen if that blighted weapon came too close to the Primordial!" Wind billows around me, a tempered zephyr threatening to become a cyclone. I push back against it, creating a gust of my own that blows Irene's neatly combed hair all about her face.

Elder Henness holds up a hand, and we both stop. "You were told what we were permitted to tell you. Now, let us move past it. You have returned with questions. Speak them."

The flippant way in which she tries to shift the conversation only serves to stoke the fire of my rage all the more. But then I remember that I have others depending on me, waiting on my return; that they wait on the wrong side of the Eyve, unprotected and defenseless against the behemoths that will soon rise from the Labyrinth. At least, that is what I expect. We were told the only way to remove the blighted blood from my system was to allow Qaeus' heart to expunge it from me. Despite the Shadowthorn absorbing back into the Primordial, I fear that the demons and behemoths still reside where they were.

Sighing away my irritation, I think back to Dimitri's suggestion. "Is there any way to contain the Primordial now that she's been released? Trapping her, taming her, anything?"

Elder Henness dips her head low in acquiescence. "The

humans were able to trap Qaeus centuries ago, but that was with the aid of the mages, a race they no longer deign to ally with."

"Yes, I am well aware of the history of Qaeus' entrapment and the feud between humans and mages. I was hoping the druids might be able to help, that we might have certain powers that could persuade her to leave Arcathain alone or keep her contained somewhere safe."

The Elders exchange a worrisome glance.

Elder Irene sits taller. "The druids will offer no aid on this matter. Not yet."

"What do you mean you will offer no aid? The people of Arcathain—"

"The people of Arcathain are not our concern. The people of the Broken Realms are."

"They *are* people of the Broken Realms!" I argue, blood pumping to my neck and cheeks. "We have to help them. They don't deserve to pay for their ancestors' sins as Qaeus seeks her vengeance on them."

"It is irrelevant, I'm afraid." Carelessly, Elder Henness flicks her wrist. "We will offer no information on this matter. You will have to figure out how to handle Qaeus on your own, or face the consequences of the inevitable peril of your homeland."

Disgust sinks into my belly like stones. In the few short days I've spent in the Eyve, never have I experienced the ugliness present here now. I thought this place had been untouched by cruelty, that the druids had overcome the pettiness of rivalry and conflict. But if the revered leaders of the druids can hold such contempt for the humans, such apathetic disregard, then what does that mean for the rest of the population? How deep does their hatred run?

Is our realm destined to forever be at odds with itself?

"Fine," I growl. If they won't help us with Qaeus, then we'll figure out another way. I've survived my entire life without the aid of the druids. Arcathainians have survived centuries of being hunted by Qaeus' demons. We will find another way.

Remembering my true purpose for coming here, I veer the conversation to another matter.

"I need to know where Ryven has gone. He left before we found the heart, forcing me to take the breath of life for myself and…I need to find him. I need to help him before it's too late. I can't do that if I don't know where he is."

Henness tilts her head. "You can't do that regardless. No other breath of life exists to protect him."

"I don't care what you think to be true," I snarl. At her stunned expression, I bite back my irritation. She doesn't deserve this courtesy, for me to speak to her with respect, but Ryven doesn't deserve to be lost to the darkness simply because I pissed off one of the druid Elders. "With all due respect, I understand that *you* don't know how to save him, but that doesn't mean there isn't a way. You said so yourselves that there are some things you do not know. So if you would be so kind, summon your critters, your winds, your trees, and tell me where to find him."

Elder Henness sinks back into her chair as if she intends to tell me nothing.

"We have no need for such theatrics," Elder Irene says, placing a gentle hand on her sister's knee. "We already know where he is."

"Where?" I beg, stumbling forward, desperate to hold on to her every word.

"He's at the border of Eyve. He's approaching the front gate as we speak."

DEMON, BECOME

FORGOTTEN FOREST OF EYVE

I ricochet out the front entrance of the Elders' home, a whirling cyclone of desperation and resolve. Wild and reckless, I zip through the trees, bouncing between the branches and disturbing the swarms of fireflies as I make my way through the Eyve and back to the place where I left them all. My sister. My friends. My colleagues. Even Ryven, unbeknownst to me.

How long had he been back? Had he ever even left, or has he spent the past day waiting in the outskirts, hidden in the trees until the deed had been completed?

My landing is the least graceful of any I've had yet. My consciousness pulls into itself and I return to my solid form too soon, my shoulder smacking into the ground before the rest of my uncoordinated limbs flail, bouldering behind me. As I crash, I'm grateful that for some reason my garments of clothing remain with me when I shift back into solid matter, unlike what happens to my aunt, sister, and all the other druids who take the form of an animal. I imagine there's a reason, some mechanic of the magic that I don't quite understand, but I haven't had the time to truly think on it yet.

Dimitri rushes to my side, my sister not too far behind him, as I stand myself upright. I smack the dirt from my clothes, but a burning ache in my shoulder makes me wince, and I clutch my elbow to support the arm that had collided with the ground and popped out of its socket.

"Your arm." Kalli doesn't wait for my reply or consent. She merely presses her hand against my shoulder, and a warm light exudes from her palm, seeping into my bone socket.

In a matter of seconds, the pain has eased. I roll my shoulder, adjusting to the strangely unfamiliar sensation of my own arm again.

"So?" Dimitri asks, the rest of the group tightening in around us with palpable anticipation. "What did the Elders say about the Primordial?"

But my mind has already leapt outside of the circle enclosing around me. I shove through the crowd, their confused, concerned gazes boring into me, but I ignore them all. After all, the answers they seek, I don't have.

I scan the perimeter, glancing between the trees that still look as if they're stuck in winter, despite the season having moved onto spring. Now that the Shadowthorn has faded, it's easier to see through them, but regardless of their sparse branches, the trees are still densely packed, leaving few holes for visibility through the forest.

But I won't let that stop me. Ryven is out there somewhere. And if I can't *see* him, then I'll just have to go *find* him.

Before I can step into the underbrush, a teeth-clenching roar bellows from the forest.

I break out into a run.

I'd recognize that tenor anywhere. I hear it in my dreams. Not the agony that's twisting it into a mangled choke, but the low rumble that always makes my stomach dip. The agony ripping through it now though is soul-deep and churns my gut with oily dread.

Bounding through a break in the trees and nearly tripping over an overgrown root that's reaching up through the dirt, I stumble into a clearing and into the man I've been looking for desperately.

Ryven is hunched over his knees, his hands planted in the soil as another tormenting shriek tears through him. The black toxin creeping up his arm has spread. His entire torso is coated in darkness. The tendrils weave all the way across his chest and down his other arm. They climb up his neck and jaw like black candlewax dripping in the wrong direction.

I slide to my knees in front of him, drawing his anguished grimace.

"Stay back," he growls, jaw clenched tight. "I can't stop it."

I hold my hands out, assessing his every move and quake. I want to help him. I need to. I want to summon my druid power of healing and cleanse the toxin ravaging him, but not only do I not know how, but it would do no good anyway. No druid healing can save him from the blight-infested demon toxin.

"I'm not leaving you," I protest, my chin quivering despite the amount of effort I took to ensure my voice wasn't watery. "Why didn't you let me help you? I could've saved you. You just left me!"

"I couldn't...let you sacrifice yourself...and I couldn't...say goodbye." Every word is labored and anguished, as if he were dragging himself through a pit of broken glass and agonizing over every slice of flesh.

Another scream builds in his lungs, this one so tortured that it tears his mouth wide open. His wings splay out, as rigid as the horizon, the pain igniting every one of his muscles and leaving him raw. His fingers dig into the dirt, and I inch closer still, so desperate to take his hand into mine, to take his pain away.

"I can help you. I think—I *know* there is a way. We just have to get you to Illashore. The mages must know about another cure."

"There's no time," he pants, the pain relenting for the briefest of moments. "It's happening. I can't fight it any longer. You have to go. Get as far away from here as you can."

"No."

"You must. I don't want to…I can't harm you like Ahl'Ro did."

The name sparks one of my most tender and frightful memories. The day my parents were slaughtered. The day I lost everything. The day we both did. I lost my family as much as Ryven did that day, and we've both been paying for it ever since.

"You won't," I say. Even to me, my voice sounds pathetic, nothing more than the wishful, pointless desires of a delusional optimist. "You won't because you're not going to become one of them. I told you, we can stop this."

"It's too late," he growls, teeth bared as pain rears its ugly face again.

But there's something worse about the harshness in his tone. There's a worrisome familiarity to it. It reminds me of the last conversation we had, right before he did something drastic.

His wings twitch as if he's readying them to launch high into the sky and flee this place before he puts me in harm's way.

I dive forward, throwing my arms around his neck before he can disappear again. "I'm not letting you leave again."

The sheer shock of my embrace distracts the pain away for a moment. His body unravels in my arms, the rigid muscles in his back relaxing as we sink into each other. I pull my head back to see his face, and note the warmth of his breath on my cheek and chin.

Chest heaving, Ryven's breaths take on a new tempo, one that matches mine in desire and need and longing.

He pushes himself back onto his heels, crushing me into him with his freed arm as the other loops around my back as if this embrace is the only thing that matters; as if us holding onto each other will stop everything bad from ever happening.

He tangles his hand in my hair and our foreheads press together. We stare into other, this moment searing into our memory with timeless finality. Here, in this clearing, there is only me and him, a druid girl and boy who found each other when they'd lost everything else, when they needed one another most.

My heart hitches when I decide to bring his velvet soft lips to mine.

The ache in my belly, the one I already thought was too unbearable without him near me, swells with the expanse of a churning sea. His lips sear into mine like they're branding me as his, and I relish it. I relish the idea that from this point forward, I am his and he is mine.

I climb closer, higher, bringing myself up and over his lap to straddle him between my legs. When he deepens the kiss, a shudder whispers through me and I part my lips to meet his urgent request. I oblige him, sinking into him and embracing the hedonism that's become inflamed inside me. He tastes sweet. Like honeysuckle and mulberry wine aged in a cedar barrel, and I find myself realizing that I could drink him for an eternity. I want to. I want to never part, to hold this time in space forever and never let it go. Never let him go.

His sharp teeth nearly prick my tongue with devilish delight as I dive inside him. As I taste him. Devour him.

But the reminder of his sharpened canines is enough to shatter the façade of safety he's allowed himself to fall into. Ryven grabs my arms and shoves me away, a hollowness tearing through me and burning with icy fury in the places where our bodies had touched.

He licks his lips, lingering in the taste of me, in the indulgence. But the demon toxin continues clawing its way up his cheek like painful leeches, reminding him of his convictions.

"If you won't let me go," he says, voice gruff and drunk on passion. "Then you have to end it. As I did for Ahl'Ro."

It's like the world has been pulled out from under me. The headiness in my chest flips upside down and I'm shaking my head before he can even finish.

"What are you even talking about?" I splutter, wrapping my arms back around his neck and holding him close, clinging to the moment that's passed as if I can drag the both of us back into it, our foreheads pressing together. "I'm not doing that."

"You can't let me live like this," he says, dark eyes boring into mine. "You know that."

I'm rendered speechless, my heart too busy shattering into a thousand pieces to pump blood through my veins, much less bring life to my thoughts. I can't do what he's asking of me…I won't. I will not accept a life without him, not now that I finally have him.

"I can save you," I say again, enunciating my every word as if maybe I haven't been speaking them clearly enough until now.

Another bout of crippling pain screams through him, flinging him out of my embrace and back to where he hunched on the ground.

"Please," he begs, body shaking violently. "End it."

Horror pierces through me as the inky toxin engulfs him. My hands come up to my lips, the lips that still taste like him, and I watch in horror, terrified of what he's becoming, of what I've done, what I've failed to do for him.

The darkness consumes every inch of him. It folds over him like night consuming the sky. It is wicked. Vile. Dangerous.

The creature before me shrieks with the call of a hundred bats. I stagger backward, landing on my rear with an audible thump.

The shadowcreature's head snaps toward me, nothing but hunger and violence reflected in his black eyes.

"Ryven." My voice warbles. "Please."

The creature, now resembling one of the twisted gargoyles that stood watch over the Castle of Nigh, with the body of a mangled wolf and the wings and face of a bat, springs into the sky. Its wide wings glow with the fading light of the sun beaming down on them.

Some of the other Crusaders trudge through the forest then, arriving in the clearing with their weapons already drawn.

"Halira!" shouts Dimitri.

In skittering strides, he bounds toward me, leveling his shadowsteel sword at the shadowbat overhead—at Ryven. The horrifying creature he's become screeches at the tip of the sword and Dimitri throws himself before me. My heart lodges into my throat as I watch my best friend and the man who I failed to save prepare to tear into each other.

"Stop," I cry, clambering my feet and tugging on Dimitri's sword arm. "Stop!"

The shadowbat sees his weapon falter, and he dives.

Dimitri wraps his arm around my waist, diving the two of us out of the shadowbat's trajectory.

"What are you doing?" he growls when we land. "You nearly got us both killed!"

"You can't kill him," I beg. Hearing the own desperation in my voice nearly shatters me all over again. But it's the look of understanding in Dimitri's eyes that takes the final blow. It starts as confusion: why would anyone want to defend a demon clearly bent on slaughter? But the longer he watches me and the way my mournful eyes follow the shadowbat as it lifts back into the sky, looping around to strike again, disgust wars with the heartbreak in his grim expression.

Demons stampede through the clearing, drawn to the scent of a fight like leeches are drawn to blood. A wall of them crash into the Crusaders on the sidelines, a battle of black bone and silver shadowsteel.

Just as the shadowbat is about to dive at us again, Eparah barrels into the clearing, the remaining handful of Crusaders charging in behind her. If Ryven's attention had been set on us, he's easily redirected by the new feast that's presented itself.

His batlike head rears back, a chilling shriek tearing from his lungs, before he plunges downward. The Crusaders raise their weapons, a raucous roar following them as they move. But they will stand no chance. Not without strategy. Not without surprise. The shadowbat is too big, its wings giving it too much of an advantage.

Dimitri shakes his arm out of my stiff grip.

"No," I beg again.

"We can't just let them die. I'm sorry. Whoever he is…we can't."

He runs off to aid his fellow Crusaders before I can think of anything to say. He won't reach them in time though. The shadowbat, with its mighty wings and sharp talons, will shred Eparah and the others to ribbons before Dimitri has even made it across the field, and then the creature will rip him apart as well.

And this is all my fault. He begged me to end it. He begged me to let him go so he wouldn't put anyone in harm's way, and I'd forced him to stay.

My cheeks warm with fresh tears, but I wipe them away as quickly as they came. I made a promise—two in fact. I told him I would never let him hurt anyone. I told him I'd find a way to cure him.

And I intend to keep both of my promises.

The shadowbat nears the ground, his talons open and ready for the kill. There is no time to lose. Necessity and desperation are my assets, and I lean into them, hard and uninhibited.

The weight of me dissipates at my will. I melt into the air, becoming part of it, *becoming it.* I am the wind that blows all across the continent. I am the air that fills the entire atmosphere. And nothing can contend with me.

I bellow from my mouthless core, a powerful gust of wind erupting from inside me. It knocks Dimitri and the Crusaders flat on their faces. It topples and tumbles the demons fighting with our friends.

The trees surrounding the area creak and groan, but I do not relent. I keep screaming, keep pushing into the shadowbat that's battering against me like a cat thrashing in water.

With a final blast of power, I shout, "Stop!"

The current rolls over Ryven, his enormous body crashing backward and into the trees.

My energy spent, I regain my mass, staggering forward on hands and knees. No matter how exhausted I am, no matter how little left of me I have to give, I force my feet under me, and on wobbling, knocking knees, I stagger after the shadowbat.

My ears are ringing, drowning out the cries of my friends as they beg me not to be so foolish, so reckless, but they don't understand that's precisely what's gotten me this far. It is who I am. I make rash decisions. I act on impulse and feeling. And right now, every fiber of my being knows I am meant to go after him, that I can do *something,* even if I still don't know what.

I find the shadowbat contorted and upside down with his back against a tree. It's dazed, but coherent enough that when it sees me, its eyes pop wide. I stare into them, hoping to find any remnant of Ryven left, ignoring the sinking feeling in my stomach that tells me there is nothing.

His eyes, though almost just as dark, had never been so feral, so dangerous, so animalistic.

A sudden hopeful thought crashes into me, spiraling up my core and tightening around my chest. He is so very animalistic, that is true, as are all of the other demons we've encountered. At the Castle of Nigh, we're even trained to think of some of them as animals: how the ones who resemble wolves travel in packs; how there are those that look like bears and as such can be momentarily frightened by loud noises and giving oneself the appearance of being larger.

If the demons are so close in nature to animals, then I might just have one more trick up my sleeve…

The shadowbat slumps down from the tree, primal instinct reawakening as it watches me. I don't have much time. In seconds, the creature will strike, and should I fall victim to its bite, it won't stop until my life is gone.

I can't let that happen, can't let Ryven become the thing he feared most of all.

Frantic for a solution, I think back to the day I spent in the library at Nigh, to the moment I'd inadvertently commanded the mice. I'd already gone through dozens, if not hundreds, of books on my own in search of anything that might've proven useful to help me better understand what I'd witnessed in my parents' cottage. I'd been disheartened and wearied, but I wasn't ready to give up. I knew in my bones, like I know now, that the answers I needed were out there somewhere, I just needed to know where to look.

Again, there was that *need*. Every time I have used my druid power, it is because of some instinctual necessity.

I *needed* to understand what had happened to my parents.

I *needed* to teach Alphonse a lesson while we were sparring, and again when I was fleeing into the Shadowthorn.

I *needed* to ensure our survival in the Labyrinth.

To survive the fall from the Primordial's hand.

To find Ryven.

And right now, I need to protect him from his worst nightmare. I need him to listen to me, to obey.

The shadowbat stands upright, its talons scratching through the soil as it wails one final cry.

I hold out my hand as it prepares to lunge.

"Stop." I breathe the word like I spoke Imryll's name in that dungeon, like it is electric and all-powerful, something stronger than blood and life and death.

The moment the words strike the air, Ryven's snarl vanishes. The wrinkles above his upturned, bat-like nose settle on his changed face.

"You will not attack anyone here," I command, stepping forward and into the power thrumming through me.

The shadowbat blinks in confusion, its legs straighten as it watches me from curious eyes. It tucks its wings behind its knobby shoulders and tilts its head. *His* head.

I chance a step forward, reminding myself that this creature is no *thing*, but Ryven. A man I've come to care for and trust. A man who taught me what it means to feel alive, to feel passion. A man who I vowed to protect.

I take another step, watching Ryven in the shadowbat's body with my heart in my throat. The only time I've been this close to a demon, they've been snarling and vicious, and moments later I sliced my shadowsteel clean through them.

But I have no axe and no dagger now.

And Ryven isn't snarling.

Reflected in his onyx gaze, I see only a deep well of sadness, a revulsion that quivers in the pools of his eyes that almost cracks me in two again. He didn't want this. He begged me to end him before he could become this…this monster. But I couldn't do it. I couldn't kill him, not when the twisting tendrils of hope still linger in my belly.

"I have sworn to protect you from yourself, as long as is

necessary, until I can rid you of the evil inside you," I say to him, taking another step closer until we are so close that the heat of his body warms my skin and I have to crane my neck to look him in the eyes—the only part of him that still resembles him. But even that is enough to fuel my hope. "I will not allow you to hurt anyone, nor will I allow them to harm you," I promise him.

They said it couldn't be done. They said that once he turned, he would be lost like all the others. But they were wrong.

I am Halira Devonshire of the Wallows of Gravenburg. I am a druid descendant who survived being blighted. I alone am responsible for awakening Qaeus.

I alone will stop the Primordial.

And I alone will save Ryven from the darkness that's infested him.

To be continued
Immortal Return
Book 3 of Primordials of Shadowthorn

PREORDER NOW!

Thank you for reading *Blighted Heart*!

Leave a Review
Help other readers find this dark saga by leaving a review on
Amazon, Goodreads, Bookbub, or any other reading website.
Even a simple "I loved it!" can really help!

ARC Team
If you're someone who loves leaving reviews and you're excited
by the idea of having early access to all of my books, check out
my website for more information on how to join my ARC
Team: www.jessacawillis.com/ARC

Social Media

And last but not least, if you'd like to stay connected, you can find my social media links here: https://linktr.ee/jessaca_with_an_a

363

*In a realm where murderers are taken by
the Councilspirits and forced into becoming Reapers,
one girl is on a path to redemption...*

Sinisa is a Reaper of Veltuur, an assassin born from the under-realm, with fatal magic coursing through their veins.

For three years, she's slain her targets dutifully. Now she just needs one more kill to ascend as a Shade, a coveted status of power. And when the King of Oakfall requests a Reaper to execute his daughter for an unforgivable crime, Sinisa is first to volunteer for the job.

It *should* be easy.

But when the Prince discovers his sister is in danger, he flees the palace with her, leaving Sinisa with only two options: journey through the mortal realm to find and slay her mark, or face the consequences of returning to the underrealm empty-handed.

It's no choice at all. She has come too far to stop now.

Besides, no one can outrun a Reaper… Or can they?

~Check out the Reapers of Veltuur Trilogy on Amazon~

Supernatural powers destroyed the world...
Now four unlikely heroes have to save it.

The world ended two years ago. They called it the Awakening: the supernatural event that gave some people powers and left others normal. Nations went to war and millions died.

Sean was one of the first to Awaken, but it wasn't until he walked in on his brother's brutal murder that he learned of the darker nature of his power: blood calls to him, and he to it. And in that moment, he showed his brother's murderers no mercy.

Now Sean must fight to keep his inner demons in check, and his path to redemption begins with the establishment of a sanctuary for people like him, people with powers: the Awakened.

But not even in the apocalypse are the Awakened safe...

Can Sean and three strangers unite the remnants of mankind when everything else has fallen apart? Can they face the darkest horror this new world has yet to offer?

~Check out The Awakened Quadrilogy on Amazon~

ACKNOWLEDGMENTS

This acknowledgment is going to look a little different than some of my others. While I'd still like to honor the impressive efforts of my editors **Sandra Ogle** and **Kate Anderson**, and give an especially grateful shout-out to **Evelyne Paniez**, my cover designer, I want to focus most of this section on honoring the people who helped me complete this book in the final stages of the process.

This was by far one of the most difficult books to finish. I did a major rewrite about a month away from the deadline, and by the time the edits were returned to me, I only had a week and a half before publication. As luck would have it—because life loves burying you in dirt when you're already at the bottom of a ravine—a few major things happened during the last few days I had to finish the book. I honestly thought I was going to have to cancel this book altogether, and maybe even quit writing on a whole. But because I'm surrounded by truly unbelievably supportive and inspiring people, I pushed through.

First and foresmost, I would not have survived the week before this book's publication without my Platypi writing friends. **Tiff**, **Chani**, **Reina**, **Cass**, **Dee**, **Colby**, and **Dani** were there for me every second of every day, boosting me up, reassuring me that I could do this, and just being there for me. I am so unbelievably grateful for you all.

Also, literally everyone on Instagram and Facebook who reached out to me to let me know that they supported and believed in me. After reading through the first five comments out of the dozens left, I was sobbing. You brought love into my life when I felt like I had little of it, and that motivated me to push through the darkness and finish this book for you all.

Last but certainly not least, my **mom** and **brother** were also instrumental in the final days leading up to the publication of this book. I literally had two days left to submit the files and my mom was willing to watch my son for a couple hours every day, while my brother helped me brainstorm a few minor edits I needed to make. They were my rocks.

I'm sure I'm missing a million people, but if you're not named on this list specifically, just know that I appreciated your support, outreach, resource-sharing, conversations, love, and motivation during that dark week. You helped keep me afloat and, as such, I was able to make sure this book landed on the shelves in time.

ABOUT THE AUTHOR

Jessaca is a fantasy writer with an inclination toward the dark, epic, and adventure sub-genres. She draws inspiration from books like the Nevernight Chronicles & ACOTAR, videogames like Dark Souls III, and television shows like Game of Thrones and The Chilling Adventures of Sabrina. She is a self-proclaimed nerd who loves cosplay, video games, and comics, and if you live in the PNW, you just might see her at one of the local comic conventions in one of her favorite RWBY cosplays!